A MILLION MILES FROM NORMAL

Dear lauren,
Hope you enjoy.
love paige.

A
MILLION
MILES
FROM
NORMAL

Paige Nick

PENGUIN BOOKS

PENGUIN BOOKS

Published by the Penguin Group
Penguin Books (South Africa) (Pty) Ltd, 24 Sturdee Avenue, Rosebank, Johannesburg 2196, South Africa
Penguin Books Ltd, 80 Strand, London WC2R 0RL, England
Penguin Group (USA) Inc, 375 Hudson Street, New York, New York 10014, USA
Penguin Group (Canada), 10 Alcorn Avenue, Toronto, Ontario, Canada M4V 3B2 (a division of Pearson Penguin Canada Inc)
Penguin Ireland, 25 St Stephen's Green, Dublin 2, Ireland (a division of Penguin Books Ltd)
Penguin Group (Australia), 250 Camberwell Road, Camberwell, Victoria 3124, Australia (a division of Pearson Australia Group Pty Ltd)
Penguin Books India Pvt Ltd, 11 Community Centre, Panchsheel Park, New Delhi – 110 017, India
Penguin Group (NZ), 67 Apollo Drive, Mairangi Bay, Auckland 1310, New Zealand (a division of Pearson New Zealand Ltd)

Penguin Books (South Africa) (Pty) Ltd, Registered Offices:
24 Sturdee Avenue, Rosebank, Johannesburg 2196, South Africa

www.penguinbooks.co.za

First published by Penguin Books (South Africa) (Pty) Ltd 2010

ISBN: 978-0-143-02651-8

Typeset by Nix Design in 11/16 pt Minion Pro
Cover design: mr design
Printed and bound by CTP Printers, Cape Town
ISO 12647 compliant

For my mum

This wasn't quite what Rachel Marcus had imagined five days earlier when she'd been forced to pack up her life and run away from Johannesburg in search of a fresh start in New York City. She had been hoping for an apartment that was more inner-city chic than inner-city shithole.

'It's small, isn't it?' said Rachel, eyeing Doreen as she turned on the kitchen tap. The top burped and murky water splashed out in epileptic fits. Rachel stared at it in horror. She had never seen lumpy water before.

'Actually, I'd say it's rather spacious for your price range,' the letting agent replied, her face inscrutable.

Doreen had a remarkable talent for real estate: she could turn any negative into a selling point. She had already shown Rachel nineteen apartments and had managed to find something nice to say about every one of them. A feat Rachel wouldn't have achieved, even with the help of a thesaurus.

Rachel pictured the letting agent standing in front of the mirror that morning. Doreen must have imagined her lips to be about half a centimetre bigger than they actually were and had applied her lipstick accordingly. In the two hours they had been together the fat, glossy colour had bled off into the deep smoker's crevices in the corners of her mouth – Doreen was what Rachel's friend Shaun called a two-pack-a-day divorcee. Her hair was bright red and teased so high she left low-hanging light bulbs swaying in her wake. Conventional wisdom would tell a woman with this colour hair that bright pink lipstick may not be the best idea. But clearly conventional wisdom was not something

Doreen paid a great deal of attention to.

Rachel's feet hurt. With each passing viewing both her heart and her standards had dropped significantly. 'What's that smell?' she asked.

'Disinfectant?' Doreen said mechanically.

'No, not that smell.'

'Cat pee?'

'No, the other one, underneath those smells.'

The letting agent raised her nose in the air and sniffed.

'It's like something's burning,' said Rachel.

'Oh, that ...' The agent nodded. 'One of the neighbours must be cooking something.'

'It's got a chemical edge to it, hasn't it?' said Rachel.

'Yes, I think you're right,' said the agent, wiping her nose with a tissue.

'Doreen.'

'Yes, dear?'

'I don't think I can live somewhere where my next door neighbours are cooking crack at three o' clock on a Monday afternoon. Do you have anything else you can show me?'

Doreen looked at her watch, clearly irritated. She shuffled through the pages on her clipboard. 'I've got two more,' she finally said. 'The one is three blocks from here, but it's a bit of a fixer-upper.'

'All right,' shrugged Rachel, looking around and wondering how much more of a fixer-upper you could get. 'It can't be worse than this, right?'

Rachel wasn't sure but she thought she saw Doreen raise a painted-on eyebrow as she led the way out of the door.

The next apartment was on the seventh floor of a nice-looking brownstone and Rachel's hopes began the slow climb up the stairs while she and Doreen took the creaky claustrophobic box of an elevator. On the seventh floor, they walked down a long, well-lit corridor and Doreen poked at the doorbell with a pink, rhinestone-studded fingernail.

An enormous man opened the door, filling the doorway with

his bulk. Rachel tried to look past him into the apartment, but there was barely a gap. 'Hello, Doreen,' he said in a nasal twang, 'we weren't expecting you.'

'Hi, Martin, sorry to barge in like this. I would have called, but we were just around the corner, and we didn't think you'd mind. This is Rachel Marcus, she's looking for an apartment, and I was wondering if I could show her around? We won't get in your way.'

'Of course,' he said, nodding as he stepped aside in a wobbling Mexican wave of skin and fat.

Rachel followed Doreen inside. An equally large woman, wearing what looked like a patterned tablecloth with holes for her arms and head, was sitting on the couch watching TV and barrelling through a bucket of popcorn. She glanced over at Doreen and Rachel disinterestedly and then turned her attention back to Jerry Springer.

'Hi, Wanda,' Doreen said. 'Don't mind us, we'll be out of your hair in a moment.'

Rachel scratched her head subconsciously as she glanced at Wanda's greasy blonde bob.

Martin closed the door behind them and waddled across the room, dumping himself onto the couch next to Wanda. He scooped a mountain of popcorn into a meaty paw and shovelled it into his mouth. Kernels rained down through the gaps between his fingers, bouncing off his chest and gut and lodging themselves in every available crack and cranny in the couch. The buttons on his shirt strained to meet their buttonholes and Rachel could see Martin's hairy belly button gazing out at her from a stretched-out gap between the fabric. A small white kernel had lodged itself inside his navel next to a piece of what Rachel hoped was lint. Between them they must have weighed two hundred and eighty kilos. Rachel wondered whether they could both fit in the tiny elevator at the same time or whether they had to take turns.

She tore her eyes away from the couple and began to evaluate the apartment. For a start it was twice the size of the previous one they'd looked at. However, it was old and grubby and Rachel could see what

Doreen had meant by 'fixer-upper'. Linoleum curled up in disgust on the kitchen floor and the walls were a dirty grey colour that may have once been white. Rachel leaned against a counter top and snapped her hand back quickly; the counter was moist and sticky. She reached for the hand towel next to the sink but it was covered in suspicious stains, so she wiped her hand down the side of her jeans several times. The apartment was bad, but now that she thought about it, it was no worse than some of the other holes she'd seen so far and nothing that couldn't be solved with a bit of paint and the liberal application of some industrial-strength bleach. Rachel looked around the rest of the apartment as she mentally washed her hand in a vat of anti-bacterial disinfectant. Her hope reached the third floor and carried on climbing, gaining speed and momentum as it went.

'It's got high ceilings, original wooden floors and one bedroom, one bathroom,' Doreen said as if she was selling Rachel gold-plated taps or a diamond-studded jacuzzi. 'Come take a look, it's even got a tub.'

Rachel followed her into the bathroom and turned on the tap. Clear water poured out freely and Rachel's hope knocked on the door. Just three days earlier only a view of the ocean from every window, a built-in tennis court or an indoor swimming pool would have elicited the kind of excitement Rachel was now feeling over functioning indoor plumbing.

'The bedroom is over here,' said Doreen, continuing the tour.

Rachel followed her into a small bedroom with a double bed, a wardrobe and an actual window. 'It's fully furnished, right?' asked Rachel.

'Yup, this is it.'

'Why didn't you show me this place first, Doreen?' asked Rachel. 'It's fantastic. When are they moving out?'

'When are who moving out, dear?'

'That couple who live here?' Rachel asked, waving her hand in the general direction of the pair on the couch.

Doreen laughed. 'No, dear,' she said, 'you misunderstand. They're not moving out. You're moving in with them. They're looking for a tenant.'

Hope picked up its suitcase, walked out the door and took the elevator straight back to the ground floor.

'But where would I sleep?' Rachel asked, horrified.

'You'll get the couch. And you'll all share the kitchen and the bathroom as communal areas, and the living room, when you're not sleeping in it. And what's great is that they both work the night shift at McDonald's, so they'll be out most nights and home sleeping during the day, while you're at work. Chances are you'll barely even know they're here. In fact, you might even be able to negotiate some kind of deal where they get the bed during the day and you get it at night, then you won't even need to sleep on the couch. It will be just like timeshare.' Doreen smiled, clearly proud of her problem-solving abilities.

Rachel felt sick. The thought of sharing the same bed, let alone the same living space with Martin and Wanda made her feel like she was suffocating. She took a couple of deep breaths and shook her head at Doreen emphatically. 'I need to live alone, Doreen,' she said. 'How about we go look at that last place you mentioned?'

Doreen heaved another sigh and referred back to her clipboard. 'I don't have the keys. Why don't you meet me at the agency tomorrow, and we'll go together. How does three o' clock sound?'

Rachel nodded.

They parted on the street. Doreen hurried off in one direction and Rachel made her way back to her hotel on foot. It took her over an hour to get there, but she needed to be conservative with her money, so a taxi was out of the question, and she wasn't in the mood for the subway. She needed to think.

Rachel made it back to her room miserable, sweaty and starving. A thick film of New York filth covered her body. It was in her nose, in her hair and her white T-shirt was a dull grey colour. She had to blow her nose four times before the mucus came out clear. As glamorous as New York was, she was starting to realise that it was also very dirty. Rachel collapsed in a chair, pulled off her shoes and socks, and after examining the severity of her blisters, closed her eyes and breathed deeply.

There was a knock at the door. Rachel peeled herself off the chair and opened it to find a room service waiter standing on the threshold holding out an envelope. Rachel grabbed one end and pulled but he wouldn't let go. They stood for a tense moment, playing tug of war, until Rachel clicked that he was waiting for a tip. Still clutching her end of the envelope she dug in her pocket with her free hand and pulled out a five dollar bill.

'Do you have change for a five?' she asked.

'Nope,' he said, snatching the bill out of her fingers quick as a crocodile and letting go of his end of the envelope at the same time. Rachel had been clutching desperately onto her end and suddenly, without any resistance from his side, she lost her balance and stumbled back into the room. By the time she'd regained her balance he was gone and so was her money.

Rachel tore the envelope open. It was a letter from home. She wiped her hair out of her face with a grubby hand and devoured it.

Dear Rachel,

Dad and I were so disappointed when you lost your job and left in such a hurry. We worry about you traipsing around New York on your own like this, without a job and with nowhere to stay. Uncle Jules says he's looking for a receptionist at his zip factory and he would be more than happy to give you a go. Dad and I have discussed it and agree that we could temporarily turn my craft room and your dad's exercise room back into your old bedroom, just until you find your feet.

Also, I know things didn't end so well with you and Phillip. It's such a shame; he was a lovely boy. You didn't tell us the details, but maybe if you apologise for whatever you did wrong, and begged him, he might consider taking you back.

We can't wait to have you home safe.

Love,

Mom and Dad

Rachel felt a mixture of irritation and homesickness. She reread the letter, then took out a sheet of paper and wrote a reply.

Dear Mom and Dad,

Thanks for your letter. It's always very exciting to get actual mail. You'd be surprised how few people still write letters these days, with the invention of the computer . . .

Please thank Uncle Jules for his kind offer, but things here are fantastic. Today, I found the perfect apartment. It's downtown, in a lovely area. It's got one small bedroom, a lounge and a kitchen and a bathroom. The view from my apartment is of the city skyline. The building also has a communal rooftop garden. I'll send you the address as soon as I've moved in and settled down. Until then, please carry on sending your letters to the hotel.

I know we've discussed it before, but you and Dad should really consider getting a computer. It would make communicating so much easier. It's pretty amazing, but an email takes just a couple of seconds to get from me to you. And computers really aren't as complicated as you think.

As far as a job is concerned, I have interviews lined up at some of the top agencies here over the next couple of weeks, and I'm sure one of them will snap me up in no time. I will keep you posted. So, you really don't need to worry, your craft and exercise room is safe for now.

And with regards to Phillip, Mom, he really wasn't as lovely as you think.

Anyway, I must go, I've got dinner plans.

Love you guys,
Rachel

PS: I was wondering if you could send me a box of Five Roses tea with

your next letter. They don't sell anything that tastes like it here and I'd
really love a cup.

Rachel put the letter in an envelope and sealed it. Then she lay on the bed, creating a grimy body-shaped mark, and had a good cry as the realisation dawned on her that she'd just paid five dollars to feel even worse about her situation than she already did.

Rachel woke up the following morning still fully clothed, lying on top of her bed. She felt disgusting – her stomach churned with an almost constant desire to vomit and she could feel a massive outbreak of adult onset acne across her face. She wasn't sure if she wanted to laugh or cry. Day six in New York and she hadn't seen a single apartment that was even close to liveable. She felt desperate, lonely and disillusioned. This wasn't how her fresh start was supposed to go.

Rachel booted up her laptop, logged onto Facebook and wrote her first status update as a New Yorker:

Rachel Marcus is now on USA time and is wondering if it's possible to still be severely jet-lagged after six days?
March 10 at 9:42am

Five minutes later Rachel dragged herself into the bathroom to try clean herself up, well aware that she wasn't going to like what she saw looking back at her in the mirror.

'Here we are, dear,' Doreen said as they climbed the steps outside a run-down brownstone apartment block later that afternoon.

Pulling out a bunch of keys, Doreen opened the front door and Rachel followed her inside and up the stairs. 'I'm afraid this one doesn't have an elevator,' she said, already huffing after only four steps.

They climbed three flights and made their way down a poorly lit corridor with peeling wallpaper. Rachel recognised pockets of different smells. They walked out of boiled cabbage, through a section of wet dog, then through a smell that reminded her of manure, before, finally, she caught a faint whiff of damp and something metallic, like cordite. They reached a door on the right-hand side at the end of the corridor and Doreen fiddled with the keys – there were four locks and she worked her way conscientiously through each one. Then, with the door finally open, Doreen stood aside so that Rachel could enter. Rachel assumed she was being polite, but once inside she realised it was only because there wasn't enough space for two people to stand comfortably in the apartment's minute entrance at the same time.

The entire apartment, what there was of it, was open-plan. The front door led directly into a kitchenette, which had a bar fridge, a sink and a stove top with two rings. To the right of that was the bathroom, which reminded Rachel of an aeroplane toilet. It contained a sink, a toilet, a tiny medicine cabinet with a mirrored door and a shower that was so narrow Rachel knew she wouldn't be able to lift her arms up once she was inside. Certainly, neither Martin nor Wanda would have been able to wedge themselves into it, with arms either up or down.

Rachel continued the grand tour. To the left of the kitchen was what Doreen referred to as the 'livingroomdiningroombedroomlounge', in the middle of which sat a grey couch, a coffee table, a TV set and a small table with two mismatched chairs. A little cupboard stood next to the TV set, doubling as a very basic divider between the bedroom area and the lounge area. The bedroom area was home to a single bed, pushed up against the far wall. There was just one window in the entire apartment and that was situated in the kitchen, directly across from the front door. And that was it.

This one certainly wasn't the biggest or the nicest of the apartments Rachel had seen, but she'd seen enough shitty little crack dens to realise that in her price range they didn't get much better. For now she'd have to share with the rats and the cockroaches. She couldn't blow money on a hotel every day for very much longer.

'So, what do you think?' asked Doreen. 'You'd better hurry, this one will go fast.'

'It will?' mumbled Rachel. 'To whom? A suicidal dwarf?'

Fortunately the agent didn't hear her. Or at least pretended not to.

'Okay,' Rachel finally said. 'I suppose I'll take it. Can I move in tomorrow and have it on a month-to-month basis?'

'Sure,' said Doreen. 'You've made an excellent choice, Rebecca.'

'It's Rachel, and it's not for long,' Rachel assured her. 'As soon as I get a job I'll move somewhere a little more bearable.'

'Of course you will, dear,' said Doreen. 'Now, I'll need a deposit and the first and last month's rent.'

Doreen handed Rachel a piece of paper with all the figures scratched out on it in red ballpoint pen. Rachel almost swallowed her tongue. It was quite a bit more than she'd been hoping to spend. She did the sums in her head. Back home this kind of money would afford her a mansion, with a staff of four and a double garage. Rachel pulled out her purse and counted out a wad of cash.

'Can I give you the rest tomorrow?' asked Rachel as Doreen recounted the money carefully, her pink fingernails flashing.

The agent appraised her through false eyelashes. 'Oh, goodness, is that the time?' she said, suddenly distracted by the enormous diamante-studded watch on her wrist. It looked like it weighed a ton and a half on her skinny, fake-tanned arm. Doreen shoved the cash into her oversized almost-designer handbag. 'I have to dash or I'm going to be late picking up Cha-Cha from day care.'

'Oh, cute,' said Rachel. 'Your daughter's name is Cha-Cha?'

Doreen looked at Rachel as if she had two heads. 'No, dear, Cha-Cha is my Chihuahua. She's in doggie day care uptown, but they close at five. Here are the keys, lock up on your way out and pop into the office first thing tomorrow so we can sign the lease and do an official handover, okay?'

'Sure,' said Rachel. 'Doggie day care, hey? Only in New York!'

Doreen whirled out of the apartment, leaving a cloud of CK One and stale cigarette smoke in her wake. Rachel could hear her click-clacking down the corridor and shuddered as she pictured her cracked heels shoved into those one-size-too-small pink sandals clattering down the stairs.

Turning around, Rachel evaluated her new home. An enormous cockroach, the size of a remote-controlled toy car scooted through the kitchen and disappeared into the shower and down the drain. Rachel shrieked and jumped backwards instinctively. Something brushed her arm and she wiped at it with a paranoid hand. She would have to buy bug spray, she decided. Lots and lots of bug spray.

Rachel opened the window and stared out at the view. About a metre away from the window was the brick wall of the apartment building next door and three floors down was a slim alley filled with trash cans. And that was the view. Home sweet home, for now. Or rather, hovel sweet hovel, she thought. She felt excited to have finally found an apartment but sheer revulsion at the state of it.

Something in her peripheral vision caught her eye. On high alert, she stepped aside and saw first one fat, round orange and then another roll past her foot. Turning, she stared as a trail of rolling oranges came through her open front door. Across the hall stood the most petite woman Rachel had ever seen. She must have been about thirty and was beautiful in a girl-next-door kind of way. She had long strawberry blonde hair and perfect skin. The woman was trying to balance two full brown-paper grocery bags on one bent knee while she struggled to get the key in the front door of the apartment across the hall. Somehow, the bottom of one of the bags had torn and the rest of the oranges, a carton of milk and a cucumber rained out of the bottom.

'Damn paper bags!' she muttered in a soft Southern drawl.

Rachel couldn't help notice that she was wearing an amazing pair of black and red boots she'd recently seen in *Cosmopolitan*. She remembered because she had coveted them from the second she'd seen them.

Rachel bent down and started to gather the stray oranges. The woman started. 'I didn't see you there,' she said, turning to face Rachel, still clutching the bags and her keys.

'Sorry, I didn't mean to give you a fright,' said Rachel, walking towards her with an armful of wayward fruit. 'I love your boots.'

'Thanks,' said the woman. 'My husband worries that I like shoes more than I like him. I tell him not to worry, but between you and me, he probably should.'

'Here you go,' Rachel held the oranges out to her.

'Cool accent, where you from?' the woman asked.

'I'm from Johannesburg in South Africa, but I'm moving in here tomorrow. My name's Rachel.' Rachel would have offered a hand to shake, but they both already had their hands full.

'It's about time someone moved in. Nice to meet you, I'm Sue,' the woman said, dumping the torn bags on the floor and turning to face Rachel with her hands on her hips. 'Hopefully you'll have better luck than the last people who lived there.' Sue gestured into Rachel's apartment with her head.

'What happened?'

'Marcelle and Trevor lived there for a year, but she killed him in there a couple of weeks ago. She shot him in the face.'

Rachel thought maybe she hadn't heard right, Sue had said it so casually.

Sue saw the look on Rachel's face. 'Don't worry,' she said. 'They cleaned it up real nice. You can barely see the stains. Look, I gotta get this ice cream in the freezer, you wanna gimme a hand with those oranges and come in for a cup of coffee?'

Rachel considered Sue's offer and wondered if it was a good idea to go into a complete stranger's apartment in New York? Was she about to become another headline in *The New York Times*? *South African woman brutally murdered with oranges in minute apartment.*

Considering the luck she'd had over the last couple of months it wasn't entirely out of the question. But Rachel shook off her paranoia. After all, she thought, what are the odds of there being two murders in the same apartment block in less than two months? And, anyway, she couldn't really blame Marcelle. If she'd have had to live with a man in such a small apartment she'd have probably ended up shooting him in the face too. 'That sounds great,' Rachel said, following Sue inside.

Putting the oranges on Sue's kitchen counter Rachel went to lock up her new apartment. Back in Sue's kitchen she took a look around. The entire apartment was about twice the size of Rachel's, which made it almost palatial in New York real estate terms. 'This is a great apartment,' said Rachel. 'How long have you and your husband been here?'

'We moved here from Alabama a year and a half ago. Brian, that's my husband, he got a job in finance. He's going to be an investment banker, but he's got to spend a couple of years jumping through their hoops before he can get there, so we're living here till then.'

Rachel nodded.

'Coffee, or can I interest you in something a little stronger?' Sue asked, holding up a bottle of wine.

'That sounds like a damn fine idea,' said Rachel.

'So, what do you do?' asked Sue.

'I'm an advertising copywriter. Well, at least, I was a copywriter back home. Things kind of got out of control. I guess you could say that a series of unfortunate events got me fired. So I left, so things could cool down a bit. I got here a week ago, so I haven't got a job yet, but I'm working on it.'

Rachel knew she was rambling, but she couldn't stop herself. This was the first actual conversation she'd had with anyone since she'd left Joburg, other than ordering food or booking her hotel room or talking to Doreen about finding an apartment. Rachel felt like she'd pulled out a plug and all her words were rushing out, splashing all over her feet and out onto the floorboards. She took a deep breath. Evaluating the story she'd just relayed to Sue, she realised she would probably have to think of a better way of wording it when she spoke to headhunters. Put like that her life didn't sound very impressive.

Sue popped the cork and poured two large glasses. 'That sounds interesting, I'm glad I bought two bottles of wine.'

'Less interesting and more horrific really. So, what do you do, Sue?' she asked, desperate to change the subject.

'I'm a freelance illustrator. I work from home. I'm busy with a series of children's books at the moment, but they've got a ridiculous deadline, hence the wine. Cheers!' she said, raising her glass. 'Here's to you finding a job.'

'And to you meeting your deadline,' said Rachel, chinking glasses.

They chatted about some of the apartments Rachel had looked at. Sue filled their glasses a couple of times and talked about her work. Talking to Sue was easy. Rachel felt like she'd known her for years. And Sue seemed only too happy to have the company. They ploughed their way easily through the first bottle of wine and it wasn't long before they were halfway into the second bottle – she was impressed, for such a small person Sue seemed quite adept at holding her liquor. Rachel felt tipsy and relaxed for the first time in weeks.

Some time after seven Rachel heard a key in the door and it opened to reveal one of the tallest men she had ever seen. He must have been almost seven foot tall and Rachel couldn't help but stare. Sue was so petite that she had to stand on tiptoes to reach up for a kiss, and even then Brian still had to bend down halfway to meet her lips. They were such an odd looking pair. Rachel couldn't decide whether Sue made Brian look even taller or Brian made Sue look even smaller.

'Honey, this is our new next-door neighbour, Rachel. She's from South Africa,' Sue said. 'Rachel, this is my husband, Brian.'

Brian strode over to Rachel with his hand held out. She shook hands with him expecting a bone-crunching grip, but instead she was surprised to find it light but firm.

'Nice to meet you. Are you moving into poor Trev and crazy Marcie's old place? Please tell me she doesn't own a firearm?' he said to Sue in mock horror.

'Sue told me about that … Don't worry: no boyfriend, no weapons, just me.'

'That's a relief,' he said. He eyed the empty bottle of wine and the second half-empty bottle next to it and smiled at Sue. 'Sweetheart, I take it you and Rachel haven't spent the entire afternoon cooking a gourmet dinner for your darling husband then?'

Sue shook her head. 'Nope,' she said. 'We've been celebrating Rachel's first apartment in New York City.'

'Well, I'm starving, how about pizza?' he asked, picking up the phone.

Pizzas ordered they moved to the kitchen table and Sue got Brian a beer.

Rachel watched Brian take Sue's hand in his and she thought about Phillip back home in Joburg. She wondered what he was doing at that precise moment. She did a quick calculation: it would be about three a.m. in Joburg. She pictured Phillip asleep in the bed they'd shared. He usually slept on his side with one arm laying over her waist. The memory felt like it came from another lifetime. She wondered if he was alone and an acute sense of grief shot through her. She put her hand up to her heart and held it there. Since she'd left home she'd managed to file the events of the preceding weeks away in a dusty unused compartment in her mind. When thoughts of either Phillip or the incident at work tried to snake to the surface she would poke them back down with a mental stick. She was here now, this was her new life and she wouldn't let the sour memory of Phillip be any part of it.

Sue filled their glasses again and Rachel realised she was feeling quite drunk. At least that gave her an excuse for allowing Phillip to filter into her thoughts again. Rachel thought about the mess she'd made of just about every relationship she'd ever been in. But this was her fresh start; she was in New York now and things would be different. Things would be great. 'How did you two meet?' Rachel asked, forcing herself back into the now.

Sue looked lovingly at Brian. 'We met in high school,' she said. 'Brian, his mom and younger brother moved to Alabama in our final year. We were in the same class.'

'I caught her checking me out in Spanish class,' Brian said.

'That's not true!' said Sue, punching Brian on the arm. 'I didn't even know you were there until I caught you checking me out in geography.'

The door buzzer went and Rachel reached for her handbag. 'Don't even think about it,' Brian smiled, 'dinner's on us.'

Around midnight Rachel dragged herself out of Sue and Brian's apartment and caught a cab back to the hotel. Sue and Brian had tried to convince her to sleep on their couch, but it was her last night in the hotel and she'd already paid for the room. That and she didn't trust herself to watch the two of them disappear off into the bedroom together, leaving her lying on the couch alone, drunkenly contemplating her failures. She also had a feeling she'd be seeing a lot of the inside of their apartment and she didn't want to wear out her welcome quite yet.

When Rachel got back to her hotel room she booted up her laptop and logged into Facebook to update her status. She had big news for anyone back home who was interested in hearing it.

Rachel Marcus has a new box-sized flat in the world's most amazing city. As well as three new flatmates. All of whom are cockroaches.
March 11 at 1:38am

Rachel Marcus is moving into the world's smallest apartment today.
March 11 at 12:15pm

'Good morning, Miss Marcus, we trust you had a good stay with us here at The New York Inn?'

'Yes, thank you,' said Rachel, steadying herself on the concierge's desk. She had a hangover and the sunlight kept seeping in through the sides of her sunglasses.

'You're all checked out, ma'am. Can Miguel help you with your bags and call you a cab?' the guy behind the desk asked, raising his hand above the bell on the edge of the desk.

Rachel looked across the foyer and recognised the guy who had embezzled five dollars from her two days earlier. He smiled widely when he saw her and walked towards her rubbing his palms together – the international symbol for windfall. 'No!' she snapped, a little too loudly, batting the concierge's hand away from the bell. 'I've got it, thank you.'

The concierge nursed his stinging hand and stared at her, shocked. Grabbing the handle of her enormous wheelie suitcase, Rachel swung the strap of her tog bag across her chest, pulled her overnight bag over her shoulder and clasped her handbag in front of her with both hands. Then, stumbling under the awkward weight of her load, she made her way out of the hotel, getting caught in the revolving door for a tense moment before she realised that her overnight bag was still stuck on the inside while she was on the outside. She backed up, released her bag and staggered the rest of the way, unglamorously, out of the hotel, already perspiring like a donkey. 'I got it, I can manage, I'm fine,' she yelled out to a disappointed Miguel. 'I'll be damned if you get another cent out of me,' she muttered as she burst out onto the sidewalk.

She caught a cab to the letting agency to finalise the deal on her apartment and then she made her way to what was now officially home. When she arrived she buzzed Sue's apartment from the street.

'Hello,' came Sue's voice through the small square speaker.

'Hey, it's Rachel, I made it. Are you as hung-over as I am?'

'I'll come down and give you a hand,' said Sue.

Sue appeared and held the door open so Rachel could lug all her stuff inside. Sue grabbed Rachel's tog bag and overnight bag and they began dragging everything up the three flights of stairs together.

'One of the reasons I took this apartment was because it doesn't have an elevator. I thought it would be good exercise, you know, save me having to go to the gym,' Rachel huffed when they stopped for a break on the second floor.

'This bag feels like its got twenty pound weights in it, are you sure you didn't bring the gym with you?' asked Sue, wiping the sweat off her forehead.

'No, just lots of shoes. When things got so messed up at home I sold everything. This is all I've got left in the whole world,' Rachel said, gesturing at her bags. 'It's hard to believe, but less than four weeks ago I was group head at one of the top advertising agencies in South Africa. I had a beautiful apartment, a personal trainer and a sexy fiancé.' Rachel shook her head and picked up the handle of the wheelie suitcase to continue her trek. 'Just look at me now.'

'It's not that bad, everything always feels worse when you're hung-over,' said Sue, dragging Rachel's bag along the floor.

'Come on,' said Rachel. 'As soon as we get this stuff inside I'll make coffee and you can be the first person I ever have over in my new apartment.'

'Sounds good,' said Sue. 'I think I've earned it.'

'Have you got any coffee I can borrow?' asked Rachel with a grin.

'Sure,' said Sue.

'How about some milk and two cups?'

Rachel Marcus is jobless and hung-over, but at least she's not homeless.

March 11 at 1:15pm

Rachel Marcus is still job hunting.
March 24 at 8:13am

Rachel Marcus has yet another job interview today. Please hold virtual thumbs for her.
April 3 at 9:03am via Mobile Web

'You've got a fantastic book.' Jerrod Craig stood over his desk, leaning forward with his fists on the table, examining a page of Rachel's portfolio intently.

'Thank you,' she said, her voice cracking like a fourteen-year-old boy's.

Jerrod Craig was, in Rachel's opinion, ridiculously good-looking. But more importantly he was also an internationally awarded art director and a creative group head at Richmond&Phillips, New York – one of the top ten most creative advertising agencies in the world in 2008, according to *Campaign* magazine. Rachel remembered seeing him go up on stage with his R&P colleagues countless times to pick up awards when she'd gone to the Cannes International Advertising Festival in the South of France the previous year. Rachel tried to calm herself. She wanted to come across as sophisticated, professional and controlled; the diametric opposite of how she was actually feeling. It was massively important that she didn't screw up this interview. She'd already been job hunting for forever and this felt like her millionth interview. She was broke and her list of potential agencies was shrinking by the day.

'This radio station campaign is amazing. I remember seeing it at all the award shows. It won at Cannes, right?'

'Yes,' said Rachel, feeling a bit more confident. 'A silver.'

'Impressive,' he said, nodding. 'So, is this your first time in New York?' She felt his green-eyed stare burn down her spine. He was deliciously tall with dark hair, greying slightly at the temples. He wore a pair of perfectly fitting Diesel jeans, a crisp white polo button-down shirt and a pair of Nike sneakers that he could park under her bed any day.

'I've been here before, but only on holiday,' she said.

'And where did you say you worked in South Africa?'

'An agency called Barker, Massa and Trout.'

'That's Matthew Barker, isn't it?' said Jerrod. 'He's great. I judged D&AD with him a couple of years ago in London. I must email him and say hello.'

Rachel giggled on the outside and convulsed with horror on the inside. The possibility of Jerrod getting in touch with her ex-boss made her break out in internal hives. She wiped her sweaty palms on her skirt under the table. It was bad enough that the whole of the South African advertising industry knew her shame, but the thought of the story spreading to New York was more than Rachel could bear.

'Look,' said Jerrod, getting back to business as he paged through the last few pieces in her book. 'I'm not going to bullshit you, you've got a great portfolio here, world-class in fact, but you've come at a bad time. We're all feeling the recession right now and we're not looking to hire. And even with your British passport, papers are tougher to get these days, so even if we were looking I'm not sure ...' Jerrod trailed off.

Rachel nodded and tried not to look shattered.

Jerrod looked her up and down. 'But,' he said, brightening as he closed her book, 'I've got your number and if anything comes up I'll call you, okay? Or, maybe I can call you and we can go for a drink some time? I could show you around.'

Rachel gulped and instantly worried that he'd heard it. 'Absolutely,' she said, standing up and tugging on her skirt, which had snuck all the way up her thighs while she was sitting and was now more like a belt. 'I'd like that,' she added.

A smile played at the corners of Jerrod's lips and his hand touched hers as he passed her the portfolio case. 'Excellent,' he said, guiding her out of the boardroom with his hand in the small of her back. Perhaps she was imagining it, but Rachel was sure his hand was placed slightly lower than necessary. A thrill shot down her spine and exploded in her crotch.

Alone in the elevator, floors dinging by, Rachel breathed out for what felt like the first time since she'd met Jerrod half an hour earlier. She let her head drop and closed her eyes, wondering whether it had been the worst interview she'd ever had or the best.

> Rachel Marcus is still jobless. Unfortunately, being a professional job-hunter is hardly a viable career path and doesn't pay very well. Bread and water anyone?
> *April 3 at 12:57pm via Mobile Web*

On the subway Rachel tried not to touch anything. In the beginning making her way around the city on the underground had been a novelty. There was endless people-watching to do and finding her way around had been an exciting challenge. But soon she'd started to see things going on down there that had made her wish her eyeballs would shrivel up. Besides the masses of tourists and businessmen and women there was also an endless stream of freaks and lunatics. She would never be able to unsee the homeless man peeing his pants in the seat across from her or the drunken punk teenager who'd spent ten minutes kissing his girlfriend as if he had three tongues after Rachel had seen her vomit into a trash can on the platform ten minutes earlier. These things had jaded her to the point where she was careful to make as little contact as possible with the surfaces around her. There was some pride in these little actions, they meant that a month into her life in Manhattan she was no longer a wide-eyed tourist and more like a hardened local commuter.

Rachel was headed uptown for an appointment at Val's office. Val was one of the directors of an employment agency specialising in creative positions within the advertising industry. Rachel liked Val; she reminded her of a school friend's mum or a member of the PTA. Val was in her fifties, but she wore it well. She was kind and friendly and spoke in the excited kind of over-explainy voice that preschool teachers use on their six-year-old students. But Rachel wasn't fooled; she knew that behind the mumsy persona Val was every inch a tough businesswoman. She was also Rachel's best shot at getting a job.

At their first meeting Val had looked at Rachel's portfolio and instantly recognised her talent, but regardless of the standard of Rachel's work, Val was conservative and quick to remind her of the global recession and the effects it was having on the industry. So far Val had sent Rachel on a record twenty-six interviews. She'd been to just about every above-the-line agency in New York and the most fruitful meeting had been the one with Jerrod Craig. Not that anything had come of it.

Rachel reconsidered her options. She was running out of money faster than she had anticipated. Roach spray wasn't cheap in New York and Rachel had planned to have a job by this stage. She did some quick mental gymnastics. Assuming she was cautious with her money she could manage another two weeks max before she would no longer be able to afford the rent on her cubby hole. Then what, she wondered? Brian and Sue's couch? The street? A homeless shelter? There was nothing exciting about her prospects. Rachel was terrified. This was the opposite of making it big in New York. She sighed. She knew she was going to have to lower her standards. Going home to the carnage of the life she'd left behind wasn't an option. Not quite yet anyway.

Since she'd started in advertising ten years earlier, Rachel had always worked as an above-the-line copywriter specialising in traditional, mainstream media: television commercials, magazine ads, press campaigns, billboards and radio commercials. She had no experience and even less passion for below-the-line advertising like promotions, branding and point-of-sale. Sitting there on the subway after yet another failed interview, close to tears, Rachel briefly considered prostitution, but then she caught a man sitting across from her staring directly at her crotch, the tip of his tongue sticking out from between his fleshy lips. He caught her stare and smiled lecherously at her. The few teeth he still had looked like pieces of burnt corn and Rachel imagined she could smell his dog breath from where she sat. Suddenly prostitution didn't seem like such a good idea anymore, the thought of his foul mouth on any part of her body made her want to vomit. So she sat up straight, looked away from him and started loving advertising again.

'Hello, Rachel,' said Val. 'So, how'd it go with the interview?'

Rachel shook her head and plonked herself down on the chair across from Val's desk, trying hard not to cry. 'I'm so sorry, Val, I tried.'

'Now, I told you it wouldn't be easy, but the best things never are.'

'Val, I've been thinking that maybe it's time we widened our search a little.'

Val looked at Rachel and took off her glasses. 'Okay, what did you have in mind?'

'To be honest,' said Rachel, 'at this stage, if it comes with a pay cheque and it doesn't involve a stripper pole or giving blow jobs in the back seat of a cab, it'll work for me.'

Val nodded.

'I was thinking,' said Rachel. 'It might be time to start looking into a below-the-line position.'

Val clapped her hands together. 'Fantastic idea, Rachel. In fact, something just came in and I think it might work for you. Give me a second.' Val turned to her computer, put on her glasses and clacked at her keyboard. 'It's not really the kind work you're used to,' she said. 'It's a small agency you've probably never heard of called Target Advertising, in a below-the-line writing position. The creative director there, Dan Charter, has been looking for someone for a couple of weeks already. He's about to go on a trip, and I know he'd be keen to fill the position before he goes. What do you think?' Val took her glasses off and peered at Rachel.

Rachel looked at her hands lying in her lap and thought about it. This was hardly the kind of job she would be able to impress everybody back home with, but she would go for it anyway and use it to pay the rent while she waited for something better to come along. She knew she didn't really have any other choice unless she fancied being homeless. She took a deep breath and tried to reassure herself that this was just a blip. Only fifty per cent of her believed it.

'It's not the kind of salary you're used to either,' Val went on, interrupting her mental pep talk. 'But, Rachel, you can make this work, I know you can. And we'll keep on looking for something else in the meantime, I promise.'

Rachel nodded, trying to rein in the tears – she would not cry in front of Val. 'Okay,' she said, clearing her throat. 'I'll give it a bash. When's the interview?'

'How's Monday at nine?' Val smiled broadly and handed Rachel a printout of directions to below-the-line, brochure-writing, AV-editing, promotion-making advertising hell.

Rachel Marcus has her seven gazillionth interview tomorrow. Okay, no need to exaggerate, maybe it's only her five gazillionth.
April 5 at 10:02pm

'What does Google say?' asked Sue, leaning over Rachel's shoulder in the kitchen.

'It says here that Target Advertising specialises in consumer promotions and competitions, corporate identities, audio visuals, in-store materials, point of sale and brochures. Their clients include a sock company, a sanitary pad company, a toilet paper company and quite a big pharmaceutical company.' Rachel paused as the full horror of the situation sank in. 'Shit, Sue, I'm used to working on TV commercials, magazine ads and radio campaigns for brands like Levi's and Nike and Mercedes-Benz ... How am I going to get excited about writing a medical brochure for nipple cream or a packaging insert for toilet paper?'

'Johnnie Walker doesn't grow on trees, Rachel, you'd better start getting excited about it!' said Sue.

Rachel nodded. She couldn't argue with that kind of logic.

Rachel Marcus is parking her pride.
April 6 at 7:51am

Target Advertising's offices were conveniently located in mid-town Manhattan. From Rachel's apartment it was a twenty minute subway ride followed by a five minute walk. The area was home to a number of meat markets and the rank smell of raw meat hovered in the streets. Rachel wasn't quite sure where she was supposed to be going. She was on the right street, but she couldn't see any kind of signage that might point her in the right direction. She stopped and fished Val's directions out of her pocket. Head down, focused on the directions, she took a step forward and was almost knocked off her heels by a giant pink pig carcass as a man in a white apron and white gum boots crossed in front of her carrying his porky load. If Rachel's nerves weren't completely shot before, they were now. This was not a good omen for a Jewish girl arriving at a job interview. In Rachel's mind it was the equivalent of breaking a mirror and she wondered if running into pork also carried the statutory seven years bad luck.

Rachel eventually tracked down the entrance. She smoothed her skirt, took a deep breath and walked through the doors of Target Advertising. A young blonde with absolutely enormous breasts sat behind a large reception desk, smiling widely. She was otherwise so petite that Rachel was immediately concerned that if she stood up she would find herself too top heavy to stay upright and would fall forward, landing flat on her face.

'Hello, I'm Rachel Marcus. I have a nine o' clock with Daniel Charter.'

'Please have a seat,' the receptionist said, her smile never wavering for a second. 'Dan will be right with you.'

Besides having a sore back from lugging around those impressive double Ds all day, Rachel thought the receptionist's mouth must also get incredibly sore after a full day of smiling. She couldn't imagine that she would ever smile outside of the office; it would just be too painful.

Rachel looked around, trying to get a feel for the agency. The decor was stark and modern; everything was white and minimalist. The reception area felt like a cross between some kind of futuristic film set and a doctor's rooms. The only shock of colour came from an enormous flower arrangement on top of the receptionist's desk. Large red blossoms shot out of the angular glass vase in a designer spray, accompanied by an odd assortment of what looked a lot to Rachel like sticks. A handful of plastic goldfish floated around inside the vase and a yellow plastic duck bobbed around on the surface of the water.

There were five chairs in the reception waiting area and Rachel contemplated which one would be the safest to try and sit on. In fact, Rachel wasn't sure whether any of them were chairs at all, rather, she thought, they were more likely pieces of art. Maybe that was why the receptionist was smiling so much. Perhaps this was how she got her kicks. Every day she sat behind her massive desk with her enormous breasts and waited for innocents like Rachel to come in. Then she invited them to sit down, waiting for them to plonk their asses down on the installation. Rachel thought she would grin endlessly too if she got to watch that all day.

The first chair she considered was styled on a giant white Pilates ball. Rachel ran her hand over it. It was made of nylon and was like a large inflated balloon. The thought of sitting on it scared her. What if it rolled away, delivering her onto the floor? She tried to remember what panties she'd put on earlier that morning and was reminded of her mother who had always instructed her to wear her good knickers all the time, just in case she got in an accident. Rachel wondered whether this was the kind of accident her mother had always envisioned.

Another of the chairs had a seat that hovered just above the ground. The entire thing was made of leather and seemed of a very complicated design. It was so deep that if she sat in it her bum would be almost touching the floor and she might never be able to get out of it again.

Eventually, Rachel chose the 'chair' that looked the easiest to get into and out of. It was in the shape of a giant white stiletto. The seat part was situated in the arch of the shoe and the backrest was the heel. Rachel felt like an idiot climbing into it and she wondered if it might have been wiser to have simply stood while she waited.

'You must be Rachel.'

A squeaky, high-pitched voice shot Rachel back into reality and she jumped out of her shoe and extended her hand. 'Yes, hello, I'm Rachel.'

The person ignored her outstretched hand and her restatement of the obvious and came in for a hug. Rachel's first surprise was that the voice belonged to a man. Her second surprise was the hug. She stood stiff as a board while this perfect stranger pressed his body up against hers. His head reached to just below her chin, and a strong smell of patchouli wafted up while he clung to her. Rachel crumpled her nose; she'd never been a big fan of incense.

'We don't shake hands at Target Advertising,' the man finally said. 'Around here we like to hug, to show how we truly value each other. I'm Daniel Charter, but you can call me Dan, everybody does.'

'Hello, Dan,' said Rachel. 'I'm Rachel Marcus.' She shook her head, realising that she'd already said her own name one too many times.

'Please, come on through,' he said.

Rachel followed him down the corridor. Walking a couple of steps behind him she managed to take her first really good look at him. He was short for a man. He wore spectacles and he had a receding hairline in front and a long ponytail down his back, which had obviously been dyed an unnatural jet black. He wore khaki pants, Birkenstocks with socks and a pale blue button-down shirt.

Dan's office was large and patchouli-scented. The first thing Rachel noticed was that instead of carpet or tiles, the floor was covered in bright-green plastic grass. Dan took his shoes off at the door, visibly enjoying the texture of the fake grass between his toes as he made his way into the room. Rachel noted that, aside from a computer, his desk was home to a number of model Porsches, a small, twisted bonsai, a miniature wooden Buddha and a couple of framed photographs. One whole wall was a glass window that looked out on a traditional Japanese Zen garden. An Indian man in a robe and turban stood in the middle of the sand, carving it out with a giant rake. Back inside the office Rachel took in a large black leather couch, a big screen TV set and a pinball machine. A whale sounds CD played gently in the background.

Dan sat down on the couch and patted the seat next to him. 'Come join me, Rachel,' he said. 'Can I get you a carrot juice or maybe a wheatgrass shake?'

'No, thanks, Dan,' said Rachel, smiling politely.

'So,' he said, rubbing his hands together. 'According to Val, you come highly recommended, Rachel. Let's take a look at your portfolio.'

Rachel settled next to Dan and laid her book out on the table. Dan paged through it, grunting. He had small, perfectly manicured fingers and wore a simple gold wedding band. While he was absorbed by her work, Rachel snuck a look at the photographs lined up on his desk. She recognised him in the first photograph. He was on a skiing trip, posing next to a tall, pretty, young-looking blonde, who could have been either his eldest daughter or his second or perhaps even third wife.

'Do you believe in synchronicity, Rachel Marcus?' Dan asked, still paging.

'I think so,' she said, although she wasn't a hundred per cent sure what he meant.

'Well,' he said. 'It's an incredible thing. My swami gave me an alignment of the chakras this morning and he told me that today would be a great day for allowing new things to enter my world.'

'Wow,' said Rachel, not quite sure how else to respond to such a statement.

'And so,' he continued. 'I feel a certain connectedness to you today. It feels almost spiritual ... Also I really like this campaign you did for Mercedes-Benz.'

'Thank you.'

'Look, Rachel Marcus,' he said, taking off his glasses and steepling his fingers in front of his face as he spoke. 'I'm not going to lie to you. We work hard here at Target Advertising, but I think you'll find it rewarding and satisfying on a much deeper, more spiritual level than anything else you've ever experienced. We consider ourselves the true shepherds of our brands. And I think you have a great deal to offer us. So, what I'm asking, Rachel Marcus, is ... would you be interested in coming to help me tend my flock, here at Target Advertising?'

Rachel had to clear her throat to stifle a laugh. She looked at this strange, strange man with a dyed ponytail who wore Birkenstocks with socks. This was it, she thought. This was who she was going to work for. Could she do it, she wondered? But then it wasn't like she had much of a choice. As Sue had so kindly pointed out, Johnnie Walker didn't grow on trees. Although on the kind of salary Target Advertising was offering she might have to change her taste in Scotch. The money was drastically less than what she'd been earning in Johannesburg, even with the pathetic South African exchange rate, but for now it would have to do.

'Yes, Dan,' said Rachel, pasting an enormous receptionist-inspired grin on her face. 'I would love to help you tend your flock.' But, even as she said it, inside, a little piece of Rachel Marcus shrivelled up and died.

Dan stood up and clapped his hands together in delight. 'That swami, I tell you,' Dan squeaked. 'He's a genius, even with all that enema talk!'

Rachel extended her hand so they could shake on it, thinking that maybe if she made it clear early on that she wasn't really the huggy type it would set the tone for a more professional working relationship.

Dan looked at her hand, shook his head and smiled, moving in for his hug. 'Can you start tomorrow morning?' he asked, mid-clench.

Rachel Marcus finally has a job in New York City. Champagne (of the screw-top variety) is on me.
April 6 at 9:57am via Mobile Web

When Rachel got home from her interview there was a small package wrapped in brown paper waiting for her. She tore it open frantically. It was a letter from home and a box of rooibos tea. She read the letter, then sat down and wrote a quick response.

Dear Mom and Dad,

Thanks so much for your letter and package. I can't tell you how nice it is to hear from home. I'm sorry to hear all the details of Uncle Hymie's prostate problems. Really sorry.

The detailed description of Cousin Elaine's wedding was also fascinating. It sounds lovely, even though the catering wasn't up to scratch.

Great news, I've landed a fantastic job at one of New York's hottest advertising agencies. Three or four different agencies all made me offers, but ultimately I chose this one (it's called Target Advertising) because I'm going to get to work on some very exciting accounts and the money is great. Way more than I was earning at home, so there's really no need for you and Dad to worry about me so much.

All right, must go, I've got a party tonight.

All my love,
Rachel

PS: Thanks for the tea. But I'm not really a huge fan of rooibos. Five Roses is really the one I'm looking for. I can't find it here anywhere. Please ask anyone at any shop over there and they will point it out to you.

PPS: Please tell Uncle Cyril that computers don't cause brain cancer and the government isn't reading everything you write on them. Ninety per cent of the population of the first world use computers, Mom. Why don't you just pop into Incredible Connection some time and have someone show you around? For me. Please.

'Ready for your first day?' asked Sue, buttering a piece of toast.

'Bye, sweetie,' said Brian, whipping through the kitchen, clutching his tie and briefcase in one hand. He grabbed the toast off Sue's plate and gave her a kiss. 'Good luck, Rae,' he added, ramming the toast between his teeth and ruffling Rachel's hair as he whirled past her.

Rachel growled and tried to put her hair back in place.

Once Brian had left Rachel did a little twirl so Sue could evaluate her outfit. 'What do you think?' she asked. 'Does it say, don't fuck with me, I'm a professional?'

Sue looked her up and down and nodded. 'Yes, and even better than that, it says don't fuck with me, I'm a professional and I'm hot.'

Rachel Marcus is off to her first day at a new school. She's gong to try play nicely with the other children.
April 7 at 8:15am

The receptionist was still smiling when Rachel arrived for her first day of work at Target Advertising. Rachel introduced herself, trying hard not to stare at the woman's enormous breasts – she didn't want to be rude. Then again, she reasoned, if she had gone to all the effort, agony and expense of having her breasts made so enormous, maybe it was rude not to stare.

'Nice to meet you, I'm Heather,' the receptionist said, extracting herself from behind the big white desk. 'Come on, I'll show you around.'

Heather led the way efficiently through the agency. 'These are the bathrooms, this is the kitchen,' she said as Rachel ran to keep up with her. 'Over here is the executive Zen garden, but it's strictly for upper management only ... There is another Zen garden for the rest of the employees on the other side of the studio, okay?'

Rachel stumbled straight into the receptionist, who had stopped suddenly and spun around to make sure she had taken in this important piece of information. Heather smiled at her through gritted teeth before continuing with the tour. Along the way she stopped to introduce Rachel to some of the employees scattered around the office. Rachel would later recall Deborah the traffic lady, who was in charge of scheduling all the work that moved through the agency, Sam, one of the account executives, and Amanda, another account executive, but after that all the names and faces blurred into one another. Rachel shook hands with everyone, thankful that hugging wasn't the agency norm, although she suspected that when Dan was around it was a different story.

The rest of the agency was furnished in line with what she'd seen in the reception area and Dan's office – modern, minimalist and white (although there was a notable lack of plastic grass and employees sat on standard office chairs, not shoes and Pilates balls). However, unlike Dan's office and the reception area, the office walls were dotted with giant framed posters of clichéd pictures of sky divers and bears in the woods. Beneath them were printed motivational statements like *Seek and You Shall Find* and *There is No Question so Small That it is Not Worth Asking*. A couple of the more lofty ones were even attributed to a certain Dan Charter. Rachel rolled her eyes. Those, she thought, would get very old, very fast.

'This is your office,' Heather finally said, pointing through a door. 'You'll share it with your art director, Justin Coley.'

'What's he like?' Rachel asked, stepping into her new office.

Heather gave Rachel a knowing smile and left without saying a word, following her breasts down the corridor and back to the reception desk to continue her smilathon.

The office contained two desks – each with an Apple Mac and a telephone – a small couch and a coffee table. The desk that faced the door was empty, while the other one was covered in layout pads, pens, papers and magazines. A picture, torn out of a magazine, of a woman wearing what might be considered a bikini, if you were feeling generous, was pinned to the pinboard behind it.

Rachel walked over to the empty desk in the office, which she assumed would be hers, sat down, turned on her computer and waited. Bored, she swivelled around in the chair, lifting her legs and watching the computer flash by as she swung past it over and over again.

'You must be Rachel,' said a clear voice with a strong British accent.

Rachel dug her heels into the carpet, gripping the arms of the chair as it came to a dangerously squeaky stop. Blushing, she looked up and saw a man with curly blond hair standing in the doorway, a welcoming smile on his face. 'None of this hugging bollocks, all right?' he said as he crossed the room and held his hand out to her.

'Thank God,' said Rachel, shaking his hand, trying hard to curb her dizziness and embarrassment at being caught spinning around on a chair like a six-year-old. 'Justin, right?'

'I'm so glad you're here at last. I haven't had anyone to play with for months. You're not a vegan or anything stupid like that, are you?' he asked.

Rachel flushed with relief. She'd also been nervous he'd be some kind of weirdo hippie hugging machine, like Dan. 'No,' she laughed, 'I'm definitely not a vegan.'

Rachel watched as Justin crossed the office and collapsed onto the couch. 'So, Rachel, welcome to the wonderful world of New York City advertising. Can I offer you a line, partner?' he asked, wiping his hand across the top of the small table that stood squarely in front of the couch.

Rachel had to try hard not to look surprised. She knew how important first impressions were and she didn't want to come across as ignorant, or uncool, or, even worse, as some kind of prude. After all, she thought, this is a New York advertising agency; it was probably standard to be offered a line of cocaine to kick-start the day. But on the other hand, she didn't want Justin to think she was a druggy. She'd done coke back home; it was an industry standard. She'd enjoyed it, but mainly she'd found it a grubby and expensive habit. One she'd never really liked enough for it to become anything more than a rare distraction on a big night out. 'No, thanks,' she finally said. 'I usually try to hold off on the cocaine before breakfast.'

Justin burst out laughing and Rachel grinned back at him. He was obviously just testing her, but she couldn't quite figure out whether or not she had passed.

As the day wore on Rachel tried to settle in and memorise more names and the faces that matched them. Ultimately, however, she resigned herself to the fact that for the first week or two, other than Heather and Justin, they would have to remain in her mind as 'girl with bad hair', 'guy with limp', 'girl with scar on chin', 'emo chick', 'halitosis boy' and 'slimy bald guy' ...

Rachel Marcus can now be found at r.marcus@targetadvertising.com
April 7 at 10:36am

The IT guy set up her agency email account and she shot off a couple of emails to friends at home and updated her Facebook status. Then, after lunch, she and Justin filed into one of the boardrooms with a client service guy to meet a client and get a brief on the first job they would work on together, an in-store promotion for the agency's sock client, RightSole.

In an advertising agency it's client service's job to be the agency and client go-between, translating the client's needs to the agency, managing the budget and attempting to keep both the client and the agency happy. From what Rachel could gather the RightSole client service guy had traded in his sense of humour long ago. Rachel had been introduced to him just before the meeting, but for the life of her she couldn't remember his name, he was that beige.

Mr Beige kicked off the meeting with introductions. The client's name was Clive something, and Rachel thought he definitely resembled a Clive something. Tall and thin, and quite bent around the shoulders, he wore a meticulous brown suit with a brown knitted tie. He looked like a forty-two year old man trapped in an eighty-nine year old man's body – something between her high school history teacher, Mr Fiske, and Mr Burns from the Simpsons.

After the introductions Clive stood up to speak, which Rachel thought was unnecessarily formal considering that there were only four of them in the boardroom. 'Good afternoon,' he said. 'To kick off, I've brought some research I think your team might benefit from. Lights, please.'

Mr Beige sprang up and dimmed the lights. What followed was a video of over a dozen lengthy research sessions. Each one showed octogenarian men and women looking earnestly into the camera and answering questions about socks. It was excruciatingly boring, and after the first four minutes Rachel's mind started to wander. With both eyes seemingly riveted to the TV, she used her peripheral vision to examine the RightSole client who was fully focused on the screen, even mouthing some of the words. Then, as Rachel watched, he paused and puckered his lips into something tight and fleshy that reminded Rachel of a cat's bum. She caught Justin watching her watch the client. He smiled at her and pursed his lips, mimicking the client's.

When the tape finished, Mr Beige turned the lights back on and Clive stood up and addressed them once again. 'As you have no doubt gathered from the footage,' he began, 'we've discovered a very exciting niche market. As you saw, once men retire they simply continue to wear the same old socks they've always had and don't find much need to purchase new ones.'

He paused for effect as Rachel stifled a yawn and nodded violently, pretending she'd been paying attention and these insights were the most fascinating things she'd ever heard. Then she wrote a fake note on her pad to make her enthusiasm seem more believable.

'So,' the client finally continued, his eyes sparkling with the deranged excitement of a man whose only real passion in life is socks, 'we're aiming to get more retired men to buy new socks. Which is why we're here, looking for something targeted, catchy and hard-working.'

'That sounds like a very smart move, Clive,' said Mr Beige, nodding.

'I think you'll all agree with me when I say that socks really are the fabric of our society,' Clive went on. 'And that's why this project is so very important. We need old men to buy more socks, goddamnit!'

The client slammed both hands down on the boardroom table to emphasise his point, and Rachel saw a gobbet of spit fly out of his cat-bum mouth and land on Mr Beige's balding forehead. Either not noticing it or choosing to ignore it so as not to offend the client, Mr Beige allowed the shiny speck to remain untouched for the remainder of the meeting. It made Rachel feel ill.

This was what she had been lowered to, she thought on the subway on her way home – hugging her boss and selling socks to old people. This was her life at a Manhattan advertising agency, hardly high-flying glamour.

Rachel Marcus is one day down, the rest of my life to go.
April 7 at 6:49pm

41

Rachel Marcus is in need of a drink. In fact, better make it a double.
April 22 at 6:35pm

'So, how's it going at Target?' asked Sue. Brian was working late and they were relaxing on the couch at Sue's place.

'Urgh, you don't even want to know, Sue,' groaned Rachel. 'The work is truly awful. In the last three weeks I've written and copy-edited a brochure for a mosquito spray and worked on a million promotions. Text-based promotions, call-in promotions, in-store promotions; there isn't a promotion I haven't done.'

'I didn't know there were so many different kinds of promotions,' said Sue.

'Me either! It's completely mindless. We just finished this terrible promotion for RightSole.'

'Aren't they the sock guys?'

'Yes. Justin·and I came up with this incredibly bland campaign based on putting your best foot forward and the client loved it. You would have thought we'd invented the shoe, he was so excited.'

'What's Justin like?'

'He's like a spoilt four-year-old fed on nothing but Coca-Cola. I don't know how I'm going to work with this asshole, Sue!' Rachel buried her head in her hands. 'He's a complete nightmare.'

'He can't be that bad, can he?' she asked, handing Rachel a whiskey.

Rachel took it gratefully – ice cubes clinking against glass was one of her favourite sounds in the world. 'Trust me, he's worse!' she said. 'Today, we had a meeting with the toilet paper client at ten, and at five past they call to tell us the client's waiting for us in the boardroom, but his royal highness still isn't in yet. So, I pick up the layouts, figuring I'll just go in there and deal with it by myself, when out of nowhere he pops out from under his desk, in the same clothes he was wearing yesterday, high and stinking of booze. He scared the crap out of me.'

'He was sleeping under his desk?' asked Sue, wide-eyed.

'Yes. Sue, I dread going to work. I never know what state I'm going to find him in. And he spends more time in the bathroom shovelling coke up his nose than he does at his desk. A partner is supposed to support you, carry some of the load, but he just cruises. He knows if he doesn't do it, I'll just pick up the slack.'

'That doesn't sound good,' said Sue.

'And it's not just the booze and drugs,' Rachel continued. 'I hate sharing an office with him. He's completely inconsiderate. Like he'll get totally into a song, so he'll put it on repeat on his computer. Then he'll leave the office to go flirt with a secretary or something, and twenty minutes later I realise I'm sitting at my desk feeling like I'm going crazy because I've been listening to the same song over and over again. I could kill him.'

'Have you spoken to your headhunter?' asked Sue. 'Maybe she can find you something else.'

'I call her every week,' Rachel replied. 'I'd call her every day if I didn't think she'd take out a restraining order on me. She says there's nothing right now.'

'Makes me glad I work for myself,' said Sue.

'The most frustrating thing is that I think he might actually be talented, but he's so lazy and unprofessional. And I don't think there's a single girl in the entire agency that he hasn't already shagged or isn't in the process of lining up to shag.'

'Gross,' said Sue. 'What do they see in him?'

'I dunno. I suppose it's his looks and that British accent. And he's always got drugs. I think a lot of these girls like that personality trait in a man.'

'Yeah, girls are funny,' Sue nodded, 'we just generally have terrible taste in men.'

'I really think he's got a serious drink and drug problem, Sue. I don't know how he's made it in this industry all these years.'

'That's probably exactly how he's made it in this industry all these years,' said Sue. 'Does your boss know about any of this? What's his name again, Doug?'

'No, Dan ... He's a whole other train smash. I don't think he has any clue what's going on in the real world. He's been away on business, schmoozing clients, ever since I joined, and get this, he takes his swami with him wherever he goes.'

'His what?'

'It's like this guru guy; he's Indian; he gives him spiritual guidance or something.'

'American Indian?' asked Sue.

'Nope, I'm talking Indian Indian: turban, robe, the works!'

'Sounds like you work at a circus,' Sue said and took a sip of Scotch. 'So, other than Justin and Dan, what's everyone else like at Target? Any nice guys?' she asked with a glint in her eye.

'Gross!' yelled Rachel.

'You should try Internet dating,' said Sue. 'You never know, you might just meet someone nice. This girl I knew from art school went online and met this guy from Utah, and they emailed for like months, and then she flew over to meet him and they were married six months later.'

'And,' asked Rachel, 'how are they now?'

'Oh, no,' said Sue, shaking her head, 'they had a terrible divorce and he took her for everything she had. But the marriage lasted just under two years ... That's something, right?'

Rachel rolled her eyes.

'Okay, so maybe that wasn't the best example,' said Sue. 'But it works for lots of people. I bet there are tons of amazing guys online, especially in New York. Seriously, you should think about it.'

'Yeah,' said Rachel. 'I'll think about it. Hey, pass the fortune cookies.'

Sue reached across the post-dinner Chinese-food war zone and grabbed a couple of fortune cookies. She tossed one to Rachel before opening her own. 'Great love and happiness will be yours forever,' she read out loud.

Rachel cracked hers open as Sue shrugged her shoulders, crumpled her fortune up and tossed it into an empty chow mein container. She looked for the fortune. Nothing. Not a thing. No little slip of paper for her. 'Typical,' she said, holding up the empty cookie casing for Sue to see. 'Even these guys don't know what's going to happen to me. How about another drink, Sue? If I'm not going to wake up tomorrow morning with a good job or a boyfriend I at least want to wake up with a decent-sized hangover.'

Later, Rachel stumbled out of Sue's apartment and made her way unsteadily across the hall to her own apartment.

'Promise me you'll think about the Internet dating thing,' Sue slurred from her front door as Rachel fumbled with her keys in the multitude of locks.

'Yeah, yeah,' said Rachel as she got the last key into the last lock by pure fluke and the door to her apartment burst open, depositing her face-down on her apartment floor.

Alone in her apartment, Rachel pulled her dress off over her head and tossed it and her underwear onto the chair that was currently doubling as a laundry hamper. She turned on the TV. 'Rock and Roll All Nite' by Kiss was playing on VH1. Rachel, feeling rather tipsy, stood naked in the middle of the lounge and headbanged along to it, screaming out the lyrics. See, she thought, it wasn't so bad being single. You got to have drinks with your newest best friend and then dance around your apartment naked, headbanging and playing an air guitar if you wanted to. You couldn't do that if you had a boyfriend cluttering up the place, watching golf or Grand Prix. Only losers went online looking for a date, she thought. Anyway, there wasn't enough room for a man in her life or in her apartment. Right now she needed to focus on making things work at Target and she could do without complications. She felt confident that when the time was right the perfect man would come into her life of his own accord. Screw Internet dating.

When the song came to an end Rachel took a bow to an adoring imaginary audience and made her way into the bathroom. She climbed into the shower and turned on the hot tap. Then she countered the hot water with cold water until she had the perfect shower raining down on her. Humming, she poured out a palm-full of shampoo and lathered up her hair. The shower was so tiny she could only raise one arm to her head at a time and so, with eyes squeezed tightly shut, she turned her head upwards, massaging her scalp with one hand and letting the stream of water splash down her face and wash the dirt and difficulties of the day down the drain.

Eyes still closed Rachel thrust her hand past the shower curtain, out of the shower and felt around the edge of the sink, looking for the bar of honey scented aromatherapy soap that lived in the soap dish. That was the upside of having such a tiny bathroom, she thought, everything was always within arm's reach.

Rachel grabbed for the soap, but instead, for just a split second, she clutched hold of something that was about the same size as her bar of soap, only it was warm and fat, with a course bristly texture. She snapped her hand back into the shower in horror as the 'soap' bolted out from between her fingers, her eyes suddenly wide with terror as she tried to establish what she'd touched. Biting back the pain caused by the suds seeping into her eyes, she looked cautiously past the shower curtain and saw a fat black blob darting across the floor. It was a rat. Black and hairy with a thick long wiry tail. The revolting creature had obviously been nosing around her honey scented soap.

Rachel shrieked and the rat scampered across the floor and

disappeared through a small hole between the tiled floor and the wall in the corner of the bathroom. She had never noticed the hole before, but now she couldn't take her eyes off it. Horrified, she burst out of the shower screaming and ran out of the bathroom, leaving the shower running. She leapt onto the couch and stood there shivering, shampoo dripping down her face and huge tears rolling from her stinging eyes. She was suddenly very sober.

Rachel stood there shivering for what felt like hours; too scared to climb off the couch. Finally, shoulders heaving, she realised she was going to have to do something. She couldn't stand dripping wet and naked, a hostage on her own couch all night. Rachel had never felt so alone. She had absolutely nobody she could call. Brian was away on business and Sue would only jump up onto the couch and scream next to her. She didn't know any other men in New York other than Justin. And he would either be coked out of his skull at this time of night, or shagging some poor unsuspecting victim. There was no way she could trust him to rescue her.

Soggy and shivering, Rachel climbed off the couch and grabbed a dishcloth off the kitchen sink, which she used to try and dry herself off before wrapping it like a turban around her dripping, soapy hair. She yanked the bathroom door closed, threw on a pair of jeans, a T-shirt and some shoes, grabbed her keys and her purse and raced out of the apartment with the towel still wrapped around her head. On the street, she crossed the road and went to the all-night supermarket, where she bought four rolls of heavy duty duct tape.

Back in the apartment Rachel could still hear the shower running. She wondered what the rat was doing. She felt sick. It was the most disgusting thing she'd ever held and she knew she was lucky she hadn't been bitten. She must have surprised the revolting thing as much as it had surprised her.

Rachel made her way slowly towards the bathroom, clutching the rolls of tape. 'I shouldn't have to do this!' she shouted to nobody in particular as she pushed the bathroom door open, on the lookout for any kind of movement. Her whole body was on edge, every nerve-ending sharply attuned to potential danger, and only when she was absolutely positive that the rat wasn't still in the bathroom did she crouch in front of the small hole and begin to cover it up with strips of tape.

Once she'd used up one whole roll of tape, plus half of the second roll, and the hole was untidily but securely plastered, Rachel turned off the shower, which had been running the whole time, and left the steamed-up bathroom, closing the door behind her. Then she knelt down and stuck the rest of the second roll of tape between the floor and the gap under the bottom of the door, so there was no way anything could get from the bathroom into the apartment.

Having sealed the bathroom off from the rest of the flat, Rachel moved slowly around the apartment, her eyes darting into the corners as she looked for more uninvited visitors. Finally satisfied that she really was alone, she tried to rinse the rest of the soap out of her hair in the minute kitchen sink and scrubbed her ratty hand raw using dishwashing liquid. Then she towel-dried her hair as best she could with another dishcloth. She would have to get used to washing in this tiny kitchen sink, she thought, because there was absolutely no way she was going back into the bathroom, ever. Why was it other people got flatmates but she got ratmates?

Finally, Rachel climbed into bed with all the lights and her clothes and shoes still on. She had never felt more homesick, despondent or lonely. This life was no good, she decided. She needed someone. Someone who was good in an emergency situation. Someone who wasn't scared of rats. She didn't want to do this by herself anymore.

Rachel Marcus didn't shower alone tonight, and there was nothing sexy about it.
April 23 at 3:34am

Four hours later Rachel woke up feeling shattered; a part hangover, part nightmare headache torturing her frontal lobe. But she didn't have time for self-pity. Climbing into bed with wet hair had left her with the kind of frizzy, out-of-control bouffant that Tina Turner would have been proud of and she needed to summon up all her courage and go into the bathroom. She needed her hair-taming tools and she needed to brush her teeth, an act she'd decided to forgo the night before, but one that she couldn't avoid much longer. And then she needed to get to work.

Rachel lifted up the wad of tape between the floor and the bathroom door, then she turned the door knob and gave it a little kick with her toe. The door glided open and she evaluated the bathroom. It was as she had left it the night before and there was no sign of any movement, but then she saw the duct-taped hole in the floor. A large hole had been gnawed through the tape. Rachel scratched at her hand in horror as her eyes darted around the bathroom. The honey scented soap that still sat on the edge of the sink had a series of what she presumed were rat bites out of it. Completely revolted, Rachel picked the soap up gingerly between her thumb and forefinger and backed out of the bathroom, grabbing the rest of her toiletries on the way. Back in the kitchen she closed the bathroom door, retaping the gap between the floor and door as best she could. Then, realising tape was clearly a delicacy for rats, she piled up whatever she could in front of the bathroom door – books, towels and, eventually, the coffee table turned on its side.

An hour later, on the way to work, Rachel tossed what was left of her honey scented soap into a dumpster, then stopped in at a shop where she picked up a fresh bar of scientifically formulated anti-bacterial soap and three boxes of rat poison.

Rachel Marcus is The Terminator, coming soon to a bathroom near you.
April 23 at 10:11am

That afternoon Rachel sat at her desk and looked across the office. 'Justin?'

'Yeah.'

'How would you describe me in twenty words or less?'

'What kind of question is that?'

'Don't think about it too much,' urged Rachel. 'Just say the first thing that comes to mind.'

'I'd say you've got great tits,' he said, standing up and walking over towards her desk.

'Justin, that's not helpful at all ...' Rachel grumbled. 'I mean how would you sum up my personality?'

'What are you doing?' he asked, popping up behind her desk.

Rachel tried to close the active window on her screen, but he was too quick, whipping the mouse out from under her hand before she could stop him. 'Online dating!' he shrieked. 'You're not, are you?'

'Well, it's not like men are falling at my feet since I moved here. And I only hang out with you and Sue and Brian, and none of their friends are single, and you only hang out with bimbos ... So, I thought I'd take matters into my own hands and try widening my circle a bit.'

'Aw, Rach ... I'd be happy to shag you if you want.' He winked. 'I'll be everything you ever wanted in a bloke.' He squeezed her arm.

'Funny one,' said Rachel, slapping his hand away. 'I knew you would tease me.'

'No, really. I'm being serious,' Justin said, looking meaningfully into her eyes. 'You really do have great tits!' Then, roaring with laughter, he headed back to his desk.

'Oh, whatever! You're such a pig!' Rachel said, looking back at the flashing cursor. 'Don't bother, all right. I'll manage on my own.'

The header read: *Describe yourself in under twenty words.* Rachel thought about it. She wasn't really a long walks on the beach or horse-riding in the moonlight kind of girl. After a couple of false starts she settled on:

I'm a double-jointed heiress, whose dad owns a brewery. Okay, sorry, not really. Here goes for real: I'm new to Manhattan, so I'm looking for someone to show me around. I think you'll find me low-maintenance, loyal, driven and independent. I like to laugh and I do so as often as possible. Ultimately, I'm looking for someone who's as good a friend as they are a lover.

She moved on to the next question: *What is your ideal match?*

Again Rachel faltered. She looked at the letters on the keyboard, hoping they would come together in some sort of order all by themselves. But of course they wouldn't. Stubborn fuckers, she thought.

Rachel took a couple of seconds to construct the ideal man in her head. She was looking for someone tall, mature, caring and established. Pretty much everything Justin wasn't. And of course, she thought, whoever he is can't be afraid of rats or cockroaches. Tentatively, Rachel began to type, picking up speed as she gained momentum. She wrote:

I'm looking for someone who makes me smile more than they make me frown, so sense of humour is a must. Throw in honesty, which at this stage of my life is incredibly important to me, as well as intelligence, maturity, drive and a bit of a naughty streak, and I think we've hit the jackpot. If this sounds like you, please drop me a line and we'll figure out the rest as we go along.

There, she thought, clicking the Submit button and pushing her chair back from her desk. Now all she had to do was wait and see if anyone was interested. It was all up to the Internet-dating gods. Rachel looked across at Justin, sitting behind his computer, probably surfing for porn, and wondered if a human sacrifice would speed things along and whether Justin would be a suitable candidate.

'Are you really going to do that?' Justin asked, sensing her gaze.

'Why not?' she asked, feeling empowered by her decision. 'It's not like I've got any better options.'

Justin held her stare. 'Come on,' he finally said, throwing down his pen and heading out of the office. 'We've got the Pharmicorp antidepressant audio visual briefing in Boardroom One now.'

'Great,' said Rachel, picking up her pad and a pen and following him out of the door. 'Maybe they'll give us some free samples.'

Rachel Marcus is to hell with it, she's putting herself out there.
April 23 at 3:59pm

That night Rachel donned her yellow plastic gloves and got to work with the rat poison in her bathroom. First, she cleared away the chewed-through tape, and then she shoved enough rat poison to kill twelve rats into the hole. When this was done, she taped it up with another roll of extra-strength duct tape. She knew it wasn't the best rat barrier in the world, but it was all she had for now, and hopefully the rats wouldn't make it past the poison. She would get the hole plastered up as soon as possible. Finally, she got to work disinfecting the bathroom with buckets of hot soapy water and a truckload of industrial strength bleach. When she was finished, she washed and moisturised her hands for the hundred millionth time since she'd first touched the rat the night before, then she re-barricaded the bathroom door before collapsing, exhausted into bed. One could never be too careful, she thought, especially when it came to New York City rats.

Rachel Marcus is washing her hands like Lady Macbeth. Out damn rat.
April 23 at 11:47pm

Rachel Marcus is getting a pedi. Because if you want nice shoes, you need nice feet. *April 25 at 12:35pm*

'So,' asked Sue, 'how's the online dating going?'

'Okay, I guess,' said Rachel. 'This place is great, how'd you find it?'

'I don't know exactly,' said Sue. 'It was one of the first places I discovered when we moved here, and I've been coming ever since. They give the best foot massages.'

Rachel looked down at the small Asian lady working quietly at her feet. Sue was sitting next to her with another Asian lady bent over her own toes.

'I told you online dating was a good idea,' said Sue.

'We don't know that yet,' said Rachel quickly. 'Some of them are real freaks: axe murderers, ex-convicts, postal workers … And the rest are potential stalkers, at the very least.'

'Well, they're men, what do you expect?' said Sue.

'I was emailing with this one guy for a couple of days,' said Rachel. 'Eventually, I asked him to send me a picture of himself, and he sent me two …'

'See, that doesn't sound so bad. How did he look?'

'I don't know. Both pictures were of his penis!'

Sue burst out laughing. 'He didn't!'

'Yup!' said Rachel.

'Why two?' asked Sue.

'One was of it erect and the other was of it flaccid.'

Sue threw her head back, guffawing, while Rachel smiled and looked down at the pair of Asian pedicurists. They both carried on filing and polishing without even exchanging a glance. Either, Rachel thought, neither of them speaks English, or they've simply heard it all before.

'Anyway,' continued Rachel, 'I don't know what he was so proud of, it was hardly the most impressive thing I've ever seen.'

'What a freak!' roared Sue, wiping the mascara tracks off her cheeks with her fingers. 'What about the others? There must be someone at least half decent?'

'Well, I suppose there is this one guy ...'

'Yes?'

'His name's Peter and he's a quantity surveyor. We've been emailing quite a bit this week.'

'That sounds interesting. What's he like?'

'Well, he hasn't sent me a picture of his little Peter yet, so that's a good start.' Rachel caught her pedicurist crack a small but visible smile.

'Rachel, you should let him take you out. Maybe he's the one.'

'Maybe,' said Rachel.

Rachel Marcus is surveying her quantity.
April 25 at 3:54pm

Rachel Marcus is trying to block out memories of last night.
April 30 at 8:32am

'So, how was your date?' asked Justin from deep under a baseball cap. 'Should I order my tux for the wedding? You're not thinking white are you, 'cos you wouldn't be kidding anyone.'

Rachel could tell Justin was massively hung-over. He'd limped into the studio after eleven, and the numerous trips he'd made to the bathroom signalled he was still sticking cocaine up his nose as if it was the Eighties. He was also in his usual foul mood – before this sarcastic barb he'd only offered her four grunts and a shrug.

'So, who's this charmer then?' He grimaced. 'Mr Lawyer Guy? Mr Accountant Man? Mr Big-Cock Chap?'

Rachel shook her head. Her first date with Peter the quantity surveyor had been a disaster. 'No,' she said. 'He's a quantity surveyor.'

'And?' grumbled Justin. 'Was it love at first sight?'

'No,' she said. 'It didn't work out.'

'Why?' prodded Justin, swinging his feet off the couch and sitting up to get a better look at Rachel, who was trying to hide behind her computer.

'He took me to quite a nice restaurant.'

'Yes,' said Justin. 'So, what's the problem then? Too handsome was he, or just too rich?'

'No,' she said, pulling a face at Justin. 'He was wearing tracksuit bottoms and a grubby white T-shirt that said "Eat Me" on it.'

'What?' exclaimed Justin.

'Yup. And I went to so much effort. I got all dressed up to meet him and all he could muster was sweats . . .' Rachel paused as the full horror of the evening came flooding back. 'The way I see it, if he's wearing tracksuit bottoms and a grubby T-shirt on our first date, what does that leave for down the line? What will he be wearing on our tenth date, or on our five-year anniversary? Nothing but a pair of crusty, skid-marked Y-fronts, I suspect.'

'That's grim,' said Justin. 'Maybe he came straight from the gym?'

'I thought about that, and I asked him, but he looked at me like I was crazy. I really think that's just what he wears.'

Rachel detected a smile playing around Justin's mouth and her hackles rose. She knew he would tease her about all this and she instantly wished she'd never mentioned she was going on a date at all.

'So what happened with Don Juan after dinner?' he asked.

'Oh, fuck off, Justin!' spat Rachel.

'No, I'm being serious,' he pleaded. 'C'mon, Rachel, please tell me. I won't tease you, I promise. I'm really interested. Really. I want to know what constitutes a bad date in a woman's eyes. Think of it as research. I could pass my findings on to bachelors everywhere. You'd be doing it for all of womankind.'

Rachel was reluctant to continue with the conversation. It was bad enough that she'd had to live through the experience the first time, but reliving it in the telling was excruciating. 'When the bill came I did that thing that girls do on a date,' she finally said. 'You know, I reached for my purse, as if I was going to pay, but I never thought he'd actually make me pay. But he did! He made me pay my half. He literally asked the waitress for a calculator and then he worked out exactly what I owed down to the cent. And, even worse, he didn't leave a tip . . . I had to slip the waitress a twenty on our way out. And then he still tried to make-out with me outside on the street. It was revolting. I almost lost the dinner I'd just paid for. I had to knee him gently in the nuts just to get him off me!'

'Well, you know what they say about quantity surveyors right?' Justin said, mock seriously.

'No, what?' asked Rachel.

'All ruler; no tip!'

Justin left the office, roaring with laughter. No doubt he was heading off to the bathroom to top up his nostrils, thought Rachel. Man, she hated his guts.

Rachel Marcus is in dating hell right now.
April 30 at 10:16am

After lunch Rachel sat at her desk staring at her computer screen. She had two choices; she could give the process another go or she could follow her gut and abandon the whole Internet dating thing. She considered her options. Life would be so much simpler if she gave up on the idea of ever meeting anyone. Then she could eat chocolate and pizza, in that order, for breakfast, lunch and dinner, give way to the pimples and wear baggy drawstring pants in public. She could stop waxing and tweezing and hold back on washing her hair so often. And without these chores in her life she would have so much more time to herself. Time she could use to develop a fun hobby like scrapbooking or alcoholism. She would become Crazy Aunty Rachel, who had a hairy chin and always got drunk at family functions. She would grow old alone and die alone and fight off the rats and the cockroaches alone … Her other choice was to persevere. She recognised that it was naive to believe that the very first guy she met online would be the one she'd been waiting her whole life to find. After all, if she was going to meet men in a bar or a laundromat or yoga class, the first man who asked her out wouldn't necessarily be perfect. Even in the real world she would have to troll through some disasters before she found her prince (or someone who wasn't an ex-con, a quantity surveyor or an unemployed whack job). Surely, she thought, she should give the virtual dating world the same chance she would give the real world? She wasn't a quitter, she decided. So she logged back into manhattanlovematch.com, blocked Peter the cheap, groping quantity surveyor out of her mind and her inbox and looked to see who else was out there.

First she clicked through to a section called *Matches*. It was a simple 'search' function. You ticked the box or selected your choice in a series of drop-down menu options, ranging from age to race, hair colour, religion and various other criteria. Rachel clicked away at her preferred requirements for a match. She thought her needs were actually pretty basic. How hard could it be to find a single, heterosexual male between the ages of twenty-eight and forty-two living in New York?

She had no preference of hair colour, eye colour or star sign. She would however want him to be taller than her, so she put that in. She also ticked the 'must be employed' box and the 'no disabilities box'. Then she specified a handful of other preferences like marital status (single, obviously) and body type (no hairy fatties, please), and finally she clicked the search button. The computer took a couple of minutes to find the relevant matches. Rachel imagined a miniature man sitting inside her computer's hard drive in front of a giant Rolodex, whipping through all her options and discarding the ones that were too weird, too short, too fat, too hairy or too unemployed, putting together a dossier of potential matches that were hopefully just right.

Her computer bleeped. It was ready to reveal its selection of potential future Mr Rights and Rachel clicked the button and waited for her fate to scroll down before her eyes. There were over a thousand matches – a somewhat scary number – and top of the list was a character by the name of *STAR TREK VOYAGER*. Rachel cringed and made a mental note: next time she would look in the advanced search section of the website to see if there was a *No Trekkies/Sci-Fi Fans* box she could check. Really, what kind of forty-one year old man still dreams about being beamed up and says things like, 'May the Force be with you'?

She scrolled further down. Next she came across *HOLE-IN-ONE*. He was a thirty-one year old accountant. The handle he had chosen told her a couple of things that instantly turned her off. Firstly, he was clearly an avid golfer. Secondly, he liked to make creepy golfing sex puns. And, thirdly, he obviously had no concept of what women really look for in men. No woman actively goes out there looking to become a golfing widow.

So far this wasn't going very well, Rachel thought as she scrolled down even further and caught sight of a chap who had imaginatively called himself *CUTE FRIENDLY ME*. Rachel cringed. If she wanted a 'cute, friendly me' she would buy a puppy. It may chew on her shoes, but at least it wouldn't pee on the toilet seat, leave the cap off the toothpaste or fart in bed and then trap her in with it under the duvet, thinking it was the funniest thing in the world.

Rachel was still within the eighty to hundred per cent matches. She wondered what would happen when she hit the forty to fifty per cent matches. Would they be one-legged psychopaths and schizophrenic mass-murderers? Rachel scrolled down even further. She passed on *TROPICAL DREAMZ, BIKERCRAZEE, SPORTSFAN100, HOT LOVER, HORNY-OLD-GOAT, FIRE STARTER, DR FEELGOOD, FREAK ON A LEASH* and *WATERBED GUY*. Were these guys mad? Did they really think that women would flock to them if they called themselves these ridiculous names? Surely they realised that some elements of their personalities were best left a secret till well after the third date? They'd have been better off admitting that they liked to wear adult diapers and have their testicles crushed by stilettos. And what about all the abysmal spelling? Rachel really didn't want to date anyone who hadn't managed to finish high school or didn't know how to spell a simple word like 'crazy'.

But it wasn't all completely scary; there were a handful of profiles that seemed relatively normal. Rachel set a couple of these aside to take a closer look at. The sadly short shortlist included *ANTHONY*, which she thought was at least honest and straightforward, *SOD IT* and *GOOD GUY*. But one profile stood out from all the others. His handle was *LONG TALL DAVE*. She liked the look of him, despite the tautology.

In one of his pictures he wore glasses and held a glass of wine and in another he was asleep in a hammock with a book resting open on his not-too-hairy chest. On closer inspection the book turned out to be *The Shipping News* by Annie Proulx. Rachel approved. It was one of her all-time favourite books. He looked easy and friendly and like the kind of guy Rachel might like to get to know a little better. She read through his profile. He was divorced with a child and was in the medical/dental category of profession. He liked cooking and reading and socialising with friends, and not that it mattered that much but his favourite colour was blue. He was a non-smoker, which made sense if he was a doctor or a dentist. And he had a dog. To hell with the old-fashioned notion of waiting until the guy made the first move, Rachel decided, and before she lost her nerve she typed off a quick mail to him, introducing herself. Then she sat back and let the man inside her computer do the rest.

That was Thursday. By Friday evening Rachel and *LONG TALL DAVE* – or just Dave, as she liked to call him – had gotten to know each other fairly well over email. Rachel counted forty-three emails that had bounced between them over a twenty-four hour period – a period in which, needless to say, she hadn't gotten much work done. Dave, the doctor, was charming and witty, and when he invited Rachel out for coffee on Saturday afternoon she accepted, hardly believing what she was doing.

Rachel Marcus is going to see the Lurv Doctor.
May 2 at 2:45pm

Dave had selected a restaurant in the middle of Central Park and as Rachel made her way there from the subway station she admired the blossoming cherry trees. New York could be an amazingly beautiful city when it wanted to be, she thought.

Rachel arrived on time and looked around for Dave. She was sure that with his height he would be easy to spot, but there was no sign of him. Nervously, she ran her eye over the crowd a second time, but she still couldn't see anyone even vaguely resembling the man she was supposed to meet. It was on her third loop that her eye caught that of a gentleman who looked to be in his sixties. He was seated at a table over to one side of the restaurant and was staring right at her, smiling. Rachel looked behind her for the intended recipient of that welcoming smile, but there was nobody there. Then the gentleman got up and started walking towards her. Rachel started to panic. Perhaps the old man had Alzheimer's and had confused her with his granddaughter. She scanned the crowd again, hoping to spot Dave so he could come rescue her, but there was still no sign of him. Maybe somebody had ruptured a spleen or swallowed a clutch pencil and he'd been called to the emergency room. It had better be a matter of life or death if he stood her up, she thought, otherwise he'd be the one being raced to the emergency room.

The old gentleman reached Rachel with a big smile on his face. 'Hello,' he said. 'You must be Rachel.'

Startled, Rachel gaped at him like a confused guppy.

'It's me,' he said. 'Dave.'

Rachel gaped some more, struggling to get enough air into her system. 'But ... but ...' she stuttered.

'It's great to meet you in person at last,' he said, pecking her on the cheek.

'How old are you?' blurted Rachel, unable to contain herself. Where was her thirty-one year old doctor?

Dave laughed nervously. 'About that ...' he began. 'I'm sixty-six.'

Rachel shook her head in astonishment. 'I thought you said you were thirty-one?'

'Well,' he said, 'that's not exactly a lie. I feel like half my age and I think you'll find I'm very young at heart.' He smiled.

He wasn't a bad looking guy, Rachel thought, but he was old enough to be her father. She shuddered at the thought. 'What about those photos?' she asked. 'The ones online and those other ones you sent me?'

'Oh, that's my son, Dave Junior,' he said, with a charming smile and a nod, as if his response made it all quite clear.

'And the bit about you being a doctor?'

'All true,' he said, looking up at her eagerly. 'Only I'm retired now. See, I've got plenty of time to spend with you, I'd spoil you rotten.'

Rachel clutched her handbag in front of her. 'I'm sorry Dave,' she said, backing away and shaking her head. 'You seem like a lovely guy, but you're so far out of my age range and it's such a massive lie. I don't think I can do this.'

Outside the restaurant Rachel stopped to catch her breath, watching through the glass as Dave made his way back to his table, put on a pair of spectacles and began to study the menu. Seconds later she was at his table. 'Dave,' she said, startling him.

'Yes?' he said, taking off his glasses and looking up at her expectantly.

'Your son, Dave Junior, he isn't single, is he?'

'As a matter of a fact he is,' said Dave Senior.

Rachel smiled. Perhaps this could be the funny story her and Dave Junior would tell their children. About how mummy and daddy met when mummy went on a blind date with Grampa Dave, who she met on the Internet.

'But,' continued Dave Senior, pulling Rachel back from her fantasy. 'He's a gay orthodontist.'

Rachel clutched her bag even closer to her stomach, turned around and left again.

Rachel walked through Central Park trying to process what had just happened to her. What was wrong with her? Why couldn't she just meet a nice, normal, honest guy? A vision of old man Dave swam into her mind. She imagined him kissing her neck and touching her skin with his liver-spotted hands. It made her shiver with revulsion. How could those young women who married rich old men bear it?

Rachel sat down on a bench and tried to force herself to relax and breathe. She stretched her arms out along the back of the bench, closing her eyes and letting the feeling of the sunlight on her face ease away all thoughts of men named Dave.

A few minutes later Rachel opened her eyes and looked around the park. About a hundred metres away a guy sitting on another bench caught her eye. He was tall and handsome, she thought, in a kind of rugged way. Well built, he had dark hair and a stubbly chin, and was wearing blue jeans, a black T-shirt that hugged his muscled arms and a black beanie. As she stared at him he looked up and saw her. Caught and flustered, Rachel looked away from him quickly, pretending she hadn't been staring. Then, as casually as she could, she ran her eyes around the rest of the park, slowly allowing them to wander back to the guy. He was still staring right at her. She blushed and looked away again quickly. His stare was so intense that she felt instantly shy. He knew she'd been checking him out; she'd never been particularly good at being subtle. Rachel pretended to study a leaf lying on the ground intently, but by now she was magnetised to him and seconds later she looked back towards him again. He was still staring at her, but this time he was smiling. He had a perfect smile and Rachel forced herself to hold his stare and managed a small, coy smile back.

Shocked by her own forwardness, and too shy to continue the eyeball tennis, Rachel stood up and walked in the opposite direction. Enough flirting, she thought. She would go home and tell Sue about her disastrous date, over one, or maybe three very stiff drinks.

As Rachel started walking she picked the guy up in her peripheral vision. He was watching her leave. Then he got up and she could see he was walking after her. Rachel felt her pulse pick up the pace a little bit. He was so hot and she wasn't quite sure what she would say to him if he started talking to her. He was quite far behind her, so she slowed her pace to give him a chance to catch up. Her skin prickled with excitement. The path she was on rounded a bend and dipped into a small bicycle-path tunnel that was shaded by a large flowering tree. The area was deserted, so as she rounded the bend Rachel ran her hand through her hair to make sure it was in place, wishing she'd thought to put on a bit of fresh lipstick before she'd left the restaurant.

'Excuse, Miss,' he shouted from behind her as she approached the entrance to the tunnel.

Rachel smiled to herself. His voice was deep and rich and she detected a thick accent, perhaps Spanish. She turned and fidgeted nervously with the collar of her dress as he caught up to her. He was even better looking up close, she thought. He had an incredibly sexy scar running down the side of his cheek and Rachel wondered whether he was a model. 'Hello,' she said.

'Hello,' he said, locking eyes with her, still smiling his sexy smile. 'You give me your phone, yes?'

Rachel smiled back at him. She found the accent and the broken English incredibly attractive. 'You want my phone number?' she asked. Perhaps, she thought, this day wasn't going to turn out so badly after all.

'Si,' he said. 'You give me phone. You give me money. You give me necklace. You give me watch!'

Rachel's eye caught a glint, and suddenly he was holding a large switchblade in her face. Rachel sucked in air as her heart fell twelve storeys. Suddenly he didn't look so good anymore. And that scar was no longer in the least bit sexy.

'Do it,' he said, jabbing the knife towards her.

Rachel thought she might be sick. She reached slowly into her handbag and pulled out her purse and her cellphone and handed them over. Then she peeled off her watch and her necklace and passed those over too.

The man looked around skittishly and pocketed the items, still clutching the knife in her face. Then he walked a couple of steps around Rachel, turned and strode away through the darkened tunnel and out the other side.

Rachel didn't think. Instead she bolted after him, losing a shoe as she ran. As she burst out the other side of the tunnel there were suddenly dozens of people around her: cycling, rollerblading, walking their dogs and children in the park. It was as if the whole world had been on pause while she was being mugged and now everything had gone back to normal.

'That man stole my purse!' she shrieked out to the park.

She looked around trying to catch a glimpse of him, so she could point him out, but he was long gone. A couple of people glanced at her and then looked away, a mother grasped her child closer to her side, and Rachel suddenly realised she was just another screaming, ranting, shoeless loony New Yorker with crazy hair. She sank onto the grass. It was damp and she felt it soak through the back of her dress. Despair filled every inch of her and she couldn't stop her hands from trembling. After a few minutes she stood up on shaky legs and went back for her shoe which had landed in the only puddle in sight for miles. Then she left the park with a wet bum and one foot squishing with every miserable step.

Without money or a phone Rachel felt lost. There was no point going to the police. What would they do? She knew it was her own fault for being so naive. She decided she wouldn't tell anyone; the whole thing was just too embarrassing. She'd lived her entire life in Johannesburg, the crime capital of the planet, and had never been mugged. She was completely stunned by her own stupidity.

Unable to catch a cab or take the subway because she didn't have a cent Rachel walked back to her apartment deep in thought. She thought about what a vain idiot she had been to think the hot mugger was trying to pick her up. She thought about what a mess her life was. She thought about all the money in her purse, gone. She thought that she could have been stabbed and left lying bleeding in the tunnel. And then she thought that if she could have just found herself a decent boyfriend, like a normal human being, and hadn't had to go online, none of this would have happened to her in the first place.

Rachel Marcus **is destroyed, devastated and now broke!**
May 2 at 6:59pm

Dear Mom and Dad,

It was lovely to get your package and letter in the mail. I see from the postmark that it took twelve days to get from you to me.

Did you manage to look at any computers yet? Mom, they're not only good for emailing, but you could also play bridge online with people all over the world, and Dad, you would be able to read up on all sorts of different birds. Please look into it, you won't regret it.

Thanks for the big bag of Earl Grey tea. Strangely enough, it's the exact same brand I can get here at the supermarket on the corner. If possible, could you send me a box of FIVE ROSES tea next time? That's the one that's not available here and I'm desperate for a cup.

Some great news – I've met a fantastic guy. It's early days and we've only just started dating, but he's really nice. Anyway, must go, he's taking me for dinner, and I don't want to be late. Don't forget the FIVE ROSES tea, pretty please.

All my love,
Rachel

Rachel Marcus **is not best friends with Monday.**
May 4 at 9:05am

Rachel stared into her coffee, looking for answers that weren't there. She was feeling bleak; the symptom of a terrible weekend. After the disgusting date with Long Tall Dave's father and the disastrous pickup/mugging in the park, Saturday night and Sunday had been torture. Miserable, broke and arrangementless, there had been nothing Rachel could do to dull the angry throb of homesickness, and at one point on Sunday night she had even almost looked forward to going back to work on Monday morning.

'That's it,' Rachel said across the office. 'I've made a decision: no more Internet dating!'

Justin raised his head from behind his Mac. 'Why, what happened?'

'After Tracksuit Pants Boy and Grandpa I don't think I can do this anymore. It's just too depressing. Maybe the universe is trying to tell me something. Maybe I'm just not supposed to be in a relationship right now.'

'You just need a good shag, that's all!' Justin said.

Rachel was just preparing to tell him to fuck off when the office phone rang. She picked it up.

'Hello, is Justin there?' a young woman asked.

'Who may I say is calling?' Rachel asked.

'It's Britney,' said the girl.

Rachel rolled her eyes and glanced over at Justin. She held the phone out at arm's length towards him and mouthed the words 'It's a Britney for you.'

Justin jumped up gesticulating wildly. 'I'm not here!' he whispered. 'You have to take a message.'

Rachel held her hand over the receiver and glowered at Justin. She hated this. Every week it was a different woman. Justin scribbled wildly on his layout pad and held it up for Rachel to read. It said: *Tell her I don't work here anymore, or I'm dead, or in Peru!*

Rachel pulled a face at him.

Please, he scribbled on the pad, and held it up for her, mouthing the word at the same time.

He looked pathetic.

Rachel put the phone back to her ear. 'I'm so sorry,' she said. 'Justin doesn't work here anymore.'

'That's strange,' said the girl. 'I met him two nights ago and he said he worked there.'

'Yes,' stumbled Rachel, 'it was very sudden, somebody died and he had to go to Peru.'

'Oh,' said the girl, sounding disappointed. 'Do you have a forwarding number for him?'

Justin had his hands clasped in front of him as if he was praying.

'No, sorry,' sighed Rachel.

'That bastard!' the girl said. 'He owes me a hundred bucks!' And the line went dead in Rachel's ear.

'Justin!' Rachel shouted. 'You're such a pig. I've told you before, I don't want to have to lie for you. That poor girl.'

'Oh, she'll be all right,' he said. 'Although, it's a pity I had to let her go, she's got a fabulous arse!'

'You're a fabulous arse!' Rachel yelled, picking up her empty coffee cup and storming out of the office. He was such a jerk, she thought. Him and every other man on the planet. What was it about men that made them so dishonest? Rachel scanned the files in her mind as she walked down the corridor and entered the communal agency kitchen, trying to pinpoint one honest man she'd known in her life. A picture of Phillip flashed in front of her and his betrayal leaked back into her thoughts. They were all the same, she thought, every single one of them. Not one of them capable of an honest act or a deep emotion.

Rachel returned to her desk with a chocolate doughnut she'd found on the kitchen counter. She didn't know whose it was, how long it had been sitting there or why nobody else had snapped it up, which made it one very suspicious doughnut, but at that point she really didn't give a damn. She needed something, anything that might cheer her up a little.

The agency kitchen was a communal space that contained a toaster, a toasted-sandwich machine, a coffee machine and an urn. Employees were allowed to help themselves to as much tea and coffee as they required, all of which was freely supplied by Target Advertising. The kitchen also housed the agency's communal fridge where, in theory, staff could store their lunch or other provisions. But only particularly brave, incredibly stupid or very new employees made use of this facility. Rachel had learned quickly that the kitchen was the Bermuda Triangle of food. In her first week alone she had unwittingly sacrificed a loaf of rye bread, a brick of mature cheddar, several Diet Cokes and three tuna salads. The jar of peanut butter with the words *DANGER THIS BELONGS TO DELIA, IF YOU TOUCH YOU DIE* written on the lid in black marker, may as well have said *PLEASE HELP YOURSELF* for all the notice people took of it – on a number of occasions Rachel had seen various people dipping into the jar, and if their Adam's apples were anything to go by they weren't Delia. Simply put, the agency kitchen was a free for all, and if something belonging to you was taken you had only yourself to blame for leaving it unguarded. So, when Rachel walked into the kitchen looking for coffee, cursing Justin and all men in general under her breath, and saw a plate sitting on the counter with an unattended chocolate doughnut lying right in the middle of it, she didn't feel guilty about taking it for one second. In fact, she only felt curious as to why nobody else had nicked it first.

Justin wasn't in their office when she got back from the kitchen. Good riddance, she thought, putting the doughnut down on her desk and then realising that she'd left her coffee behind. She swore and went back to get it.

When she walked back into the office, fresh cup of coffee in hand, Justin was standing with his back to the door. 'Justin ...' she said, rounding the corner of her desk and noticing her doughnut was missing.

He turned around, mouth full, shoving in the last piece of doughnut.

Rachel knew it was only a doughnut, a stolen one at that, but it was her stolen doughnut and the only good thing that had happened to her in days. Like every man she'd ever known, he'd taken her good thing away from her. 'That was my fucking doughnut, you asshole!' she shouted, tears welling up.

Justin looked at her innocently, licking the last bit of sugar off his lips. 'Oh, it was?'

'Yes, you shithead. It was on my desk, whose did you think it was?'

'Chill out, it's only a doughnut,' he said, swaggering back to his desk, wiping his mouth with the back of his hand. 'And I hate to complain, but it wasn't really all that fresh. Listen, I'm having a boozy lunch with Double D Heather, and I'm hoping it ends up back at my place ... You don't have fifty bucks you can loan me, do you?'

Rachel picked up the closest thing she could grab, which was a Sellotape dispenser. She raised it high above her shoulder and hurled it across the office, aiming for Justin's head. As if in slow motion he watched it glide past his shoulder and smash into the wall behind him, crashing into the plaster and then dropping to the floor, leaving a massive hole in the wall.

Justin grabbed his jacket off the back of his chair and made for the door. 'I take it that's a no?' he said, winking at Rachel. 'I'll see you later, yeah.'

With Justin gone Rachel could finally do what she'd wanted to do all morning. She put her head down on her desk and started to cry.

Later, soothed by her tears, she wiped her eyes and nose on her sleeve and opened a blank page in Microsoft Word. She decided to ignore Justin and take her mind off the disaster zone that was her life by getting started on the Pharmicorp antidepressant audio visual script. She knew she couldn't count on him at all and if the job was going to be finished in time for the presentation in just over two weeks she was going to have to get going by herself. Anyway, she told herself, she didn't need him. He was just another idiot she could add to the long list of idiots she had met in her life.

Rachel stared at the blank page and the flashing cursor. She sipped her now cold coffee and considered her nails – she could do with a manicure, not that she could afford one. Her eyes darted back to the blank page, hoping something had magically written itself while she had been looking at her nails. Nope, nothing, still blank. She bashed on a couple of keys, and the words *Men are assholes* appeared. Rachel copied them and then pasted them all the way down the page. Too irritated to work she toggled over to Outlook Express and opened her inbox. She scanned her received messages. There was a new mail from a friend back home. She would respond to that later with a scalding account of Justin's disgusting behaviour. A good rant to a captive audience would make her feel better, it always did. There was also a notification from the online dating website:

A member at manhattanlovematch.com by the name of NEWYORKGUY has sent you a message. To read it, please visit the site and find the message in your manhattanlovematch.com inbox.

She trashed the notification immediately. She wasn't interested. Justin had just confirmed what she already knew. Men were all selfish, lying bastards and only really good for changing tyres and getting rid of bugs and reaching things on top shelves, if that. She was completely done with dating. To further cement her decision she opened up her Facebook page and changed her status update:

Rachel Marcus is never dating again.
May 4 at 12:25pm

Satisfied that she had now cleared the path to a smoother, happier, better way of life, Rachel decided to treat herself to a greasy, fattening, celebratory lunch. If she was going to make it through the rest of this bleak Monday with her wanker of an art director she was going to need sustenance, and after all, she thought, she may as well take advantage of the fact that she was never going to go on another date again and let herself go.

Rachel went to a small deli a couple of blocks down the street from Target. It was a typical New York eatery. It had a long counter with stools for customers facing into an open-plan kitchen where three loud Italian short-order cooks screamed and shouted over each other in a mix of English, Italian and kitchen code while they cooked food on a row of open-top grills. Along the opposite wall of the long, thin establishment was a row of booths tended by two waitresses. The restaurant, which seemed unnamed, was home to fast-paced, indigestion-inducing, organised chaos. If you were focused you could get in a three-course meal and be in and out in under fifteen minutes.

The deli was packed but Rachel only had to wait a minute before a stool at the counter became available. She looked at the menu and ordered a cheese burger, fries and a strawberry milkshake. She needed comfort food. Minutes later a plate piled high with food landed in front of her. She ate and drank and slowly started to feel a little better. Clearing her plate, she ran her finger through the last of the ketchup she had squeezed onto her plate and licked it. Then she put her knife and fork together.

She'd barely even released the knife when the shortest, fattest and ugliest of the short-order cooks swooped in to clear away her empty plate. 'You gotta good appetite,' he said loudly, nodding at the empty plate. 'Not like those skinny model girls. You like to eat, eh?'

Embarrassed, Rachel put the milkshake glass she was clutching down on the counter. There was a couple of centimetres of the icy pink goodness left in the bottom of her glass and she really wanted to finish it, but she knew if she wanted to maintain any kind of self-respect, after the chef's cruel appetite comment, she would need to leave it behind. She eyed the bottom of the glass and then eyed the Italian, who was still standing watching her with a leering smile on his face. Screw him, she thought. Screw them all. From now on she would say and do exactly as she pleased. Just like a man. As he reached across her for the glass she picked it up and slurped what was left of the milkshake through the straw, racing the end around the base of the glass, loudly sucking up any remnants of pink foam. Satisfied that the glass was now a hundred per cent empty she put it down on the counter and burped loudly. Then she smiled, dropped her money on the counter, grabbed her handbag, slid off the stool and left the restaurant.

Rachel went back to her desk. The flashing cursor on the blank document, which she had over-enthusiastically named *Pharmicorp AV Draft One*, mocked her. Rachel tried to think about antidepressants, but she couldn't concentrate. Something was tugging at the back of her mind. She double-clicked the deleted items icon and reread the email from manhattanlovematch.com. What the hell, she thought, anything to avoid working on the AV. Rachel opened Internet Explorer and clicked through to manhattanlovematch.com. She filled in her username and secret password and watched as the home page loaded painfully slowly. *You have one new message* said the man inside her computer. Rachel clicked through to the message. It couldn't harm, she thought. She'd see what he had to say, send a polite but firm mail back to say she wasn't interested and then she'd trash her account. After that she'd be able to write the audio visual in peace, without the unread mail nagging on her conscience.

Rachel read the message, it said:

Hi, I found your profile intriguing. I'd love to chat to you and get to know you a little better. Let me know if you're interested. Hope to hear from you soon. Until then, Robert.

There wasn't a single bad pun, dodgy pickup line or spelling mistake. Intriguing, she thought. He finds me intriguing. Rachel also thought the 'until then' part was a nice touch, it made her feel like he really wanted to hear from her, in a chivalrous, old-fashioned kind of way. Curious, Rachel clicked through to his profile and scanned it. She wondered what the chances were that this guy was different from all the others.

NEW YORK GUY'S PROFILE

Age:	*33*
Star Sign:	*Aquarius*
Height:	*6'0"– 6'5" (180–89cm)*
Body Type:	*Above average*
Hair Colour:	*Light brown*
Eye Colour:	*Blue*
Occupation:	*Lawyer*
Income:	*Above average*
Drinking Habits:	*Regular drinker*
Smoking Habits:	*Non-smoker*
Hair Style:	*Short*
Facial Hair:	*I'm clean-shaven*
Eyesight:	*I've got 20/20 vision*
Fashion Sense:	*Casual (I'm usually in my favourite jeans)*

Why you should get to know NEW YORK GUY?

I feel a little awkward being on an online dating site, but anyway here goes:

I'm friendly, successful and can do basic algebra. I can spell and I've never been intimate with a cousin or any other family member. I also don't have a criminal record or a hunchback.

This guy was funny. Rachel carried on reading.

I believe that a romance has to consist of both physical and mental attraction, otherwise it is just a friendship. I'm looking for someone who is passionate about something — even if it's bird watching. It's not so much the object of passion, it's more the presence of it that's important to me. I care about the things that matter. I'm a thinking, feeling, questioning kind of guy.

I like my fun, but I'm also happy on my own. I'm okay in crowds, but can be a little shy, which means I'm best one-on-one or with a small group of good friends.

Rachel scrolled down.

NEW YORK GUY describes his ideal match as:

I'm looking for someone who is easy to be with — relaxed, fun and interesting. A woman who enjoys the simple pleasures as well as the finer things in life. Someone who can talk for hours about the things that are important to her, or just lie together for hours in comfortable silence. Perhaps you just haven't been able to find that one person who is your physical, emotional and mental match? Or maybe you're looking for something exciting and real. And so, like me, you've resorted to this medium, which you are still trying to justify by telling yourself: 'it's the new age of communication'. If anything I've said above strikes a chord in you, please say hi, because then I think I'd love to get to know you a little better.

Rachel read through *NEW YORK GUY's* profile again, this time a little less greedily, trying to be as critical as she could. Then she clicked through his posted photographs. There were two. One was a holiday snap of him in front of the Eiffel Tower and the other was a casual shot taken at a party. He looked comfortable and relaxed. Rachel liked the fact that neither picture was posed.

What if he's actually the one and you miss out because you're so angry and too stubborn to send one little response, nagged a voice in her head. This will be the last one, it said. Anyway, he took the time and trouble to write, responding is really just the polite thing to do.

'What the hell,' Rachel said out loud, to the empty office. She shot a response off to him, settling for a short, simple message that read:

Hi NEW YORK GUY, thanks for your mail. I enjoyed your profile. Rachel.

She wheeled her mouse over to the Send button. Her finger hovered above the button. Should she or shouldn't she? She wavered for a second, then she clicked it and the email sent itself.

Rachel Marcus is going to give this Internet dating thing one more bash. It's unlikely, but just in case there are any good men left out there.
May 4 at 4:13pm

'Hello, darling,' Justin slurred, falling in the door.

Rachel checked the time: it was just after four. 'Nice lunch then?' she asked.

'Fan-fucking-tastic.'

'Jesus, Justin, I can smell you from here,' said Rachel as he closed in on her desk. 'It's after four, what's the point coming back to work? It's not like you're going to sit down and work between now and six ... You can barely even stand.'

Rachel went back to her typing, bashing at the keys to highlight her anger, but when Justin continued to stand swaying in front of her desk she looked up again. 'What do you want?' she snapped.

Justin wobbled and pulled a white cardboard box out from behind his back. He placed it in front of her. Then he turned around and staggered out of the office.

When he was gone Rachel opened the lid cautiously. Inside were six perfect assorted doughnuts.

Rachel Marcus has butterflies in her stomach.
May 8 at 7:15pm

Rachel had decided to pull out The Killer White Dress for this date. It came to just above her knee and the neckline was cut so low it scraped her belly button, making it one of those dresses that required a whole roll of strategically placed double-sided tape to keep everything safely contained. It was a bold choice, but it was a Friday night in Manhattan and Rachel had a date with a hot lawyer. If ever there was a time for bold choices, she thought, it was now.

Rachel and *NEW YORK GUY*, Robert to his friends, had emailed for a few days and then moved the relationship to the next level, the telephone. From what Rachel could tell he seemed smart and quite funny, for a lawyer. And damn hot if his photos were anything to go by. Their emails, text messages and phone conversations had become increasingly more intimate and raunchy over the last two days, until finally Robert had asked her to meet him for dinner.

Rachel struggled to get her hair to behave. She stuck a diamanté clip in it to try coax it into some semblance of a 'do' and applied a generous lathering of lipstick. Robert had offered to pick her up but she was already nervous of meeting him and she thought it would be better to meet in a public place. She also didn't like the idea of him knowing where she lived. If her last couple of dates had taught her anything it was that men weren't to be trusted.

Rachel decided to treat herself to a cab – the thought of facing the subway in a white dress and heels was too much to bear. So, fashionably late, at around ten past eight, she stepped into the restaurant.

She nodded at the maitre d'. 'Hi, I'm meeting someone, Robert ... um ...' Rachel suddenly realised she didn't know his surname and that he probably didn't go by *NEW YORK GUY* in his day-to-day life. 'Um ... sorry,' she said. 'It's a table for two ... It's under Robert somebody ...'

'I believe your date is waiting for you at the bar,' the maitre d' said, with an evil glint in his eye.

'Thank you,' she said, scanning the crowd at the bar.

Black man who must be at least fifty. No.

Fat man in grey suit. No. Please, no.

Three businesswomen clutching cosmopolitans. No.

Then she saw him. He'd already spotted her and was watching her with a satisfied look on his face. When she caught his eye he smiled and waved. Rachel was relieved. He looked even better than his photograph, which, she'd learnt the hard way, was as rare as men with a full set of teeth and all their own hair in the Internet-dating world. Rachel double-checked. Nope: no colostomy bag, no false teeth, no hair plugs. Just six-foot four of yum. Rachel walked towards him and made it all the way across the restaurant and into the bar without tripping or embarrassing herself. So far this was the best date she'd had in months. And she hadn't even spoken to him yet.

'Hello, Rachel,' he drawled, pulling her towards him and giving her a kiss on each cheek. Her skin burned where his lips made contact. He smelled delicious and expensive. 'Can I just say, you're much more stunning in real life than in your pictures,' he whispered in her ear as she pulled away from his kisses reluctantly.

'Thank you,' she stuttered. 'It's very nice to meet you at last.'

'Come on then,' he said. 'Let's go to our table, I'm starving.' He winked at her and led her to a table with a reserved sign prominently displayed on it.

'How about some vino?' Robert asked once they were settled in and a waiter had appeared.

'Sure,' said Rachel, smiling.

'Red or white?' he asked as the waiter handed him the wine list.

'Maybe white?' she said.

'I think I feel like red. You don't mind do you?' He smiled at her and her heart fluttered.

'Sure, I'm easy either way,' she said.

Robert chose something French and the waiter bowed and scurried away.

'So, tell me,' said Robert, looking Rachel straight in the eye, 'what's a gorgeous woman like you doing on an Internet-dating site?'

A warm feeling flushed through Rachel's body. She liked this guy and it didn't hurt that he was easily the most handsome man in the room.

A few minutes later the waiter brought their wine and Robert tasted it, licking his lips. Even his teeth were sexy, Rachel thought as he nodded approvingly at the waiter who filled their glasses.

'Allow me to tell you about our specials,' the waiter said. 'We have an asparagus and artichoke tart with a mustard mayonnaise; a prawn, caviar and lobster risotto; chicken breasts stuffed with brie and a trio of vegetables on a bed of truffle linguine …'

Rachel watched the waiter's lips attentively as he spoke, trying desperately to focus, but unable to concentrate. Instead of listening to him she savoured the memory of Robert's lips on her cheeks.

'So,' said Robert. 'Any of that sound appealing?'

When Rachel pulled focus back into the moment she discovered the waiter had left the side of their table. Then the realisation dawned on her that she wouldn't have been able to repeat even one of the specials if her life had depended on it. There might have been something to do with seared sirloin, but she couldn't be sure. She smiled at Robert. 'Maybe I'll just choose something off the menu,' she said.

'A toast.' He raised his glass. 'To us.'

Rachel grinned. She couldn't believe this was her, sitting here, in this room, with this incredible man. She took a deep breath and clinked his glass with hers. For a split second she thought about Phillip, a million miles away on what felt like another planet. Rachel wondered what he was doing. Then she shoved him out of her mind and focused instead on this moment. Her moment. She knew she'd earned this happiness and she wasn't going to let anything ruin it. She took a deep sip of wine. It was sweet, dark and delicious, and it slipped easily down her throat and warmed her stomach.

They studied their menus in a comfortable silence. The waiter returned, took their order, and then disappeared again.

Robert picked up their conversation where they left off. 'I've been working sixty-hour weeks for the last nine years or so, working towards making partner, so online dating is really the only way I've had to meet women. And that's my excuse. What about you?'

'Meeting men in this town is a lot harder than I thought it would be,' Rachel said. 'Especially when you don't really have a circle of friends. So I thought I'd try it. Although, I must tell you, I was on the verge of giving up when I got your mail.'

'Well,' said Robert, reaching across the table and covering her hand with his. 'Thank goodness I found you in time.' His hand was cool and dry and Rachel was relieved her hand was facing palm-down on the table. She could feel the sweat in the creases of her hand against the tablecloth.

'So ...' he said later, as the waiter placed their food down in front of them. Rachel had ordered the salmon and Robert was having a steak. He waited for the waiter to fill up their glasses and leave before he continued. 'So,' he repeated, reaching for his knife and fork. 'Tell me more about the exciting world of advertising.'

Rachel smiled and reached for her glass. A phone rang.

'Hold that thought,' he said. 'Sorry, I have to get this. Please start. Don't let it get cold. I won't be long.' He reached into his pocket and pulled out his cell as Rachel picked up her knife and fork and started eating, carefully following the one side of the conversation she could hear.

'Hi,' he said. 'Sure. Of course. Absolutely. I'll pick some up on my way home. I know, two per cent. You already said. Yes. Of course. But I might be late, okay? Yes, me too. Night.'

Robert cut the call and put the phone back into his pocket. 'I'm so sorry,' he said. 'I had to take that. Where were we?'

Rachel chewed a small mouthful of salmon. 'Was that work?' she asked.

'No, that was just my wife,' he said, slicing into his bloody steak with his knife.

Rachel choked on her mouthful. 'Your wife?'

'Yes, please don't let me forget to pick up some milk when we leave here, okay?'

Rachel dropped her knife and fork. They clattered loudly on her plate and some of the diners at the tables surrounding theirs looked over. 'You never said you were married!' she blurted, pushing her chair away from the table.

Robert looked up at her. 'Well, you never asked. But, yes, almost five years now.' He said it so casually, Rachel was horrified. 'But, of course, we're not happy,' he continued, reaching for her hand again. 'You know how it goes?'

Rachel pulled her hand violently out from under his, knocking the bottle of wine over in the process. Red wine cascaded onto her plate, pouring into her food and splashing all the way down the front of her white dress. Almost instantly the waiter appeared out of nowhere with a fistful of napkins, righted the now almost empty bottle of wine and reached towards Rachel's chest to try mop up some of the half litre of red wine that was dripping down her cleavage and bleeding across the front of her dress. The other diners gaped as Rachel jumped up in a shocked haze, her chair falling over backwards onto the floor with a clatter. Somehow the red wine had affected some kind of chemical reaction, causing the double-sided tape to unstick itself. So there Rachel stood, in the middle of an upmarket restaurant in Manhattan, with both breasts popping out of either side of the neckline of her saggy, uncooperative dress. Every eye in the restaurant was on her. Rachel felt tears prickle at her eyes as she desperately tried to cover herself with both hands.

Robert made to get up and reached for her, trying to help. 'Rachel …' he said.

'You monumental fucking shit!' Rachel swore loudly, grabbing her tiny evening bag and trying desperately to use it to cover her breasts before turning and fleeing the restaurant.

Rachel Marcus is so over white clothes, red wine and yellow lawyers.
May 8 at 11:49pm

Rachel Marcus feels like a right tit.
May 9 at 9:27am

Rachel stood in her kitchenette wearing a Springbok rugby jersey, which was a couple of sizes too big. It had belonged to an ex-boyfriend and she had long thought that it was the only good thing she had gotten out of the relationship. She nursed a cup of coffee between her palms. The milk in her fridge had been spectacularly off, but she was desperate for a cup, so she was drinking it black. She blew over the top of it and took a sip, scalding her tongue on the molten lava.

In just a couple of hours the Springbok rugby team would be taking on the New Zealand All Blacks in a massive grudge match in Johannesburg. Rachel had emailed and Facebooked with everyone back home and she knew her folks were going to a box in the stadium and all her friends were going to someone's house to watch the game. At least nobody back home knew that she'd shown her tits to half of Manhattan the night before, Rachel thought, her cheeks burning with shame. If she wanted to go out in public again she'd have to wear a baseball cap and sunglasses.

Not for the first time since she'd arrived in New York, Rachel wished she was home. She felt miserable, alienated, homesick and, of course, alone. What she wouldn't give for a stick of biltong, a boerie roll off the braai, a bag of Nik Naks in her lap and, more than anything, a good old cup of Five Roses tea.

Rachel looked out of the window at the view, which was still a brick wall. Things weren't quite working out as planned. Her job was a joke, her art director was a nightmare, she had one-and-a-half friends and she lived in a shithole. And now, to make matters worse, the whole of New York City had seen her tits.

There was a quick knock and Sue popped her head around the door. 'Hiya,' she said, cheerfully.

Rachel didn't respond.

'Hey, why aren't you dressed? I thought we were going shopping?'

'I don't want to go. I feel miserable.'

'Was last night terrible?' asked Sue.

'Worse,' said Rachel.

'Throw on some clothes; we're going shopping. Come on, you can tell me all about it.'

'Can we spend obscene amounts of money on shoes we don't need?' asked Rachel, through trembling lips.

'Of course,' said Sue. 'Isn't that what we always do on a Saturday?'

Rachel poured the bitter, steaming coffee down the sink and walked the one and a half steps into the bedroom to find a pair of jeans. 'Fine,' said Rachel. 'I'll go out. But I'm not brushing my teeth.'

'Great,' said Sue with a grin. 'But then no tongue-kissing me.'

Rachel cracked a smile. It was faint, but it was there.

Rachel Marcus is going incognito.
May 9 at 10:02am

They took the subway into SoHo. Rachel could tell Sue was trying to cheer her up, but it would take more than an amble around the shops to make her feel better. After a couple of hours they stopped off at Dean and DeLuca and sat at the counter facing the street, eating chocolate croissants.

'So,' said Sue. 'Spill the beans.'

'Do I have to?' asked Rachel.

'It was the lawyer guy you've been mailing with for the last week, right?' prodded Sue.

'Yes,' said Rachel, through gritted teeth. 'He's a partner at a law firm uptown.'

'Nice.'

'No, not nice,' said Rachel. 'He's married.'

'No!' said Sue.

'Yes. And I showed my tits to the whole of New York City,' continued Rachel. 'And I ruined my favourite dress.' She felt tears of shame welling up as the night replayed itself in gruesome clarity.

'Well,' said Sue, jumping up and grabbing her bag. 'We'd better go find you a new favourite dress then, hadn't we?'

Rachel followed Sue, pulling her baseball cap as far down as it would go over her face.

Rachel Marcus had all four of the main food groups today: chocolate, sugar, salt and whiskey.
May 9 at 11:32pm

Rachel Marcus is not a poster child for the American dream right now.
May 13 at 9:32am

'What are you doing?' asked Rachel.

'Surfing the net,' said Justin. 'I'm doing research for the AV.'

'Read out the URL you're looking at right now, Justin.'

Justin looked over at his monitor, then back at Rachel. 'www. girlswholikeitdirty.com,' he said.

Frustrated, Rachel stared into her coffee cup, a knot of anxiety eating away at her stomach.

'Hello, team,' squeaked a voice as the door to their office burst open and Dan Charter wafted in on his cloud of incense.

Rachel and Justin sat up straight and acted like they were hard at work. Dan strode towards Justin first because his desk was closer to the door. Justin jumped out of his seat, and in an attempt to prevent Dan from seeing the porn on his monitor threw his arms open and swooped in, giving Dan a massive bear hug. 'Welcome back, Dan. How was California?' he asked, winking at Rachel from over Dan's shoulder.

'California is California. My swami says it has a yellow aura and my wife likes the shopping, so at least they're both happy,' Dan said, extracting himself from the man-clinch and turning to face Rachel. 'So, Rachel Marcus, how's my favourite South African?' he asked, moving in for a hug.

Rachel stayed sitting at her desk, hoping it would throw him off, but her luck wasn't that good. 'How about a big, karmic, energy-filled hug, Rachel?' asked Dan.

Rachel pasted a fake grin on her face and realising there was no way she was going to get out of it, stood up to receive her hug. He was shorter than her, so she always found hugging him awkward. Particularly since he liked to put his arms up over her shoulders in a hug, which meant she generally had to bend a little at the knees and place her arms below his. She'd never really thought about hugging too much before, but now she was struck by the thought that even in hugging, one person always seemed to get the upper hand. As he squeezed her she found her nose lodged in the crook of his neck. She retched on the smell of patchouli mixed with sweat and hair gel and pulled out of the hug as quickly as she could without offending him.

'We've missed you, Dan,' Justin lied.

Dan settled into the couch. 'So, team, how's my Pharmicorp AV?'

'It's great,' replied Justin. He was lying again; they had absolutely nothing.

'Excellent,' Dan purred, dangling a leather Birkenstock from the end of his big toe. 'This is such an important piece of work. The Pharmicorp guys are really counting on us to pull through for them. If they're happy they've hinted that they might give us the laxative and premature-ejaculation business, and that's big money. I don't need to tell you two how important this is, do I?'

'No, of course not,' said Rachel. 'I think we've got some great stuff.'

'That's what I like to hear from my star team,' said Dan. 'All right, let's hear it then?'

Justin shot a worried glance in Rachel's direction. Dan had discovered a stain on his khaki tunic and was trying to wipe it off. He licked his finger and gave the stain a good rub. Rachel thought it looked a bit like hummus.

'Shit!' mouthed Justin to Rachel.

'Dan, we'll be ready to show you when we've got the work done up nicely,' busked Rachel. 'Maybe tomorrow?'

'Rachel, Rachel,' said Dan, forgetting his battle with the hummus stain for a second. 'Through the years many people have told me that I'm a man of great vision. So, why don't you tell me your idea and I'll use the power of my mind to visualise it. All right? In fact, I may even be able to help you craft it a little. So, let's hear it.' He clapped his hands together, took off his glasses and steepled his fingers in front of his face, staring at Rachel, fully focused.

'Okay,' said Rachel, running her eye desperately over some of the scribbles on her layout pad even though she knew she wouldn't find anything of use there – she'd spent the morning writing Robert's name, followed by as many disgusting expletives as she could think of and then surrounded the whole thing with little doodles of skulls and crossbones.

'So,' said Justin, jumping in. 'This is what we were thinking …' He paused as if to gather this thoughts. 'We were thinking that … Well, we were thinking … Well, it's kind of difficult to explain, you know …? How should I put this …? You see, the way we see it, the problem with people suffering from depression is that they feel alone and isolated, like they're stuck under a dark cloud. Research tells us that they feel like nobody understands them and then that tends to deepen the depression. And so half the problem is that they actually make themselves inherently more unhappy.'

Justin stopped to take a breath and Rachel looked across at Dan, who seemed to be totally focused on what Justin was saying. She wasn't sure where Justin was going with this, but so far it was working.

'So, with all this in mind,' Justin continued, 'we want to create more than just an audio visual. We want to use all the modern tools at our disposal, things like social networking and branded content, to create a virtual community for these people, so they don't have to suffer alone. The big idea we want to mine is that this antidepressant isn't just physiologically making people feel better, but it's also enabling them to actively help themselves get better and play a role in their own mental health. Let's not just make an audio visual; let's make a call to arms.

Let's create an invitation that will help us find people to join our army and help us fight this disease together, with Pharmicorp, as a team, and not alone as individuals. We want to make a recruitment video, not just a boring old AV. It should become a living, breathing, organic thing. Part of it could be that we invite people who suffer from depression to send in their own artwork or poetry or music, or any other creative outlet, and we could use that in two ways. First, as artwork and content for future campaigns in different media – we could even go as far as initiating and sponsoring art shows or live events and readings. And, second, we could use it to entice other sufferers to join in. The added benefit of this strategy is that sufferers could use their art to express themselves, which is a form of healing in itself, isn't it?' Justin stopped, nodded at Dan and sat back down behind his desk.

Silence.

Rachel held her breath and contemplated what kind of job she would look for when she could no longer work in advertising – perhaps something secretarial. She wondered absently if one needed to be able to type with more than two fingers to get that kind of job.

Dan tapped his fingers against one another, deep in concentration. 'What about meditating?' he finally asked. 'Can we include meditating in it somewhere? Maybe with a swami?'

'Sure!' said Justin, 'It's not exactly what we had in mind, but I think we could work it in somewhere.'

A broad smile spread over Dan's face and he got up. 'I like it,' he said. 'I wasn't sure about it at first, but now, with the meditating touch, I think it's good. No, actually, it's great. Nice one team!' Dan high-fived Justin, gave Rachel a thumbs-up and swooshed out of the office.

Rachel and Justin took one look at each other and burst out laughing.

'What hat did you pull that rabbit out of?' asked Rachel between hysterical fits of laughter.

'I don't know,' said Justin, beaming. 'It just came to me right then, in a moment of panic.'

'Well, thank heaven for you,' said Rachel. 'I didn't have anything. I thought we were screwed for sure.'

Justin smiled.

'And it's actually a really good idea, Justin,' Rachel went on, surprised to find herself so impressed. 'I love the social-networking angle. I think it can really work. And I think it's added value that the client can really buy into. You're right, this doesn't have to be your typical old AV where they take the big Carmina Burana-type soundtrack and lay down some boring stock shots and whack on a James Earl Jones or Sean Connery voice-over. This can be completely different, maybe even fresh.'

'See, I'm not just a pretty face,' said Justin, still smiling. 'Come on, we cracked it, I think that deserves a celebration! How about you let me buy you a drink?'

'Sure,' said Rachel. 'I was looking for someone to help me drown my sorrows tonight anyway.'

'Hey, what the hell have you got to be sad about Rachel Marcus?' asked Justin, a smile playing on his lips. 'You've got great tits, you work with an incredibly handsome and talented art director and you were just integral in helping Dan Charter win this country's biggest laxative account.'

Laughing, they shut down their computers.

Rachel Marcus and Justin Coley are out of the office for the rest of the day, so bugger off!
May 13 at 2:56pm

'It's not fair,' whined Rachel. 'What Sue and Brian have … Why can't I have that?' She knew too much tequila made her whiney, but it hadn't stopped her drinking it.

Justin leaned over the bar, trying to get the bartender's attention. 'We need another drink,' he said, slurring. 'Okay, maybe we don't need anything more to drink, but our glasses are almost empty and that always requires immediate action.'

'Aren't I good enough? Don't I deserve that?' asked Rachel.

'What's wrong with this bartender, is he blind or something?' shouted Justin. 'Can't he see we're about to die of thirst over here?'

Rachel sniffed. 'It's like they're soulmates.'

Justin handed her a paper napkin off the counter before trying to catch the bartender's attention by waving both arms in the air as if he were guiding in an aeroplane.

'It's like Sue and Brian are two people,' Rachel slurred, 'but really one person at the same time …'

Justin gave up on the bartender and grabbed Rachel's hand instead. 'Come with me,' he said. 'I've got something that will make you feel better.'

Steering her through the bar to the toilets, Justin opened the men's toilet door and looked inside. 'Quick, follow me,' he whispered.

Rachel was feeling quite drunk, so she didn't spend much time questioning the intelligence of following Justin into the men's toilet in a dark and dodgy bar at four o' clock on a Wednesday afternoon. Instead, she trailed in behind him, wishing she hadn't abandoned what was left of her drink back on the bar.

Justin opened a door to one of the stalls and indicated for her to go inside. Squeezing in behind her, he locked the stall door, put the toilet seat down and crouched on his haunches in front of it. Rachel stood swaying next to him as he pulled off a couple of sheets of toilet paper and used them to wipe down the seat. Then he dug in his pocket and took out a small white paper envelope.

'You've done coke before, hey?' he asked her, looking up into her face.

'Sure. Of course,' she slurred. 'We do it back home all the time.'

Justin raised a sceptical eyebrow at her.

'Okay, not ALL the time,' Rachel said. 'Now and then … at parties and awards shows … whatever. Hurry up already, I'm thirsty and it stinks in here!'

Justin turned back to the toilet lid, opened up the envelope and emptied a pile of off-white crystals onto the top of the toilet seat. Satisfied, he folded the little envelope closed. Then, seeming to change his mind, he opened the envelope again and emptied more out onto the seat.

Rachel watched with detached fascination as Justin took out a twenty dollar bill, laid it out flat over the pile of rocks and used his gym card to crush them under the note. This done, he used the side of the card like a razor and cut four enormous lines. Finally, Justin rolled the twenty dollar bill up like a straw and offered it to Rachel.

'Here you go, love,' he said, 'this will make you feel better.'

'Justin, you do too much of this shit,' Rachel slurred, leaning back against the wall.

'And you don't do nearly enough of it,' Justin retorted, offering her the rolled-up note again.

Rachel shook her head. 'You first,' she said.

Justin shrugged, shoved the rolled-up note up his right nostril and expertly hoovered a fat line up his nose. Then he transferred the note over to his left nostril, held his right nostril shut with his finger and hoovered up another line. Standing, he handed Rachel the note. She looked at it for a second then bent down. As she did so, her hair brushed over the perfectly lined up soldiers of cocaine and sent granules flying around the toilet seat. She couldn't help giggling, which made her lose her balance. Steadying herself she stood up, still laughing.

Justin bent down again, took up his gym card and reordered the coke, pulling the soldiers back into line. Then he stepped aside so Rachel could have her go. This time as she bent down she felt his hand cool on her neck as he swept up her hair and held it in a ponytail so it wouldn't get in the way again. Rachel shoved the rolled-up note up her right nostril, held her left nostril closed and snorted half the line up her nose, then she swapped nostrils and sent the other half up the left nostril. Woof! The coke shot up into her brain, delivering a massive jolt of electric energy. She could taste it dripping down the back of her throat. She'd never really liked the hard, chemical taste of cocaine, but the effect was all right – the chatty confidence it gave her was fun in small doses.

She stood up and Justin smiled at her, letting go of her hair. 'That other one is yours too,' he said, pointing at the last line left on the toilet seat.

Rachel shook her head, not trusting herself to speak straight away. 'Are you sure?' he asked.

She nodded and smiled widely at him as the coke perked her up.

Justin took the note and snorted up the last line efficiently. Then he ran his finger along the top of the toilet seat and rubbed the remaining coke onto his gums. He may as well have licked the top of the toilet seat, she thought. For an expensive drug, it always amazed her just how dodgy cocaine culture was. The rich elite congregating in public toilets, licking toilet seats and shoving dollar bills that had been who knew where up their noses – very glamorous indeed.

Justin put a finger to his lips, silencing Rachel, who hadn't realised that she was rabbiting on about something she'd already forgotten. Opening the door, he checked to make sure the bathroom was still empty, then he led her out of the cubicle. Rachel followed him back into the bar before slipping into the ladies. She studied her reflection in the mirror. Coke made her feel invincible and completely in control – she could see how Justin could get so addicted to it. She thought about him. At thirty he had a full head of thick curly blond hair, flawless skin, great teeth, naughty eyes and a naturally olive complexion, which hid the fact that he was rarely out in the sun. He also had a surprisingly good body, considering how little effort he put into working out. Even though he put his gym card to regular use, Rachel knew it wasn't used for exercising.

Rachel dried her hands on her jeans, not trusting the once-white towel hanging on the rail, and returned to the bar where Justin was waiting for her with fresh drinks. She slid back up onto the stool. 'Thanks for that,' she said.

'No problem,' he replied. 'So tell me what you're looking for in a guy?'

'I don't know,' Rachel admitted. 'I usually pick such losers. I can't think of a single guy I've ever dated who wasn't a complete jerk. It's like I attract them or something. That's it, I figured it out, that's my problem – I'm a jerk magnet. That's my fate. Maybe I was seriously bad in a previous life, like a serial rapist or a politician or something, and now this is my punishment.'

'Don't be ridiculous,' Justin said, patting her hand, 'there are lots of amazing guys out there.'

Rachel looked up at him, surprised by his sincerity, but he wasn't looking at her. He was looking over her shoulder. She swivelled on her stool and saw that he was eying out a pretty blonde waitress wiping down a table across the bar. Rachel suddenly felt furious at him. 'Don't touch me, you shit!' she shouted, pulling her hand away from his 'What the fuck do you know about amazing guys? You're all the same! Why do you all have to be like that?'

'Like what?' he asked.

'Like that!' she said, nodding towards the waitress. 'Like a dog! Like every asshole guy I've ever known! You're the king of dysfunctional relationships! When last did you tell a girl the truth or want more from her than a good fuck? You're just like the rest of them. In fact, I think you may be worse! I think you're the biggest asshole I've ever met!'

As Rachel gesticulated with her hand to emphasise her point, whiskey sloshed out of the glass she was holding and landed in her lap. She swallowed what was left in her glass and then she slammed it down on the bar counter with a massive thunk, for effect.

Justin eyed out her empty glass and waved to get the barman's attention again.

'Hi, guys, another round?' the barman asked, clearing away their empties.

'I don't want to be here with you anymore!' Rachel said to Justin, ignoring the bartender and climbing off her bar stool. But when her feet touched the ground she suddenly realised that she was a dozen times more drunk and stoned than she'd thought she was. Her legs gave out below her and she slipped to the floor with a hiccough.

'You two have had enough,' said the barman. 'I'm cutting you off.'

Justin crouched down next to Rachel and helped her up. 'Come on, feisty,' he said. 'Let's get you home. After all, we've got an antidepressant AV to write in the morning.'

Justin must have been more sober than her because he managed to hail a cab and direct it to her apartment. Rachel vaguely remembered that she had shouted at him for most of the ride home, then he'd had to practically carry her all the way up the three flights of stairs before holding her hair back for the second time that night, this time while she'd vomited heroically into the toilet. Then he had helped her to her bed, taken off her shoes and covered her with a blanket. And the last thing Rachel sort of remembered, before she slipped into a cocaine, whiskey and tequila-fuelled coma, was Justin forcing her to take two aspirins, putting a glass of water and a bucket next to her bed and letting himself out of the door.

Rachel Marcus has a hangover the size of Canada or Australasia, whichever's bigger.
May 14 at 9:38am

Rachel could have done with a second pair of sunglasses to put on top of the pair she was already wearing. Anything to stop the daylight burning into her eyeballs and eating away at her brain. She lay on the couch at work, groaning.

'Are you sure you're going to be okay?' asked Justin, passing her a cup of coffee and then disappearing back behind his Mac to look for references for the antidepressant mood board.

'Now I remember why I never do coke: it gives me the worst hangover,' whispered Rachel. 'How could you let me drink so much?'

'If I'd known you couldn't handle your liquor I would have stopped you,' Justin said and laughed.

'Not funny,' said Rachel. 'Anyway, how come you look so good today? You look like you went to church, sang in the choir and were at home and in bed by nine.'

'I guess I've had more practice than you.'

Rachel nodded. He was right. In comparison to Justin's usual Wednesday night, the previous evening must have been tame. Home by two, only one bottle of Scotch, one bottle of tequila and one gram down, child's play for someone of Justin's partying calibre.

'I'm sorry if I talked your ear off last night,' Rachel said. 'Tequila makes me a bit batty!'

She remembered arriving at the bar and then matching Justin tequila for tequila and Scotch for Scotch. Then she remembered being very drunk and following him into the bathroom and snorting cocaine with him, but after that it all became vague. 'And thank you for holding my hair back when I vomited. Imagine how much worse I would be feeling if I hadn't got rid of some of that last night?' Rachel went on, covering her face in embarrassment.

'Don't stress, that's what partners are for. Anyway, it's the Art Directors Club Awards tonight and I'm hoping you'll return the favour.'

'What?' Rachel shrieked, sitting up straight and wincing at the sudden movement. 'Don't tell me that's tonight?'

Justin nodded.

'I totally forgot. Shit! What am I going to wear? And I'm so hung-over! Why does it have to be tonight?'

'How could you forget? It's been in our diary for ages.'

Rachel bent down and grimaced as she picked up her handbag. 'Justin, you have to cover for me, okay?' she said. 'I need to go and find a dress and some painkillers. And I'm going to need an afternoon nap if I'm going to make it through tonight.'

'Of course,' he said. 'On condition you buy a dress that's shockingly short, particularly see-through and massively low-cut.'

Rachel pulled a face at him and snuck out of the door.

Rachel Marcus is sneaking out. Shhh.
May 14 at 12:18pm

'You never really told me what actually happened to your white dress,' said Sue.

'I don't have time and it's too embarrassing,' Rachel grumbled. 'Just trust me, it's wrecked, and even if it wasn't, I don't think I could ever wear it again. The memories are just too painful.'

'So, what's this shindig tonight?' Sue asked. She was lying on

Rachel's bed eating a bag of Cheetos and had managed to get Cheeto dust all over her fingertips and lips. There was even a streak of it across her cheek where she had tried to wipe it off, but in the process had only managed to make it worse.

Rachel smiled at her. 'How come you can eat that shit and never gain any weight?' she asked as she squeezed into her new red dress. 'I only have to look at a pastry to put on a kilo.' And she must have inadvertently looked at four, or maybe even five pastries between buying the dress earlier on and putting it on now, she thought, because it suddenly felt a damn sight smaller than it had in the shop.

'Art Directors Club is an advertising awards show,' Rachel finally said, taking a break from fighting with her dress to answer Sue's question. 'Agencies from around the world enter their best work and a jury of internationally recognised creative directors judge it. Tonight is the ceremony where they give out the awards, and then there's a massive party afterwards. We always entered it back home, but of course I've never been able to actually go before tonight.'

'It sounds fun. Will there be snacks?'

Rachel gave her a look. 'Yeah, and lots of booze,' she groaned. 'Pity I had to go and get so hammered last night. I hate being so hung-over. Here, Sue, give us a hand with this zip won't you?'

'Deep breath, sugar,' said Sue, pulling the zip up the length of Rachel's back. 'Deeper.'

Rachel sucked in till she felt the zip give and slide all the way up her back. 'What do you think?' asked Rachel, turning to face Sue. 'Be honest.'

Sue was so stunned that she gaped at Rachel with a mouth full of half-chewed chips. 'Honestly,' she finally said, 'that's some dress.'

'Really?' asked Rachel. 'And the bags under my eyes, are they bad?'

'Bags!' Sue laughed. 'Darlin', with those tits, in that dress, nobody is going to be looking at your eyes. You look like a million bucks!'

'Thank you, Sue. Pity I only feel like four dollars fifty.'

'Don't thank me, thank whoever ruined your white dress. Lord knows, they did you a big favour. Come on, put on some shoes and come next door. Brian has to see this.'

Brian was sitting on the couch watching NFL, but he forgot about the game as soon as Rachel walked through the door.

'Well, don't just stare, dummy,' said Sue, climbing into Brian's lap. 'What do you think?'

'Jesus, Rae,' Brian choked, gawping. 'Where's the rest of your dress?'

Rachel smiled. She was still amazed by the size difference between them. In his lap Sue looked even tinier. Rachel had once asked Sue how they had sex without Sue being completely squashed. It turned out they made a plan. Often.

'So,' said Sue, 'have fun. I wanna hear all about it in the morning.'

'Absolutely,' said Rachel. 'What are you guys up to tonight?'

'I dunno …' Sue drawled, winking at Brian. 'Maybe we'll have an awards show of our own. What do you think, honey?'

Brian smiled widely and Rachel took this as her cue to leave. 'And the award for the handsomest man in the world goes to …' she heard Sue say as she closed the door behind her. 'Drum roll, please …'

Back in her apartment Rachel picked up the vintage black Dior alligator-skin clutch Sue had agreed to loan her and changed into the pair of Jimmy Choo stilettos she had bought with her first month's pay cheque. She had barely been able to afford tampons by the end of the month, but it didn't matter, she was wearing Jimmy Choos. This, she thought, was why she'd come to New York.

Rachel Marcus is all dressed up, with everywhere to go.
May 14 at 7:03pm

The cab pulled up in front of the Kodak Theatre at a quarter to eight, which gave Rachel fifteen minutes to have a glass of champagne and find Justin and the rest of the Target Advertising crowd before the ceremony started. She would have rather been attending as a member of Wieden+Kennedy or Richmond&Phillips or any of the other above-the-line agencies, but she knew she was lucky to be going at all. Anyway, she thought, as she paid the cab driver, this gave her something to work towards. She'd show them all; she just needed a little more time.

An escalator carried throngs of fashionably dressed people to the gallery for pre-show cocktails and champagne. Rachel grabbed a glass from a passing waiter and took a sip. She needed it to calm her nerves, but the champagne didn't go down very well – her hangover lay in wait at the back of her skull. She took another sip. This one went down slightly more easily, pushing her hangover back into the shadows. With the champagne doing its thing, Rachel found a spot to leave her glass and made her way through the crowds. Eventually, she saw Justin and the rest of the Target crew and elbowed her way towards them. Justin was wearing a modern take on a tux: a pair of vintage black suit pants, with a velvet stripe down the sides of the pant leg, a matching dinner jacket and a crisp white shirt that was open at the neck. He was holding a Scotch and had his hands all over a PA. He didn't see Rachel coming. She snuck up and tapped him on the shoulder. 'Evening,' she said.

Justin turned around. He looked at her blankly for a second and then a smile of recognition broke out on his face. 'My God, woman, you look incredible!' he said. 'Last time I saw you I thought I might have to call you an ambulance.'

Rachel blushed. 'Thank you.'

'Can I get you a drink?' he asked. 'I was just getting one for Lisa here.'

'It's Bridgette!' said the pouty PA.

'Yeah, Bridgette,' he said.

Rachel shook her head at him in disgust, but before she could tell Justin just what she thought of him the lights in the gallery began to flash on and off.

'It's starting,' said Justin. 'Come on, let's get decent seats.'

'What about the rest of them?' asked Rachel, pointing at the other Target Advertising people. She saw Dan Charter, standing in the middle of a group of creatives and suits from the agency. He was wearing a long black silk tunic over a pair of black linen trousers and a pair of slip-on black shoes. His ponytail was tied back with a diamanté-studded hair band.

'Screw them,' said Justin, grabbing her hand.

Inside the hall the seating was set up cinema-style. Rachel and Justin managed to elbow their way to two seats in the middle and towards the back, giving them a perfect view of the stage. The others weren't so fortunate and as the ceremony began she noticed that Dan Charter hadn't managed to get a seat and had been forced to sit on the floor in one of the aisles towards the back of the auditorium. She pointed him out to Justin who couldn't resist catching Dan's attention and giving him a facetious wave.

'Here,' whispered Justin, shoving something into Rachel's hand as the ceremony began. She felt cold metal and found herself clutching a hip flask.

Rachel took a small sip. It was so strong it burned her gullet going down.

The ceremony lasted an hour and a half and Justin and Rachel passed the hip flask between them as they watched the awards being handed out. Target weren't up for anything, of course, this was way out of their league, but for Rachel just being there was enough. Eventually, they got to the Gold Award for the Broadcast Television and Cinema category.

'And,' said the Master of Ceremonies, who was wearing a completely see-through dress, 'the Gold for Broadcast Television and Cinema goes to Stewart Southworth and Jerrod Craig of Richmond&Phillips for their Telecon Three, mobile phone campaign.'

The audience erupted and Rachel watched the spotlight search the auditorium before landing on two seats near the stage. Jerrod was wearing a dashing black tuxedo jacket with a white shirt and dark blue jeans and Rachel felt her pulse quicken as she remembered her meeting with him. The spotlight followed him and his partner onto the stage, where they received their award and made a big fuss over kissing the half-dressed emcee. Rachel wasn't sure which she wanted more; the gold award or the man currently holding it.

When the ceremony finally ended an excitable crowd of thirsty ad folk poured back into the foyer space where the organisers had set up a dance floor. Rachel and Justin pushed their way over to one of the bars to queue for a drink. 'I'll be back in a bit,' said Justin, grabbing her arm. 'I just need to go powder my nose. Want some?'

Rachel glared at him and mock vomited. 'Absolutely not, thank you very much.'

Justin shrugged. 'Hey, will you get me a Scotch?' he asked as he disappeared into the crowd.

Rachel jostled, waiting for a gap to open up, then she felt a warm hand on her shoulder and turned around, wondering how Justin had managed to make it back so fast.

'I thought that was you,' said a man's voice.

Rachel looked up straight into Jerrod Craig's green eyes. He was clutching his Gold Cube in one hand.

'Remember me? Jerrod. From the interview at R&P?'

'Yes, of course I remember you,' Rachel stammered. 'Congratulations on the Gold.'

'Thanks, but it's only advertising, right,' said Jerrod as someone behind him slapped him on the back, shouting their congratulations. 'It's not like we're saving lives or anything.'

'Well, still,' said Rachel, 'it's very impressive.'

'Thanks,' he said, eyeing her out from top to toe. 'I believe I owe you a drink, young lady. I've been meaning to phone you ever since your interview. I wanted to let you know that a spot might be opening up at R&P in a couple of months, and it could be just the kind of thing you might be interested in.'

Rachel nodded with enthusiasm. 'Really? That sounds fantastic!' she said, trying to look unphased at still having his warm hand resting on her shoulder.

'Let me make it up to you for not calling, okay?' he said. 'Will you let me buy you a drink? And I'd love to chat to you more about the

Mercedes-Benz campaign you worked on.'

'Of course,' said Rachel. 'I was just going to get a Scotch for myself and my art director; he just popped to the bathroom.'

'Excellent, let me buy it for you, it's the least I can do.' Jerrod moved his fingertips gently down her arm and placed his hand on her elbow, guiding her closer to the bar. Electricity pulsed down her arm, directly into her crotch as he pressed close into her back, pushing her forward into the crowd, protecting her from the shoving behind them. Rachel could smell his aftershave and she regretted having to stop breathing in, in order to breathe out.

Rachel tried to move closer to the bar, but even with Jerrod helping her through the crowd it was pretty hopeless. 'This is crazy,' Jerrod whispered into her ear. 'We're never going to get to the bar. What do you say we get out of here and go get a drink somewhere that isn't so crowded, where we can talk?'

Rachel turned and looked up at him. She was so close she could see that he hadn't had a close shave. She felt a sudden and desperate urge to run the tips of her fingers across his five o'clock shadow. 'But don't you want to celebrate with your team?' she asked.

'No, I want to celebrate with you,' he said.

Wow, Rachel thought, this dress was worth every cent. 'Okay, let's wait for my art director. He'll be back in a second, all right?'

'Fuck him,' said Jerrod with a smile. 'Come on, let's get out of here.'

Rachel scanned the crowd quickly and saw Bridgette standing across the room with a group of creatives from another agency. She grabbed Jerrod's hand and pulled him with her.

'Hey, Bridgette,' Rachel said as soon as she was close enough to make herself heard above the din of the crowd. 'If you see Justin, won't you tell him I left and that I'll see him at work in the morning?'

Bridgette eyed Jerrod and nodded. 'Sure thing, Rachel,' she said.

'Thanks,' said Rachel.

'You'd better warn him that she might be in a little late,' said Jerrod.

Rachel waved at Bridgette as Jerrod grabbed her free hand and pulled her towards the escalator, down, down, down to the ground floor and out into the fresh night.

'So where to then, darling?' he asked as they stood on the pavement outside the theatre.

'I don't know,' Rachel said, suddenly feeling a little shy. 'You're the local; you tell me.'

'Okay,' Jerrod said, hailing the first cab that passed. 'Don't worry, I know just the place.'

The cab came to a screeching halt in front of them, Jerrod opened the door for her and Rachel climbed in, feeling a little self-conscious about the length of her dress – when she was sitting it crawled up even further. She tugged at it, trying to drag it back down to earth again as Jerrod climbed in next to her.

'Do you know the Ivory Tower?' Jerrod asked the cab driver as he pulled out into the traffic.

On the way Rachel tried to push him for details, but Jerrod just smiled, refusing to answer her questions. They drove for about fifteen minutes before coming to a stop in front of an ordinary looking building. There was no signage and although Rachel looked up and down the block and across the street she couldn't see any bars or nightclubs. Jerrod paid the fare and climbed out, then he came round to the curbside and opened the door for her, reaching in and taking her hand to help her out.

'Is this it?' asked Rachel. 'I don't see any bars or anything like that?'

'You'll see,' he said.

Holding his award in one hand and Rachel's hand in the other Jerrod pulled her along behind him as she tugged at her dress, desperate to get it back to a respectable length.

'Jerrod …?' said Rachel as he nodded at the doorman, who let them in. If this was his apartment he was being very presumptuous, she thought.

'You'll see,' he said, cutting her off.

The entrance hall was carpeted in something that looked like red velvet and lit by low-hanging crystal chandeliers, but there was no clue as to where they were actually going. The elevator was already waiting and Jerrod ushered her inside before pressing the button for the forty-sixth floor. As the doors closed Jerrod took Rachel's hand. Her ears popped as they hit the nineteenth floor and around the twenty-third she started to feel a little strange, but all that was forgotten when they hit the forty-sixth floor and the elevator doors opened onto a massive candle-lit lounge furnished with plush velvet couches and chairs. The walls around the perimeter of the large room were all glass, giving a three-hundred-and-sixty degree view of the city, waitresses served drinks from a giant round bar centred in the room and a jazz band played softly from one corner. 'Wow,' whispered Rachel. 'This place is unbelievable.'

'Yeah, isn't it?' he said proudly. 'I love it here.'

The hostess escorted them to a small unoccupied lounge space that looked directly out over the magnificent skyline. A comfortable-looking velvet couch covered in scatter cushions and a low wooden coffee table awaited them. A dozen candles covered the table, providing a gentle glow. Jerrod put his award down and they settled into the couch.

'Good evening, can I get you a drink?' asked a waitress.

'How about some champagne?' Jerrod said, nodding at the award. 'We're celebrating. A bottle of Veuve Clicquot please.'

Rachel purred internally like a small diesel engine. 'Jerrod, how did you find this place?' she asked.

'I told you I'd show you New York.' He smiled. 'When you've lived in a city your whole life you find the places that tourists don't know about. Special places where only the locals go.'

The waitress reappeared with their champagne and two crystal flutes and poured them each a glass, then she disappeared. Rachel felt like they were alone on top of the city. She raised her glass and looked at Jerrod. 'Here's to your success,' she said.

'Yes,' he said. 'Running into you again really was a success.'

'No,' Rachel giggled, 'I mean the award.' She pointed a manicured

Jimmy Chooed toe at the statuette.

'Oh, that!' he said with a naughty laugh.

'I'm being serious, it was totally deserved, the work really stood out.'

'Thank you. So did you.'

The champagne was cold, bubbly and delicious and Rachel felt the pleasure centres of her brain light up.

'I have a bit of a confession to make,' Jerrod said.

'What's that?' asked Rachel.

'After I met you the other week, I emailed Matthew Barker.'

Rachel winced.

'He told me what happened at your last agency.'

Rachel took too big a sip of champagne and it bubbled up into her nose. She coughed and sputtered, struggling to catch her breath and her composure. 'Excuse me,' she said, putting her glass down and standing up suddenly. 'I'll be back ... ladies' room ...'

Casting her eyes around, Rachel made her way across the plush carpet to the bathroom. She drank water from the tap to try ease her coughing fit. Then, once she'd managed to get the choking under control, she took a proper look around. It was definitely one of the most incredible bathrooms she'd ever been in – even the toilet handles were crystal. But she felt like she couldn't fully enjoy the plush beauty of her surroundings knowing that Jerrod had heard about the fiasco back home. She had known she wouldn't be able to keep the embarrassing disaster at her previous job a secret forever, but she had hoped it wouldn't come out quite yet, and especially not to someone like Jerrod Craig. She applied fresh lipstick and tried to formulate some kind of plan. She knew she didn't have long. What would Jerrod think she was doing if she spent half an hour in the bathroom?

Rachel took a deep breath and tried to calm herself – nobody ever solved anything in a panic. She faced herself full on in the mirror. She couldn't just ignore it; she would have to tell Jerrod her side of the story to salvage some kind of dignity. After all, who knew what version of the story Matthew Barker had told him. Rachel put her chin up, her shoulders back and took another deep breath, then she made her way back out into the lounge with as much grace as possible.

When she got back to their couch Jerrod was leaning back, with both arms stretched out along the top of the sofa, smoking a cigar and taking in the view. 'You okay?' he asked when Rachel sat down next to him.

'Me?' she asked, picking up her champagne. 'Oh, yes, fine. Sorry. The bubbles just went down the wrong way.'

'So, as I was saying,' he said, with another naughty smile. 'I hear when you mess up, you do it good and proper.'

Rachel's cheeks burned. 'What did Matthew tell you?' she asked.

'Just that you screwed up and they had to fire you,' he said. 'I was hoping you'd fill me in on all the gory details?'

Rachel took a big sip of champagne, searching for a bit of Dutch courage. 'It's a horrible story, Jerrod,' she finally said. 'It's the reason I had to leave home and come here in such a hurry.'

'Oh, well, then you see, it's not that bad, at least it has a happy ending,' Jerrod said, clinking her glass with his.

'Nope, it was pretty bad. It was like a chain reaction.'

'What happened?'

'Things were amazing ...' Rachel began. 'I was working at Barker, Massa and Trout, which is a great agency. Anyway, I was a creative director: great job, huge salary, lots of awards. And I was engaged and planning a wedding. Everything was perfect.'

At the mention of her engagement Jerrod raised an eyebrow, but he didn't say anything, he just leant forward, filled their glasses and nodded for her to continue.

'I suppose it all went for a ball of shit when I found out my fiancé had fucked me over,' Rachel went on. 'It was like I was just in a haze after that. I felt like I was feeling my way around my life, like the lights were out and I was in a heavy mist. I suppose then I kind of lost concentration ...' She paused to think how best to continue. 'So, then this job came across my desk. We'd been working on this huge campaign for a local dog food company and we'd done a massive television commercial and a national print and magazine campaign. For the last element of the campaign I had to write some label copy for a tin of promotional dog food. It was the tiniest, simplest job, the promotional element of which was a win free dog food for a year competition. Anyway, so when I put together the first draft of the copy for the label there wasn't a competition phone number supplied with the brief, so I made one up. I just filled in 234 5678, assuming that when it went to the client they would supply the correct number. But, like I said, I'd totally lost my focus, and the whole job passed through the system, the client signed it off and I signed it off and it went to print. Just like that. The Johannesburg city telephone code is 011, so nobody picked up that 011 234 5678 wasn't the right number …'

Jerrod sucked in a breath.

'We printed twenty million labels with the wrong phone number on them. And then we distributed cans with them on to every supermarket in every town and every village across South Africa.' Rachel took a sip of champagne, her hand shaking a little as she raised the glass to her lips. 'Anyway, so it turned out that the number belonged to a local businessman, and of course he started getting thousands of phone calls. We offered to buy the phone number off him, but he wouldn't sell it to us. Instead, he sued the agency for millions. Needless to say, we lost the client and I lost my job. End of story. End of life in Joburg.'

Rachel felt a tear drop down her cheek and watched as Jerrod reached out to wipe it away with his thumb. 'Shit, Rachel,' he said. 'That's terrible!'

'It's okay,' she sniffed, 'it's not a life sentence. I'm all right now. Everything happens for a reason, right?'

'I think so,' Jerrod said with a smile. Then he leaned in to her and held her chin in his hand. Raising it up, he kissed her on the lips. 'See, like I said, happy ending. Look where it's led you.'

Rachel laughed, embarrassed that she'd let herself cry in front of him. 'What can I say? When I mess up, I do it in style.'

Jerrod winked at her. 'That's the only way to do it, darling.'

'Okay, definitely time for a subject change,' Rachel said, downing the rest of her champagne and holding her glass out for a refill. Maybe it was the champagne, maybe it was the release of finally getting the story off her chest, but at that moment she felt relaxed for the first time in months. Jerrod was the first person who had managed to make her feel anything other than shame over what she'd done back in South Africa.

Later, when the bottle was finished, Jerrod looked at her from under the longest, darkest eyelashes Rachel had ever seen. 'So,' he said. 'I've got another amazing city view I'd love to show you, that is if you're up for a nightcap?'

Rachel looked at her watch: it was 2.15 a.m. She wondered how it had gotten so late so soon. Last time she'd looked at her watch was when they'd left the awards show around midnight. She weighed up her options. She wasn't going to sleep with him, she told herself. She wanted this to be more than that. This man was something special, something that only came along once in a lifetime, and she didn't want to screw it up. But, she thought, she wasn't completely devoid of self-control, what harm could one more drink do?

'Sure, why not?' said Rachel. 'But I've got to be home by four at the latest; I've got work tomorrow.'

Jerrod paid the bill, picked up his award and they left the bar hand-in-hand. In the elevator Jerrod pushed her up into a corner and kissed her as they whooshed from the forty-sixth floor down to the ground. Rachel's knees wobbled beneath her, her ears popped and her heart raced. If she died that very second, she thought, it would most certainly be of a heart attack and she would die one very happy woman.

Somewhere in the background Rachel heard the elevator door open, but Jerrod carried on kissing her. It was only when the elevator door started to close again that he pulled away, reluctantly catching the door as it was about to close on them.

Out on the street they stood on the curb while the doorman hailed a cab. It started to rain while they waited, big romantic tears of rain, and Jerrod took off his jacket and covered Rachel's bare shoulders with it.

Seconds later a cab pulled up and they piled in out of the rain. Once they got going Jerrod gave the driver his address and in between thinking about the kiss in the elevator and worrying about her hair, which did terrible things in wet weather, Rachel wrote a virtual status update in her mind:

Rachel Marcus is in heaven and she's wearing her new, all-time favourite lucky dress.
May 15 at 2:27am

The elevator opened directly into Jerrod's apartment. Rachel had only ever seen that on TV – yet another item to add to the long list of things that impressed her about Jerrod Craig.

He lived on the nineteenth floor and much like the bar they had come from one entire side of the apartment was glassed in. The only difference was that Jerrod's view was of the Hudson River, Ellis Island and the Statue of Liberty, which towered in the distance.

'Wow,' Rachel gasped, 'this place is something else.'

'Thanks,' he shouted from the kitchen. 'What can I get you to drink? I've got beer or whiskey.'

'Whiskey please,' she shouted. He was a whiskey drinker, she thought, this evening just keeps on getting better.

Jerrod's apartment was straight out of a decor magazine. Everything was white and clean and each piece of furniture was a classic designer piece.

'This is quite some collection you've got,' she shouted, appraising one of his paintings. It was a gorgeous portrait of a very naked woman that covered one entire wall of the lounge.

'Thank you,' whispered a voice behind her, very close to her ear.

Rachel started, she had thought Jerrod was still in the kitchen, but he had somehow snuck up behind her. She turned around and took a step away from him as he passed her a Scotch on the rocks. You will not sleep with him on the first date … You will not sleep with him on the first date … she repeated to herself over and over as she clinked the ice cubes in her glass and then took a sip.

'Your accent is incredibly sexy,' he said, stepping towards her again. 'I can't get enough of it. I could listen to it all night.'

'Good thing, 'cos you pretty much have been,' she said.

'I'm just warning you,' he said, pulling her towards him. 'I'm going to kiss you now.'

In that moment, as Jerrod kissed her and ran his fingers along the back of her neck Rachel instantly and conveniently forgot her earlier mantra.

'Come with me,' he said gently, taking her hand.

Rachel floated behind him as he led her out of the lounge. She couldn't take her eyes off the back of his neck. How could the back of someone's neck be that sexy?

Suddenly Rachel heard a loud clunk and a searing pain shot through her shin. She'd been concentrating so hard on the back of Jerrod's neck that she'd walked right into a small white modernist cube placed between the couches in the lounge. 'Fuck!' she swore, unable to hold it in.

'Are you okay?' he asked.

'Fuck! Fuck! Fuck!' Rachel cursed, hopping and rubbing her fingers over her shin.

'That stupid cube,' Jerrod said, dropping to his knees in front of her as he realised what had happened, 'I'm forever walking into it too. I'll get rid of it tomorrow. Are you okay?' He rubbed a warm hand over the quickly forming bruise. 'Is that better?' he asked, kissing her shin gently and running his other hand slowly up and down the back of her leg.

'Mmmm,' Rachel said as the pain in her shin dissipated and was replaced with a rush of heat.

'Good,' Jerrod said, standing up again and facing her. 'I wouldn't want you to sue me for negligence …'

'Too right, I have a great lawyer,' Rachel teased him, running a finger down the front of his chest. 'That cube could have killed me, you know ...'

'I don't suppose there's anything I could do to change your mind about litigation, is there?' he said with a naughty smile, wrapping both his arms around her waist. 'Perhaps we could negotiate some kind of out-of-court settlement?'

'Hmmm, I don't know. What did you have in mind?' Rachel asked, smiling.

Jerrod pulled her in towards him and kissed her. He was the ideal height and her body moulded perfectly into his.

'Still planning on suing me?' he asked when they eventually stopped kissing long enough to speak.

'It depends,' Rachel said. 'First let me hear the rest of your argument.'

Jerrod laughed and took her hand, leading her through a door and into his bedroom where another whole bank of windows lined one of the walls, looking out at the Statue of Liberty. 'You know, I've wanted to do this since the second I first laid eyes on you in that interview,' he said, turning back to her, his voice suddenly serious. He kissed her again, reaching his hands around her back and unzipping her dress.

'And I've wanted to do this,' she said, pushing him backwards onto the king-sized bed as her dress fell obediently to the floor.

Jerrod grabbed her hand, pulling her after him, and rolled her over onto her back. Taking both her wrists in his hands he pinned them above her head, then he bent down towards her, first kissing her ear lobe before moving on to her neck and finally her mouth. Rachel closed her eyes and enjoyed the sensation of his tongue, savouring the pressure of his hands circling her wrists and pinning them to bed.

When Jerrod let go of her wrists Rachel reached down and slowly began to unbutton his shirt. His chest was smooth and muscled and Rachel couldn't resist running her fingers across it before reaching for his belt. As she undid it Jerrod shucked off first his one shoe and then the other with his toes, then he tossed his pants and shirt across the room to join Rachel's dress on the floor. Pushing him back onto the bed she moved over him, straddling him. He groaned as she gently took his ear lobe between her teeth before backing her way down his body, kissing and stroking his chest and then his stomach, going lower and lower until eventually she pulled off his Calvin Kleins and took him in her mouth.

'My turn,' Jerrod said, some minutes later, his voice raspy. Reaching down he pulled her up to join him at the top of the bed. He tickled his fingers across her back, unfastening the clasp of her bra in one easy action, then he ran his hands down her body and pulled off her panties. Rachel sucked in her tummy, glad the lights were off and the moonlight was on. She was nowhere near stick-insect thin, and she suspected that was probably what a guy like Jerrod was used to. But her self-consciousness was soon forgotten as Jerrod ran his fingers over her. She pushed herself against him and groaned as he zeroed in on her. At the same time she took hold of him in her hand and he growled with pleasure.

It felt to Rachel like they never stopped kissing. Eyes closed, their tongues met over and over again. Then, just before she couldn't take it any more, she whispered his name. Jerrod didn't need any further invitation; he took a condom from the drawer next to the bed, tore the packet open with his teeth and slipped it on. Then he manoeuvred himself over her and allowed her to guide him deep inside her. Jerrod moaned into her ear, kissing her neck, and a rush of bliss coursed through her. This was the moment she would remember and replay in her mind – the moment he pushed inside her.

He moved with her, perfectly in time, then harder and faster, until she felt her orgasm climbing its way up to the top of the hill, ready to barrel down the other side. She orgasmed hard and a couple of seconds later she felt his muscles tighten. He groaned once with incredibly intensity, his body perfectly still, then, slick with sweat, he rolled over and lay beside her. Seconds later, Rachel felt him reach for her, pulling her close into him as he covered their breathless bodies with the duvet. I could get used to this, she thought.

Rachel lay there until she heard Jerrod's breathing even out. When she was sure he was asleep she slipped out from under his arm and went into the bathroom. His entire en suite was carpeted and she couldn't help but run her bare feet over the decadent shag.

After going to the toilet and washing her hands Rachel pulled on an old T-shirt she found folded next to the sink. It smelled like him. Then she looked at herself in the mirror, watching as the afterglow of sex slowly edged its way out of her face. 'You stupid girl!' she whispered at her reflection. 'I thought you weren't going to sleep with him on the first date?'

Rachel splashed cold water on her face and thought about the last time she'd had sex. It had been with Phillip, just before everything had fallen apart back home. She shook the memory out of her head, then she slipped back into the bedroom.

Jerrod was spread out on his back, snoring quietly. She took a closer look at him; he had an incredible body with those defined cuts on his hips that drive girls crazy. Rachel had to tear her eyes away from him to scout around on the floor for her clothes. She found her shoes, dress and bra quite easily, but she couldn't find her panties anywhere. Finally, looking across the bed she saw them wedged underneath Jerrod's sleeping body. She reached for the small corner of fabric sticking out from under his left hip, but when she pulled at it gently he started to stir. Rachel backed up as quietly as she could, terrified that he might wake up and find her looming over him. Oh, well, she thought, she'd have to leave them behind. It was a small price to pay for an inconspicuous exit.

Rachel took one last long look at Jerrod. She may as well engrain this image on her memory, she thought. Chances were she'd never see him again. She knew his type. He could have any girl in the city and probably did. She shouldn't get her hopes up that this was anything more than a wild night of celebration.

Picking up her shoes, Rachel tiptoed out of the bedroom. Back in the lounge she pulled her dress on, inhaled the smell of Jerrod's T-shirt one last time for good measure, then she folded it and left it on the back of the couch.

Sneaking out of his apartment, Rachel looked at her watch: it was a quarter to five. Only three hours till she had to be up for work.

Rachel Marcus is more hung-over than she was yesterday, and that's saying a lot.
May 15 at 11:38am

Rachel didn't remember turning her alarm off when it *beep-beep-beeped* at seven thirty, but she must have. She opened her eyes for the first time at half-past ten, then closed them again – it was just too painful. She opened them again half an hour later, got out of bed and crawled the few feet on her hands and knees to the kitchen where she drank the tap dry. Then she groaned all the way into the bathroom, first doing her obligatory rat check, and finding it all clear, then trying to find her personality and sense of humour, which she concluded weren't there either. Finally, she climbed under an icy shower and let the water wash over her in an attempt at shaking off some of her hangover.

Feeling only marginally better, Rachel climbed out of the shower. As she wrapped her aching head in a towel flashbacks from the night before rushed in and her cheeks began to burn. Thank goodness she'd left Jerrod's apartment and hadn't slept over, she thought. Not only did she not look so great this morning, but she was also relieved to have avoided the humiliation of the dreaded morning-after conversation that would have been unavoidable had she woken up there. She flushed, ashamed all over again, as another flashback flooded her memory. It must have been all that champagne. Yes, she would blame it all on the champagne.

Rachel slumped down on the edge of her bed and turned on her cellphone. Nine missed calls flashed up on the screen. She dialled into her voicemail. 'You have five new messages,' said the electronic voice. 'First new message.'

Beep.

'Oi, Rachel, it's Justin. Where are you? I'm standing by the bar where I left you, but I can't see you. What happened? Are you lost? I got you a Scotch. I'll wait for you by the DJ decks.'

'Message left at 11:13 p.m.,' said the electronic voice.

Beep.

'Rachel, what the hell? Bridgette said you left with that Jerrod Craig prick from R&P! I didn't even know you knew him!'

'Message left at 12:06 a.m.'

Beep.

'Rachel, it's Justin,' he slurred. 'I can't believe you went off with that wanker and abandoned me here.'

'Message left at 3:47 a.m.,' said the electronic voice.

Beep.

'Morning, Rachel, it's Deborah. We were wondering if you're coming in to work today? Give us a call, okay, love?'

'Message left at 10:15 a.m.'

Beep.

'Rachel, it's Deborah again. Won't you give us a call, we're starting to worry about you.'

'Message left at 11:06 a.m.'

Rachel dialled frantically.

'Target Advertising. Good day, this is Heather speaking. How can I make your day?'

Rachel cringed at Heather's smiley voice. 'Hi, Heather, it's Rachel Marcus, can I speak to Deborah?'

'Morning, Rachel, heard you had a blast at Art Directors Club last night,' Heather twinkled. 'Putting you through.'

Deborah picked up after two rings. 'Deborah speaking.'

'Deborah, it's Rachel.'

'Oh, thank God, Rachel. We were starting to worry about you.'

'I'm so sorry, Deb, I turned off my phone before the awards show last night and forgot to turn it back on again. And then I had a ridiculously late night and slept through my alarm, so I only just woke up and picked up your messages now.' She paused. 'Deb, I need a huge favour, I'm absolutely trashed, I need to take a day off. Is that okay?' Rachel held her breath and crossed her fingers and toes.

There was silence on the other end of the line. 'You'll have to fill in a leave form on Monday when you get in,' Deborah eventually said begrudgingly.

'You're a lifesaver, Deborah,' said Rachel, breathing out a huge sigh of relief. 'I owe you one. If Dan asks, won't you tell him I needed a personal-space day?'

'See you Monday, Rachel.'

Deborah hung up and Rachel collapsed backwards onto the bed, feet still dangling off the edge.

The next time Rachel opened her eyes it was just after three in the afternoon and she felt almost human. She went to the fridge, looking for something to wash down the dirty old sneaker lodged just behind her tongue.

Rachel Marcus is excited to wake up without a hangover for the first time in days.
May 16 at 9:23am

Rachel looked in the mirror and figured that her extra-curricular activities over the last couple of days had only aged her by about a year, which wasn't as bad as she'd expected. She checked her cellphone again. Nothing. She wondered for the millionth time whether Jerrod would call. Then she tried to push the thought out of her mind. She was crazy to think he was interested. The best she could hope for was that when they bumped into each other at the next industry function he'd remember her name. Rachel shoved Jerrod Craig into the bottom of a filing cabinet stored at the back of her mind in a file marked *Delicious but Stupid Mistakes*.

To get away from her stubbornly mute cellphone, Rachel went to the gym to try sweat out some of the poison from the last two nights. Later, she balanced out all the exercise with pizza at Sue and Brian's place.

'Want a beer?' asked Sue, passing Brian a fresh one. He was sitting on the couch watching an action movie.

'No, thanks.' Rachel winced. 'After the week I've had I think I'll stick with iced tea.'

'You're such a party animal,' grinned Sue, opening a beer for herself. 'So then, what happened?'

Rachel had reached the point in the story where they had arrived back at Jerrod's apartment. 'You know, stuff...' Rachel smiled.

'You're such a ho! I can't believe it!' shrieked Sue.

Brian eyed them suspiciously then went back to his movie.

'So, how was it?' asked Sue.

'Amazing,' said Rachel, grinning.

'And is he ...?' asked Sue.

'Enormous!' confirmed Rachel.

They burst out laughing as behind them Brian turned the volume up so he could hear Steven Segal slay twelve ninjas over their shrieking.

'But I think I messed up, Sue,' said Rachel, suddenly serious.

'Why? Didn't you swallow?' Sue burst out laughing again.

'No!' said Rachel, masking a smile. 'I'm being serious. I think I messed it up. I don't think he's going to call me.'

'You don't know that,' said Sue, jumping immediately to her defence.

'Guys don't call girls who sleep with them on the first date, Sue.'

'How did you leave things the next morning?' asked Sue.

'Are you mad?' said Rachel. 'I didn't sleep over. I crept out while he was sleeping, like a complete coward.'

'No!' shouted Sue. 'Why?'

'I wanted to avoid that awful uncomfortable morning-after thing that always happens. I always think it's so weird, and anyway I'm not one of those girls who look as good in the morning as they did the night before.'

Sue eyed Rachel over her beer. 'Don't be ridiculous, Rae. Just wait and see what happens, okay. Don't jump to conclusions. It's still only Saturday. It hasn't even been a few days yet.'

Rachel nodded. She'd give Jerrod till Sunday night, she decided, and if he hadn't called by then she'd know it was over before it had even begun.

Rachel Marcus is watching her telephone very carefully. She's waiting for it to make its move.
May 17 at 9:45pm

Dear Mom and Dad,

Thanks so much for your newsy letter and the package. I was very excited. But, unfortunately, the tea you sent me is still not the right kind. Like I said in all my letters, we get lots of different types of tea here, but what I can't seem to find anywhere here is Five Roses. So, thanks for the green tea, but please can you send me Five Roses tea next time. Please. Five Roses!

On a different note, Mom, what a nice surprise to hear that you bumped into Selwyn Schmeisenberger. Of course I remember him. He got a dreidel stuck up his nose at Jewish Camp when I was twelve and they had to take him to the emergency room in Gordon's Bay. How could I forget him? Thank you for giving him my email address, postal address and telephone number, both office and cell. It's always nice to catch up with old friends unexpectedly. You also mention twice in your letter that he's a single podiatrist (which by the way isn't really a real doctor) and that you play bridge with his mom, which is all very interesting, but as I mentioned to you in my last letter, I have actually met someone special here. So it's probably best that you don't hand my details out to anyone else you bump into, even if they are single Jewish podiatrists.

Did you go to Incredible Connection yet? Maybe when you go, you could pop into a Pick 'n Pay and buy me some Five Roses tea. That way you could kill two birds with one stone.

Work is hectic and I'm really enjoying the challenges of a big New York City advertising agency. It's what I've always dreamed of and I realise how lucky I am.

Okay, can't wait for your next letter, and most of all, that package.

Love,
Rachel

Rachel Marcus is back at her desk and this week she's on the straight and narrow. She's never drinking again. Ever.
May 18 at 9:08am

By Monday morning Rachel had resigned herself to the fact that she wasn't going to hear from Jerrod Craig ever again. At the office she made two cups of coffee, one for herself and one for Justin, and decided to focus all her attention on finishing the Pharmicorp job, in an attempt to shove Jerrod out of her system for good. The presentation was only a couple of days away and she was starting to get tired of having the job lying on her desk. She'd always believed advertising briefs were a bit like fish and house guests, they all start to stink after five days.

When Rachel returned from the kitchen Justin was in his usual position, slouched behind his computer, wearing a baseball cap pulled down low over his eyes. She put his coffee down next to his mouse. 'Hey, how are you?' she asked.

'I'm fine!' Justin grunted, ignoring the coffee. 'What happened to you on Thursday night after the awards?'

'I bumped into an old friend.'

'Jerrod Craig?' he asked.

'Yes. I interviewed with him at R&P when I first got here and I hadn't seen him since.'

Justin slumped further behind his computer. 'And where were you on Friday?'

'Oh, you know,' Rachel grinned, 'late night. Hey, I'm sorry I left without saying goodbye, it's just he wanted to get out of there and I couldn't find you. But I left a message with Bridgette. I figured you would have done the same if some hot chick had wanted to drag you out of there, right?'

'So how are things with Mr Craig, then?' he grouched. 'When's the wedding? Can I be your best man?'

'No!' said Rachel, smarting a bit. 'It's over. I mean, it was nothing. We're just friends.'

The office door opened and Heather's breasts appeared closely followed by her smile and then the rest of her. 'Morning, guys,' she said.

Heather was carrying a massive bunch of at least two dozen ice-white long-stemmed antique roses, which she handed over to a very stunned Rachel. 'Wha ...?' she stammered.

'These came for you first thing on Friday morning,' said Heather. 'Oh, and this too.' She handed Rachel a yellow message slip.

Rachel laid the armful of roses on her desk while Heather hovered, smiling expectantly. Rachel looked up at her and cleared her throat gently.

'Fine!' Heather said, grimacing as she turned to leave the office.

Justin was still in his seat, but his body language had changed completely – he was peering over the top of his monitor, watching her every move. Rachel shrugged at him and fished for the card that was tucked in amongst the stems. She read it to herself:

Rachel, it was a pity you left in such a hurry last night. xJ.

Next Rachel read the little yellow Target Advertising message slip:

Message from: *Jerrod Craig*
Received: *3:45 p.m., Friday*
Thanks for last night, I had a great time. Call me so we can get together.

Below that Heather had scribbled his phone number.

Rachel sat down in her chair, almost missing the seat which had swivelled around while she was standing. She stared at the message and the flowers in shock.

'What is it?' asked Justin.

'Jerrod,' said Rachel. 'It's all from Jerrod Craig.'

'I thought you were just friends?' Justin sulked, retreating back behind his computer monitor and picking up his coffee.

'I thought so too,' said Rachel with a big grin on her face.

'Fuck!' Justin swore, standing up and pounding his hand on his desk, startling Rachel. 'This is the crappest coffee I've ever tasted,' he shouted. 'What the hell did you make it with, water from the toilet? I'm going out. I need decent coffee!'

Rachel was so busy reading and rereading her messages she didn't even hear him leave. Flowers and a phone call, she couldn't believe it. She picked up the phone and dialled Jerrod.

'Hello,' said Jerrod's sexy voice.

'They're beautiful, Jerrod, thank you so much,' gushed Rachel.

'Who is this?' he asked.

'It's me, Rachel.'

'Oh, hello, I was wondering what happened to you?' he said. 'Where did you slink off to?'

'I needed to get home; it was so late,' she said.

'Well I missed you. I wanted to wake up with you.'

'Thank you for the flowers, they're gorgeous,' she said, trying hard to stay cool, a hot flush rushing up her neck.

'The what?' asked Jerrod. 'Rachel, I can't hear you, I've got ... bad ... signal ... losing ...'

'Jerrod, hello, can you hear me?'

'Tonight ...' said Jerrod through a whole lot of crackle. 'My place ... dinner, seven thirty ... talk to you then ...' Then the phone died.

Rachel tried to call him back but his phone went straight to an electronic message telling her that the subscriber was not available to take her call.

Rachel couldn't believe it – he actually wanted to see her again. Maybe her bad luck was shifting. She looked at her watch: it was still early. The day stretched out ahead of her endlessly.

Rachel Marcus is counting the hours and they feel like days.
May 18 at 9:34am

Rachel found a vase in the agency kitchen. She filled it with water and arranged her flowers. Walking back to her desk she saw the other girls giving her 'the look'. The one girls reserve for other girls who get flowers sent to them at work. But she felt so good that she didn't care if they all hated her guts. She had been sent flowers by Jerrod Craig. The Jerrod Craig. They should be jealous.

When she got back to her desk Rachel put a call through to Sue.

'Sue, it's me.'

'Hiya, sugar, what's up?'

'Jerrod sent me flowers.'

'Fantastic! See, I told you to be patient. What kind?'

'Antique roses,' fired back Rachel.

'Colour?' asked Sue.

'White.'

'How many?'

'Two dozen . . .' Rachel smiled. This was why girls needed girlfriends.

'That's good,' said Sue. 'White roses show he's got taste.'

'And he called on Friday, but I didn't get the message because I wasn't at work.'

'You see, I told you not to give up on him so soon. I'm so happy for you, Rae. So, what's next?'

'He asked me over to his place tonight.'

'For dinner?'

'Yes, I think so,' said Rachel. 'We kind of got cut off before we could discuss the details. I wonder if he'll cook?'

'Wow, that's results, Rae.'

'Can I borrow your purple Pradas?' Rachel asked. 'I know it's a lot to ask, but I promise I'll look after them.'

'Of course you can. You probably won't be wearing them for very long anyway ...' Sue snickered. 'Anything else?'

'There's no way I'd fit into anything else of yours, you skinny cow,' said Rachel, laughing.

When they hung up Rachel opened up her Pharmicorp document and tried to concentrate on the script. So far she had only managed to write six minutes of it and it needed to be twenty minutes long.

The next time Rachel surfaced from behind her computer it was late morning and she'd managed to make a severe dent in the script, but looking across the office she realised that Justin still hadn't returned from getting coffee.

Rachel picked up a sandwich for lunch. Ordinarily she would get a ham-and-cheese baguette and follow it up with a chocolate-chip cookie, or chips, or a brownie and a Coke, but if she was going to be shagging Jerrod Craig the way she hoped she would be shagging Jerrod Craig she needed to watch what she was eating. So, instead, she ordered a tuna sandwich on wheat and a pomegranate juice. It was a sacrifice, but it was worth it.

There was still no sign of Justin when Rachel checked her watch again at around two. At three thirty Dan popped his ponytailed head around the door. 'Hi, Rachel, we missed you on Friday.'

Rachel had to disguise a guffaw as a cough. Dan was wearing a colourful floor-length dashiki, a green fez and pair of neon-green Crocs. 'Dan,' she said. 'I'm so sorry, I felt like I needed a personal-space day to truly explore my inner thoughts, to really connect with my inner child's mind, so I could come in today refreshed and energised, ready to conceive this antidepressant AV as if it were my first born.'

Dan looked at her, his eyes wide. He nodded furiously. 'Yes, Rachel Marcus, yes!' he said, striding towards her with great purpose, his man-dress flapping around him. 'Don't be afraid to open your chi. You've come so far.'

Rachel knew she wasn't going to get out of this one and with no other option she stood up and allowed Dan to embrace her. Then she made a personal pledge. She would draw the line at wearing Crocs. She would spew as much shit as she thought he needed to hear but she would always draw the line at wearing Crocs, even if it meant losing her job.

'Actually, Rachel,' Dan said as he finished hugging her, 'I'm looking for Justin. Have you seen him?'

'You just missed him, Dan,' Rachel lied, crossing her fingers behind her back. 'He popped out to get a coffee a minute ago. In fact, I'm surprised you didn't bump into him on your way in.'

'Oh, that's a shame. I'll pop back and try catch him a little later,' Dan said. 'I wanted to see how he's going on the storyboards. I have some thoughts on how the swami should look.'

'Great,' Rachel said. 'I'll tell him you're looking for him when I see him.'

Dan left, tripping over his hemline as he went, and Rachel cursed under her breath. Justin had made her lie for him again and this time it was a little too close for comfort. She took a deep breath and decided to put in another hour or so on her script before popping home for a shower. She would pick up a bottle of something on the way to Jerrod's – she didn't want to arrive empty-handed. Closing her eyes, Rachel allowed herself to daydream briefly, images of her and Jerrod rushing into her mind's eye, then she opened her eyes again and forced herself to focus on her work.

Just before five Dan popped back in. 'Justin around?' he asked.

'Dan, I can't believe you missed him again,' Rachel said as smoothly as she could. 'He actually just went looking for you. He was on his way to your office. I'm sure if you head back that way you'll bump into him.'

Dan nodded and reversed out as Rachel shut down her computer.

Rachel arrived on the street outside Jerrod's apartment clutching a bottle of perfectly chilled rosé a full sixteen minutes too early. She decided to walk a couple of blocks to kill some time – she didn't want to seem too keen, even though she felt part puppy with a tennis ball and part seven-year-old on Christmas morning. The devastatingly high heels on Sue's purple Prada slingbacks proved a slight problem as she click-clacked down the street. They weren't the most comfortable things she'd ever worn but she loved them so much she didn't care.

Rachel kept walking, looking for a shop, so she could stop and buy gum – surely, she thought, that would waste at least ten minutes. But she still found herself back outside Jerrod's apartment, armed with a pack of sugar-free strawberry flavoured chewing gum at an unfashionably early 7.22 p.m. Just as she was about to ring the buzzer at the front door to the apartment block a small Asian delivery man opened the door from the other side, held it open for Rachel and then let himself out.

Inside, the doorman nodded at Rachel from behind his desk, recognising her from Friday morning's walk of shame. 'He's expecting me,' she said, trying not to look too embarrassed.

The doorman gave her a lascivious grin and opened the elevator, turning his security key in the lock to allow it to take her up to the nineteenth floor.

The elevator doors opened to a delicious smell. Candles flickered around the apartment. 'Hello,' Rachel shouted out, her nerves jangling at the thought of seeing Jerrod again. 'Anybody home?'

'Hello?' Jerrod appeared from the dining room, barefoot, holding a glass of wine in his hand. 'Rachel?' he said, his voice filled with surprise.

'Hi, Jerrod.'

'What a surprise! Come in, we're in the dining room,' Jerrod said, leading her out of the lounge.

Surprise! We? Rachel started to panic. She felt like she'd turned up at school on a Saturday by mistake. Alarm bells started clanging in her head and suddenly she knew she'd made a horrible mistake. Jerrod wasn't expecting her for dinner at all. She replayed the earlier phone conversation in her mind and felt beads of panicked sweat forming on her top lip as a sinking feeling gripped her chest.

The dining room table was laid for two and sitting at the table was the most beautiful blonde woman Rachel had ever seen. 'This is Tessa,' said Jerrod. 'Tessa, this is Rachel.'

Tessa stood up, towering over Rachel. She had flawless skin, piercing blue eyes and naturally high cheekbones. Rachel wanted to die. Tessa smiled and revealed the final straw, a set of perfect white teeth.

'Hi, nice to meet you,' Tessa said, holding out a smooth, beautifully manicured hand.

'Oh, my goodness, Jerrod,' Rachel said, covering her mouth with her hand. 'I'm so sorry, I didn't realise you were having someone else over for dinner. When we spoke on the phone earlier you said ... I thought ... I mean ...' Rachel looked down to make sure she wasn't suddenly naked, figuring that it was the only thing that could have possibly made this encounter any worse. 'You said something about dinner at seven thirty,' she finally choked, bowing backwards out of the dining room. 'It was a very bad line, but I assumed ... I'm really sorry.'

'Wait, Rachel, it's absolutely fine, really,' Jerrod said, following her out of the dining room, but Rachel had already raced to the elevator and was stabbing at the button repeatedly. 'Rachel,' Jerrod shouted, more assertively now. 'Where are you going? Why don't you stay? There's plenty of food.'

Rachel turned to face Jerrod, 'I'm such an idiot. I'm so sorry I interrupted your date. I don't know what I was thinking.' To Rachel's relief the elevator opened and she stepped inside. 'Have a lovely evening ...'

'This isn't a date, Rachel,' Jerrod said, holding back the elevator door. 'Tessa is my cousin.'

'Your cousin ...' Rachel repeated.

'Yes, you fool. She lives in Milan and she's in New York overnight. She's off to LA on a job tomorrow. She's a model. Now, stop being such a freak and come have dinner with us.'

Grabbing Rachel by the hand Jerrod yanked her back into the apartment. 'I think what I said on the phone was that I was having an early dinner with my cousin at half-past seven, and I would call you after she left,' he said, grinning at her. 'Now, shall we try this again? Hello, darling ...' He pulled her towards him and kissed her on her lips. Rachel melted into him.

'Is that for me?' he asked when he eventually pulled away from her, pointing at the bottle of wine Rachel was still clutching in a now very sweaty palm.

Rachel held it out to him, speechless.

'Thank you,' he said, taking the bottle. 'Now, come talk to Tessa and I'll pour you a glass, you look like you could do with a drink.'

Back in the dining room Tessa stood up again with her big, friendly smile still on her perfect face. 'Now, let's try this again,' Jerrod said. 'Rachel, this is my cousin, Tessa. Tessa, this is Rachel.'

'It's so lovely to meet you,' gushed Rachel. 'I'm really sorry about earlier ... I didn't mean to gatecrash your dinner.'

'Don't be silly,' said Tessa. 'Anyway, I don't know who Jerrod thought he was catering for here, there's far too much food for just the two of us.'

Jerrod set another place on the table and together they tucked in to bowls of spicy Thai chicken with basmati rice. Once Rachel got over her initial embarrassment and settled into the evening the conversation was easy and Rachel was relieved to find that she still thought Jerrod had a sharp, witty sense of humour, even when she hadn't drunk copious amounts of expensive champagne. Tessa was also great and Rachel wondered what was wrong with her. No single human being could be so gorgeous, friendly, smart and funny. There had to be a flaw somewhere.

'So, tell me about the agency you work at?' Tessa asked as Jerrod disappeared into the kitchen with their empty plates. 'I only ever get to see advertising from the other side of the camera.'

'Do I have to?' groaned Rachel.

'It can't be that bad, can it?' Jerrod said, reappearing with ice cream and a bowl of bright red strawberries.

'Trust me, its worse,' said Rachel. 'It's called Target Advertising.'

Jerrod shook his head.

'See,' Rachel said. 'You've never even heard of it. We're busy working on a campaign for a pharmaceutical company launching a new antidepressant. That includes a brochure for the medical reps, a twenty minute audio visual, new packaging and the packaging insert. It's a nightmare.'

Jerrod laughed. 'I'm sorry, I don't mean to laugh, but that really doesn't sound like much fun.'

'But I thought advertising was all glamour and excitement?' said Tessa.

'Not this kind of advertising,' said Rachel.

'Who do you work with there?' asked Jerrod.

'Well, that's the other problem,' Rachel said, sucking on a strawberry as seductively as she could and wondering how they'd gotten onto the subject of her inadequate job – it was more than mortifying. 'I work with this British guy, Justin. He's got some serious issues.'

'Not Justin Coley?' asked Jerrod.

'You know him?' said Rachel, surprised. The New York advertising industry was so big and Target Advertising was so small and insignificant that she never could have imagined that Jerrod would have even heard of Justin.

'So, that's where old Justin Coley ended up. And he's still a complete screw-up then, is he? Some things never change.'

'How do you know him?' Rachel asked, still completely taken by surprise.

'Didn't you know? He used to work at Richmond&Phillips.'

'No, I had no idea.'

Jerrod laughed. 'It's a classic story, a little piece of New York advertising history in fact. I'm surprised you haven't heard it yet.'

'He never mentioned anything. What happened?'

'He was part of a team with this guy Chuck Watson. They worked together for something stupid, like six years. They were a good team, great mates, attached at the hip. You know how it goes with teams; you work together pretty much twenty-four seven. It's a bit like being married.'

Rachel nodded. She knew. Some of her closest friendships had been with the art director partners she'd had over the years.

'Anyway,' Jerrod continued, 'Justin had been dating this girl Vanessa for a really long time, something like two years, and he was crazy about her. Completely whipped. Back then I was a senior art director, so me and my partner were just a couple of offices down from them. Anyway, one day we hear this huge commotion coming from their office, crazy loud screaming and shouting. Turns out Justin had just found out that Chuck had been banging Vanessa behind his back for months. Everybody knew about it except Justin, but that day he found out somehow and he went completely mad, he totally lost it. Chuck was this big guy, smoked heavily and had this habit of always fiddling with his Zippo. It used to drive me crazy. He used to snap it open and light it, then close it again. He did it all the time, like a nervous tic. Even when he wasn't smoking, he was forever fiddling with that thing. Anyway, so when Justin found out about the affair he attacked Chuck in their office. He just launched himself at him and started beating the crap out of him. I'm not surprised he was upset, Chuck was like his brother, and then he finds out he's been sleeping with the love of his life, and not just once, for months ...' Jerrod paused and took a sip of wine. 'So, when Justin attacked him, Chuck must have been fiddling with his Zippo,' Jerrod continued, putting his glass back on the table, 'and I don't know how it happened but the next thing we all knew the fire alarm was going off and all the sprinklers came on. They evacuated the whole building, but they couldn't put out the fire; there was just so much board and paper in the office. By the time they managed to put the fire out, Justin had burned down the entire floor – all the computers, all the work, gone. Luckily nobody got hurt, but he gutted the place. They had to rebuild the entire creative studio …'

'That's hectic!' Tessa said, covering her mouth with her hands.

'I can't believe it,' Rachel said. 'He never said a word.'

'I don't blame him; it was hardly his finest hour. Of course, they fired both of them. I think Chuck and Vanessa moved to Chicago, together, and Justin just kind of fell apart. Lots of booze and drugs. What a fuck up. I wondered where he'd disappeared to. So, he's at Target?' Jerrod laughed. 'That's classic!'

'Why didn't someone tell him?' Rachel asked. 'If you all knew she was cheating on him, why did nobody say anything? You were his friends and colleagues and you all just watched it happen.'

'It wasn't anyone's business, Rachel,' Jerrod said. 'You know what it's like; nobody wants to get involved. But he was really hacked off at all of us about it. He hasn't spoken to any of us since. Not that we've seen him around. After he fell off the rails he fell off the planet.'

'I'm not surprised,' Rachel said. 'I would have been completely destroyed too. With friends like you guys …'

Rachel trailed off. She thought about Justin and his situation. It was such a sad story: public humiliation, betrayal and then, on top of it all, losing his job. In fact, Rachel thought, it sounded a little familiar, a little like her story. No wonder he's such a mess, she thought.

'So, Tessa,' Jerrod asked, breaking into Rachel's thoughts. 'What are you shooting in LA?'

'It's a Victoria's Secret catalogue,' she said.

Of course it is, Rachel thought.

'Speaking of which, I'd better get going,' Tessa went on, pushing back her chair. 'I've got an early flight tomorrow and I need my beauty sleep. Rachel, it was wonderful to meet you. I'm so glad you came over. Look me up next time you're in Milan, okay? Jerrod's got my details.'

'I'd love that, Tessa. Thank you.' Rachel stood up and Tessa leaned down and kissed her on one cheek, then again, European model style, on the other one. Once again Rachel felt inadequate. Tessa could stay up partying all night and then fly to LA and still look magnificent; she didn't need beauty sleep, she didn't need anything.

'I'll see you out, Tess,' said Jerrod, escorting her out of the dining room.

Rachel cleared away the dessert dishes and took her wine into the lounge. When Jerrod returned ten minutes later he joined her on the couch.

'Jerrod,' she started. 'I am so sorry about being such a freak earlier. I totally misheard you on the phone. I feel like such an idiot.'

'Rachel, you have to stop apologising.' He reached for her hand and held it up against his, palm to palm. His hand dwarfed hers. She felt his long, soft fingers caress hers. 'I'm really glad you came over. In fact, I was worried I was never going to hear from you again. I called you at work on Friday and I waited for you to call me back the whole weekend. All I had to remember you by were the panties you left me on Friday morning. My little souvenir. I carried them in my pocket all day Friday.'

Rachel giggled shyly. 'I missed your call on Friday morning,' she admitted. 'I didn't quite make it to work. I guess I was all shagged out. I only got your message and the flowers this morning.'

'Well the important thing is that you eventually got them,' Jerrod said, tracing his fingers up Rachel's bare arm. Her stomach did flick-flacks. He was so good-looking. What did he ever see in her? Panic rose in her throat and her heart started to race as she thought about being alone in this perfect apartment with this amazing man. She took a couple of deep breaths to calm herself down. 'So, who do I have to sleep with around here to get another drink?' she asked, holding up her almost empty glass.

Jerrod disappeared into the kitchen to open another bottle of wine and Rachel went to stand in front of the window, reminding herself to carry on breathing steadily as she looked out at the Statue of Liberty.

'Did I mention how pleased I am that you came over tonight?'

whispered a husky voice close to her ear.

Startled, Rachel almost dropped her wine glass. He had snuck up on her again.

Rachel watched their reflection in the darkened window and saw Jerrod move even closer behind her. He put his arms around her from behind, taking her wine glass from her and putting it down next to the freshly opened bottle on the coffee table, then he turned her around and bent down towards her. First their lips, then their tongues met and Rachel had to lock her knees to avoid slipping to the ground like an invertebrate. She could smell his now deliciously familiar, woody aftershave mixed in with the aroma of spicy Thai green curry. 'You smell good enough to eat,' she whispered, nuzzling his neck.

'You're a very dirty girl, you'd better come with me,' he said, leading her through to his bedroom and into the en-suite bathroom – Rachel careful this time to avoid the shin-height modernist cube sitting between the two couches.

In the bathroom Jerrod ran a deep bubble bath and while the tub filled he undressed her slowly, kissing every centimetre of revealed skin before slipping out of his own clothes and climbing into the bath.

'I think this is the most fun I've ever had on a second date,' Jerrod said as Rachel followed him into the tub, leaning her back against his chest.

'You're very lucky, you know,' Rachel said. 'I don't normally sleep with men on a second date, let alone a first one.'

'You could have fooled me,' he teased, soaping Rachel's chest with a soft, thirsty sponge and turning on the hot water tap with his big toe.

'Well, in this case there are extenuating circumstances,' she said. 'On the first date you wore a tux, which is hard for any woman to resist, and then you sent me flowers at work. What woman wouldn't sleep with you?'

Jerrod paused. 'What can I say? I'm one charming guy.'

The bar of soap leapt out of his hand and plunged into the depths of the soapy bath. He made a big show of pretending to try and locate it and hot water sloshed over the sides of the bath as she squirmed and giggled under his soapy touch. Then, when neither could take the teasing any more, they climbed out the bath and made love on the carpeted bathroom floor.

'So, is that why they call this carpet shag?' asked Rachel as they lay catching their breath under Jerrod's fluffy white bath sheets.

Jerrod laughed and kissed her on the shoulder.

Rachel woke with a start. It was pitch dark and she couldn't get a handle on where she was – a deep blackness swallowed everything that wasn't three centimetres away from her face. She sorted through the files in her mind. Joburg? No. New York? Yes. But where? Not her apartment. Then it came rushing back, her mind flooding with images and her body with heat. She was at Jerrod's place.

Rolling over, Rachel found Jerrod lying next to her in the bed, breathing steadily. She raised herself up on her elbow and looked at the alarm clock on the bedside table: 4.15 a.m. Climbing out of bed, her eyes now adjusted to the darkness, she tiptoed into the bathroom to pick up her clothes and then she snuck out of the apartment. The doorman smiled knowingly but hailed her a cab without saying a word. Rachel made it home and into bed, still floating on a cloud, by ten past five. The walk of shame had never felt so good.

Rachel Marcus is happier than you today.
May 19 at 9:38am

Considering Rachel had had less than four hours sleep she felt remarkably alive when her alarm bleeped her back to the land of the living at seven thirty. Leaping out of bed, she walked the four or five steps to the bathroom, made her cautious rat inspection and, satisfied she was alone, climbed into the shower.

Rachel stood under the stream of hot water with a ridiculous smile on her face. Although she could not deny that she was a very dirty girl, chances were that there wasn't much actual dirt left on her body after their marathon bath the night before. And so, after a couple of minutes, she stepped out of the shower and wrapped herself in a towel that was considerably less fluffy and luxurious than the ones she'd been treated to at Jerrod's place. This towel had once been white, but that had been a very long time ago. It was now more of a gummy shade of grey. Rachel made a mental note never to invite Jerrod back to her place, even if it was a matter of national security. She couldn't allow him to see how she lived.

Stepping out of the bathroom in a dramatic cloud of steam Rachel heard a knock on the door. 'Morning,' said Sue. 'I just wanted to check you made it home last night.'

'Eventually ...' Rachel smiled.

'So, how was it?' Sue asked, filling the kettle as Rachel went into the bedroom area to get dressed.

'Sue, it was incredible, I don't even have words to describe it.' Rachel said, slipping into a pair of jeans.

'Really?' asked Sue. 'Did he make dinner?'

'Yup. Thai chicken curry, then ice cream and strawberries.'

'What about breakfast?' Sue winked.

'No, I snuck out while he was still sleeping and ran away,' said Rachel.

'I can't believe you! You're such a coward!'

'This guy, Sue ... I've never felt this way about anyone so fast before.' Rachel sat on the edge of the bed and pulled on a pair of socks, then reached for her black boots.

'Well, you seem happy,' said Sue. 'Just be careful, okay? I don't want you to get hurt. Oh, and Rachel ...'

'Yeah.'

'Your socks don't match.'

Rachel looked up at her with a silly, smitten smile on her face.

Rachel Marcus can't wipe this stupid grin off her face.
May 19 at 9:18am

Rachel was at her desk that morning when her cellphone beeped with a text message from Jerrod:

Thanks for incredible evening. You disappeared again. Am going to have to handcuff you to the bed. Chat later.

Rachel fired back a response:

Thank you for dinner. Have massive deadline for tomorrow. Working late. Chat later. x

Rachel was busy analysing Jerrod's message for hidden meanings when Justin loped in. He looked like he'd either come from a street fight or a fifty per cent off sale at Bloomingdale's. His left eye was swollen shut and was every imaginable shade of black and blue, the bruising extending all the way down to a fat lip with a cut through it.

'Oh, my God, Justin!' Rachel said as soon as she saw him. 'What the hell happened to you? Are you all right?'

Justin smiled and then winced as Rachel helped him onto the couch. He wheezed out in agony as he sat down; clutching at his ribs. His breath was sour with bourbon.

'I'll get you some ice and coffee, okay. Don't move I'll be right back.'

Rachel raced to the kitchen where she made Jerrod a strong cup of black coffee. Then she opened the freezer. She had never looked in the freezer section of the communal agency fridge before and now she knew why she had subconsciously avoided it. There were only three items in the freezer and of those only the ice tray was even vaguely recognisable, although it, like everything else, was held captive in a thick layer of hungry, suspiciously yellow ice. Rachel picked up a sharp knife and chiselled the ice tray out of its dirty igloo. Then, grabbing a dishcloth, she filled it with uneven chunks of ice. She'd never tried this before, but she'd seen it in lots of movies, so she was sure it must work. Finally, she heaped three large spoons of sugar into Justin's coffee and hurried back to their office.

Justin was sound asleep on the couch, snoring quietly. Not knowing what to do, Rachel abandoned the coffee she had made for him and the ice in its grubby dishcloth, sat down at her desk and chewed on a nail. The Pharmicorp presentation was the next day and she knew her side of it would be ready in time, but Justin clearly wasn't coping. He looked like he'd been the only cat in a dog fight.

Rachel had never felt so frustrated with anyone. On the one hand she understood that he'd had some traumatic experiences and she felt that she more than anyone could relate to the kind of humiliation and betrayal he'd been through. But still, she reminded herself, that was no excuse for derailing his own life and hers in the process. Fair enough, Justin had been to hell and back, but then instead of dusting himself off and trying to staple his life back together, the way she was, he'd simply started his very own pity party and it had been going on ever since.

The most frustrating part, she thought, was that it was Justin who'd cracked this campaign, but he couldn't even hold it together long enough to put it down for the presentation. She decided she would give him a good talking to when she next found him sober, whenever that might be. Although she suspected it wouldn't make an inch of difference.

Justin woke up around eleven and limped over to his desk to get going on his storyboards.

'Justin, do you want to talk about what happened to you?' Rachel asked him.

'I'd really rather not,' he lisped through swollen lips.

'Can I at least take you to the emergency room so they can take a look at you? I think you may have broken some ribs.'

'I'm fine,' he said, reaching for a fat blue marker. He took off the lid and sniffed the nib, sucking in as much of the inky smell as he could get before putting pen to paper.

'So, are you just going to pretend nothing happened?' she asked.

'I'll tell you what I'm going to do, Rachel. If you'll stop bugging me, I'm going to get to work on these storyboards and then later I'm going to take my camera and I'm going to go film some sample footage for tomorrow's presentation. That's what I'm going to do.'

At least he's finally focused on the campaign, Rachel thought, going back to her script.

They both worked on in silence until just after lunch when Justin left with his camera. With the office to herself Rachel's mind toggled between thoughts of the amazing time she'd had with Jerrod the night before and her complete and total annoyance with Justin.

Some time later Dan strode in followed by an entourage. 'Team,' he shrilled. 'How about we run through tomorrow's presentation?'

'Hiya, Dan, sure thing. Justin's out getting some reference footage, he'll be back later to finish up, but I'd love to take you through everything,' lied Rachel.

Dan dropped onto the couch closely followed by his swami, who was dressed in a robe and turban. The swami was a large, bearded man, but he squeezed in next to Dan nonetheless. The couch was clearly too small for both of them at the same time, but the swami didn't seem too bothered by it. Once settled he pulled a small Zen garden and miniature rake out from the folds of his robe and busied himself, combing the sand methodically. Dan appraised the swami, shifted his bulk as far away from the other man as he could, in an attempt to make himself as comfortable as possible, and then focused on Rachel. Two client service people had also traipsed into the office and with nowhere else to sit they hovered beside the couch, trying to look important.

Rachel did a run through of the work. The team nodded, the swami combed and Dan scratched his chin thoughtfully.

'So all that's left is the storyboards and then we should be good to go,' said Rachel, trying to sound confident as she wrapped up her run-through.

'Very good, Rachel. Any questions?' Dan asked the client service team. But before either of them could answer or comment he clapped his hands to end the exchange and then struggled to pull himself out of the couch. Tumbling free, he pulled his dashiki up to just below his knees and strode from the office, with the client service team and the swami scurrying out after him.

Justin reappeared at the office around six. He looked slightly better, but not much. He had showered and changed clothes, but his wet dirty-blond hair straggled around his face and he still looked bruised and miserable.

They had a lot of work to do and not much time to do it in, so Rachel parked her planned lecture for the time being and ordered dinner for them from an Italian restaurant down the street. When the food arrived they took a break from behind their desks, ate in silence and then went back to work again. The work list for the meeting was long and Rachel ticked off each item as she finished it.

   Twenty minute audio visual ✓
   Social networking element and feel boards ✓
   Experiential element ✓
   Branded content ✓
   Medical brochure ✓
   Full packaging insert ✓
   New packaging ✓
   Point-of-sale material ✓
   Theme for the annual sales conference held in Vegas ✓

It was hardly the cutting edge advertising of Rachel's past, but she felt proud of the work. It was good for what it was. Drained and exhausted she finished up just after ten and got up to stretch.

'How's it going over there?' she asked Justin.

Justin shrugged. 'Not too bad, I've probably got about three hours of work left.'

'Justin, are you okay?'

Justin eyed her out of his one good eye. 'Of course,' he said sarcastically. 'I'm fine! Never better!' He paused and grimaced. 'How are you? How are things with our man, Superhero Craig?'

'Actually, I didn't realise you knew each other,' said Rachel. 'He told me you met at Richmond&Phillips. I didn't know you'd worked there.'

'Yeah, well, I wouldn't believe everything Jerrod Craig tells you, Rachel.'

'What's that supposed to mean, Justin?' asked Rachel. He was starting to infuriate her again. There was only so much bitter sarcasm a girl could take in one day.

'Nothing, just be careful. He's not always as charming as he comes across.'

'Don't worry about me, I'll be fine,' snapped Rachel. 'I'm not an idiot. I can look after myself.'

'Whatever,' sighed Justin. 'Look, I don't have time for a petty argument about your boyfriend, I've got a ton of shit to finish before tomorrow and I'm hanging for a drink.'

'You're not going out after this are you?' asked Rachel, trying to control her temper. 'Tomorrow's going to be huge, and you look like you could do with some sleep.'

'I'm not an idiot, Rachel,' Justin snapped back sarcastically, parroting her. 'I can look after myself.'

'You could have fooled me!' Rachel said, nodding at his black eye.

Justin didn't answer, he just nodded once and then went back to his work in a sulky silence.

Rachel cleared off her desk, binned the crumpled-up papers and old scripts and took all the empty coffee cups out of their office. When she got back she laid out her scripts and documents, ready for the meeting in the morning, updated her status on Facebook and shut down her computer. 'Justin, I'm going to head out now,' she said. 'Is there anything I can help you with before I go?'

Justin shook his head. 'Nope, I've got everything under control.'

'Don't forget, the meeting's at nine. Do you want me to give you a wake up call?' she asked.

'Don't worry,' he said, through clenched teeth. 'I won't let you down.'

'I know you won't,' she said, careful to use her softest voice. It was late, it had been a long day and she really didn't want to argue with him anymore. That and she needed him in a good mood for the meeting. So, while every fibre of her body wanted to go over there and shake some sense into him she knew she couldn't let it show. 'Call me if you need anything, okay,' Rachel said as she left the office. 'My cell will be on all night.'

Rachel Marcus is looking forward to sleep. Nighty-night all.
May 19 at 10:24pm

Rachel got home feeling the effects of a very long night, followed by a very long day and another very long night. She sat on the edge of her bed and gnawed at her fingernails, which were already chewed to pieces. She felt stressed about the Pharmicorp meeting and half angry, half worried about Justin. Eventually Rachel pulled herself off the bed, did her obligatory rat and duct-tape check, climbed into a hot shower and tried to wash off the day.

Just as she was trying to dry herself off with her inadequate towel she got a text message from Jerrod:

Hey, you home yet?

She fired a quick response back to him:

I just got home from work. Been a ridiculous day. How was yours?

Rachel pressed send and her phone rang almost immediately.

'Hello, gorgeous,' Jerrod's voice came down the phone line like electricity, 'I was going to text you back, but then I thought how nice it would be to hear your voice.'

'Close your eyes,' said Rachel, 'I'm naked. I just got out the shower and I don't want you to see.'

'It's nothing I haven't seen before. Want me to come over and help you dry off, dirty girl?'

Rachel lay back on the bed wrapped in her towel. 'Aw, babe, I'd love that,' she said, 'but it's been such a long day. Justin got into some kind of fight, you won't believe the state he's in, and then he disappeared all afternoon and I had to deal with the whole team on my own. And I've got that big presentation tomorrow. I think I need an early night. I know it's hardly a million dollar TV production, but it's important to Target.'

'That's not cool of him, angel,' Jerrod drawled. 'I told you, he's a loser. You need a better art director and a better job. I'm going to try find you something at R&P, okay. I promise.'

Rachel's tired, beaten heart lifted its head and wagged its tail. 'Jerrod, that would be incredible,' she sighed, 'I need to get out of that

144

place before it drives me crazy. How was your day?'

'Usual shit … We just finished production on a twelve-spot TV campaign for Nescafé.' He paused. 'Oh, yeah, and we got briefed on an awesome new job. It's a seriously confidential pitch for a massive international car account. There's a team in the London office working on it too. The client is going to flight the campaign that they select internationally. It's massive, Rachel. This is the big time.'

'Jerrod, not only are you incredibly well endowed, but massively talented too, I have no doubt that you guys will nail this one easily.'

Jerrod laughed. 'Hmm, a one-woman PR machine, I like it.'

'I suppose I should get some sleep,' whispered Rachel.

'Okay, but will you have dinner with me tomorrow night, to celebrate the success of your big presentation and my big brief?'

'I'd like that.'

'Okay, good luck,' he said. 'Night.'

'Night,' she said and hung up.

Rachel didn't even bother putting on pyjamas. She tossed her towel on the floor, pulled the covers over her damp body and snuggled into her duvet with a satisfied groan.

Rachel Marcus is all about antidepressants today.
May 20 at 8:09am

Rachel paced the office chewing on the edge of her thumb. She'd picked out a pinstripe suit and a pair of tall heels to show she meant business and a low-cut shirt to show she meant pleasure too. It couldn't do any harm and if there were any male representatives in the presentation it might even do some good. She hovered over Justin's desk. It looked like he'd worked very late – coffee cups and pieces of paper were strewn all over the place – but a stack of presentation boards lay neatly on his chair. She flipped through and found them all there and in good order. So far so good, she thought, breathing a deep sigh of relief. It wasn't that she didn't trust him, she'd seen how creative he could be when he was up against it, it was just that she never quite knew which Justin she was going to get. The talented art director Justin or the bitter, hung-over, trashed Justin. She didn't doubt his design ability; it was just his staying-sober ability that was in question.

She thought about Jerrod, the other art director in her life. She was excited to see what he'd do with this new international brief. And then a thought suddenly struck her: she might even put her mind to it, if he was willing to tell her the brief. If she played it right it could be her ticket out of Target Advertising. Rachel shook her head, banishing the thought. Right now she had more pressing things to contend with. Where was Justin? She had hoped to do a run-through of the presentation with him before the client came in at nine.

'Morning team,' Dan Charter said, bursting into the office.

Rachel was surprised to find him wearing an actual suit for the first time since she'd met him: tie, closed shoes, the whole nine yards.

'Dan, you look smart,' she said, stepping forward and opening her arms for the embrace she knew was coming. At this stage there was no point in fighting it.

'How's my A-team?' asked Dan, giving her a squeeze. Rachel thought she might have even smelt aftershave on him, instead of the usual tang of incense and sweat. 'Are you ready to blow those Pharmicorp boys away?'

'Absolutely, Dan, the work's looking great.'

'Where's Justin?' he asked, looking around the office, suddenly concerned.

Rachel panicked: What to do? What to do? She took a deep breath and opened her mouth, but before she could help herself the big lie had already fallen out of it. 'He just popped to the bathroom, Dan. He'll be back any second.'

Dan eyed Rachel suspiciously. 'All right, well the client's here, so come through to the boardroom as soon as he gets back.'

Just then Justin walked in. Dan's eye's widened as he took in the state of Justin's face. Justin had managed to avoid Dan the day before, but there was no avoiding him now.

'What the Krishna happened to you, Justin?' Dan asked.

Justin's swollen eye, bruised face and bust lip weren't as angry as they had been, but he still looked like a piece of hamburger meat.

'All right,' said Dan, when it was clear he wasn't going to get a response out of Justin. 'I don't have time for this right now. The client's here and they're expecting both of you, so get your stuff together and come through. I don't have to remind either of you how much is riding on this presentation, do I?' Dan looked at them both sternly, shook his head at the state of Justin and left.

Justin remained planted in front of Rachel's desk. She noticed he was swaying slightly. 'Are you hammered, Justin?' she asked.

Justin looked at her through his one good eye. 'Maybe just a little …' He snickered, swaying some more.

'Fuck, Justin! Fuck! Fuck! Fuck!' Rachel wailed. 'Listen, we don't have time for this … Here, chew this.' She handed him a stick of chewing gum. 'Come on, we'll have to get you some coffee. What the hell are we going to do? Look, whatever happens you'd better not say anything in the meeting, all right. Just sit next to me and let me handle the presentation. Can you do that? Okay? All right?'

'Sure thing,' he said and hiccoughed.

Rachel smoothed out her jacket and tried to rein in her temper, which was pulling at a very short leash. She picked up her scripts and Justin's layouts and pushed him roughly out of the door. 'Come on then,' she said through gritted teeth, 'we'd better go in. Just remember, you're not going to say anything.'

As Rachel followed Justin out of the office door she shook her head, wondering how everything had gone so wrong so fast. She berated herself for not escorting him home the night before to ensure he was in one piece for the meeting. 'Dammit,' she cursed under her breath. If everything blew up in her face, she only had herself to blame. Why couldn't he stay sober just this once? He knew how important this meeting was. What was wrong with him, she wondered, that he had to fuck this up for both of them, and after all their hard work too?

Standing outside the boardroom Rachel appraised him. There wasn't much she could do about the smell of him. She'd just have to hold thumbs that no one got too close to him in the meeting. 'Come on, let's go,' she said, readjusting her grip on the storyboards. She had to force herself to contain her anger, it wouldn't help her now.

When they walked into the boardroom a huddle of grey suits turned around and took them in. Rachel counted twelve people from Pharmicorp, add to that the client service team from Target – made up of the two gimps from the briefing session – and then of course there was Dan and now Rachel and Justin, all filling the boardroom to capacity. The swami seemed to be the only member of the team missing. A table packed with coffee, tea and breakfast pastries stood at the back of the boardroom and the dull-looking suits shuffled around it in their Hush Puppies, drinking coffee and eating Danishes in an awkward, formal way.

'Excellent, our star team has arrived!' exclaimed Dan. 'Everyone, allow me to introduce Rachel Marcus, our most senior copywriter, and her partner, senior art director Justin Coley. Please forgive the state of Justin, he was in a minor vehicle accident, but as you can see, he's on the mend, right Justin?'

Justin nodded, swayed and gave a thumbs-up. Rachel held her breath. The boardroom crowd let out a collective sigh of pity and smiled at Justin generously. Perhaps, Rachel thought, this might just work to their advantage. Maybe they would get the sympathy vote. Justin's swaying might even be confused with a slight concussion.

'Team, I'd like you to meet Brewster Masterson, CEO,' Dan continued, 'Darlene Phillips, Marketing Director …'

Dan reeled off a list of names and their corresponding titles as they worked the room, shaking hands with smiles pasted on their faces. Rachel's was a smile borne of pure terror, but she suspected Justin's was one fuelled by booze and cocaine.

Finally, with the introductions complete, Rachel managed to escape from Dan, sit Justin down in the chair nearest the door and bring him a cup of strong, sugary black coffee and a pastry. Everyone took their seats and the small talk tapered off into expectant silence.

Dan stood up and rubbed his hands together. 'First of all,' he began in his now familiar squeaky voice. 'I'd like to welcome you all to Target Advertising. We can't wait to take you through our brand vision for the coming year. We've been focusing all our energies on this task for weeks, taking our time to carefully learn your brand. Our aim was to turn over every stone and hunt down the perfect marketing solutions for this important, life-changing product.'

Dan paused and was rewarded with twelve synchronised grey-suited nods

'As I'm sure you're all well aware,' Dan continued, 'we at Target Advertising are action and solution driven, so enough talk. I'd like to hand you over to the team who will take you through this ground-breaking work.'

Dan sat down and started clapping, prompting a spattering of awkward executive applause.

Rachel stood up and went almost immediately onto autopilot. She opened her mouth and was amazed to discover that whole, smart-sounding sentences came pouring out of it. Rachel started with the big idea, talking them through it with the use of feel and mood boards. She discussed the social networking angle and the call to arms strategy. Then she took them through the design for the product packaging and moved steadily through the product insert, reading the copy aloud. Finally, she talked about the medical brochure and the conference theme, before working her way towards the audio visual and its neighbouring campaign elements.

Stopping to catch her breath and take a drink of water she ran her eye around the room and appraised the situation. Justin was still swaying, his one good eye blinking intermittently, but nobody had seemed to notice. Then Rachel looked over the mass of work lying spread out in front of her. She felt a surge of pride. She glanced over at Justin again. Granted he was a complete fuck up, but regardless of that he'd still managed to come up with the goods on this job. She would never have thought she'd enjoy working on this kind of thing, but she had. It was strange, but she felt a similar kind of pride in this campaign as she'd felt in the massive above-the-line campaigns she'd worked on back home. And, she thought, both their skill and their talent had shown through in the work they were presenting. Relative to the rest of the work in this category the campaign was fresh and original. It was just a pity that Justin wasn't technically around to enjoy the presentation and all the fruits of his labours, because although he was sitting right there, he certainly wasn't present.

Forging ahead, Rachel presented the audio visual, taking the executives through the script and the storyboards and then finally finishing off with the video references Justin had shot the previous afternoon and a music reference she'd downloaded off the net. The executives sat with their funeral faces on. She couldn't tell whether they liked the work or found it putrid, but at least none of them had fallen asleep or taken a telephone call while she was presenting, which she always considered a good sign. An even better sign was that none of them seemed to have noticed that Justin's one eyelid was now starting to droop and he was alternating between swaying and drooling. If she could only keep their attention off him for just a little longer, she thought, this might actually all work out okay.

Rachel wound down her presentation and brought it to a neat and tidy close. 'So, once again, we'd like to thank you for your time,' she said. 'We hope that you see the potential we see here, so that we can take this incredible brand to the next level, together. Thank you.'

Rachel sat down, heaving a massive internal sigh of relief. She'd done it, she'd presented the work – which had looked great – and nobody had any clue that Justin had been beaten to a pulp, was wired to the hilt, slammed drunk and probably hadn't slept in close on forty-eight hours. Rachel crossed her fingers under the table and said a little prayer, deciding that even though she really wasn't particularly religious, now was as good a time as any to use whatever means were available to sway the odds in her favour.

Dan jumped up out of his seat. 'Excellent! Excellent, Rachel Marcus!' he cried, throwing out his arms. 'Does anybody have any questions?'

Brewster Matheson, the CEO cleared his throat. 'Yes,' he said. 'Yes. Yes.'

Ah, a 'yes man' thought Rachel.

'Your thoughts are very interesting indeed,' Brewster continued. 'But I think I'd like to hear a little about how you envision treating the packaging. Do you see it being built around a photographic image or a cartoon illustration as per your layout? Justin, as senior art director I'd be interested to hear your input on this.'

Justin was staring at his hands on the table.

'Justin?' said Dan.

Rachel nudged him and he jerked to attention. He clearly hadn't expected to hear his own name called out. Rachel thought it doubtful that he'd been paying attention to anything that had been said and wondered if he even knew where he was.

Justin stood up, looked around the room, swayed for a couple of seconds, opened his mouth to respond and then vomited magnificently all over Darlene Phillips, the Marketing Director of Pharmicorp, a multinational pharmaceutical company that owned at least a dozen major international brands. Then he hiccoughed, wiped his mouth with the back of his hand, said 'Oh, fuck!' and passed out cold on the boardroom floor.

What happened next happened in slow motion. Dan descended on Darlene Phillips from the head of the boardroom table and in a flurry of apologies tried to wipe the vile-smelling vomit off the front of her blouse and face with the front tail of his shirt. Rachel wasn't sure if it was the effect of Justin's vomit or the sight of Dan's unnaturally hairy belly, but Darlene Phillips went a strange shade of green. She swatted Dan's hand away from her heaving chest and covered her mouth with her hand, breathing deeply before she in turn vomited all over Dan, catching Brewster Masterson in the face and all down his left-hand sleeve.

Heather was summoned to bring towels and call in a couple of guys from the studio to carry a confused and woozy Justin off to their office couch. It was carnage. Rachel sat down in her seat and dropped her head into her hands. Well there goes the Pharmicorp account, she thought.

Rachel Marcus is 'Oh, shit, shit, shit!'
May 20 at 11:31pm

Half an hour later Rachel found herself at her desk staring into a cup of chamomile tea. Justin was on the couch, staring at his knees. Suddenly, Dan appeared in the office doorway. His hair was wet and he'd changed into a pair of khaki cargo pants and a light-blue denim shirt. 'Rachel, Justin, you're both fired,' he said. And then for the first time in the history of Target Advertising Dan Charter turned around and left the room without having given anyone in it a hug.

'Oh, fuck!' said Justin.

'No way!' yelled Rachel, slamming her mug of tea down on the desk, splooshing it everywhere. 'I can't believe this is happening to me!' Rachel was livid. All the anger, all the frustration, all the homesickness from the last couple of months rushed through her veins. 'I'm totally fucked! I can't believe you've done this to me, Justin! Is it too much to ask that you don't fucking vomit on the client? I was just fired from my last job back home and now again! What the fuck! This wasn't even my fault. This was all your fault, you selfish bastard! You've really fucked up this time!'

'You've been fired before?' Justin asked, startled.

'Don't you dare talk to me! I can't even look at you right now!'

'I'm so sorry, Rachel,' Justin said. 'I really didn't mean to screw everything up like this. I don't know what happened. I was planning on going straight home after I finished last night, but then a mate called and I thought I'd go meet up with him for a quick drink. And my face hurt so much ... I thought it might help me sleep ...'

'You're just the fucking Mayor of Excuseville, aren't you?' Rachel shouted at him, shaking her head in rage.

'Rachel, I'm sorry, I'd never do anything to jeopardise your career on purpose. I swear it!'

Rachel stormed out of their office, slamming the door hard behind her. She flew down the passage. Motivational posters tacked to the wall, shouting out *Yes You Can!*, flew up and curled their edges from the sheer fury of her passing. Outside Dan's office Rachel paced up and down the carpet a couple of times, breathing deeply and trying to calm herself. She knew what she had to do. There was no way she could be without a job; she would be completely screwed and she'd probably have to pack up and go home. This wasn't her happy ending, and she would accept nothing less.

Rachel tapped on Dan's closed door and walked in. The sound of pan pipes wafted from a series of strategically placed speakers. Dan was standing in the middle of the office, barefoot and bent over, so both his hands and his feet were flat on the floor, his buttocks raised high in the air. Dan's swami was standing directly behind him, his groin level with Dan's backside. The swami had a hand on each of Dan's hips, helping to steady Dan's ridiculous yoga pose, and if Rachel had been less furious she would have found a week's worth of humour in the image.

When the swami saw Rachel's face he immediately let go of Dan's hips. Dan lost his balance, landing on the grassy carpet.

'Dan, I need to talk to you.'

'There's nothing to talk about, Rachel,' he said, standing up. 'I'm trying to reassert some positive energy in my soul right now. After today, it's much depleted.'

'Dan, I've come to beg you not to do this.'

'Rachel, you guys have got serious problems. I don't know what's going on with Justin or with you for that matter. Sometimes I get the sense that you're not really all that passionate about what we do here at Target Advertising. I'm very well attuned to that kind of thing. I also think he's stoned half the time. He's barely ever here and he owes us a ton of money. Did you know he's advanced on his salary by a month? And now he comes to work so drunk he vomits on my client. Do you realise how serious that is, Rachel? We could lose Pharmicorp ... That's millions, even without the laxative business.'

Rachel wanted to make a 'flushed down the toilet' pun on losing the laxative account, but she recognised that her timing may be a little off for that kind of humour. 'Dan, he wasn't drunk, I swear it,' Rachel said instead. 'It was food poisoning. He just ate some bad duck last night; it wasn't his fault. It's amazing that he even made it in to the office in such a state. He should probably be in hospital on a drip or something.'

Dan looked unconvinced but Rachel ploughed on regardless. 'Dan, it's such bad karma to fire someone,' she continued, trying a different tack. 'Please, please, give us another chance. I will take full responsibility for Justin, you have my word. If he fucks up again you can fire us both. I guarantee from now on he will be nothing less than a perfect employee. And you don't have to pay him his salary for the next month; that way he'll be caught up on the loan. If you fire him now, you'll never get your money back. Please, Dan, please, just give us one more chance. I'm totally committed. I love the work I'm doing here. I've never felt so spiritually fulfilled at an agency before, ever. This is my home, Dan. Don't take away my home ...' she pleaded.

Dan turned to his swami and Rachel used all her available mental energy to burrow into the Indian man's turbaned head, willing him to grant a stay of execution. The swami looked at Rachel and then back at Dan then back at Rachel. Finally, he moved his head in a barely noticeable nod.

'Okay, Rachel Marcus,' Dan sighed, 'you both get one more chance. But Justin is now your responsibility. Sort him out or you're both gone for real. I'm not kidding here, Rachel, you've got one month, and if I don't see a vast improvement ... Well, then I'm sorry, but you can't say I didn't give you a chance.'

Relief flooded Rachel's body. 'Thank you, Dan,' she said, bowing as she backed out of his office. 'I promise you won't regret this.'

Rachel was too furious to face Justin straight away. She needed to calm down if she was to do anything other than kill him. This should have been a moment of triumph – the work had been great and she had presented like a star – but instead here she was on her knees, begging Dan not to fire her, lying for Justin yet again. She locked herself into a cubicle in the bathroom, put the toilet seat down and sat on it. Unaware of what she was doing with her hands while her mind raced she unravelled the toilet paper from the roll, looking down at it unseeingly as the creamy waves gathered in a pile on the floor at her feet. Rachel thought Justin was the most selfish, self-centred, ill-disciplined person she'd ever met. And now she was going to have to babysit him just so she could keep the crappiest job she'd ever had. A job she'd never wanted. A job she couldn't stand.

When she walked back into the office Justin was still in a dismal heap on the couch. The combined effect of his black eye and busted lip and the scent of defeat that oozed out of his pores should have made Rachel pity him, but she was still too angry.

'What happened? Where've you been?' he asked.

'Dan said we can stay on trial for a month. But there are terms!' she said. 'And if we don't follow them, we're gone.'

Justin nodded.

'I mean it, Justin. This is serious shit. You just got me fired too!'

'Rachel, I know I fucked up and I'm really sorry,' Justin spoke in a small voice that sounded to Rachel like it came from somewhere very deep inside him. 'I think sometimes you have to sink to the bottom of the shit pile to realise how screwed up your life is.'

'Justin, this has to stop,' Rachel continued. 'I told Dan I would be responsible for you. If you fuck this up we're both out on the street with nothing, okay? It's not just your reputation you're destroying here, it's mine too, you selfish, immature child!'

Justin looked straight at her and nodded again.

'You need to stop drinking and pull your shit together, starting now!'

'Rachel?'

'What?'

'I don't have anywhere to live. I lost my apartment and all my stuff.'

'When?' asked Rachel, horrified.

'A couple of weeks ago. I'm completely skint. I've got nowhere to live. I've been showering at the gym.'

Rachel knew somewhere inside her she felt sorry for him, but all she could see at that moment was that he'd done this to himself. He'd taken a perfectly good life and shredded it. 'Jesus, Justin! Dan said he's not paying your salary for the next month to cover your staff loan. What the hell are you going to do?'

He couldn't look at her. He dropped his head, shrugged his shoulders and covered his face with his hands.

Rachel sighed and rubbed her eyes in frustration. 'You'll have to stay with me until we figure this thing out,' she finally said.

'I'm sorry, Rachel,' he whispered.

'Fuck! What a mess!' Rachel grumbled. 'Let's get out of here ... You need a shower.'

Rachel Marcus is not a big fan of vomit.
May 20 at 2:21pm

They sat on the subway in silence. Out of her peripheral vision Rachel saw a fat tear roll down Justin's black-and-blue cheek, but he swiped it away quickly with his fist.

As they got closer to her stop Rachel began to wonder how they would both fit into her apartment – she could barely squeeze into it by herself as it was. Perhaps, she thought, she wouldn't have to stay with Justin. Maybe she would stay at Jerrod's place a little more often now. She smiled inwardly. She could live with that.

Rachel showed Justin around the apartment, a job that took eleven seconds. 'Bathroom, kitchen, lounge, bedroom,' she said sharply.

'What happened there?' Justin asked, pointing at the badly duct-taped hole in the bathroom wall.

'I had a rat problem,' Rachel said, shuddering at the memory. 'You may not have noticed, but this is hardly The Ritz Plaza. I've been meaning to get it fixed but I haven't had a chance. I've been putting down rat poison once a week, and I haven't seen any more of them, but keep an eye open.'

Justin nodded.

'Help yourself to whatever you find here and make yourself at home,' Rachel continued, 'but there's one rule.'

'Anything.'

'No booze and no drugs. If I even suspect you're doing either you'll find yourself out on your ass, Justin. I mean it. This is serious!'

'I know,' he said. 'Thank you, Rachel.'

'Are you going to be okay here by yourself tonight?' Rachel asked, tossing a towel at him a little too hard. 'I've got a date with Jerrod.'

'I'll be fine ...' Justin sighed. 'I'm exhausted. I haven't slept in days. I'm going to have a shower and crash. Then, tomorrow, I need to re-evaluate what I'm doing, try to figure some stuff out.'

'Are you okay to sleep there?' she asked, pointing to the couch.

'Rachel, compared to some of the places I've slept lately this is seriously five-star.'

Rachel shuddered. She could only begin to imagine some of the places he'd seen from inside the bottom of a bottle.

Opening the fridge Rachel pulled out half a bottle of vodka from the freezer and a bottle of whiskey and two bottles of wine and packed them safely inside a backpack – she would leave her booze at Sue's place to make sure he had no temptations. Then she went to the medicine cabinet in the bathroom, returning with a couple of aspirin and a glass of water. 'How are you feeling?' she asked.

'Shite,' he said, taking them from her, 'but I suppose I deserve this hangover, right?'

'Yes, you do,' she said. 'I've got to head over to Jerrod's place now, but I mean it, okay, no booze and no drugs. I'll have my cellphone on me the whole time and Sue's just across the hallway if you need anything.'

Justin nodded.

'I won't be home late,' she said. Then she picked up the backpack, let herself out of the front door and walked across the hall.

'Hey, how did your presentation go?' asked Sue as she opened the door. 'What are you doing home so early? And what's that on your sleeve?'

For the first time Rachel noticed the spattering of vomit patterned down her sleeve. 'That,' she said, 'is vomit!' She shrugged off the jacket and let it drop to the floor, suddenly too exhausted to be alive.

'Vomit!' shrieked Sue, picking up the jacket between her thumb and forefinger and holding it away from her body as if it were radioactive. 'Why on earth did you vomit?'

'It's not my vomit, it's Justin's.'

With a scrunched up nose Sue opened the bathroom door and tossed the jacket into the bathtub, then she reached for a couple of mugs. 'That does not sound good. What did he do now?'

'Sue, it was disgusting!' Rachel said, slumping down on the couch. 'He came in so trashed that I had to do the presentation by myself. He just sat there drooling. And I almost made it all the way through without anyone noticing, but then right at the end he vomited all over the client!'

Sue covered her mouth in disgust, her eyes wide.

'Then the client vomited all over her boss and Dan!' Rachel put her head in her hands. 'It was revolting ... And then ... And then Dan fired both of us!'

'Shut up! Oh, my God, what are you going to do?'

'It's okay ... It's okay ...' Rachel gasped. 'I don't know how, but I managed to convince Dan to give us another chance. I said I'd take responsibility for Justin and we'd sort our act out. But it turns out he doesn't have a cent, Sue. He's been living on the street.'

'Oh, my goodness,' was all Sue could repeat as Rachel filled her in.

'So now he's staying next door with me, just till we can get him straightened out!' Rachel spat out the last sentence and breathed in deeply. She still felt incredibly angry but now it was mixed in with such a deep-boned exhaustion that it was all she could do to hold her neck up straight on her shoulders.

'You mean he's here? Across the hall?' asked Sue.

Rachel nodded again.

'Rachel!'

'I know, but I don't have a choice, I need this job otherwise I'm out on the street; there's nothing else out there for me. I have to do something; plus he's got nobody else.'

Sue handed Rachel a cup of coffee and they sat in companionable silence. Rachel thought of half a dozen things she wanted to say, but she was all out of words.

'What can I do?' Sue asked eventually.

'I'm going to need help keeping an eye on him,' Rachel replied. 'I've got to get him straight and sober and back on track. I've got a date with Jerrod tonight, so I was thinking … Would you mind checking in on Justin in a couple of hours?'

'Of course, Rachel, I'll do whatever I can,' said Sue. 'But first things first,' she scrunched her nose up, 'you need a shower. There are fresh towels in the bathroom.'

'Sue, thank you. I owe you one,' Rachel said, heading for the bathroom.

'No problem, just leave me that bag of booze, and we'll call it quits.'

Rachel Marcus has a date with Prince Charming now. And she really needs it after the day she's had.
May 20 at 6:12pm

'Jerrod, I promise you won't even know he's there.'

Rachel was sitting on the couch with her bare feet in Jerrod's lap. They had finished dinner and he had been massaging her feet until a minute ago when she'd come to the part in her story where she had explained how Justin had become her new temporary flatmate.

'But where will he sleep when I stay over at your place?' Jerrod asked.

'You're not going to stay over at my place,' said Rachel, horrified at the thought.

'Why not?'

'Well, I don't really want you to see my place.'

'Why not?'

'It's such a dump, Jerrod.'

'But you don't mind if Justin sees it?'

Rachel could sense this wasn't going well and she knew she needed to do something to stop the situation from spiralling completely out of control. 'He's different, babe,' she said, dropping her feet off of his lap and crawling across the couch towards him. She buried her face in his neck and nibbled at his ear in an attempt to distract him.

'How is he different?' asked Jerrod, not so easily distracted.

'Well,' said Rachel, taking a break from his ear lobe and sitting up straight, 'for one thing I don't have any feelings for him. In fact, he's a complete pain in the ass. I'm so angry with him right now I can barely look at him. He got me fired, remember? He's only staying at my place because he's got nowhere else to stay, and I need to keep an eye on him to make sure he stays sober and gets to work every day.'

'What if he sees you naked?' asked Jerrod.

'If anything, that would turn him off,' Rachel said glibly and smiled.

Jerrod looked at her blankly; he clearly wasn't in the mood for a joke.

'I'm only kidding, Jerrod.' Rachel sighed. 'He won't see me naked, I promise. I'll change in the bathroom, okay? Anyway, this just means I'll have to stay over here more often, if you'll have me?' She dropped her face back into his neck and tried to change the subject manually, because changing it verbally didn't seem to be working.

Jerrod dropped his head backwards and Rachel hoped it was a sign he was easing off the subject. Just to be sure she put a throw pillow down on the floor and dropped to her knees between his legs. She undid his belt buckle, pulled his jeans and his Calvin Klein's off and tossed them across the floor. There was one foolproof way she knew of putting an end to a confrontation like this one. Rachel looked up at Jerrod, 'Babe, let's not fight about this anymore tonight, okay? Anyway,' she said, looking down at his growing excitement and then back up into his sexy green eyes with a naughty smile, 'everybody knows that it's rude to talk with your mouth full.'

Jerrod smiled at her and she knew she had him, even if only for the next fifteen to twenty minutes.

Rachel Marcus knows how to win an argument.
May 20 at 11:25pm

Rachel snuck into her apartment. Justin had left the bathroom light on and from the spray of left-over light that spilled into the rest of the apartment she could make out the shape of his body on the couch. After checking for rats, she brushed her teeth and slipped into a pair of pyjamas. Then she pulled the bathroom door closed and went through her nightly ritual of taping up the gap between the floor and the door. She hadn't seen another rat since The Incident and she no longer barricaded the door, but taping it up still helped her sleep a little more easily.

Finally, she tiptoed over to her bed – she was exhausted; her legs ached and her brain felt like it was three sizes too big for her head – but as she snuggled gratefully into her duvet she heard Justin tossing and turning, followed by a massive thump.

'Ow! Fuck!' he cried.

'What happened?' whispered Rachel.

'You're home? I didn't hear you come in. I fell off the couch.'

Rachel heard him clamber back onto the couch and rearrange his pillows. 'Bad dreams?' she asked.

'Yeah,' he said. 'How was your date?'

'It was amazing, thank you,' she said. 'He's amazing.'

There was a long dark silence.

'Rachel, I can't thank you enough for everything you're doing for me,' Justin whispered. 'I swear I won't let you down.'

'You'd better not,' Rachel said. 'Now get some sleep, okay. We've got a lot of vomit to clean up after tomorrow.'

Rachel Marcus and **Justin Coley** are walking on eggshells.
May 21 at 8:30am

They moved around the apartment getting ready for work, both far too aware of the other person's personal space, forming crop circles in the carpet as they walked large loops around each other. The mood was sad and polite. Neither of them brought up the events of the day before. At least having him living on her couch meant she had some control over getting him to work sober and on time, Rachel thought, trying hard to look on the bright side.

Justin and Rachel slunk into the office half an hour early. Double D Heather still smiled at them when they walked through the reception area but it was a controlled smile, one that kept a tight rein on all her teeth.

'Team!' Dan said sternly, walking into their office at around ten.

'Morning Dan,' Rachel said, sitting to attention. She eyed him up and down: he was wearing a floor-length blue dashiki, a pair of leather Jesus sandals and his mouth was set in a perfect, thin, straight line.

'Dan,' said Justin, standing up. 'I just want to tell you how grateful I am that you're giving me this opportunity ...'

Dan cut him off at the knees. 'Save it, Justin, I just got off the phone with Pharmicorp. They've decided to put the business out to pitch. They felt we had a "clash of cultures". Dan made rabbit ears in the air with his fingers as he said the words.

Rachel felt her windpipe contract. She looked at the clear plastic ballpoint pen she was holding and wondered whether she would be capable of giving herself an emergency tracheotomy with it if at any point her throat closed completely and she stopped being able to breathe altogether. She'd seen it done in a documentary once and it didn't look all that complicated. Just aim and pierce.

'Oh, Dan ...' began Justin.

'Don't say anything, Justin!' Dan snapped. 'Tomorrow morning I'm leaving for Nepal for three weeks. I've decided to take my swami and my wife to a Buddhist retreat. I need to cleanse. In the meantime client service are going to brief you on a promotion for Sanitex sanitary pads. This is your last chance here. I want to see this put to bed by the time I get back. I've got my people watching you both. Sort it out or get out. Justin, you're lucky Rachel convinced me to give you another shot. If it was up to me, karma or no karma, you'd never trample the employee Zen garden again!'

Dan swooshed out of the office. There was a prolonged silence. 'What, no hug?' Justin finally asked.

Rachel shot him a glare. It had finally happened: she'd been reduced to sanitary pads. She wanted to cry.

Rachel Marcus **has reached the pinnacle of her advertising career. Not!**
May 21 at 2:30pm

Rachel Marcus is going on a double date tonight. How Eighties is that?
May 30 at 4:41pm

'You're going to love them, Jerrod,' Rachel said in the cab on their way to dinner.

They were going out with Sue and Brian for the first time and Rachel had invited Justin at the last minute because she didn't want to leave him home alone, unsupervised.

'What does he do?' Jerrod asked, running a hand through his hair.

'Brian's in finance, remember, I told you. And Sue illustrates children's books.'

'I can't believe you invited Justin!' Jerrod said.

Rachel closed her eyes and took a couple of deep breaths. She felt nervous. It was ridiculous, she knew. Hell, it wasn't like she was introducing him to her parents or anything, these were her friends. She was sure they'd love him. And Jerrod already knew Justin ... If they could only get over the past and move on they might even like each other. It wasn't like Jerrod had had anything to do with the betrayal. Sure, he could have said something to Justin at the time, and it had been wrong not to, but the unfortunate set of circumstances had hardly been Jerrod's fault.

'I can't have a late night tonight, okay?' said Jerrod, 'I need to go into the office for a couple of hours tomorrow to work on the pitch.'

'Come on, grumpy,' Rachel squeezed his knee, 'it'll be fun.'

'Pass the salt, please, Jerrod?' asked Justin.

Jerrod's head was down and he seemed to be focusing all his powers of concentration on the burrito on the plate in front of him. The salt was right next to him, but he either didn't hear Justin or he was blatantly ignoring him.

They were sitting in a booth at a Mexican restaurant in Greenwich Village. Jerrod at the end of the table, next to the window, with Rachel next to him, Sue and Brian across from them and Justin at the head.

'So, you mean to say that you've never seen my airline commercial with the monkey in a pilot's uniform?' Jerrod asked Brian, finally looking up from his burrito as Sue handed the salt cellar to Justin.

'I'm really sorry,' Brian said. 'I don't really watch all that much TV, mainly just the news and sports, isn't that right, babe?'

Sue nodded.

'I've seen the ad with the singing tennis shoe, though,' Brian went on. 'I love that one; it's classic. Did you do that one?'

'No, I didn't do that,' Jerrod growled. 'That's a piece of crap! I can't believe you like it.'

'Is everything all right here?' asked the waitress. 'Can I get anybody another drink?'

Rachel could have kissed the waitress for interrupting them. Dinner so far had been a complete disaster. 'Anybody want another virgin margarita?' Rachel asked cheerfully, holding up her almost empty glass.

A volley of nos bounced around the table and the waitress disappeared. Rachel suspected that the lack of alcohol may have been one of the main reasons for the way the evening was going. Both Justin and Jerrod had hit major sulks the second they saw each other and Jerrod and Brian hadn't found a single subject they agreed on all night. And to make matters worse Rachel was desperate for the bathroom – her two virgin Margaritas had gone right through her – but she was too terrified to leave the boys alone at the table with only Sue as a buffer.

'I don't see why I can't have a proper drink.' Jerrod said.

'I told you, babe, we're trying to support Justin,' said Rachel, putting her hand on Jerrod's thigh in an attempt at appeasement.

'I'm not the one with the drinking problem,' snapped Jerrod. 'I don't see why I have to suffer because he can't manage his alcohol.'

Justin looked down at his plate awkwardly.

Rachel pulled her hand off Jerrod's leg and glared at him. 'Jerrod, that's really unnecessary,' she said through gritted teeth.

'Please,' said Justin, shifting uncomfortably in his seat, 'like I said earlier, I really don't mind if you guys drink.'

'Well, we shouldn't be drinking anyway,' said Brian, smiling at Sue. 'So we don't mind.'

Now it was Sue's turn to glare, but her glacial stare was aimed at Brian.

'Why not?' asked Rachel, her anger instantly dissolving into curiosity.

'We're trying to have a baby,' Brian blurted out, his smile radiating pure joy. He put his arm around Sue's shoulders protectively.

Sue smiled and tucked herself neatly under Brian's arm.

'That's fantastic!' shrieked Rachel. The people at the neighbouring tables craned their necks to see if they could catch a glimpse of whatever the drama was, before returning to their plates. 'You guys are going to make the best parents ever. I'm so excited for you.'

Rachel nudged Jerrod in the ribs with her elbow. 'Yeah, that's great, good luck,' grumbled Jerrod through a mouthful of food.

'Congratulations!' said Justin, shaking hands with Brian.

Rachel thought it was strange to congratulate someone simply for shagging a lot, but at least Justin's gesture felt genuine, unlike Jerrod's barely audible mumble. Jerrod was so grumpy tonight and sulk wasn't a good look on him.

'Oh, my goodness,' said Rachel, 'I just thought of something. If you guys have a baby you'll have to move out. There's no way you could fit three of you in that apartment. What will I do without you?'

'I didn't think of that,' said Brian. 'Hey, babe, maybe we can move somewhere with higher ceilings? Look, I've got this permanent bruise from always forgetting to duck when I walk out the bathroom door.' Brian raised his fringe and pointed at a small bruise on his forehead.

'Guys, don't you think this discussion is a little premature?' said Sue. 'There is still a very long way to go. We just started trying, all right. We weren't even going to say anything yet …' She glared pointedly at Brian again. 'Can we please change the subject?'

'Please, excuse me,' Jerrod said, pushing his empty plate towards the middle of the table. 'I'm going to the bar. I need a real drink.' He scraped his chair back and stood up, then bent down and kissed Rachel on the lips before making his way to the bar, shooting a pointed glare at Justin on his way.

'I'm so sorry he's so unpleasant tonight, it's not you guys, I swear,' said Rachel once Jerrod was out of earshot. 'I think he really likes you guys, he's just hectic at work right now and he's not getting much sleep. They've got this huge project on the go, it's a pitch and it's all he can think about. He's not always like this, I promise.'

Rachel knew that this wasn't entirely true. Jerrod had made it abundantly clear how he felt about Justin living in Rachel's apartment. His jealousy bothered her but at the same time it managed to stroke her ego a little too. And Rachel also suspected that Jerrod found Sue and Brian a little too small-time for his liking.

'Can I offer anyone dessert or coffee?' the waitress asked cheerfully as she cleared the plates.

'No thanks, just the cheque,' piped up Brian. 'Sue, you ready to go, sweetheart?'

Brian was obviously keen to get Sue home and Rachel suspected that they wanted to get to work on making their baby. It was sweet really.

'Can Rachel and I share a cab home with you guys?' asked Justin.

'Oh, Justin, do you mind going without me?' Rachel asked. 'I think

I'm going to go back to Jerrod's place.'

'Oh, yes, of course, I wasn't thinking,' Justin stuttered. 'Sure, no problem. Sorry, I didn't mean to presume ...' He trailed off.

'You sure you'll be okay?' Rachel asked him.

'We're right across the hall if he needs anything,' said Sue.

Jerrod arrived back at the table at the same time as the bill and Jerrod, Brian and Justin all pulled out their wallets. Rachel cast a glance over at Justin, who was looking into his wallet anxiously. She kicked Jerrod under the table. Jerrod rolled his eyes and reached for the bill. 'Please everyone,' he said, 'let us get this. Our treat ... To celebrate your exciting news and Justin's fresh start.'

Outside on the street Justin and Jerrod each hailed a cab as Brian fussed around Sue, helping her with her coat. Everyone said polite goodnights and thank yous and the two cabs went off in opposite directions; one uptown, one downtown.

'Thank you for paying for dinner,' Rachel said through gritted teeth once they were in the cab and on the road heading home. 'But I don't know why you had to be such an ass all evening?'

She felt hurt and upset by his behaviour. He'd been embarrassingly rude to Justin and he'd barely made any effort to get to know Brian or Sue.

Jerrod ignored her and carried on looking out of the window, his sulk reflecting back at Rachel in the glass.

'How long are you going to act like this?' she asked.

'How long is he going to be around?' asked Jerrod.

'Justin? Is that what this is about?' She paused, exasperated. 'Jerrod, Justin is my friend and my art director, nothing more. I'm coming home with you, aren't I? I know you're not crazy about him. Well, here's some news for you, neither am I right now. And I don't expect you to be best mates, but you're going to have to get used to having him around. At least till he gets back on his feet, okay? What happens to him now impacts on me. He needs to sort his shit out and I'm the only person who can help him at the moment. I need your support, babe. Without him, I'm out of a job!'

They drove on and Rachel watched Jerrod clench and unclench his jaw.

'I also thought you could have been a little nicer to Brian,' she said.

'Jesus, Rachel, Brian's another story. What kind of grown man has never seen my airline commercial with the monkey in a pilot's uniform?' Jerrod said. Then he grumbled something incoherent and they drove four blocks in cold quiet.

'Jerrod, this is stupid,' Rachel eventually said. 'I really don't want to fight. Especially not about a monkey in a fricking pilot's uniform! We've both had a stressful week and tonight's been crap. Why don't we try salvage what's left of it?'

Jerrod looked at her, but he didn't answer.

'Exciting news about Sue and Brian isn't it?' she said cheerily, trying to change the subject.

Jerrod shrugged his shoulders.

Rachel eyed him out, he was even sexy when he was being an asshole, she thought. She put her hand on his leg and slipped it up his thigh, brushing his crotch with her fingertips. 'Do you think you'll ever want kids?' she asked, smiling coyly. 'I think you'd be an amazing dad.'

Rachel noticed Jerrod's jaw start to relax a little and he eventually smiled slyly, a naughty look in his eye. 'I don't know,' he said, 'but I sure like the practicing.' He kissed her hard and Rachel tasted bourbon on his tongue.

Back at Jerrod's apartment Rachel went into the en suite to get ready for bed. She'd started to leave items of clothing in one of his drawers and she'd also cleared a space in his medicine cabinet. It hadn't been an easy task. Every inch of shelf was already filled top-to-bottom with assorted hair gels and moisturisers. Rachel had shuffled the products around and had eventually managed to clear just enough space for her toothbrush, some perfume, night cream, a razor and a stick of deodorant. So far Jerrod hadn't mentioned it.

'It feels like you haven't stayed over in ages.' His voice came from the bedroom. 'Keeping an eye on Justin is like your full-time job.'

'It's not just my fault we've barely seen each other,' Rachel said defensively. 'You've been so busy on the pitch. I think you've worked late every night this week.'

Rachel ran dental floss between her teeth. She was looking forward to stretching out next to him in his king-sized bed under his expensive linen.

Climbing into bed Rachel tried a couple of positions until she found what she thought was her sexiest, most flattering pose. She pretended to read her book and listened, excitement building as Jerrod padded around the apartment turning off lights and making sure everything was locked up. Then he walked through the bedroom, winked at Rachel and popped into the bathroom. Rachel listened to him getting ready for bed. She felt he had an extensive routine for a man. He always did a couple of sets of push-ups, then he washed his face with a cleanser and then a toner before applying a moisturiser and a night cream. Finally, he combed his hair, brushed his teeth for at least two minutes with an electric toothbrush, flossed and then finished off with a gargle of mouthwash. The entire routine took him about fifteen minutes.

Eventually he climbed into bed, naked. Rachel put her book down and turned off her bedside light, plunging the room into darkness. She felt Jerrod envelope her in his arms. He pulled her black silk slip off over her head and ran a hand down her warm, naked body. Kissing her neck and then her lips, he ran his hand down her stomach and felt for the warmth of her. She lifted her hips, moaning as he teased her a little, before slipping a couple of fingers inside her. Then, suddenly, he rolled on top of her and entered her, kissing her on the shoulder. Surprised by his quick approach, Rachel lay with her eyes open as he moved above her urgently. He came a couple of seconds later, grunting with the effort and pleasure of it. Then he rolled off of Rachel, kissed her on the cheek and turned onto his side, falling almost instantly into a deep, calm, satisfied sleep.

Rachel sat up in bed and glanced across his prone body at the digital alarm clock on the bedside table. The entire event had taken just eleven minutes. She felt disappointed. By her calculations it had taken him longer to wash his face.

Rachel Marcus **is doing Sunday things.**
May 31 at 11:40am

'**I**'m sorry if last night at the restaurant was a little awkward,' Rachel said, licking a finger and running it through the crumbs on her plate.

Rachel and Sue were parked at their usual Dean and DeLuca table surrounded by shopping bags, empty cappuccino cups and what was left of a couple of chocolate croissants.

'That's okay,' said Sue. 'I'm sure it's not so easy on Jerrod knowing that Justin's living in your apartment. I think Justin is doing really well, by the way. He seems to be pulling himself together slowly.'

'He is, isn't he?' said Rachel. 'He says he hasn't touched a drop since the whole Pharmicorp incident and I believe him.'

'What's it like having him at the apartment all the time?' asked Sue, licking cappuccino foam off her spoon.

'It hasn't been easy. Things are kind of intense right now, working together nine hours a day and living together, but I've started getting used to it, even though he can be a giant pain in the ass.'

'Well, I like him,' said Sue. 'I find him, I don't know, genuine. Even though he is kind of fucked up.'

'Yeah, he is, isn't he?' said Rachel.

'What? Fucked up?' asked Sue.

'No genuine,' said Rachel.

Sue raised an eyebrow and picked the chocolate off a corner of what remained of her croissant.

'Jerrod takes every opportunity to bash Justin,' said Rachel. 'I can't stand it. It's the only thing we ever really argue about. And if I stick up for Justin it just makes him more mad.'

'Yeah, those boys definitely don't have each other on their Christmas card lists this year,' said Sue, shaking her head.

'What does Brian think of Jerrod? Has he said anything? Was he upset last night?'

'Oh, you know Brian, he's thick skinned and he doesn't say too much. Both of us just don't want to see you get hurt,' said Sue gently. 'Promise me you'll be careful with Jerrod, Rach, I'm not so sure about him yet.'

'I promise,' said Rachel. 'He really was just very stressed last night, Sue. He's not normally such a dick.' Sue was just being overprotective, Rachel thought. She would be the same if the tables were turned. 'So, you and Brian were in an awful hurry to get out of there last night!' Rachel grinned.

'I'm sorry I didn't tell you about us trying to have a baby.' Sue sighed. 'I'm still getting used to the idea, but Brian's on a mission, he wants us to be pregnant before the end of the year.'

'What do you want?'

'I dunno,' said Sue. 'I'd like to have kids, but I'm not sure if I'm ready yet.'

'I think Brian would make a wonderful dad.' said Rachel. 'He's so committed to you and you know I've always thought you would make an amazing mom.'

'If I tell you something,' said Sue, 'will you promise on your life never to repeat it to another living soul, as long as you live?'

'Of course ...'

'Promise you won't even tell Jerrod, or your family, or a cab driver, or anyone?' said Sue.

'I promise,' said Rachel. 'You have my word. Anyway, if I did tell a cab driver you'd be pretty safe, none of them speak any English!'

'I mean it,' said Sue. 'You can't repeat this.'

Rachel nodded.

'I had an abortion when I was thirteen.'

'Wow!' said Rachel.

'I've never told another living soul,' said Sue.

'What happened?'

'I was a dumb thirteen-year-old with too much curiosity and not enough sense. It was the worst experience of my life and it tore my family apart.'

'Does Brian know?' asked Rachel.

Sue grabbed Rachel's arm, knocking over the milk jug in the process. 'No, and you can't ever tell him! You promised!'

'I won't,' said Rachel, taken aback by Sue's intensity. 'I'd never tell Brian if you didn't want me to. But I still think he would understand. He loves you more than anything.'

'Rachel, he can't find out, okay, I need to be able to trust you on this.'

'Of course you can trust me, Sue, on my life.' Rachel crossed her heart with her fingers and then wondered if that worked for Jewish people.

Rachel Marcus is drinking coffee.
June 2 at 8:48am

Rachel Marcus is finishing her coffee.
June 2 at 9:03am

Rachel Marcus is going to get another cup of coffee.
June 2 at 9:14am

Rachel Marcus will do anything to avoid working on sanitary pads, including drinking too much coffee and changing her status update way too often.
June 2 at 10:48am

Angelica, the horsey client service lady who was responsible for the Sanitex sanitary pad account, cantered into the office just after eleven. 'Client loves the initial thoughts for the promotion that we presented on Friday and can't wait to see the rest of the campaign,' she said, beaming as if she'd just announced the arrival of the Queen.

'Excellent,' said Rachel.

'Thank fuck for small mercies,' said Justin.

'There are just a couple of tiny little changes they're suggesting,' said Angelica.

'Of course,' said Justin sarcastically, slumping back behind his desk.

These days Rachel was terrified of bad news; always waiting on the one sentence that would send Justin back down the slippery slope he'd clawed his way up over the last couple of weeks. She felt like he was balanced precariously over an abyss. Maybe these were the words that would finally topple him over the edge again.

The first two weeks he was clean had been the worst. Detox had given him horrific mood swings, sweats, bad dreams and the shakes, which still bothered him. But now when Rachel looked at Justin she could see how much better he was. His skin was clearer and he'd put on a bit of weight. But even with all his progress she knew he was still far from better. Most days she felt like he was held up by a very thin piece of fishing gut, a couple of staples and some duct tape.

'What does the client want?' Rachel asked, resigned.

'Well,' began Angelica, pulling a sheaf of papers out from behind her back and referring to them. 'They say we can't use the words "blood", "bleed", "red" or "period", and we can't refer to "that time of the month" either.'

'But they're sanitary pads!' said Rachel.

'They'd prefer it if we used the word "menstruation" and also they are "feminine hygiene products", never "sanitary pads".'

Justin shook his head.

'Also, they like the visual of the girl in white jeans playing volleyball but they thought maybe she could be playing another sport, like tennis or badminton. Research shows that volleyball isn't so big with our demographic. Oh, and they're not so sure about the headline, and they thought maybe she shouldn't be wearing white jeans. Finally, they asked if we could reconsider the background colour and the font, and make the logo and the pack shot at least fifty per cent bigger.'

'I thought you said they loved it?' said Justin.

'Oh, but they do,' gushed Angelica. 'It's just a couple of teensy-weensy tweaks. And they're only suggestions; they're not insisting.'

'And if we don't make these suggested changes?' asked Justin.

'Well, then I don't think they'll buy the work,' said Angelica.

Rachel looked at Justin. 'Let's just do it, okay. It's not worth pushing back on this, Justin. Dan is back in four days, and we need to have this thing buttoned down by then.'

'This is pathetic!' Justin shouted. He glared at Rachel and Angelica, threw his pen down on the desk, grabbed his cellphone and stormed out of the office, slamming the door behind him.

Rachel chewed on a fingernail and wondered whether or not to go after him – if he fell off the wagon now it would be a complete disaster. She reached for her bag, but as she was getting up Angelica blocked her. 'Rachel,' she said. 'There are a couple of small body copy changes I need to take you through quickly. Client wants to see the revised copy this afternoon.'

Angelica put a piece of paper down on the desk. Rachel barely recognised her own words. Someone had scrawled all over them with a red pen. Barely a word on the document had been left untouched and notes bled out from the copy, filling the margins. Rachel took a deep breath, sat back down again and counted to ten while Angelica twittered on in her ear.

Rachel Marcus is minus one art director. Has anyone seen Justin Coley?
June 2 at 7:05pm

'You're where?' asked Jerrod.

'In a bar on Forty-Second Street,' said Rachel.

'What the fuck are you doing there?'

'I'm looking for Justin; he disappeared and I need to find him.'

'Of course, I should have guessed it would be something to do with Justin.'

Rachel held the phone away from her face; Jerrod's shouting was hurting her ear. 'I thought you were coming over here and bringing dinner from Wanton Gardens!' he yelled. 'You said you'd be here at half six. We were going to have an early dinner so I could get in some work on the pitch tonight. I'm starving, Rachel!'

'Oh, shit, I forgot!' Rachel said into the phone.

'Well, that's just great, Rachel,' he ranted. 'I just love it when my girlfriend forgets about me!'

'Well, I'm hungry, tired and stressed too,' Rachel yelled back into the phone. 'I'm sorry I forgot we had plans, Jerrod. But I didn't do it on purpose. I could do with a little support here too, you know. I've been looking for him for hours already and I don't know what to do. Where do you think he is?'

'I don't care where he is!' Jerrod yelled. 'I care where you are and I care where my dinner is! You know what, Rachel, this isn't working for me. I can't deal with all of this right now!'

'What the fuck is that supposed to mean, Jerrod? Stop being such a jackass! I said I was sorry; I'll head over to you now.'

'Don't bother,' Jerrod said, slamming the phone down.

Rachel's heart sank. That was not the conversation she had been hoping for. She looked around the bar one more time but Justin wasn't there. Rachel had spent the last three hours looking for him in every bar she knew he frequented. She'd even tried the one they'd been to the night they'd done cocaine together, but there was no sign of him and his cellphone was off. Rachel dialled Sue's number and spoke immediately when she answered, not even giving Sue a chance to say hello. 'Have you seen Justin?' she asked.

'No, wasn't he at work with you today?' asked Sue.

'Sue, we had a bad meeting and he stormed out ... He's disappeared ... I need you to take a look at my place and see if he's there.'

'Hang on,' said Sue.

Rachel imagined Sue padding to her front door and then out across the hall on her tiny bare feet.

A moment later she was back. 'There's nobody home,' she said.

'Are you sure?' asked Rachel, her panic overflowing into her voice.

'Well, it's not like there are that many places to look in your apartment,' said Sue. 'He's not there.'

'What if he's fallen off the wagon, Sue?' asked Rachel, close to tears.

'Rachel, take a deep breath, okay. You can't possibly do more than you've already done for him. At some point his sobriety has to become his own responsibility.'

'I know, Sue, but I'm terrified for him.' Rachel sniffed into the phone.

'Look,' said Sue, 'I'll keep checking, and I'll call you as soon as he comes in, okay? Please, don't cry. Everything is going to be fine.'

'Thanks, Sue, I've been to all the bars around work but nobody's seen him.'

'Rachel, that's crazy, you can't walk the streets all night looking for him. There must be thousands of bars in New York where he could be hiding.'

'I know,' Rachel sucked in a deep, steadying breath, 'and the worst part is that Jerrod and I had a massive argument because I forgot we had dinner plans tonight. He just slammed the phone down on me. I think it's over, Sue.'

'No, Rachel, you're both just upset.'

'What if he never wants to speak to me again?' Rachel choked. 'I think I've really fucked up this time.'

'Don't be silly, Rachel, he's just grumpy with you. You should go over there and try smooth things over. Couples should never go to bed angry with one another.' Sue paused. 'Hey, you know what I do when I screw up and Brian and I have a fight and I want to make up?'

'No, what?' asked Rachel.

'I buy a sexy outfit; something naughty like a French maid or a Playboy Bunny or something.' Sue giggled. 'It always works. There's no way a man can stay angry with you when you're half dressed and you've gone to all that effort with him in mind. It's a hundred per cent foolproof. Trust me, he'll take one look at you and he won't even remember why he's mad.'

'That's not a bad idea, Sue,' said Rachel. 'Do you really think it will work? I've never done anything like that before.'

'C'mon, think about it, Rae. You in a Playboy Bunny outfit, what's not to work?'

Rachel nodded into the phone.

'Seriously, Rachel, you should do it. It'll take your mind off Justin. You and Jerrod will make up, and before you know it Justin will be back and everything will be sorted.'

'Maybe you're right,' Rachel said.

Sue shrieked with delight.

'A sex shop in New York, that shouldn't be too hard to find, right?' Rachel said and they both laughed. 'Hey, Sue, speaking of finding things, do you think Justin's okay?'

'He'll be fine, sweetie. I'll call you when he comes home.'

'Thank you, Sue.'

Rachel tried Justin's cellphone one more time, but she got his voicemail again. Then she tried Jerrod's cellphone. It also went straight to voicemail.

Taking a cab to Jerrod's apartment Rachel asked the driver if he knew of any lingerie or sex shops in the neighbourhood. He smiled at her lasciviously in the rear-view mirror and radioed into his control room in a loud Middle Eastern language.

The cab dropped her off outside Jimmy's XXX House of Fun. The facade was painted black and covered with neon signs proclaiming *XXX Adult Movies* and *Toys and Girls*. She stepped inside. The shop was well lit with florescent bulbs and packed with stock. One wall was covered in movies and the opposite wall was covered in dildos, while racks of dirty magazines ran the length of the shop. A couple of men were browsing the movie section. Rachel avoided making eye contact with any of them and hurried over to the sales lady – a petite, bored-looking Asian girl with heavy eye make-up and multiple piercings in her nose, chin and eyebrow. Strangely, Rachel noticed, the only place she wasn't pierced was her ear lobes.

'Hi,' Rachel said quietly.

The salesgirl looked her up and down.

'I'm looking for a sexy costume, like a French maid's outfit. Do you have anything like that?'

'What you?' asked the salesgirl, tapping her nail file on the edge of her fingers. 'Size fourteen?'

'Actually, more like an eight,' said Rachel, trying hard not to feel offended.

'We're all out of French maid,' said the salesgirl, walking out from behind the counter.

Rachel followed her down the middle of the shop and noticed that she had a tattoo on the back of her neck that said *Made in Japan*. At the end of the magazine racks they reached a rail, stacked with outfits. The girl rifled through them and pulled out two. 'In big size we only got witch and bee,' she said.

'Any Playboy Bunnies, schoolgirls or cheerleaders?' asked Rachel.

'Only witch and bee!' snapped the salesgirl loudly.

Rachel took a closer look at both outfits. The witch had a scary mask, a tall pointy black hat, a very short, very skin-tight, plastic off-the-shoulder dress, a black cloak and a particularly phallic-looking short plastic broomstick. Rachel thought it was the most unsexy outfit she had ever seen. 'I don't want to be a witch,' she whispered to the salesgirl. 'I don't think men want to forgive witches that have been bad.'

'Only got witch and bee for you, big girl,' repeated the salesgirl, her voice booming across the shop.

'All right! All right!' Rachel said, appraising the bee outfit. It consisted of a miniscule yellow-and-black striped strip of fabric, that was a boob tube but could have also been a belt, a minute ruffled miniskirt made out of bright yellow plastic and a prosthetic black plastic sting on a belt. The final touches were provided by a pair of bright yellow pleather crotchless panties, a pair of black-and-yellow six-inch pointed drag-queen heels, a pair of yellow wings that would attach to her back with elastic and an yellow-and-black Alice band with bobble feelers sticking out of it. For a novelty outfit it was very intricate and well thought out. Rachel was surprised and impressed. Until this moment she'd never thought that bees could be sexy.

The salesgirl showed her to the changing room where Rachel

squeezed into the outfit and evaluated her reflection: wings, six-inch heels and all. Then she turned around and looked over her shoulder to catch a glimpse of the view from behind. She looked half sexy and half ridiculous, but mostly just ridiculous. Oh well, she thought, if this didn't make Jerrod forgive her, nothing would.

Rachel thought about the situation. Had their roles been reversed and Jerrod had allowed some girl to move into his apartment and had then stood Rachel up to go scouring the city for her, she would have been less than impressed herself. She couldn't blame him for being mad at her. She needed a big gesture, something to prove to Jerrod that she was crazy about him and that she wasn't in the slightest bit interested in Justin. And the way she saw it, you didn't get a much bigger romantic gesture than a yellow-and-black pleather, crotchless bee outfit.

As Rachel gathered her clothes she heard a host of strange noises. It sounded like there was a couple having sex in the dressing room next to hers. She wouldn't be surprised, she thought, making a mental note to avoid touching anything on her way out.

Having made her decision, Rachel put her coat on over the outfit. The wings and ridiculous sting made things tricky and uncomfortable, so she took off the coat and removed them both. She would put them on in the elevator, together with the yellow and black Alice band with its two bouncy yellow bobble-tipped feelers. Finally, she put her coat back on, parted the changing room curtain with her elbow and made her way carefully past the wall of giant dildos to the till.

'You buy big black cock?' boomed the Asian salesgirl as she rang up the outfit.

'No, thank you,' Rachel said politely as everyone in the shop turned to stare at her.

'Big black cock half price today,' said the salesgirl, waiting to ring up the final total in case Rachel changed her mind.

'No, really, not today, thank you,' Rachel whispered.

'What, you no like big black cock?' said the girl.

'It's not that,' said Rachel, running her eye around the shop to make sure she wouldn't be offending any of the other customers, who might be owners of their own big black cocks. 'I don't really have a need for one today, but maybe tomorrow.'

'Big black cock not half price tomorrow,' the salesgirl said, shaking her head and ringing up the grand total.

Rachel paid for the outfit, shoved her clothes into a Jimmy's XXX House of Fun shopping bag and ducked out of the sex shop.

Hobbling down the street in the six-inch heels, Rachel pulled her coat tighter around her to cover up the bee costume, but it was a warm June night and it wasn't long before she began to sweat. The crotchless pleather panties chafed unpleasantly on her thighs and by the time she had clopped the five blocks to Jerrod's apartment her make-up had started to melt down her face. Ah, the things we do for forgiveness, she thought. Eventually, chafed in places she hadn't even known existed, she arrived at the building, where the doorman let her in with the knowing grin of a man who had been a doorman in New York long enough to know that a woman in a floor-length coat in June was definitely hiding something.

Alone in the elevator Rachel tore off the coat and put on her wings, sting and the Alice band. Her heart was racing. She couldn't believe she was doing this.

As the elevator doors opened Rachel caught a glimpse of herself in the entrance hall mirror. She looked away quickly and shuffled into the apartment before she lost her nerve. 'Hello!' she yelled. 'Anybody home?'

Jerrod's voice came from the kitchen. 'Rachel, is that you?'

Rachel put on her sexiest walk and made her way towards the kitchen. 'Jerrod, I'm so sorry I screwed up, I was a completely selfish little bee ...'

Jerrod was at the kitchen counter with an open beer in front of him. A stylish woman in her late fifties sat next to him, drinking a cup of tea. The woman was wearing a classic pink Chanel two-piece suit with a string of pearls around her neck and when she saw Rachel her mouth made a perfect pink O, though despite her obvious horror her pinkie finger remained extended at ninety degrees to her bone china teacup.

'Fuck!' swore Rachel, the word tumbling out of her mouth.

Jerrod spluttered, spitting out a mouthful of beer.

Rachel tried to cover herself, but she didn't have much to work with. The world slowed down to a complete stop.

'Mom, this is my girlfriend, Rachel Marcus,' Jerrod eventually said between guffaws. 'Rachel, meet my mother, Judith Craig.'

Rachel reached for a nearby dishcloth to try and cover her embarrassment, clutching it over her bare crotch with her left arm as she politely extended her right hand towards Jerrod's mother. 'Hello, Mrs Craig, it's lovely to meet you,' she said, her cheeks luminous. 'I'm so sorry . . . I didn't know anybody else was going to be here.'

'My mom was shopping in the neighbourhood and she decided to pop by for a cup of tea and surprise me,' Jerrod said, doing a bad job of hiding his amusement.

Mrs Craig looked sharply at Rachel. 'Hello,' she said. 'Well, Jerrod, I think I'd better be off. Your father and I are going to the club for dinner. It's Mimi Rogers' sixtieth.'

Mrs Craig picked up her handbag and left the kitchen, carefully averting her eyes from Rachel and giving her a wide berth, ignoring her outstretched hand.

Jerrod followed his mother out the kitchen. 'Let me show you out, Mother,' he said, slapping Rachel on the ass as he walked past her. 'Nice sting,' he whispered.

Rachel remained planted to the spot, all too aware of her crotchless yellow panties, her six inch drag-queen heels and the bobble feelers wobbling on her head. She stood with her one hand clutching a red-and-white checked dishcloth over her crotch, the other hand still outstretched and still unshaken.

When Rachel heard the elevator door ding shut she covered her face in her hands, dropped the dish towel and howled in embarrassment.

Jerrod was hysterical when he came back into the kitchen. He bent over double, his hand slapping his thigh and tears rolling down his cheeks. 'That was the funniest thing I've ever seen!' he said, clutching his sides. 'What on earth are you doing?' he asked.

'It was Sue's idea!' Rachel whined. 'She said I should buy a sexy outfit so you wouldn't be mad at me anymore. I know I fucked up and I wanted to say sorry. But how can that possibly be the first time I meet your mother? She must think I'm some kind of fetish freak. And I can't believe I swore in front of her. This is a disaster! I'm so embarrassed!'

Jerrod put his arms around Rachel and tried to comfort her. 'A bee?' he said. 'That's very innovative.'

Rachel looked at him, her mouth turned down at the corners. 'They didn't have any French maid outfits left!'

'Oh, baby, I wouldn't worry too much, my mother never approves of my girlfriends, even when they're not wearing crotchless bee outfits. You look hot!'

Rachel forced a smile. 'You like?' she asked, stepping back and turning for him so he could get a good look at the whole effect.

'I like,' he said, reaching for her and kissing her hard on the lips, his fingers slipping down towards the yellow pleather panties that offered her very little privacy.

Later, Rachel pulled on her jeans and one of his old T-shirts while Jerrod fried them up a couple of omelettes which they ate on the couch. 'I know I already tried to say it with the bee costume, Jerrod,' Rachel said between mouthfuls, 'but I want you to know that I am really sorry about earlier. I didn't mean to forget about our plans. I've just been so worried about Justin. If he falls off the wagon I'm so screwed.'

'Rachel, I really don't want to talk about him anymore ...' Jerrod growled.

When they finished eating, Rachel took their plates into the kitchen. The mood was strained but Rachel tried not to let it bother her too much. It had been a stressful and embarrassing day. The stupid costume and the make-up sex had lightened the mood a little but there was still a heavy undertow from their earlier argument.

'Babe, I'm going to go work in my study for a couple of hours,' Jerrod said.

'How's the pitch going?' Rachel asked.

'Good, but slow.'

'Are you ever going to tell me who the client is?' Rachel asked with a glint.

'Babe, it's so confidential, I can't.'

'Jerrod, I'm your girlfriend, I just put on a bee costume and walked five blocks in six-inch heels for you. Not to mention humiliating myself in front of your mother ... Come on.'

Jerrod thought about it for a second then he bent down towards her and moved her hair out of her face, tucking it neatly behind her ear. He cupped his hand around his mouth and whispered the name of the brand into her ear.

Rachel's eyes lit up. 'Fuck me!' Rachel said. 'That's huge! Wow!'

'I know,' Jerrod smiled, 'but Rachel you can't tell anybody, not a soul. Seriously, we've all had to sign confidentiality agreements, so not a word of this leaves this room.'

Rachel nodded her head furiously. 'Of course, babe, I promise. I won't breathe a word of it to anyone.'

Jerrod kissed her and then slipped off into his study.

Rachel cleaned up the dinner things and then went into the bathroom where she lit some candles. Turning on the iPod in the bedroom she ran a hot bubble bath, switched on the heated towel rail and laid two fluffy bath sheets over it. Then she padded into Jerrod's study. He was sitting at his desk, drawing some scamps on his layout pad. Rachel tiptoed up to him and reached for his hand, trying to pull him out of his chair. 'I've run us a bath.' she said.

'Now's not a good time, Rachel. I have to work.'

'Come on, babe, half an hour. I'll try and inspire you.'

Jerrod shook her hand off. 'Not all of us get to work on audio visuals, Rachel. This is real work. It's important. I can't have you interrupting me all the time!'

Rachel took a step back; his words had stung.

'I'm sorry,' he said, his voice gentler now. 'But I need to concentrate.'

'Sorry,' Rachel mumbled and backed out of his office.

Smarting, she went into the bathroom and climbed into the bath by herself. She knew he was busy and under a lot of pressure, but she also suspected that Jerrod was still punishing her a little for forgetting their dinner plans earlier.

As she lay in the soapy water Rachel wondered about Justin. Sue hadn't called, which meant he wasn't home yet. She pictured him in a bar somewhere in the city.

When the bath water got cool Rachel climbed out, dried off and slipped back into Jerrod's T-shirt. She made two cups of herbal tea and then tiptoed to Jerrod's study and tapped lightly on the door. 'I don't want to disturb you,' she said. 'I made you tea.'

'That's okay,' said Jerrod. 'I'm sorry I snapped at you. It's been a long day.'

'I totally understand,' she said. 'I know how stressed out you are. And I wanted to say how sorry I am about this whole Justin thing. He'll be out of our lives in a month or so, I promise. I want you to know how much more important you are to me than him, okay?'

Jerrod nodded at her.

Rachel put his cup down next to him and went to sit on the other side of his desk, lifting her bare legs up and wrapping her arms around her shins. 'Why don't you tell me about the brief,' she said, eyeing his layout pad. 'Maybe talking about it will help?'

Jerrod considered her across the desk. 'Okay,' he said, 'but you cannot repeat a word of this to anyone.'

Rachel made the Scouts' honour signal with her hand. 'I absolutely promise.'

Jerrod laid the brief out for her point by point. He outlined the product and the strategy, the target market and the research findings. Then he took her through the media requirements. Rachel listened quietly. It was a tough brief and she knew immediately how much was riding on it. They chatted a bit about the merits of the strategy and later, when their tea was finished, Rachel left him to work and went to read in bed.

Rachel Marcus is allergic to bees.
June 2 at 11.47pm

Rachel Marcus is still looking for Justin, anyone seen him? Anyone?
June 3 at 9:49am

When Rachel woke up at seven thirty the next morning Jerrod's side of the bed hadn't been slept in and there was still no word from either Sue or Justin.

'Still no word from Justin?' asked Sue as soon as she heard Rachel's voice on the other end of the line.

'Nothing,' said Rachel. 'Are you sure he didn't come back to the apartment last night?'

'Nope, I checked every couple of hours. No sign of him, even this morning.'

'I'm really worried, Sue.' Rachel was at her desk gnawing her poor shredded fingernails. 'Do you think we need to start calling hospitals? What if something's happened to him?'

'He'll be fine,' said Sue, not sounding entirely convinced. 'Let's try not to worry. I'm almost positive he'll show up. He'll come weaving in through that door any minute with a monster hangover and then you'll be completely furious at him and everything will be back to normal. Let's talk about something else. How was Jerrod last night? Did you get an outfit?'

Rachel blushed as she remembered the incident. 'Yeah, it was ... um ... interesting. Anyway, outfit or no outfit, he's like a bear with a sore tooth at the moment. I just wish he and Stewart would finish this pitch already so we can go back to normal. What about you guys? How's the shag-fest going?'

'Good, yeah, good,' said Sue.

The conversation petered into silence.

'If Justin isn't dead already, I swear, Sue, I'm going to kill him myself for making me worry like this.'

'I'll keep checking the apartment,' said Sue.

'Thanks, Sue, chat later?'

'Yeah.'

Rachel tried Justin's cellphone again. It went to voicemail, but when she tried to leave another message it informed her that his mailbox was full.

Rachel Marcus doesn't know whether to be terrified or furious.
June 3 at 11:35am

Next Rachel called Jerrod. He answered on the eighth ring, just before it went to voicemail.

'What do you want?' he snapped.

'Babe, Justin still hasn't turned up. I'm really worried. What do you think I should do?'

'I'm busy right now, Rachel! I can't talk to you on the phone all day about this crap. Why are you so worried about him anyway? He's a complete loser! Look, I've got to go, Rachel, and I'm not around tonight, I've got to work late.'

'Babe …' started Rachel.

Jerrod cut her off. 'We'll talk tomorrow,' he said. 'Bye.' And he put the phone down.

Rachel paced the office. She wondered what Jerrod's problem was. 'What does he expect me to do?' she asked aloud. 'Pretend Justin's not missing?'

Rachel realised she was talking to herself and stopped, but she carried on pacing and shaking her head. She wouldn't talk to Jerrod again, she decided, until he grew the fuck up.

She sat down at Justin's desk. Everything was as he'd left it the day before and as she moved his mouse his screen came to life. She toggled through the open pages in his Internet browser to see what he'd been looking at before he'd left. The first page open on his screen was girlswholikeitdirty.com. Rachel smiled and clicked on the next tab. A list of Alcoholics Anonymous and Narcotics Anonymous meetings in Central New York popped up on screen and a flutter of hope burst through Rachel. As she read through the list an email arrived. It was an online flyer for a local bar, advertising a ladies' night and a buy one shooter get one free promotion. Rachel's stomach turned and she shut down his computer. Where on earth could he be? Dan would be back in a couple of days and if Justin was still gone, then so was she.

'Rachel?' Angelica's horse face peeked around the door.

Rachel was tempted to say 'Why the long face?', but she restrained herself, she was in enough trouble already.

'Good, you're here,' Angelica said, looking around for Justin. 'I have some great news for you two.'

'We've heard that one before,' Rachel said with a smirk.

'Sanitex have approved the promotion.'

'But they want to change one last little thing, right?' prompted Rachel.

'Nope,' said Angelica. 'They loved the changes you suggested and we have to start shooting on Monday if we want to make the deadline.'

'Well, they weren't really our changes, remember?' said Rachel. 'They were their own changes.'

'Let's not nit-pick,' Angelica smiled tightly, 'they bought it and that's what matters. Isn't it simply the best news?'

'Super,' said Rachel, but her stomach was in knots. She couldn't do this without Justin, and if he didn't show up soon Rachel would have to let the agency know that he'd gone missing and that would be the end of that. Rachel crossed her fingers under her desk and went for it. 'That really is great news, Angelica,' she said. 'Well done. Do you want to set up a pre-prod for tomorrow morning, first thing, and Justin will get right on it?'

'Will do, and well done again, team.' Angelica beamed and trotted out of the office.

Rachel Marcus is crossing her fingers and toes.
June 3 at 5:42pm

On her way home Rachel did another circuit of the bars Justin frequented but nobody had seen him. As she slipped her key in the door Sue's head popped out of her apartment. 'Oh, Rachel, hi,' she said. 'It's you. I thought maybe it was Justin.'

Rachel smiled sadly at Sue and opened the door. Sue looked in over her shoulder. The apartment was as Rachel had left it the day before. There was no sign that Justin had been around. 'I don't know what else to do?' said Rachel, slumping down on the couch.

'Brian and I are going to see a movie. Why don't you come? It will help take your mind off all of this.'

'Thanks, Sue, but I'd better stay here in case he calls or something.'

'Okay, I'll put my phone on silent in the movie. Call me if you hear anything.'

'I will ... Promise.'

Sue left, closing the door behind her, and Rachel went to wash her face. When she walked into the bathroom the first thing she did was to check her rat hole. Rachel rubbed her eyes, thinking she must be seeing things. There were no longer several untidy rows of grey duct tape attempting to mask the hole in the wall. Instead the wall was smooth, white and holeless. Rachel bent down on her haunches and ran her hand over the pristine surface to be sure she wasn't imagining it. Justin must have done it some time before he disappeared. Rachel had been staying over at Jerrod's a fair amount and he must have taken the opportunity when she was away. She smiled and touched her hand to her heart in an instinctive reaction.

Suddenly Rachel heard a key in the door. Shooting up straight she bashed her head hard on the underside of the sink. It knocked her down on her bum and she saw spots in front of her eyes for a second.

'Hello, anybody home?' Justin asked, knocking gently on the front door, peeking his head around it as he pushed it open.

'Where have you been?' Rachel shouted, scrambling to her feet and rubbing her head where a small bump had already started to form. 'Thank goodness you're all right.' She felt such a mix of anger and relief that she wasn't sure what to do first. 'I was so worried about you, you shit, why didn't you phone?' she asked as she hugged him and then punched him hard on his arm. 'Where have you been? You fixed the rat hole. It's amazing!'

Justin was dirty and unkempt and Rachel could see he hadn't slept. His hair was a matted mess and he had dark rings under his eyes. 'My mobile battery died and I didn't have a charger with me.'

'Justin, where have you been?'

Justin collapsed on the couch. 'I was upset.'

'I gathered,' said Rachel.

'I fell off the wagon, Rachel.'

Rachel's heart sank.

'I've just been feeling so bad and that stupid client bullshit was the last straw. I wanted it to all go away, so I went to the first bar I could find and I ordered a shot of tequila.'

'Fuck, Justin!'

'I know.'

'I wish you'd called me,' said Rachel. 'I could have come to get you.'

'It was too late already, Rachel. And I already feel terrible about the way I've imposed on you. I know I've made things difficult with you and Jerrod, and I know how much you like him, and I want you to be happy. Things are really fucked up right now.'

'But where were you all night, Justin?'

'I got arrested.'

Rachel sucked in air through her teeth. 'Jesus, Justin! What for?

Why?'

Justin put his head in his hands. 'Open container. I passed out in the park with an open bottle, so they tossed me in the drunk tank for the night. It was hell, Rachel.'

Rachel covered her mouth with her hand, horrified.

'They let me out this morning with a warning. They're not going to press charges.'

'Oh, thank God, Justin. What about today; where have you been all day?'

'I spent the day going from meeting to meeting: Alcoholics Anonymous, Narcotics Anonymous. I think I went to a different one in every borough.'

'How do you feel?' asked Rachel.

'Tired, but positive,' Justin said and sighed. 'I think with the meetings I can carry on doing this now. If you'll let me stay?'

'Of course, of course, I'm just relieved you're okay. Justin, you are okay, aren't you?'

'I think so.'

'Why don't you have a shower and I'll order us some dinner. We can deal with all of this tomorrow.'

Later, they ate dinner in silence. Justin was ravenous and cleaned his plate three times. Rachel dished up more for him each time and filled his glass with water as he emptied it.

After dinner Rachel made up the couch and he collapsed onto it as she climbed into her own bed. 'There's good sanitary pad news,' she said.

'Don't you mean good feminine hygiene product news?' he asked.

'They bought the revised campaign. You're pre-prodding it tomorrow and shooting it next week. It's a four day shoot in LA. Do you think you're up to it?'

'I think so,' said Justin.

'They're putting you up in a hotel over there.'

'That sounds cool.'

'What about the minibar, Justin'

'It was just a slip, Rachel,' he said, his voice hard. 'I'm scared. I don't want to go there again.'

Rachel nodded. She believed him. 'Well, Dan is back on Monday,' she said, 'so at least you'll miss that.'

But Justin didn't respond; he was already asleep. Rachel listened to him breathing and wondered if he would manage to stay clean on his own for four whole days. They had AA in LA, didn't they? They had to … There was probably a meeting on every corner, knowing LA.

Rachel Marcus is okay, you can all stop looking now, he's back.
June 3 at 9:51pm

Rachel lay replaying the last couple of days in her head. The fact that Justin had fallen off the wagon really bothered her. She had told him in the beginning that if he fucked up she would kick him out, but she knew now that she couldn't do that to him. He was her friend and she was all he had right now.

Rachel understood what it was like to have your heart cruelly broken and she recognised that on another day or in another time, after what had happened to her, she could have been the one who had fallen apart and he could have been the one helping her pick up the pieces instead of the other way around. He was bound to trip up, she decided, but he seemed remorseful about it and she thought he was sincerely committed to dealing with his problems and getting better, and that was all she could ask for right now. Before she fell asleep she decided she would continue to stick by him and be the friend that he so desperately needed. After all, it wasn't like she didn't have room in her life for another friend right now.

Rachel Marcus is ready for Dan the man. The question is, is he ready
for her?
June 8 at 9:04am

'Welcome back, Dan, how was your trip?' Rachel pasted a smile on
her face.

'Rachel. Yes, I'm back. Come in.' Dan glided across his office and
gave her a hug, which Rachel thought was a good sign, especially
considering how they'd left things a couple of weeks earlier.

'Hello, Shandahar,' she said, greeting Dan's swami, who was hovering
in the corner of Dan's office as usual. 'How was the retreat?'

The swami wore his standard robe, a pair of sandals and a small neat
turban balanced on top of his head. He looked at Rachel and bowed.

'No, that's Shamandar,' said Dan. 'Shandahar decided to stay in
India and further his studies.'

'Oh, I'm sorry,' said Rachel, clasping her hands in front of her chest
and bowing at the swami. Seen one swami, seen them all, she thought.

The swami nodded and bowed back at her. Was she mistaken or
was he looking at her breasts? She pushed the thought out of her mind
and focused back on Dan.

'So, Rachel Marcus,' said Dan. 'I hear that you and Justin did a good
job on Sanitex and Justin is off shooting it in LA? Well done. If you
carry on this way perhaps I might consider keeping you on, although
considering what's happened an annual increase would be quite out of

the question.'

'Thank you so much, Dan,' she gushed. Why did he have to be so damn patronising, Rachel wondered. She'd spent the last couple of months busting her butt on his crap briefs and now here she was grovelling to retain the opportunity to write the world's most boring brochures for haemorrhoid creams and pimple lotions. What she really wanted to do, she thought as she turned to leave, was stab him in the neck with his five thousand dollar Montblanc pen and kick the swami in the shins. It was only by breathing deeply and centring herself that she managed to contain her agression.

Escaping the plastic grass and sandalwood of Dan's office, Rachel headed for the nearest bathroom. It was situated just off the Target Advertising reception area and was a typical office bathroom in every respect except for one thing, it was a unisex loo. There was one large area with a row of basins down one side, a row of stalls down the other side and a bank of urinals off in the corner, which were rarely used by anyone other than Dan. There were single-sex facilities elsewhere in the agency, but they were at the other end of the offices and had only been added after Human Resources had insisted on it to avoid potential law suits. Rachel was sure Dan had stolen the idea for unisex office loos from *Ally McBeal*, a wacky television series from the Nineties which was set in a quirky law firm. Rachel couldn't stand it. She liked her privacy and she usually avoided it unless she had absolutely no other option. Today, however, she was desperate and irritable. Rachel peeped around the door to make sure there wasn't anyone standing at the urinals. Then she slipped into one of the stalls. She pulled down her jeans and panties and sat on the loo, shaking her head and marvelling at the ridiculous enigma that was Dan Charter.

Suddenly, out of nowhere an idea hit her. It arrived in her brain fully formed and completely blindsided her. It was as if it had been in the wings of her mind her whole life, waiting for this precise moment, waiting for her to pull her jeans down and sit on this exact toilet so it could jump out at her.

It was an idea for Jerrod's car account pitch. Rachel circled it in her mind, evaluating it, then, finished on the toilet, she jumped up, pulled up her pants and pulled the chain. She dashed out of the bathroom and headed straight for her office, in such a hurry that she forgot to wash her hands or check her make-up in the mirror. She also managed to trail a long piece of toilet paper that had stuck itself to the heel of her boot all the way from the bathroom to her desk.

Rachel started to make notes, trying to capture the idea while it was fresh. It was massive: TV, print, radio. It was the ever-elusive Big Idea. This had happened to her once before a couple of years earlier. She had let a difficult brief float in the back of her mind for a week or two, only to have the solution burst out of her head suddenly, perfectly formed, while she was driving, thinking about something entirely different. There was something about giving the brain time to solve a problem that allowed it to do its best work.

Rachel continued scribbling furiously. It poured out of her; all her passion flooding back as she remembered what it was she was doing in advertising in the first place. She drew up a couple of rough print ads and sketched an outline for another television commercial.

After a couple of hours spent plotting the campaign Rachel called Jerrod. His phone rang ten times and then went to voicemail. No big surprise there, she thought. But soon all that would change. Maybe Jerrod would include her idea in their presentation to the client? This could mean big things for her.

Rachel took a break from furious scamping to fantasise a little and shake a cramp out of her hand – she'd become lazy at Target and wasn't used to writing so much. If she cracked this everything would change. Maybe R&P New York or London would offer her a job. She could leave Target Advertising and return to the world of real advertising, where she would make actual real commercials, for proper brands that consumers out there really saw. Jerrod would be promoted for discovering the person who conceptualised the entire campaign. And what if it won awards? She would finally be the award-winning copywriter living in

New York that she'd always wanted to be. She'd be able to return to South Africa with her head held high, maybe even to take up a position as a creative director at a top agency or even start her own thing. Why not? That is if she decided to leave New York. Who knew, maybe she and Jerrod really did have a future together right here in this incredible city?

Suddenly New York seemed full of possibility. Rachel went back to her layout pad and leafed through the pages, rereading what she'd written. Yup, it was good. Actually it was better than that. It was really good. She carried on scamping up her ideas for the rest of the day. As she finished one thought the next one was lined up in her mind, waiting to be recorded on paper. Screw Sanitex and RightSole she thought, this is so much bigger than that.

Rachel tried to call Jerrod a couple more times as six o'clock approached, but his cell went to voicemail every time. Eventually she put her pen down and got up to stretch. She was far from finished – the idea still need a lot of crafting – but she would get there. For now, though, it was out of her head and onto paper and Rachel believed it was good.

Rachel Marcus is giving it the overnight test.
June 8 at 7:54pm

'Hi honey, I'm home,' said Rachel, knocking on Sue and Brian's door. At the beginning of their friendship she had always just walked in if the door was unlocked, but these days they might be shagging, and she really didn't want to walk in on that.

'Come in,' shouted Brian.

'Are you guys decent?' she asked, tentatively pushing the door open.

'Yes, we're decent …' Sue laughed. 'It's only half-past eight on a Monday night, what do you think we are, a pair of bunny rabbits?'

'Well, better safe than sorry, right?' said Rachel.

Sue was making dinner and Brian was opening a bottle of wine.

'We didn't expect to see you tonight,' said Brian. 'Where's Captain Advertising?'

'He's really busy at work with the pitch,' said Rachel. 'I haven't seen very much of him lately. But it's okay, I totally understand, I know it's only temporary. And Justin's away this week on a shoot in LA.'

'Can I pour you a glass of wine?' asked Brian.

'Yes,' said Sue, a little too over enthusiastically. 'Why don't you stay for dinner, there's more than enough here!'

Brian shot a glance at Sue and Rachel saw that the table was set for two, lit romantically with flickering candles. 'Thanks, guys. Maybe just a quick glass of wine and a catch up, but then I'll leave you two alone,' she said. 'Looks like you've got a romantic evening planned. Anyway, I've got work to do and I'm looking forward to having my apartment to myself.'

Brian poured the wine and passed it around.

'Guys, I've got incredible news,' said Rachel, holding up her glass to make a toast.

'What, honey?' asked Sue.

'You know that massive international pitch Jerrod is working on? Well, I think I cracked the campaign!' Rachel beamed.

'You're such a genius!' said Sue. 'When?'

'Well, don't laugh, but I was on the toilet at work today and it hit me, out of nowhere, like a lightning bolt. I'm not one hundred per cent sure, but I think it's really good.'

'Well done, Rachel,' said Brian. 'A toast: to my beautiful wife and our genius friend.'

They clinked glasses and drank.

'So, what did Jerrod say about it?' asked Sue.

'I haven't told him yet; he's not answering his phone. I think he's still at work. But maybe it's a good thing that I can't get hold of him, I want to see if my idea stands up to the overnight test, so I'll wait and bounce it off of him tomorrow. If I still like it that is.'

'Of course you'll still like it tomorrow, honey, I'm sure it's brilliant,' said Sue, stirring the pot on the stove. 'I'm so proud of you. Maybe this means you can get out of Target?'

'I really hope so. Although I did have the idea on the toilet, I hope that doesn't mean it's complete shit ...'

Sue and Brian both laughed and Rachel smiled.

'All right, there's a hot shower, some takeout and a pedicure back at my place with my name on it,' said Rachel, draining her glass. 'Have fun my little bunny rabbits.'

Brian grinned but Sue looked less happy as she waved goodbye to Rachel.

Rachel had a quiet night. She sent Jerrod a text message to say goodnight. Her phone bleeped and she attacked it, but it was only a message from Justin to say the shoot was going well and that they'd just wrapped for the day. He was on his way to his hotel room. No minibar.

Rachel Marcus **got an A on the overnight test.**
June 9 at 9:53am

At the office the next morning Rachel paged through the layout pad full of scamps, outlines, thoughts and ideas from the previous day. When she was finished she went through them again with a pencil, adding things and making changes as she went. She felt like this was potentially the best work of her career. Finally, she picked up the phone and dialled Jerrod's cell. He answered on the fourth ring. 'Hello ...' he said in a sleepy voice.

'Jerrod, it's me, did I wake you up?'

'Yeah, we put in an all-nighter last night.' He yawned.

'Do you want me to call you back later?' she asked.

'No, it's okay, I'm up now,' he said grudgingly.

'I feel like I've barely seen you,' she said.

'Rachel, do we have to go through this again? You know I've been manic at work. I really don't need added pressure from you on top of it.'

'I'm not putting pressure on you. I miss you, that's all. How's it going?'

Jerrod grunted.

'Babe,' she said, 'I've got something to show you. It's a surprise. Do you want to grab dinner tonight?'

'Nah, I'm shattered. I don't want to go out.'

'Jerrod, I really need to see you,' Rachel pleaded.

'Oh, all right then, I suppose you could come over. We can watch a movie or something.'

'I can't wait,' said Rachel.

'Okay, look, I gotta go. I need to shower and shave and get into the office...'

Jerrod hung up without even waiting for Rachel to say goodbye. That's okay, thought Rachel, in a couple of hours all that will change.

Rachel Marcus is cracking things left, right and centre.
June 9 at 10:27am

After work Rachel gathered up all her pitch scribblings. Over the course of the previous twenty-four hours she had amassed dozens of ideas, all of them based on the simple pay-off line that had struck her on the toilet. She had expanded it into a couple of television commercials, a slew of double-page magazine print ads, a whole tactical newspaper campaign and even a promotion. Rachel folded the scamps into a small black portfolio bag and left the office, hoping if all went according to plan this would be one of the last times she would make her way through the Target Advertising studio, past the executive Zen garden and the slightly smaller employee Zen garden, past the unisex toilets and Double D Heather's reception desk, past the 'art chairs' and out onto the street that stank like raw meat.

Riding the elevator up to Jerrod's apartment Rachel's cheeks burned as she recalled the bee incident. She sadly doubted she would ever be invited to the club for brunch with Mr and Mrs Craig.

When she walked into Jerrod's apartment the lights were dim and Jerrod was on the couch with a beer watching basketball on his enormous flat-screen television set that took up part of a wall across from the bank of windows. Jerrod barely raised his head when she walked in.

'Hey, sexy,' she cooed, climbing onto the couch next to him and folding her legs underneath her body, snuggling up to him.

He kissed her absentmindedly without taking his eyes off the television set, getting her on the side of the ear, missing her face all together. 'Hi, babe,' he said. 'I'm just watching the game ... Before you get settled, won't you grab me another beer?'

Annoyed, Rachel looked at him. She kind of was settled already, but she wanted a drink too, and since he obviously wasn't going to offer her one and it certainly wasn't going to grow legs and walk to her from the fridge by itself, Rachel got up and went to the kitchen. A spaghetti Bolognese simmered gently on the stove. When she saw it her mood eased. At least he'd made dinner. She was starting to get a little tired of takeaways and her skin wasn't loving it either; she'd recently discovered an outbreak of adult onset acne on her chin which she attributed fully to her diet or lack of one. She opened the fridge and helped herself to a beer, grabbing a fresh one for his royal highness at the same time.

Climbing back onto the couch Rachel nuzzled under his chin and he put his arm around her. This was the closest she'd felt to him in weeks.

'So what's this big surprise?' he asked, eyes still glued to the screen. 'Is it an ant outfit? Or, no wait, it's a wasp, isn't it?'

'Well,' she said, ignoring his teasing. 'You're not going to believe this, but I had an amazing idea for your pitch!'

'What do you mean?' asked Jerrod, looking at her properly for the first time since she'd walked in the door.

'Remember you told me the brief the other week? Well, I guess it's been percolating in the back of my mind all this time. I think my subconscious has just been beavering away at it. Then, yesterday, don't laugh, but I was on the toilet and it kind of hit me. I've been working on it for the last two days, trying to expand on it and pull it together. I tried to call you all day yesterday to tell you about it but your cell just went to voicemail. I can't wait to show you. I think it's really good, Jerrod.'

Rachel finished the speech she'd practiced over and over during the subway ride to Jerrod's place and took a deep breath, watching him closely for a reaction.

'That sounds interesting. Do you have the ideas here?'

'Yup,' Rachel leapt up off the couch, 'I brought them with me.'

'Wow, Rachel, I didn't know you were working on it.'

'You know, subconsciously, on the side. Do you want to take a look?'

'Sure.'

Rachel took her portfolio bag over to the couch. She unzipped it and Jerrod leaned over and turned on the lamp. Then he moved the two open beers and the newspaper off the coffee table, muted the game with the remote and made space for Rachel to lay the work out.

'Just remember,' Rachel said, 'it still needs quite a lot of work and I'm a writer, so it's also going to need a really strong look to pull it all together. But as far as ideas go I think it's a good start.'

Rachel started by taking Jerrod through the thinking behind the campaign line which held everything together. Then she pulled out a piece of layout paper with the line written on it in black pen. She gave Jerrod a second to take it in and then she started to go through the work piece by piece. She took him through a couple of potential television commercials and then she pulled out the magazine ads one by one, laying them out on the coffee table. Jerrod nodded his head and scratched his chin, but he remained quiet, only asking a question here or there to clarify a thought in his mind.

When Rachel was finished she picked her beer up and sat back on the couch to let him digest it all, watching him carefully as he leafed through the pages strewn across the coffee table – first the TV concepts and then the magazine work. 'So?' she asked, her stomach churning. 'What do you think?'

'Jeez, Rachel, I wish you'd told me you were working on this.'

'I wasn't really, it just kind of came to me ...' Rachel trailed off.

'If you'd told me you were going to put all this time and effort into it I would have told you not to bother ...' Jerrod sighed. 'We've already cracked our campaign idea. We know what we're going to present and now we're just crafting some of the executions. Didn't I tell you that we'd cracked it?'

'No, not really,' Rachel said. 'I guess we haven't seen very much of each other lately. Things have felt a little strained and you've been working so hard. I just assumed you hadn't cracked it yet. I didn't realise . . .'

'I feel really bad that you've gone and done all this work for nothing,' he said.

'Well maybe it's not for nothing,' said Rachel, scrambling to rescue her work. 'Maybe some of it can fit in with what you're already doing?'

'Oh, Rachel, I don't know. If this was any other pitch, but we're up against the London crew here, so the work really has to be top-drawer stuff. Baby, I don't want to hurt your feelings, but I have to be honest, I don't think this is quite the calibre we're looking for.'

'Oh,' Rachel said, a flush rising upwards from her neck. He didn't like the work. Rachel had never felt so embarrassed. Even when she'd flashed her tits to the whole city she'd felt less mortified. Of course, they'd already cracked it, what had she been thinking? Jerrod and Stewart had just won a Gold Cube at Art Directors Club, they were one of the best creative teams in the city . . .

Jerrod must have sensed Rachel's embarrassment. He took her in his arms and kissed her on the forehead, on each cheek, on the tip of the nose and on the chin. 'Baby, you're so talented and so beautiful,' he said, trying to soothe her, 'and I really appreciate all the thought you've put into this, and if we hadn't already cracked it I would definitely take this in and show the guys . . . It's just a couple of weeks too late.'

Rachel recognised Jerrod's tone well. It was one she'd used many times before when critting average student portfolios. He was trying to let her down gently. She'd been so sure this work was spot on. But maybe he was right; she had been working in a vacuum after all. Justin was in LA, so she'd had nobody to bounce her ideas off. Left in isolation a creative person can easily become so immersed in their own ideas and crawl so far up their own ass that they can't see the wood for the trees. It happened all the time and was one of the main reasons that creatives worked in teams.

Rachel let Jerrod embrace her. How could she have been such an idiot? she wondered. How could she have been so vain as to believe she could think up an award-winning advertising campaign for one of the world's foremost automobile companies, off one of the industry's toughest briefs, while sitting on the toilet? Rachel scooped the sheets of layout off the coffee table and shoved them back into the portfolio bag. 'You're right,' she said. 'It's crap, isn't it? I don't know what I was thinking.'

'Come on, dry your eyes, baby girl.' Jerrod wiped a tear off her cheek with his thumb. 'Let's go have dinner. I'm starving and I made my world-famous spaghetti Bolognese.'

Jerrod took Rachel's hand and led her into the kitchen. He took down a couple of plates and dished up, then he opened a bottle of wine and lit the candles on the dining room table. It was the first time they'd eaten in the dining room for weeks and so although Rachel didn't have much of an appetite she made an effort to finish everything on her plate; she didn't want Jerrod to think she was sulking or being ungrateful.

'You know what, Rachel, I've been so swamped that I almost forgot,' Jerrod said, swirling the last of his wine around the inside of his glass. 'Our below-the-line creative department is looking for a new writer. How about I put in a good word for you? How does that sound?'

'Thanks, babe,' Rachel said, swallowing a mouthful of pasta. 'That would be amazing. I really need to get out of Target and anything you could do to help me would be awesome.'

After dinner they washed up together and Jerrod danced with her across the kitchen floor with soapy hands to something by Jack Johnson playing on the docked iPod. Rachel knew he was trying to sugar-coat his rejection, and she appreciated his efforts, after all he could have simply told her outright that the work sucked. She was lucky he was being so nice about it.

Back in the lounge Jerrod surfed around until he found another basketball game. Rachel hated basketball, but she wasn't in the mood for anything else either. She stared blankly at the screen, watching her and Jerrod's reflection bounce back at her. Later, they went to bed and made love. Rachel was relieved it took longer than eleven minutes, but when Jerrod grunted out his orgasm she faked hers. He fell asleep straight away, leaving her to stare at the ceiling till she found sleep some time around three.

Rachel Marcus is an idiot.
June 9 at 11.59pm via Mobile Web

Rachel Marcus is going to focus on her own work from now on.
June 10 at 9:04am

The first thing Rachel did when she got back to her desk at Target was to clear away any remnants of the pitch work. She tossed the sketches and scamps into the bin, then she emptied the bin into the trash in the kitchen. Back at her desk she sent all her pitch folders to the trash icon on her desktop.

Are you sure you want to delete 'Pitch Ideas' from the trash? Yes. No. asked the computer.

'Yes!' she said out loud and clicked all her crappy, embarrassing, half-baked, toilet-generated thoughts off to the virtual trash can in the sky. Now she would be able to focus on her real work, the stuff that paid the rent and the whiskey and shoe bills. Rachel picked up the Sanitex competition campaign job bag and carried on copy-checking where she'd left off two days earlier.

Rachel Marcus is the queen of sanitary pads, or rather, feminine hygiene products.
June 10 at 1:56pm

'So, Sue, how was last night?' asked Rachel, twisting the phone cord around her fingers.

'No, you first,' said Sue. 'Did he love your pitch work?'

'No, not really.'

'What happened? Did you show it to him?'

'Yeah, but I was wrong, Sue. In retrospect the work just isn't good enough.'

'Is that what he told you?' asked Sue sceptically. 'And you believed him?'

Rachel looked down at the scamp pad where she had doodled Jerrod's name over and over with dozens of tiny pencilled hearts around it. 'I wasn't seeing the bigger picture, Sue,' she said. 'This is a massive international thing and I was crazy to think I could solve it on my own. Jerrod was right. It's never that simple.'

'Have you at least asked someone else's opinion?' Sue asked. 'Someone you trust. Surely you should get a second opinion before you accept everything Jerrod says? That's what I'd do.'

'If Justin was around I suppose I would have shown him. But he's shooting in LA.'

'When's he coming back?' asked Sue.

'Today, some time. He should be in this afternoon.'

'Well, like I said, I'd get another opinion before I toss all that hard work out the window,' said Sue

'Sue, I actually agree with what Jerrod said about my work – it really just wasn't good enough. I have to be realistic here. Anyway, it's super confidential, so I actually couldn't show it to anyone anyway, even if I wanted to. But, Sue, I'm done with all that now. Let's talk about something else. How's the baby-making business?'

'It's all right. I suppose we'll keep on trying till we get it right.' Sue sighed. 'Listen, Rae, I've got to go, I'm on deadline. Do you want to do dinner with us tonight?'

'I can't, Jerrod's taking me out. I think he's trying to cheer me up.'

'That sounds nice. So things are good with you guys again?'

'Yes, amazing. Maybe we just needed something like this to get us closer again.'

'Maybe,' said Sue. 'Chat later?'

'Absolutely,' Rachel replied, hanging up.

Rachel Marcus **is all hunky-dory.**
June 12 at 1:56pm

'Hi, babe, it's me.' Jerrod's sexy voice travelled through the telephone, into her ear and down her spine.

'Hi, is everything okay?' asked Rachel, suddenly nervous. Jerrod barely ever called her at work during the day.

'Everything's fantastic!' he said. 'Pack your bags, baby girl, I'm taking you away for the weekend.'

'Wha …?' stuttered Rachel.

'I've booked us into a little inn in Vermont for the weekend. You'd better get home and pack your bags, not that you're going to need clothes.'

'But, Jerrod, don't you have to work this weekend? Isn't your presentation next week?' Rachel suddenly felt stressed; she was seriously in need of a bikini wax.

'Yup, the presentation is next week, but like I said last night, we've pretty much cracked it all. We've got a whole team of illustrators coming in, I just finished briefing them, and they'll spend the entire weekend drawing up all the images we need for our presentation. Then we'll spend Monday and Tuesday putting it all down into presentation format, dropping the renderings into the story boards and putting in the headlines and body copy. So there's really nothing left for me to do for the next couple of days other than take you away for a DW.'

'What's a DW?'

'A dirty weekend, silly girl. Hurry, pack a bag and don't forget those yellow crotchless panties. Maybe it's time to dust them off and take them for another ride! They'll be just what we need in the countryside, a little bee action!' Jerrod laughed at his own joke.

Rachel cringed at the bee reference. She still hadn't quite gotten over the humiliation of the incident.

'I would say I'd pick you up outside your apartment, but I still don't know where you live,' he continued. 'Can you be at my place by six?'

'See you then, Jerrod.' Rachel hung up and smiled. Who needed an incredible career when you had an incredible boyfriend?

Justin was back from LA and Rachel had to admit she'd missed him. She'd become so accustomed to having him in the apartment and looking across her desk at him every day that when he was gone he left behind a large gap. She had so few friends in New York that when just one of them wasn't around she really felt it.

'That was Jerrod,' she said, looking across the office to where Justin sat behind his Mac.

'I gathered,' he said. 'How is the old chap these days?'

'He's taking me away for the weekend, so you'll have the apartment all to yourself. Will you be all right?'

'Of course, I'll be fine. I was planning to go to a couple of NA meetings and there's an exhibition I want to see at the Guggenheim … And also I need to start looking for my own apartment.'

'You're moving out?' asked Rachel.

'My month is almost up, so I'll be getting my salary back and you'll be getting your privacy and your life back.'

'Oh,' said Rachel. 'Well, there's no need to hurry, I don't mind having you around. In fact, I kind of like it. Anyway, who's going to plaster up the holes and keep the couch warm if you're not there?'

Justin shrugged.

'Hey, do you think Dan will let me off a little early today?' asked Rachel.

'I saw him in the Zen garden earlier. Good luck. Don't get us fired.'

It was a weak joke, but it still made her smile.

Rachel hummed as she walked down the corridor and straightened her hair before knocking on Dan's door. 'Hi, Dan, it's Rachel, do you have a second?'

'Come in,' he chirped in his squeaky voice.

Rachel pushed the door open. The swami was lying on the leather couch reading a *GQ* magazine but she couldn't see Dan. It was only on her second sweep of the office that she spotted him on a yoga mat on the plastic grass behind his desk. He was wearing a black leotard, underneath which were a pair of black Lycra footless tights. A pink sweatband was stretched around his forehead, matched with one on each of his wrists. Rachel didn't know much about yoga but if she had had to guess she would have said that Dan was currently in the Curled Pretzel Position. 'I'm sorry,' she blurted, looking away quickly. 'I didn't realise you were busy. I'll come back later.'

'It's fine,' he said, untwisting his body and returning to the middle of the mat with his legs crossed in front of him, each foot balanced on the opposite knee. 'Come in, Rachel Marcus, and join me in some ritual cleansing.'

Across the room the swami farted and Rachel noticed that he'd fallen asleep with the *GQ* covering his face.

'Don't pay any attention to Shamandar,' Dan said, 'his third chakra has been blocked for quite some time now and we're working on clearing it.' Dan got up, walked over to his desk and picked up a brown drink, wiping beads of sweat off his forehead with the sweatband on his wrist. 'Lentil smoothie?' he asked, offering Rachel a sip.

Rachel scrunched up her nose. 'No, thanks. I was wondering if I could have a word?'

'Of course, Rachel Marcus, my soul has many ears. Those that hear the words that you say and those that translate your karma.'

Shamandar punctuated Dan's comment with another fart and Rachel had to muffle a giggle.

Dan sat down and once again Rachel was forced to avert her eyes. Seriously, she thought, no man over forty should be allowed to wear a skin-tight Lycra leotard.

'Dan, my boyfriend wants to take me away on the spur of the moment for a weekend in Vermont, and I really need to get a bikini wax and pack a suitcase. So, I was wondering if you'd mind terribly if I left a little early today?'

The second the words were out of her mouth Rachel regretted saying them. She had debated whether to tell Dan about the wax or just make something else up, but in the interests of good karma she had decided to go with the truth for a change. The only problem, Rachel reflected, was that Dan, being the hippie he was, probably liked a fuller bush and may not appreciate the importance of a good, strict bikini wax before a dirty weekend.

Dan appraised Rachel and thought about it for a second. Then he opened his desk drawer, took out a Magic 8-Ball, shook it a couple of times and read the answer out loud: 'Probabilities seem good,' he read.

'Is that a yes?' asked Rachel.

Dan nodded. 'Have a miraculous weekend, Rachel Marcus,' he said, standing up and stepping towards her, extending his sweaty sweat-banded arms for a hug.

'Thanks so much, Dan, I really appreciate it,' Rachel said, backtracking out of the office and then escaping down the corridor before he could reach her.

Leaving early, a dirty weekend away with her sexy boyfriend and no hug from Dan, she loved her life.

Rachel Marcus is going to Vermont for a DW. See you all on Monday.
June 12 at 2:51pm

'Check this, Jerrod,' Rachel shouted from the bathroom. 'Our hotel room is so fancy it's even got a telephone next to the toilet.'

'It's not a room, it's a suite,' Jerrod said, picking up the remote control to see what channels they had got.

'And look at this view … That must be the orchard. How did you find this place?'

'Someone at work told me about it,' he said, popping open the complementary bottle of champagne and pouring two glasses.

'Well, I love it. It's so romantic and I don't think I've ever seen such a big bed. Ooh, look, here's the brochure for the spa.'

'You can have any treatments you want,' he said, kissing her neck. 'We can book them first thing in the morning. I really need a massage; my shoulders are so stiff.'

Rachel took a sip of champagne, then she put her glass down and took his glass out of his hand and put that down too. With a naughty smile she lifted Jerrod's shirt over his head and kissed him. He ran his hands under her shirt, tickling down her spine.

'Thank you for bringing me,' she said, standing on her tiptoes and curling her arms around his neck. Then she pushed him backwards forcefully till the back of his legs knocked against the bed and he fell back onto the mattress. She dropped to her knees between his open legs, unbuckling his belt and freeing him from his jeans and his shorts. Then she took him in her mouth, slowly and gently at first, and then harder and faster. She decided it was the least she could do if she was to expect a manicure, pedicure, facial, full-body exfoliating wrap and a full-body massage this weekend.

Later, they put on plush white bathrobes and ordered room service. 'Look, they have apple-picking,' said Rachel, browsing through the hotel catalogue with her mouth full of chicken Kiev.

'And there's an art gallery in town I want to check out,' he said, cutting into his sirloin.

'Or we could just stay in our room all weekend?' Rachel said.

'You see,' said Jerrod. 'You're full of good ideas.'

'Speaking of good ideas,' she said, 'I want to hear all about your pitch work.'

'Rachel, you know I can't talk about it, it's top secret.'

'Aw,' Rachel faux pouted.

'All I can say is Laurence, our CEO, was so blown away that he reckons there's not a chance London could do better. Those were his words.'

Rachel felt her face flush as she remembered the ideas she'd shown him. In hindsight her work had been nothing more than mediocre.

'And I've got more good news,' he said, lifting his glass in a toast. 'I wanted to wait till we were here to tell you, so we could celebrate.'

'What?' Rachel asked, holding her breath in suspense.

'They're flying Stewart and me to London next week to present the pitch ourselves.'

'Wow, that's incredible! Congratulations!' Rachel put her empty plate down on the coffee table and climbed into Jerrod's lap, kissing him on the lips and clinking her glass against his. 'I'm so proud of you, babe! You're such a rock star! Hey, while we're talking about work, you didn't by any chance manage to chat to the guys in your below-the-line department about that job did you?'

'Shit!' Jerrod cursed. 'Rachel, I'm so sorry, I completely forgot. What with all this excitement over the pitch and now the trip, it completely slipped my mind. I'll do it next week, I promise.'

'That's okay, I know how hectic you are right now.'

'I'm sorry I can't tell you about the work, babe, but maybe it's a good thing. This way you get to see the finished work fresh and I can get your honest opinion on it. You know your opinion means the world to me, right? Oh, wait, I almost forgot!' he said, lifting her off his lap.

He dropped to his knees on the floor and dug around in his suitcase, then turned back to her and walked on his knees till he was kneeling right in front of her. 'Rachel,' he said, suddenly serious. 'I know I've been a bit of a dick the last couple of weeks, and I haven't been easy to live with, but this weekend is my way of saying thanks for being so patient with me.'

He pulled a box out from behind his back and handed it to her. It was white and had a deep-blue silk ribbon wrapped around the outside. Jerrod picked up his champagne and stood up with an enormous boyish grin on his face as Rachel untied the ribbon and opened the box. A layer of tissue paper covered the top of the box and when Rachel moved it aside she found an intricate, deep-blue corset made of Victorian lace and threaded with the softest, most delicate silk Rachel had ever felt. She reached her other hand into the box and pulled out a matching G-string and garter belt.

'Oh, Jerrod!'

'Do you like?' he asked.

'I don't like, I love. They're gorgeous.'

'I can't wait to see it on,' he said.

Rachel held the lingerie up in front of her body and looked in the mirror. She dropped her robe and stepped into the panties, which fitted perfectly. Past her shoulder in the mirrored reflection she noticed that Jerrod had taken a video camera out of his suitcase and he was turning it on, fiddling with the settings. 'What's that?' she asked.

Jerrod, not recognising the mounting panic in her voice, walked towards her and Rachel heard the zoom as he zeroed in on her face, and then panned down. 'I brought my camera,' he said, grinning. 'I thought we could make some home movies.'

Rachel covered her naked breasts with her one hand, holding the corset limply by her side in the other, her heart pounding. Memories of Phillip and that terrible morning flooded her mind and she felt the bile rise from her stomach up into her throat. She dropped the lingerie, grabbed her robe and ran into the bathroom, locking the door behind her. Leaning her back against the door she slipped down onto the floor.

'Rachel,' shouted Jerrod. 'What's going on? You can't try it on in there if you don't take it with you!'

Rachel struggled to breathe. She heaved a couple of times and then crawled on her hands and knees over to the toilet bowl, where she vomited.

'Rachel,' he said, through the door. 'What's going on? Are you okay? Bad chicken?'

Rachel couldn't answer. Tears rolled down her cheeks as she wiped her mouth and then heaved, vomiting again.

Jerrod knocked on the bathroom door. 'What's the matter? Babe, are you okay?'

Rachel tried to remember to breathe. It was only a camera she told herself. Just because he's got a camera doesn't mean he's like Phillip.

The phone mounted on the wall above the toilet roll started to ring. Rachel stared at it as the little red light on it flashed on and off. Finally, she reached for it and held it to her ear.

'Baby, are you okay?' Jerrod's voice was gentle on the other end of the line.

Rachel sniffed into the phone and wiped her nose on the sleeve of her robe.

'What happened? Did I do something wrong?'

'It's not you,' sobbed Rachel. 'It's the camera.'

'I don't understand,' he said. 'It's just a camera. Come out of the bathroom so we can talk about this.'

Rachel replaced the handset and lay down on the bathroom floor, the cool tiles chilling her burning cheeks as she stared at a spot on the wall and waited for her breathing to even out. She thought about Phillip back home in South Africa. She knew she'd never really let herself mourn the abrupt ending of their relationship or allowed herself the time she needed to heal after his betrayal. When she'd lost her job so soon after she'd lost him there hadn't been time to mourn. She'd shoved it to the back of her mind time and time again when it resurfaced. She had thought he loved her but she'd been wrong. She just didn't understand how she could have been so wrong.

As the sun went down the bathroom darkened – the light switch was on the outside. Rachel knew she would have to peel herself off the floor at some point, but she just couldn't do it yet. She cried some more, grieving for every lost relationship she'd ever had and every man who had ever hurt her. She shed tears over the ones who had cheated on her, the ones who had lied to her and then finally over Phillip, who had ripped her heart out in the cruellest way. She was so over being brave.

Hours later she pulled herself up off the floor and checked her reflection in the mirror. Her hair and make-up were destroyed, her eyes were red and swollen and her nose had made a snail trail down her face. She washed her face, tied up her hair, brushed her teeth and opened the bathroom door. The suite was in darkness except for the blue light the TV cast across the room. Jerrod was lying on the bed watching golf, but when Rachel came out he muted the volume with the remote control. She climbed onto the bed next to him. Jerrod reached out to touch her. 'Don't,' she said.

The camera sat on the bedside table staring at her. She averted her eyes. She couldn't look at it.

'I'm sorry I freaked out,' she said in a quiet voice, raspy from crying so much. 'It's not you. Back home something crap happened to me.'

Jerrod nodded, encouraging her to continue.

'Remember I told you I was engaged?'

Jerrod nodded again.

'His name was Phillip. We were together for four years.' Rachel breathed deeply and carried on. 'For his birthday in December I bought him a digital camera. On Valentine's Day he took me out for dinner; it was very romantic and we discussed the wedding, which was supposed to be this December. After dinner we went home, we'd been living together for two years, and the next morning we fooled around when we woke up. We were naked and Phillip picked up the camera. He thought it would be sexy to take some pictures. Afterwards, he went to the shop to get a newspaper and some milk for coffee. While he was gone I started looking through the photos on the camera. I wanted to delete the ones of me that weren't flattering.' Rachel laughed and shook her head at the irony of it.

Jerrod was listening intently, still clutching the remote control.

'So, I started scanning through the photos, and I couldn't believe how many he'd taken. I deleted some. And then I saw a strange one. It was of a woman with long blonde hair, lying naked, spreadeagled and blindfolded on a bed. She was tied to the bed by her wrists and ankles with black leather straps and she had an eagle tattooed on her hip. There were dozens more of the same girl in all these different positions. And I could see bits of Phillip in some of the pictures – his hand or his leg. I had given Phillip that camera in December. This was in February. The photos were recent and the girl in the photos was lying in the same bed, on the same linen I was lying on at that moment. The same white duvet. My Egyptian cotton, four-hundred thread-count duvet! So I left him. Then a week later I got fired over the whole dog food thing. So, in the space of a couple of weeks I lost everything because of that fucking man and that fucking camera.'

'Rachel, I didn't know. I would never have brought the camera out if I'd known.'

'I know,' she said. 'I suppose I just got a little freaked out. No cameras, okay?'

'No cameras,' he said, tossing the camera into his suitcase next to the bed.

Rachel curled up under his arm and he stroked her hair. She closed her eyes and tried to stop the disturbing images from playing and replaying on the inside of her eyelids. She'd managed to banish them for all these months, but tonight they'd made a comeback with a vengeance. A few minutes later she felt Jerrod reach for the remote and heard golf commentary waft back through the room.

'I'm sorry, babe, I didn't even try on the lingerie properly,' she said in a tired, half-asleep voice. 'It is beautiful and I do love it.'

'That's all right, angel,' he said. 'There's always tomorrow night. Anyway, the US Open is on now.'

Completely emotionally drained Rachel fell head-first into sleep.

Rachel Marcus is back from Vermont.
June 14 at 8:51pm

'Hi honey, I'm home,' Rachel shouted, banging on Sue and Brian's front door.

Sue opened the door and gave Rachel a big hug. 'How was it? We missed you.'

'Here I bought you these,' Rachel said, dumping an enormous bag of fresh Vermont apples into Sue's arms.

'Cool, you went apple-picking,' said Sue.

'Not really,' said Rachel. 'We barely left the hotel room ... Oops, sorry, I mean suite. We picked those up for you on our way back into the city this afternoon.'

Sue laughed. 'Sounds like you had a good time?'

'It was unbelievable. We had a little hiccough on Friday night but it was all over by Saturday morning. There was a spa at the hotel and Jerrod bought me just about every treatment on the menu. He spoilt me completely. Look at my nails.'

'Ooh, pretty!' Sue cooed, admiring Rachel's fingers.

'How are things here? Everything okay with Justin?'

'He seems fine,' said Sue. 'He had dinner with us on Saturday night and I think he went to a couple of meetings ... Did you know he's started apartment-hunting?'

'I know. It's going to be weird without him here. And Jerrod's going to London in a week to present his pitch, so I'll be home alone.'

'Don't worry, sweetie,' said Sue, 'I'm always just across the hallway.'

'Will you call me from London?' asked Rachel, standing on the street corner outside Jerrod's apartment in one of his T-shirts.

'Of course, baby. I'll only be gone for a couple of days,' Jerrod said, rubbing his hands up and down her naked arms to try keep her warm.

'You've been working so hard, you must be exhausted,' said Rachel.

'It's okay,' Jerrod said into her hair, 'I'll sleep on the plane. They're flying us first class. Anyway, I've got so much adrenalin for this meeting, I don't feel tired.'

The taxi driver tossed Jerrod's suitcase into the trunk and opened the passenger door for him curbside, then he climbed into the driver's seat and waited impatiently for his passenger. 'I'd better go, I don't want to hit traffic on the way to JFK,' Jerrod said.

Rachel stood on her socked tippy-toes and kissed him goodbye. 'Good luck with the pitch, my sexy genius.'

'Thanks, I'll call you when we land.' He gave her another kiss and climbed into the cab.

Rachel waved as she watched the cab drive off, berating herself for the hundredth time for being so vain as to think she could come up with the campaign on her own when it had taken a team of at least twenty people made up of the top strategists, marketers, client service people, researchers and creatives that New York had to offer, all working flat out for over a month and a half to do it.

Rachel Marcus is hunting apartments with Justin, she may need a shotgun.
June 20 at 10:32am

'I don't understand what was wrong with the last one ...' said Justin, stepping over a rat carcass that was lying on the kitchen floor of the ninth apartment they had looked at that morning.

'Is that a dead dog?' asked Rachel.

'No, silly, it's a rat.'

'Are you sure? It looks big enough to be a dog.'

'I'm positive, Rachel. Now, seriously, why didn't you like that last one?'

'Well, for starters it was the size of a cardboard box and I'm not even exaggerating,' said Rachel. 'I thought I was living in the smallest apartment in New York, but that was ridiculous.'

'Oh,' he said. 'And the one before that? What was wrong with that one?'

'Other than the fact that there's a hole in the floor?' asked Rachel. 'You can see down into the apartment below you, Justin!'

'So, what do we think?' asked Doreen, popping her pouffy red head back into the kitchen.

'I think I'll take the one we saw with the hole in the floor,' said Justin.

Rachel groaned.

'Ah, yes, the fixer-upper. Good choice.' Doreen smiled and made a note on her clipboard.

'Justin, you don't have to do this,' said Rachel. 'What part of there's a hole in the floor don't you get?'

'It's nothing a strategically placed rug won't fix,' he said. 'It's cool. A rug will really tie the room together, don't you think?'

'I just don't want you taking a dodgy apartment because you feel like I'm chasing you out of my place,' Rachel said. 'Why don't you stay with me a little longer and take your time looking for something a bit more ... a bit more ...' Rachel trailed off, she was at a loss for words. 'A bit more ... you know, liveable.'

'Rachel, Jerrod will freak if I stay with you any longer. When I answered your phone the other morning while you were in the shower he just about lost his tonsils.'

'I suppose,' said Rachel, opening a kitchen cupboard and then slamming it shut again quickly to keep the bugs inside.

Justin turned to Doreen. 'When can I move in?' he asked.

Rachel Marcus is holding thumbs for her boy in London today.
June 22 at 10:41am

Rachel Marcus is calling it a day after another crazy day in advertising.
June 22 at 6:12pm

The waiter delivered plates of food to the table and Rachel, Sue, Brian and Justin redistributed them so that each one ended up in front of its rightful owner. Sue was having the chicken, Brian had a full rack of ribs and both Rachel and Justin had ordered a steak. Once everyone had their food Justin picked up his story where he'd left off when the waiter arrived.

'Where was I? Oh, yes, so I arrived at the community centre, but I was running late for the AA meeting, so I just ran into the room where I'd had a meeting before. There were already about ten or twelve people sitting on chairs in a circle, and because I was a bit late the meeting had already started, so everyone turned around and stared at me when I walked in.'

'That's awkward,' said Sue.

'Just wait,' he continued. 'So, anyway, they all made a big fuss about getting me a seat and welcoming me into the circle.'

'Were there any famous people there?' asked Rachel, interrupting him.

'No, silly, that only happens in the movies. Addicts, alcoholics and junkies are actually very boring in real life, and not very attractive.' Justin paused. 'Okay, so I joined them, and they went back to where they were in the circle. It was this big fat guy's turn. He was really ugly, with these pockmarks all over his face, and he was telling this story about how he had been sleeping with his wife's sister and his wife's best friend and his wife's hairdresser. Finally, he also admitted to having sex with his wife's mother!'

'That's disgusting,' said Sue.

'Did he say if his wife's mom was hot?' asked Brian.

Sue punched Brian hard on the shoulder.

'What? It's an important detail,' Brian moaned.

'Anyway,' Justin continued as Brian nursed his shoulder, 'he told us that he had managed to keep it all a secret the whole time. None of them had known he was boffing all the others. But then, in a fit of guilt, the wife's sister was at the hairdresser and she confessed to the wife's best friend in front of the wife's hairdresser, and so they figured out he was doing all of them. Then the three of them got together and told the wife and she kicked him out!'

'That's vile!' said Rachel as Brian and Sue cracked up.

'So, then the next guy in the circle was this very tall thin guy wearing a grey three-piece suit. He began by telling us all about how he was actually super conservative: he and his wife go to church every Sunday, he sings in the church choir, he's an accountant, et cetera, et cetera. And then he told us that he had had a threesome with these two black she-male hookers on his way home from work the day before and still made it home in time for "pot roast" Tuesday.'

'You're kidding!' said Sue.

'Nope,' Justin said. 'It's all true. But, obviously, by then I'd realised that I was in the wrong meeting. It was a sex addicts meeting, not an Alcoholics Anonymous meeting, but I couldn't leave after listening to all these people tell their most intimate stories. And I was next in line. So, I figured I was going to have to make something up, but I couldn't think of anything that was bad enough to match any of the things the other guys there had done and it needed to be realistic. I started to sweat. It was going to be my turn any second and because I was new to the group everybody was looking at me. So ...'

Rachel's cellphone rang. She looked down at the illuminated screen and clapped her hands. 'It's Jerrod,' she squealed, 'calling from London.'

She answered the phone. 'Hi, baby,' she shouted and then felt rather foolish because the line was so clear he could have been sitting at the next table.

'Hi, Rachel,' Jerrod said.

Sue, Brian and Justin watched her intently, listening in on her half of the conversation.

'How'd it go?' she asked, crossing her fingers on top of the table.

'It was awesome!' he said. Rachel thought he sounded like he'd been drinking. 'The client loved us, babe! London office went before us but they totally bombed. It was the most positive presentation I've ever been in!'

'That's fantastic,' said Rachel. 'I'm so proud of you.'

'They bought all of it Rachel. They signed it off and gave us the go ahead. We start production as soon as we get back to New York!'

'That's unheard of!' said Rachel.

'I know! They say it's the best work they've ever seen. They're so excited about it, babe. They even gave us an extra two million dollars to pump up the budget! I gotta go ... We're going out to celebrate. I'll call you tomorrow but I may be hung-over. I love you, baby!' Jerrod hung up.

'What happened?' asked Sue.

All eyes were focused on Rachel. 'He said "I love you"!' she stuttered with a dumb grin on her face.

'Oh, sweetie, that's fantastic!' shouted Sue, jumping up and flinging her arms around Rachel's shoulders.

'That's great!' said Brian, patting Rachel on the back. 'What about his presentation, how did that go?'

'Oh that,' she said, dismissing it with a wave of her hand. 'It went great. They bought it all and they go into production as soon as they get home.'

'Let's get some champagne,' said Sue, throwing her arm in the air to try and get a waitress's attention. 'Or some grape juice,' she added, casting a nervous glance over at Justin.

'Sorry, Justin,' said Rachel. 'I interrupted your story.'

'Nah, don't worry,' he said. 'I'd already told the good part.'

Rachel Marcus is three words richer.
June 22 at 11.12pm

Later, Rachel lay in bed wearing one of Jerrod's T-shirts. 'Are you all right, Justin?' she asked through the darkness. 'You barely said a word on the way home.'

Rachel didn't get a response. He was probably already asleep, she thought. She rolled onto her back and thought about how everything was starting to come together at last. Jerrod had told her he loved her. She played the phone call over in her mind again and again, wondering if it was the excitement of the moment or the booze that had made him blurt out the words. Then she thought about the fact that he hadn't really given her a chance to respond. She wondered how she would respond if he said it to her again. The answer was as obvious as the nose on her face. There wasn't a doubt in her mind; she would absolutely say 'I love you' back. She closed her eyes and imagined he was lying next to her.

Rachel Marcus is about to be alone in her apartment again. Except for the rats and cockroaches, of course.
June 23 at 5:37pm

'Have you got everything?' Rachel asked Justin.

'I think so, but if I've left anything behind you can always bring it to work for me, right? It's not as if we're never going to see each other again.'

'I know, but I feel sad. I'm going to miss you.'

'Between now and when you see me at work at nine tomorrow morning?' Justin asked incredulously. 'Think of it like this: you're not losing a housemate, you're gaining a couch.'

'You make a good point. Now I can reinstate my ban on all things football on my TV.'

'That's the way,' said Justin. 'Silver lining and all.'

'Oh, I almost forgot ...' said Rachel. She rummaged around in her cupboard and pulled out a long fat tube with a red ribbon around it.

'What is it?' asked Justin.

Rachel handed it to him. 'It's a housewarming gift.'

Justin took it from her and untied the bow, unrolling it. 'It's a rug! I love it!'

'It should fit perfectly over the hole in the floor,' said Rachel.

Justin gave her a hug. 'Rachel, I want to thank you for everything you've done for me.'

'Don't be silly,' she said, feeling her throat go thick and scratchy. 'Anyway, I didn't do it for you, I did it for myself, to protect my own job, remember? I'm actually rather selfish.' Rachel smiled and Justin laughed.

'I mean it, Rach, I don't want to get all soppy here, but I wouldn't have made it out the other side of this in one piece without you.'

'Look,' said Rachel, wiping her eyes, 'just 'cos you've got your own pad now doesn't mean any of the rules change. I expect you at work sober every morning.'

'Done.'

They hugged again. Then Justin kissed Rachel on the lips, lingering for a second before pulling back from her, still holding both her arms. Rachel stood dead still; he'd never kissed her on the lips before and she wasn't sure how to react. He blinked once, smiled and then picked up his bags and made his way out of the door.

Rachel Marcus is looking forward to a quiet night in front of the telly.
June 23 at 6:04pm

Rachel paced the length of the apartment. It took her three seconds. This was the first time she'd had the place to herself in months. She walked into the bathroom and looked at the patch on the wall where the rat hole had been. Then she looked in the fridge. There wasn't a drop of booze. She shook her head, wondering if Sue had any whiskey.

Plonking herself down on the couch Rachel thought about Jerrod flying home to her. She still hadn't brought up the 'I love you' phone call with him. She'd spoken to him earlier in the day when he'd called from the airport, horribly hung-over – Rachel could almost smell the booze fumes down the telephone – but he'd simply told her that he'd see her when he landed and that had been it. She wondered again whether he'd planned to say 'I love you' the night before or whether it had just slipped out. She also wondered whether he remembered that he'd even said it. Rachel decided not to mention it. She would wait and see what happened when he got back. Either way, he'd said it and she'd heard it and that was what mattered.

Rachel picked up the remote control. 'Hello, old friend,' she said. 'No more football, you have my word.' Then she turned on the TV and flipped through the channels.

There was a quiet knock on the door.

'What did you forget, Justin?' she shouted, climbing off the couch and making her way towards the door. 'I told you, you're going to have to buy your own hair gel now.'

Sue stood on the doorstep, arms by her sides, tears rolling down her cheeks.

Rachel pulled her inside and led her to the couch. 'What is it?' she asked, panic rising in her chest. 'Is everything okay, Sue? Where's Brian?'

Sue battled to get the words out through giant sobs that made her whole body shake. 'He's next door … We had a massive argument …'

Sue's chest heaved as she struggled to take in gulps of air. Rachel grabbed a brown paper bag from the kitchen, emptied some fruit out of it and handed it to her. 'Here,' she said. 'Breathe into this. Try taking long, slow breaths. Everything is going to be all right, just breathe.'

Sue's eyes were wide above the bag as she heaved in and out, slowly getting herself together enough to take the brown bag away from her mouth.

'I'm making tea,' said Rachel as Sue curled up on the couch, sobbing quietly. 'I would bring you a stiff drink but I got rid of all the booze while Justin was here.'

By the time Rachel carried the tea to the couch Sue had already worked her way through three quarters of a box of tissues. She looked like she was curled up on a white fluffy cloud.

'Thank you,' said Sue, taking the tea, her shoulders still shuddering.

'What the hell's going on, Sue?'

'I really screwed up, Rachel.'

'Tell me what happened, Sue. You're scaring me.'

'My period is a couple of days late.'

'Really? That's fantastic!' shrieked Rachel. 'Is that why you're crying? I would be terrified too. I think it's normal … But you don't have to be, it's going to be amazing.'

'No, that's not it,' said Sue. 'Brian noticed my period was late … He said he's been keeping track of my cycle. Can you believe that? He brought home a pregnancy test and we did it.'

'And?' asked Rachel, eyes wide.

'It was negative.' Sue broke down again, sobbing and heaving.

'Aw, sweetie,' said Rachel, rubbing Sue's shuddering back. 'It's okay, you can try again. You've only just started; it takes a while. Everything is going to be so fine. In fact, one day you'll be sitting in your rocking chair surrounded by all sixteen of your children and everyone will laugh their asses off when you tell them this story.'

Sue smiled weakly. 'No, Rae, that's not it.'

'What then?' asked Rachel.

Sue took a deep breath. 'Brian started talking about fertility. He wants us to go see a specialist. I completely lost my temper and we ended up having a terrible fight. I said the worst things imaginable to him. I was so awful. I told him I didn't want to have his baby! I can't believe I said that!' Talking about it brought the tears back to her eyes.

'Oh, honey, please don't cry,' Rachel said. 'Everything is going to be fine. You just reacted badly. It's a hell of a shock to find out you're not pregnant, especially when you're late. Maybe Brian's timing wasn't the best, bringing up fertility when you're already feeling a little raw, but he didn't mean it. Men don't have any tact. Just go back in there and talk about it. Everything is going to work out.'

'No, Rachel,' said Sue, more forcefully. 'You don't understand. There's something else I haven't told either of you.'

'What?'

'Remember I told you I had an abortion when I was thirteen?'

'Yes.'

'I didn't tell you the whole story. The boy who made me pregnant was twenty.'

'Oh, Sue!' said Rachel, covering her mouth with her hand.

'It was terrible. My parents were furious. My dad never looked me straight in the eye again after that. He was so hurt and shocked. My folks just didn't know how to deal with it. And the boy and his family left town.'

'Oh, Sue, that must have been awful,' said Rachel, 'you were just a little girl!'

'My mom took me away for the weekend. We told everyone we were going to visit my grandmother, but we went to this clinic in another state where they gave me an abortion on the Friday. We stayed at this disgusting cheap motel till the Sunday, then we drove back home again, and everybody pretended nothing had happened. But I didn't stop bleeding. The nurse said it was normal to bleed for a couple of days afterwards, but five days later I was still bleeding really heavily, so my mom didn't have a choice, she had to take me to the local doctor. He told us that I had an infection and that when they did my abortion they didn't get everything out. I had to have an emergency D and C. They gave me an anaesthetic and when I woke up the doctor told me it was all sorted out. My mom wouldn't talk to me about it, and when I was better we all just carried on with our lives, like none of it had ever happened. A couple of years later I started dating Brian and I suppose that's mainly why we left home together when I turned eighteen. Things with my folks and my sisters were never really the same after that.'

'Sue, that's a terrible story.'

'There's more, Rachel. When Brian and I started talking about having a baby a year ago I went to see a specialist on my own, just to make sure I was all sorted and ready to go. He did some tests and he told me I can't have children. Rachel, there is an absolute zero per cent chance that I can fall pregnant. There's nothing they can do about it. The abortion and the operation afterwards caused too much damage and that's it.'

Rachel looked into Sue's tearful brown eyes and her heart sagged.

Here was an amazing woman who'd found a perfect man and they'd never be able to have their own baby. 'Does Brian know you went?' she asked.

Sue shook her head.

'So, he doesn't know you can't have a baby. This whole time he's thought you've been trying?'

Sue nodded.

'Oh, my God, Sue, you have to tell him.'

'I know,' said Sue, the tears welling up again. 'I've tried, believe me. But I don't think I can do it. I don't think he'll ever be able to forgive me for not telling him. I was going to, I always meant to, but then when it actually came down to it I could never get the words out. I thought if I never actually said the words out loud then it wouldn't have to be true.'

'Sue, I really think he'll understand,' said Rachel. 'I think he'll be angry at first, and you'll have to ride that out, but he loves you so much. I mean, the two of you are like one person. It's not your fault that this happened to you, Sue. But you're going to have to tell him.'

'I don't think I can cope with losing him, Rachel,' Sue sobbed. 'His father was a bastard. He left them when Brian was just a baby. His whole life he's only ever wanted children, so he can give them all the love he never got, and now I have to tell him we can't have any . . .'

'Whatever happens I'll be here for you, Sue.'

'Promise me you won't mention a word of this to Brian. I need to tell him myself, in my own time,' sniffed Sue.

'I promise.'

They sat together in silence for a long time.

Eventually Sue stood up to go. 'I guess I'd better go apologise for what I said.'

Rachel gave her a big hug. 'Do you want to borrow my bee outfit?' she asked, trying to lighten the mood. 'You said a sexy outfit always worked for you before when you guys fought?'

Sue shook her head. 'I think I'm going to need a lot more than a sexy outfit to get out of this one,' she said and took a very deep breath, then she left, closing the door behind her.

Rachel Marcus is so much for a quiet night in front of the telly.
June 24 at 2:13am

Rachel Marcus is looking forward to having her baby back from visiting the Queen.
June 24 at 9:36am

'Jerrod, you're back!' Rachel breathed into her cellphone.

'Hi, babe, we landed at about six, but I didn't want to phone and wake you up.'

'I missed you!' Rachel said.

'It's nice to be home, but I'm exhausted. The trip was intense and we have our first pre-production meeting first thing tomorrow morning.'

'This is so exciting. I'm really proud of you.'

'Wanna do lunch today?' he asked. 'We could go for sushi. I brought you something skimpy back from London.'

'I'd love to but we're meeting the sock people to show them the copy for their new packaging.'

Jerrod snorted out a laugh. 'Body copy for sock packaging … sounds challenging.'

Rachel's ego stung. 'We can't all work on massive international car campaigns and spend our lives jet-setting first class around the planet, Jerrod. Some of us have to stay home and do the mundane stuff that pays the rent.'

'Aw, baby, I was only teasing you.' He chuckled. 'So, no to lunch then?'

'I can do dinner if you want? We could go back to that rooftop place you took me to after Art Directors Club.'

'Okay, but it can't be a late night. I need to be fresh for my pre-prod tomorrow morning.'

'Okay,' said Rachel, 'I promise not to pour enormous amounts of very expensive champagne down your throat and then drag you back to your place and spend hours performing obscene sexual acts on you. You have my word.'

They set a time to meet and Rachel hung up with an enormous Cheshire cat grin on her face.

Rachel Marcus is making promises she can't keep.
June 24 at 9:52am

Rachel chewed the end of her pen and thought about Sue. Her confession had been a shock. Rachel had always assumed she'd be aunt to dozens of Sue and Brian's either freakishly tall or freakishly short offspring and that they would all live together across the hallway from each other, happily ever after. She dialled Sue's number.

'Hey,' Sue answered after the second ring.

'You sound bleak. How did it go?' asked Rachel.

'Not so good.'

'Did you tell him?'

'No, I couldn't,' said Sue. 'But at least he forgave me for the nasty things I said last night, although it was still very raw this morning when he left for work.'

'You know you have to tell him soon,' Rachel said as gently as she could.

'I know, Rachel, but not yet, okay. I need last night to blow over a bit first; it's still all a bit too tender.'

'Whatever you choose to do I'm behind you a hundred per cent.' Rachel said,

'Thank you, that means the world to me. Just promise you won't say anything. I need to do this my way.'

'I promise, Sue, you have my word.'

'So,' said Sue, 'is Captain Advertising home yet?'

'Yup, he's taking me back to the Ivory Tower tonight.'

'Lucky girl,' said Sue.

'I can't wait to see him. He said he brought me something skimpy back from London.'

'Diamonds can be skimpy, can't they?' joked Sue.

Rachel laughed. 'You sound better today, Sue. I'm glad. Just promise me you won't hold off on telling Brian for too long, okay?'

'I promise.'

Rachel Marcus is excusing herself to go and slip into something a little skimpier.
June 24 at 5:43pm

Rachel rode in the elevator up to the Ivory Tower wearing a sexy, silver, low-cut, knee-length dress and a pair of very high silver heels. Underneath that she wore the lingerie Jerrod had given her in Vermont.

Memories of her first night with Jerrod filled her mind as she stepped into the lounge and a sudden warmth streamed through her veins. Jerrod hadn't arrived yet, but the waitress showed her to the same couch they'd occupied that first night. Rachel thought it either sheer luck or a well-planned romantic gesture on Jerrod's behalf. Hoping it was the latter, she settled in and ordered champagne.

Five minutes later Rachel felt hot breath on her neck and a pair of hands covered her eyes. She felt Jerrod's mouth on her neck and goose bumps ran all the way up the length of her left leg and exploded like fireworks in her crotch. 'Honey, I'm home,' he whispered in her ear.

Rachel jumped up to kiss him. She felt like he'd been gone for weeks, even though it had only been a couple of days. 'Welcome back,' she said as they settled on the couch. Her cheeks were flushed from the kiss and she felt like every nerve ending was on fire. The waitress poured them each a glass of champagne. 'Here's to having you back,' she said, clinking her glass against his.

'Has Justin moved out yet?' asked Jerrod.

'Yes.'

'Well, then I'll drink to having you back too,' he said and kissed her again.

'Tonight, it's just me and you,' she said, coyly rubbing her leg up against his.

Jerrod's eyes lit up and he reached into his pocket and pulled out a small package tied up with a white silk ribbon. Inside was a delicate layer of tissue paper, stamped with the La Perla logo. Rachel opened it and pulled out a lacy black G-string, the thong part of which was made up of at least a dozen perfect white pearls. 'It's gorgeous, Jerrod,' she whispered. 'I love it.'

'You can thank me later,' he said into her ear, nibbling on her ear lobe.

Later, in Jerrod's en suite bathroom, Rachel took off the lace panties from Vermont and put on the pearl G-string. It was, she was certain, the most beautiful, but also the most uncomfortable single item of clothing she had ever owned. She hobbled from the bathroom into the bedroom, trying hard to look alluring, but by the time she got round to her side of the bed she was in agony. Nothing like a bruised butt crack to make a girl feel sexy, she thought.

Climbing onto the bed Rachel said a little prayer of thanks as Jerrod slipped the panties off. She'd never been so happy to see a piece of clothing tossed across the room in her life. Surely, she thought, something so uncomfortable could only have been designed by a man. Jerrod kissed Rachel's neck and ran his hand down her body. A flush rose to her cheeks as they kissed and Jerrod's fingers feathered down her spine. Rachel rolled him onto his back, then she kneeled astride him and ran her fingers down his chest. She kissed him on his neck, and flicked her tongue over his Adam's apple and down the middle of his chest, kneading and massaging his body gently as she went. Then she began to massage his shoulders, feeling the tension start to melt away as she worked his muscles between her fingers. Slowly she moved down his chest and when she reached just below his belly button she stayed there, teasing him with her tongue and her fingers, letting her hair wash over his stomach. After a few minutes of this she raised her head, shook her hair out of her eyes and looked up into his face. Jerrod's head was turned to the side, resting on the pillow, his eyes were closed and he was snoring lightly.

Rachel Marcus is a victim of jet lag.
June 24 at 11:49pm via Mobile Web

Dear Mom and Dad,

Sorry I haven't written in a bit; things here have been crazy busy at work and with Jerrod. Thanks for the newsy letter and parcel which I received today. Imagine my excitement when I opened it and discovered a box of Five Roses tea. I was completely over the moon. I just couldn't believe it when I opened it and found it was empty.

I wasn't sure why you would send me an empty box until I opened your letter and discovered that you'd sent the box to ensure that you had the right product because you were worried that you kept sending the wrong thing.

I'm pleased to say that you have finally found exactly the right thing. Please can you put a box of this into the mail right this second, before you do anything else. I'm now more desperate for a cup than ever before. Just putting my nose in the box and smelling it, I could almost taste it. It was very difficult for me.

I'm glad you finally made it to Incredible Connection, but I'm sure the shop assistant wasn't actually fifteen and only looked like a teenager. I'm also really pleased to hear that you bought a DVD player. What great news! I've been trying to talk you into getting one for years. I never understood how you still manage to use a VHS. Do they even make those tapes anymore? Although I have to say that I was really hoping you'd take a look at the computers while you were there.

Love and miss you,
Rachel

Rachel Marcus would kill, maim and disfigure for a cup of genuine Five Roses tea right now.
July 15 at 2:29pm

Rachel and Justin were at their desks when Dan's swami walked in, closely followed by the man himself. The swami was wearing a pair of khaki chinos, a loose-fitting white cotton shirt and a pair of sneakers. In contrast, Dan was wearing a custard-yellow dashiki and his purple Crocs.

'Brother Dan is fasting today and he has taken a vow of silence,' said the swami as the two men made their way to the couch and wedged themselves in. He had a surprisingly deep voice and Rachel realised that this was the first time she'd ever heard him speak. She glanced over at Justin, who looked equally surprised.

'This is another step on the road to true enlightenment,' the swami continued, 'and so today I will be his voice. Today we are at one, together.'

Dan nodded.

'Brother Dan has asked me to discuss his needs with you while he is unable to speak,' the swami went on. 'He wants you to begin work on an important project. He needs you to reach for inspiration within yourselves and draw on the power of your creative souls in solving this most important job for the company of Target Advertising.'

Rachel felt excitement at the prospect of doing an important job and Justin also suddenly seemed more alert. She wondered about the mystery brief, hope welling up. She didn't want to get overexcited but she wondered if she could be so lucky as to finally get to work on something bigger than a packaging insert. Maybe a radio commercial or even, dare she dream, a print ad.

'Brother Dan will be visiting his psychic now, but he will return in two hours, and then he will evaluate your ideas in this most urgent matter,' said the swami, shifting in his seat.

Dan had closed his eyes and was nodding. Rachel wasn't sure if he was nodding at what the swami had said, if he was in a trance or if he was just sleeping.

'Two hours doesn't give us very much time,' said Justin.

'Yes,' said Rachel. 'Especially if it's a complicated job.'

'As the great swamis say,' said the swami, 'when there's a deadline, there's a deadline.'

Rachel and Justin glanced at each other.

'But I can tell you this,' the swami continued, raising one finger, 'brother Dan has enough faith in you to feel confident that this is a task you will embrace in these few hours. Remember, time is what keeps the light from reaching us. There is no greater obstacle to Buddha than time.'

The swami took a deep breath and Rachel and Justin watched him expectantly. He was dragging the moment out like a reality TV host before a commercial break.

'Brother Dan has requested that you conceptualise something to prove just how committed you are to making things work here at Target,' the swami finally said. 'He is in need of a birthday card for the managing director of the RightSole Corporation.'

Having delivered his message the swami stood up with his hands clasped together in front of him as if in prayer. Dan, however, remained seated, his eyes still closed, until the swami gave him a swift kick in the shin. Immediately, Dan's eyes shot open and he jumped up, bowing once to Rachel and then again to Justin before following the swami out of the door.

'Fuck!' said Rachel.

'What a pile of bollocks!' said Justin.

'I can't believe this is what we're reduced to, Justin! A freaking birthday card!'

'What do we look like, bloody Hallmark?' said Justin, kicking at the leg of his desk.

'Well, I'm not working late on this crap,' said Rachel. 'I refuse. Jerrod and I have plans tonight, and I haven't seen him in over a week.'

'Why so long?' asked Justin.

'He's busy shooting that campaign,' Rachel grumbled. 'It's been an insane schedule. They are putting in fifteen-hour days on set. Then, when he's not shooting he's either entertaining the client, who's here from Germany, or he's so exhausted that all he wants to do is sleep – to be honest, I think he's still jet-lagged from the trip to the UK. Anyway, they're wrapping early tonight and he's taking me for dinner. So, I'm going to make us some coffee and when I get back we're going to nail this birthday card. I'm not leaving any room for Dan or his stupid swami to keep us here late tonight, all right?'

Justin nodded, tearing the top sheet off his layout pad to reveal the crisp, blank sheet below it.

Rachel Marcus is working hard for her money.
July 15 at 5:45pm

'Where do you think Dan is?' asked Rachel, pacing a hole in the office carpet. 'He was supposed to be back here before half-past five.'

'Maybe his psychic told him she saw an art director punching him in the face in his very near future and it freaked him out?' Justin said, doodling on his pad.

'It's not funny,' Rachel said, starting to feel her panic rise. 'I'm going to be late for dinner. I'm supposed to meet Jerrod at his place at seven and I still need to go home and change and I'm seriously in need of a shower.'

'Tell me about it,' said Justin.

Rachel shot him an icy glare.

'I'm sure Prince Charming will understand if you're a little late and a little stinky, Rachel.'

'No, he really doesn't like it when I'm late. It makes him grumpy, and that's the last thing I need right now, it will spoil our whole evening.'

Justin put his hand over his mouth and said the word 'wanker', disguising it weakly in a cough.

'That's really mature, Justin,' said Rachel.

'Chill, Rach, I'm sure Dan will be back any minute.'

Rachel carried on pacing, watching the hands on the clock tick around past six o' clock and then quarter past. She tried to call Dan, but both his and the swami's cellphone went straight to voicemail. At quarter to seven, close to tears, she picked up the phone and dialled Jerrod's number. 'Hey, Jerrod,' she said, when he answered after the fourth ring.

'Hi, babe.'

'How's your shoot going?'

'It's been a long day, but a good one. I'm looking forward to seeing you tonight. I thought we could open some wine and throw a couple of steaks on the grill. I feel like I haven't seen you in ages.'

Rachel's stomach wrenched. 'About that,' she said. 'I'm still at the office. We're waiting to review this ridiculous job with Dan. He was supposed to be here over an hour ago, but he hasn't pitched yet.'

'Oh,' said Jerrod, sounding disappointed. 'What's the job?'

'Babe, don't laugh, okay? It's ridiculous … It's a birthday card for one of our clients.' Rachel flushed as she told him. Why did her job have to be so Mickey Mouse? She should have lied, she thought. She should have said it was a competition or a print ad, anything more dignified than a birthday card for a sock client.

There was silence on the other end of the phone. She could hear Jerrod breathing. 'What about dinner?' he asked.

'I suppose Justin and I will order something in,' she said.

'Of course,' spat Jerrod, 'Justin. I should have known.'

'What's that supposed to mean, Jerrod?' Rachel asked, her voice suddenly hardening. 'Do you really think I'd rather work on a birthday card than spend the night with you?'

'Well, you don't sound too unhappy about it. I don't understand why you have to stay late on a birthday card, Rachel, it sounds like bulshit to me!'

'Jesus, Jerrod, I only just got my job back, and it's not like I'm Dan's favourite person right now. He gave us a deadline and told us not to leave before he got back. I think he's testing us. I can hardly just ignore it because it's not a ten million dollar TV ad! I need this job, no matter how crap it might be.'

'Rachel, I could have gone out for dinner with the client and the crew, but I blew them off and came home to be with you!' Rachel recognised the anger building in his voice.

'I can come over straight after we've seen Dan,' Rachel said, trying to placate him. 'I just don't know what time it will be.'

'Don't bother, Rachel! I've got a six a.m. call on set tomorrow morning. Enjoy your dinner with Justin.'

'Jerrod . . .' she said, but the phone was already dead in her ear.

Rachel stood with the phone still balanced in the crook of her neck.

'Wanker,' coughed Justin again, into his sleeve.

Rachel glared at him. 'You're not helping matters!' she said through gritted teeth.

Dan wafted into the office. 'Sorry I'm late, team,' he said, taking his place on the couch.

'I thought you took a vow of silence?' said Justin.

'Only between nine and five,' said Dan.

'Where's the swami?' asked Justin.

'He has a date tonight,' said Dan. 'They're going for ribs. So, how's my birthday card coming? Roger Ballast is a very important client.'

Rachel sucked in a deep breath. 'Roger Ballast? From Sanitex?'

'Yes,' said Dan.

'The swami said it was for the RightSole client. We've done a card based on a sock joke!'

'Oh, dear,' said Dan. 'That's no good. You'll have to start over.'

'You were here in the room when he briefed us, Dan!' wailed Rachel. 'Sitting right there!'

'I was?' said Dan, surprised to hear it.

'Well, you can't expect us to come up with something now and have it ready by tomorrow morning,' said Justin. 'It's after seven, we've been here all day and Rachel has plans tonight, don't you Rachel?'

Rachel shrugged her shoulders and stared at her desk.

'Who said I need it for tomorrow morning?' asked Dan. 'His birthday is only on Tuesday.'

Rachel closed her eyes and let the frustration and anger wash over her. She wanted to shout at Dan. She wanted to cross the office and smack him in his stupid face. She wanted to swear at him and tell him what a dumb, short, squeaky voiced lunatic he was. She wanted to stomp on his Croced feet and pull his idiotic ponytail. She wanted to yell at him and tell him that she was a top above-the-line copywriter and she didn't want to spend another second of another minute of another day working in his two-bit business for his pathetic, ridiculous clients. Instead, she breathed deeply, counted to ten and tried to find her happy place. When it wouldn't come she counted to twenty.

After Dan left Rachel picked up the phone and dialled Jerrod's number again. 'Maybe I can still catch him?' she said to Justin as she dialled. 'Maybe this day won't be a complete write off?'

But Jerrod's phone went to voicemail.

Rachel Marcus is a series of unfortunate events.
July 15 at 11:43pm

Rachel was in her kitchenette burning a bag of microwave popcorn when suddenly she heard shouting. She concentrated on trying to isolate specific words, but the noise was scrambled by the walls. Finally, after several minutes, she heard Sue and Brian's door slam. Rachel felt stapled to the ground. Perhaps it was her imagination, but the entire apartment block seemed suddenly very quiet. Even the freak on the fifth floor had stopped playing chopsticks for four seconds. A few seconds later Rachel heard a very gentle knock on her door. When she opened it Sue stood there, shoulders quaking and quiet tears rolling down her face. They didn't need to speak. Rachel hugged her gently and then pulled her into the apartment, closing the door behind her. She led Sue to the couch and sat her down, then she took out a fresh box of tissues, made two cups of sugary tea and took the bits of popcorn she could salvage, the tea and tissues to the couch. Sue had her head bowed so low it was almost between her legs while great heaving sobs wracked her body. All Rachel could do was sit next to her, rubbing her back and passing her a fresh tissue when she had doused the one she was using.

Some time after midnight Sue eventually stopped sobbing. Rachel led her to the bed – she was like a ghost, barely present – handed her a glass of water and two sleeping pills, slipped her shoes off and covered her with a duvet. Sue sucked in deep trembling breaths of air as Rachel took the blanket and pillow Justin had used and made up a bed on the couch for herself. She lay staring up at the ceiling, thinking about Sue and Brian and what they were going through. Rachel also thought about Jerrod, so busy with his shoot and now furious with her. She wondered if he really loved her or if it had just been the booze talking back in London. She wondered if they would find it hard to fall pregnant like Sue and Brian. Then she took a deep breath, recognising, as she did so, the smell of Justin on the pillow. Oddly, she thought, he smelt like the ocean.

Hours later, still lying with her eyes open, Rachel heard Brian come home – it sounded like he was bouncing off the walls as he walked down the corridor. Rachel looked at her watch: it was after three in the morning. She heard him fumble with the lock. Then she heard him drop his keys and swear. He fumbled some more, swore some more, kicked something, swore again and then eventually, when Rachel was about to get up to go and help him, she heard him get the door open.

Rachel rolled over on the couch. At least he was home safe, she thought as she snuggled under the thin blanket and said a little prayer that Sue and Brian would get back together soon. Mainly because she really loved them, but partly also because she couldn't imagine sleeping on this terrible couch for more than a couple of nights. As she drifted off to sleep she wondered how Justin had managed it for a whole month.

Rachel Marcus is worried about her friend.
July 16 at 7:15am

'Do you mind if I stay here for a while?' asked Sue the next morning. They were the first words she'd said since she'd arrived on Rachel's doorstep the night before.

'Of course, Sue. Stay as long as you need to. What did Brian say when you told him?'

'He was furious, Rachel. He told me to get out. He said I'd ruined his life.' Sue rubbed her red, swollen eyes. 'I don't know if he'll ever be able to forgive me for deceiving him.'

'Wait, I think I hear him,' said Rachel. She ran to the door and pressed her eye against the peephole. 'He's leaving for work.'

Sue started crying again as they listened to him clomp down the passageway. 'Rachel, will you get a couple of my things for me?' she sobbed. 'I don't think I can go in there.'

Rachel waited a couple of minutes and then, still in her pyjamas, she let herself into Sue's apartment. The remnants of dinner from the night before lay on the dining room table, the sink was full of dishes and the bed was unmade. Rachel cleared up – moving around the apartment silently, making the bed and picking up the odd item of clothing – before packing a couple of Sue's things into a suitcase. Then she went into the bathroom, picked up the pink toothbrush and popped it into Sue's toiletry bag, leaving the tall blue toothbrush alone in the cup. She felt the tears start to well up as she looked at the lonely toothbrush, and sinking down onto the lowered toilet seat lid she tore off sheets of toilet paper to mop herself up with.

When Rachel walked in the door of her apartment, dragging the small suitcase behind her like a stewardess, Sue was sitting on the couch hugging a pillow. 'Sue,' said Rachel. 'This isn't going to be for long, you guys will sort this thing out soon, you'll see … He just needs a day or two to calm down.'

'Maybe, but I wouldn't blame him if he never wanted to speak to me again,' sobbed Sue.

'Sue, that won't happen and you know it, he loves you too much,' Rachel said, wheeling the suitcase to the bed, lifting it up and unzipping it. 'You just need to be a little bit patient,' she added, looking down and wondering how they were both going to fit all their shoes into her tiny apartment.

After helping Sue unpack Rachel had a shower, got dressed and made her way begrudgingly into the office, leaving Sue on the couch. Rachel had work to do – there was the revised birthday card and later, if she was lucky, a RightSole quarterly report to copy-check.

Rachel Marcus is working on stinking socks again.
July 16 at 12:37pm

'How's Sue holding up?' Justin asked.

'Not so good. She said to thank you for the dinner invitation tonight but she's not up to going out right now. To be honest, she's a bit of a mess,' said Rachel, walking around his new apartment and familiarising herself with the space.

Justin was in the kitchen, wearing an apron. He had a different pot on each of the four rings on the stove and foodie smells that Rachel couldn't quite pinpoint were billowing out into the rest of the apartment.

'The rug looks good,' Rachel said.

'I know!' he said with a grin. 'And you can't even tell there's a hole in the floor.' Justin paused. 'Okay, dinner's ready,' he announced, turning away from the stove with a full plate in each hand.

Rachel picked up his soda and her water and followed as he made his way over to the couch. 'Thanks for inviting me for dinner,' she said. 'It smells great.'

'It's my pleasure. I had to have a house-warming to break in the new place and I thought it was the least I could do considering how much you've done for me over the last couple of months.'

They sat down and Justin handed her a plate which she balanced on her knees. 'It may need salt,' he said.

'Cheers,' Rachel said, raising her glass. 'Here's to your new apartment and to being sober. Just look at how you've turned your life around; it's very impressive.'

'I'll drink to that,' Justin said, clinking his glass against hers. 'Here's to one day at a time.'

They sipped their drinks and then put them on the floor next to the couch. Rachel mixed the pasta and chunky sauce together then she twirled some onto her fork and lifted it to her mouth. The first thing that she tasted was salt, then something like leather. She chewed the piece of rubberised meat but her teeth seemed to have no effect – nothing broke down in her mouth. Justin seemed to be having a similar problem. She smiled at him and carried on chewing. Eventually, she swallowed the piece of old shoe whole, feeling it sludge its way cautiously down her throat.

'Beef?' she asked after she'd taken large sip of her drink to help push the mystery meat down her gullet.

'Chicken, actually,' he said.

Rachel raised an eyebrow in shock. 'Oh. It's very … it's … um …'

'It's fucking disgusting, is what it is!' Justin said, spitting his mouthful back out onto his plate. 'Here give me that … Quick, before I poison us both.' He grabbed the full plate off Rachel's lap and dumped it in the sink along with his own. 'That's vile … I'm so sorry. Come on, let's order pizza.'

'Oh, thank God,' said Rachel. 'I was terrified I was going to have to force that down just to be polite. What on earth was it?'

'It was supposed to be some chicken and pasta thing,' he said. 'I think I was always trashed when I made it before. Cooking sober is a whole new ball game.' He smiled and picked up the phone. 'Luckily for you, ordering pizza is something one can do drunk or sober.'

Once he'd called in the order Justin sat back down next to Rachel. 'How are your meetings going?' she asked.

Justin fiddled with his iPod, looking for something to play. 'I go every day,' he said. 'They help. Hey, what should we listen to?' Justin shifted on the couch and his leg touched hers.

During the course of an average day at work they often touched and Rachel knew it shouldn't feel strange, but for some reason under these circumstances, alone together in his apartment at night-time, everything felt completely different. Only a couple of centimetres of Justin's leg was touching hers but her leg was on fire where it touched his. Rachel wasn't sure if Justin had even noticed. He carried on scrolling through the iPod's menu casually. She didn't know what to do. If she pulled her leg away he might notice but she felt so uncomfortable that she didn't feel she could stay the way she was. There was a knock on the door. 'Pizza's here,' she said just a little too loudly, jumping off the couch, grateful for the distraction. 'I'll get plates.'

Justin paid the pizza guy and laid the boxes on the kitchen counter. Rachel stood with an awkward smile pasted on her face as Justin opened a box. Steam and the delicious smell of pepperoni and melted mozzarella wafted up towards them. As Justin bent to place a slice on a plate one of his locks of curly blond hair fell over his eye. Instinctively, Rachel reached across his face and swept it away. The action made Justin turn towards her. He reached for her wrist and wrapped his fingers around it, holding her hand up next to his face. Rachel felt her pulse beat in Justin's fingers or it could have been his pulse, she couldn't tell. Then he leaned towards her and kissed her, still encircling her right wrist with his left hand, stroking her pulse point with his finger.

Suddenly Rachel jerked her head back from his. Her eyes wide she stared at him in shock. Then, before she could think about what she was doing, she slapped him hard across the cheek.

Justin stumbled backwards from the slap, his hand going instinctively to his face as he stepped onto the rug she had bought him and fell armpit-deep through the floor.

'Justin!' Rachel shouted, putting her hands up to her mouth. She hadn't meant to slap him. 'Are you all right?'

'Oi!' shouted a very loud voice from the depths of the hole. 'What the hell do you think you're doing up there?'

'He's got my foot!' shouted Justin, a look of panic crossing his face as he started to wriggle frantically, trying to lever himself up with his arms.

Rachel ran around behind Justin and hunkered down. Then, reaching under his arms, she heaved as hard as she could until his body started to shift. Justin wriggled and slithered until at last she managed to pull him free from the hole and they both fell back onto the floor, her arms still wrapped around his chest. They lay there, him on top of her, panting. She could feel his heart racing.

'Who the fuck do you think you are!' the voice continued shouting, from the apartment below. 'I should call the cops!'

Justin jumped up and stared down into the hole. 'Give me back my shoe, you wanker!'

'It's in my apartment, now it's my shoe!' shouted the voice. 'Stay out of my fucking lounge!'

Rachel grabbed at the rug which had slipped down the hole with Justin. As she did so the man in the apartment below jumped up to try and get a hold of the corner of it that had been left dangling out of his gaping ceiling, but Rachel was too quick for him and managed to pull it up out of danger. 'Are you okay?' she asked Justin as she laid the rug back across the hole.

'I think so,' he said. 'That wanker stole my shoe!'

'You kissed me,' said Rachel.

'I remember. Right before you slapped me.' Justin stroked his cheek.

'I wasn't expecting you to kiss me.'

'I'm sorry if I gave you a fright.' Justin stepped towards her again. 'Rachel, there's something I need to tell you.'

Rachel raised both hands palm up and stepped back from him, careful to avoid the hole. 'Justin, I'm with Jerrod, I can't do this. And we work together. I just can't.'

'Rachel, I need to tell you something very important,' Justin said, taking another step towards her.

'I have to go …' Rachel turned around and searched for her bag, eventually finding it next to the front door. 'I'm sorry, Justin,' she said as she picked it up. 'I can't do this. Will you be all right here? You won't drink, will you?'

Justin shook his head. 'No,' he said forlornly.

'Thank you for dinner …' She smiled, realising the stupidity of the comment.

'Stay,' he said. 'At least have some pizza. Come on, I really need to talk to you. It's important.'

'No, I think I'd better go.'

Rachel closed the door and hurried out of the building. The night air cooled her heated cheeks and she decided to walk a couple of blocks to clear her head. Guilt flushed through her body. Why had she let him kiss her? She had a boyfriend she loved; what was she doing? Rachel reached for her cellphone and dialled Jerrod's number. 'Hi, babe, it's me,' she said, when he answered after the eighth ring.

'What is it, Rachel?' he snapped. 'I'm in an edit suite, I can't talk.'

'I just wanted to say hi and see how it's going.'

'Rachel, you can't keep calling me, I'm really busy.'

'Jerrod, I've only been calling you because we need to talk about the other night. And you haven't been answering my calls. I didn't mean to let you down, okay? Look, we're both hectic and stressed right now, and I really miss you. I'm sorry and I don't want to fight, all right?'

Jerrod softened. 'Me neither, babe. I didn't mean to be such a hardass. I'm just really tired right now. This job is taking it all out of me, and I was looking forward to seeing you the other night, so I was disappointed. Where are you?'

Rachel sucked in a breath. She couldn't tell him the truth. There was no way he would ever understand that she had gone to Justin's apartment for dinner. And if he ever found out about the kiss … She shuddered at the thought. 'I'm on my way home from work,' she said, her fingers crossed tightly behind her back. 'I'm going to have a shower and an early night.'

'Tomorrow is our last day of production. Do you want to do something tomorrow night?' he asked.

'I'd love that,' Rachel said, warmth pulsing through her body.

'I'll call you in the afternoon to let you know when I'll be finished,' he said. 'Love you lots.'

'I love you too,' Rachel said, hanging up. She'd said it! Well, first he'd said it, then she'd said it. Well, actually, he'd said 'love you lots'. She wondered if that was the same as 'I love you'. It didn't feel the same. She shook her head. He'd said it and then she'd said it, the rest was semantics.

Rachel walked to the subway her brain racing ahead of her. She toggled between pure joy and sheer guilt. On one hand she felt furious with herself: Here Jerrod was working his fingers to the bone to try secure a bright future for both of them and all she could do was prance around Manhattan kissing other men. And on the other hand he loved her and she loved him: all was right with the world.

Sitting on the subway Rachel decided not to tell Sue about the kiss or the 'I love you's. These days Sue alternated between crying feverishly, working feverishly and sleeping feverishly, and Rachel felt like she had to do everything in her power to keep her from throwing herself out of the window. Next to Sue's problems Rachel knew hers were pathetic. She was well aware that on a scale of one to serious, losing your husband and not being able to have children beat kissing your art director by mistake and then telling your boyfriend you love him hands down.

'I'm home,' Rachel said, letting herself into the apartment and waiting for her eyes to adjust to the gloom. There was only the glow of the television to light the way.

'Hello,' came the weak response from Sue, from where she was curled up on the couch.

Even in the dim light Rachel could tell that Sue was wearing a pair of tracksuit bottoms and one of Brian's old T-shirts. She recognised them instantly as the same clothes Sue had woken up in that morning. Chances were that she hadn't changed all day.

'What you watching there?' asked Rachel.

Sue moved her legs aside to make space on the couch. 'It's the home shopping network,' she said, snivelling.

'Is that Jane Fonda selling pearl necklaces?' asked Rachel.

'Yup,' sniffed Sue.

'Have you eaten anything today, Susie?' she asked.

Sue shook her head.

'Come on then,' said Rachel. 'Let's get some dinner, I'm starving.'

Rachel Marcus is wondering if 'love you lots' and 'I love you' mean the same thing?
July 23 at 11.01pm

Rachel Marcus is making like an ostrich.
July 24 at 8:10am

Justin was already at his desk when Rachel got to work the morning after the kiss. As far as she could remember it was the first time he'd been at work before her and it shook her equilibrium. She had lain awake on the couch half the night worrying about how she was going to deal with the kiss situation. She didn't want things to be awkward. Justin was her work partner and they spent up to ten hours a day together, things needed to be cool between them. At around four a.m. she had eventually settled on the ostrich approach.

'Morning,' she said cheerfully. 'You're in early.'

'Rachel, we need to talk about last night ...'

'Justin,' she said as sternly as possible. 'What happened last night was a mistake. I should never have let it get that far. I don't want things to be awkward between you and me. You're my art director and that's the most important thing. And then there's Jerrod; he can't find out about this. So, I'm begging you, please, can we just pretend it never happened?'

'Rachel,' he said. 'I'm sorry about last night. I don't want you to feel awkward.'

'Good, so then it's forgotten. Let's just move on, okay?'

'No, wait,' said Justin. 'We really need to talk, there's something I need to tell you.'

'Justin, that's not a good idea. Let's not say anything we might regret. I've forgotten it. It's over. All right? Now, what are we working on today?'

Before Justin could speak Dan walked in wearing white-linen pants and a long, loud African shirt covered with multicoloured geometrical patterns. Rachel waited for his swami to follow, but Dan was on his own.

'Morning,' said Rachel.

'Morning, team,' said Dan. 'Oops, I guess I can't call you that anymore, can I?'

'What do you mean?' asked Rachel.

'Well, since Justin no longer works here, you're no longer technically a team and so I shouldn't really call you "team" anymore.'

Rachel shot a glance at Justin.

'I've been trying to tell you, but you haven't let me. I resigned yesterday,' said Justin.

'What? Why?'

'Sorry,' said Dan, 'I hate to interrupt the chit-chat but I've got a breathing and body balance session with my swami in five minutes. Rachel, I want to chat to you about your next job.'

Mouth agape Rachel looked at Dan and then back at Justin.

'I need to brief you on an amazing project,' Dan continued. 'You won't believe it, but I've invented a miraculous, groundbreaking meditation technique. It's quite incredible, I tell you. It's going to revolutionise the way the world meditates. Anyway, we need to get going on this quick-sharp. I'm getting ready to patent it, but I need you to put together a rationale and a brand proposal for me. I think I'm going to call it The Charter Method. What do you think?'

Rachel gulped at him like a fish. 'That sounds, um, exciting ... I can't wait to get started.'

'Excellent.' Dan clapped his hands together. 'All right, I'm in a client meeting all afternoon and then I have a retreat all day tomorrow, but as soon as I get back the day after that we can sit down and I'll brief you in full.'

Rachel nodded in silent horror. Dan opened his arms and for the first time Rachel fell into his embrace willingly. She felt like she needed the hug.

'Justin, I guess when I come back you won't be here anymore?' Dan said, pulling away from Rachel. 'I know we've had our problems, but I wish you a gentle journey into the future.'

'Thank you, Dan,' said Justin as Dan closed in for his hug. 'And thanks again for all the opportunities.'

'What the fuck, Justin?' Rachel said as soon as Dan was gone.

'Rachel, I've been trying to tell you … This is what I wanted to talk about last night and again this morning. In fact, I've been wanting to tell you for days, but you've been so preoccupied with the whole Sue nightmare and all of Jerrod's shit that there's never been a good time to break the news.'

'What's going on?' She felt tears behind her eyes and tried desperately to blink them away.

'I can't stay here, Rachel,' Justin said. 'It's not you, I love working with you, but I'm serious about staying clean and I can't stay in the same place where I've been using all these years. There are just too many memories and too many temptations. I need to change my life. I also need to do work that I'm passionate about again. This sock and sanitary pad stuff is rubbish. I want to make work I can be proud of.'

'What are you going to do?' Rachel asked in a small voice.

'I've got this mate from London, his name's Dane, and he was working at this hot-shot boutique ad agency in London called Blue Monkey. Anyway, to cut a long story short, they're opening a Blue Monkey office here in New York. I've decided to focus on design for a bit, so they've hired me as a senior designer. They're a great bunch of guys.'

'Yeah,' said Rachel dismally. 'I've heard of them. They're really good. That's a great opportunity!'

'They have a couple of brands in London who wanted to align internationally, so it made sense for them to open up a shop here. One of our clients is a record label, so I'll get to design some cool CD covers, and they've got a brand of olive oil and a travel company too … I'm really looking forward to sinking my teeth into some serious design work and that's what they're all about.'

'I just can't believe it. I'm ecstatic for you,' Rachel said, not sounding anywhere near it. 'But I'm shocked, I never saw this coming.'

'Me neither, Rach,' said Justin. 'Dane called me last week out of the blue … But it's the first time I've been excited about work in years. Rachel, I have to take this opportunity otherwise I'll never forgive myself.'

'You really do,' said Rachel, trying to disguise her sadness.

'Rach, I'm so sorry, you must feel like I'm abandoning you here, but it all happened so fast and I had to resign yesterday. That was one of the reasons I invited you over last night. I had planned to tell you, but then …' Justin's voice trailed off.

'When are you leaving?' asked Rachel.

'I had some leave owing me and we're in-between jobs, so Dan said I should go straight away. I think he was kind of glad to be rid of me if I'm honest.'

'I'm so happy for you, Justin. I just can't believe it. This is all happening so fast.'

'Rachel, nothing will change between you and me, okay? We'll still be friends. We'll still talk every day, all right?'

Rachel nodded, but she felt numb.

Rachel Marcus has her office all to herself and she doesn't like it one bit.
July 24 at 11:45am

Once Justin had packed up his desk and left, Rachel stared into her monitor. He hadn't been gone ten minutes and she already felt lonely.

Just the knowledge that she wouldn't be sharing the space with him anymore made her feel bereft. She made herself a cup of coffee and foraged for anything anybody might have left lying around, but the kitchen, much like her office, was bare. Back at her desk her phone rang and she lunged for it, desperate for the company. Even a telemarketer would do, she thought.

'Hello,' she said.

'Hiya, babe.'

'Jerrod, it's you.' The sound of his voice brought tears to her eyes and this time she didn't fight them. She let the self-pity roll unabated down her cheeks.

'Hey, why are you crying?' he asked.

'Justin is gone. He resigned. He left.'

'That's fantastic news,' Jerrod said. 'Now there's nothing holding you back.'

Rachel recoiled, wondering how the man she loved could misunderstand her so much?

'I've got more great news,' he said. 'We just finished the launch commercial and they're distributing the material this afternoon. Are you all set for dinner tonight? I'm taking you somewhere disgustingly expensive.'

'Jerrod, I've really missed you. I can't wait. Where do you want to go?'

'It's a surprise. Be at my place at seven thirty. The limo is picking us up at eight.'

'Limo?' Rachel wiped the tears away from her eyes and sat up in her chair.

'Yup, nothing's too nice for my baby.'

Jerrod hung up but Rachel remained holding the warm phone to her ear. What would she wear? she wondered.

The beeping in her ear brought her back to planet earth and she replaced the receiver. Then she looked over at Justin's desk to tell him the exciting news, but of course he was gone.

Rachel sat back in her chair and chewed on the end of her pen, she didn't like being alone in the office, it was way too quiet without Justin there. Just four months earlier she would have been ecstatic if he'd left, but now she missed him – Target wasn't going to be any fun without him. She wondered whether Jerrod had remembered to put her forward for the job at R&P like he'd promised. He'd probably forgotten, she thought. He'd been so hectic with the shoot. Rachel wrote the word *Job* with a large question mark next to it on the layout pad in front of her and doodled around it. She'd ask him about it when she saw him later.

Rachel Marcus has never been in a limousine before. Tonight's the night and she's taking Jimmy Choo with her.
July 24 at 5:27pm

Rachel fixed her hair in the elevator's floor-to-ceiling mirrored wall and applied her twelfth layer of fresh lipstick since she'd left home. Her stomach felt like it was being used as a jumping castle. It seemed like a very long time since she'd spent any quality time with Jerrod at all and she was excited at the thought of seeing him. She'd really missed him.

Rachel was wearing a short, sequinned, chocolate-brown dress with spaghetti straps and a ridiculously non-existent back – in fact, she'd had to change panties a couple of times to ensure that they didn't peak out the back of her dress. She'd splashed out that afternoon and bought the dress on her emergency credit card. An invitation to dinner with her amazingly sexy and successful boyfriend, transport by limousine and nothing to wear; in Rachel's mind that constituted an emergency.

The elevator door dinged open and Rachel stepped into the entrance hall of the apartment. From where she was standing she could see Jerrod on the other side of the apartment. He was leaning on the kitchen counter with his back to her, talking on the phone. When he heard her come in he turned around and broke out in a broad grin. He waved and pointed at the telephone, shaking his head – the phone was attached to the wall by a curly umbilical cord that held him hostage in the kitchen. He was wearing a black Paul Smith suit and tie and Rachel thought he looked more handsome than ever.

Rachel took a couple of steps towards the kitchen. 'Yes, Mom,' she heard him say. 'I know I've been busy, but I'm tired, okay. We're going to have to do dinner at the club another time, maybe next week.'

The second she heard that he was talking to his mother Rachel took a step backwards. She hadn't seen her since the incident with the bee costume and, frankly, she wouldn't have known what to say to her if she had.

'I know I haven't seen you guys, Mom,' Justin continued, rolling his eyes. 'But I was in London on business, remember? And since then I've been flat out, shooting and doing post-production on this job. All I want to do is have some dinner and a hot bath and climb into bed.' Jerrod grinned at Rachel and winked.

Rachel wandered into the dining room while she waited for Jerrod to finish on the phone, leaning over the back of one of the dining room chairs to smell the flowers arranged in a vase in the middle of the table. She didn't notice Jerrod's briefcase perched precariously on the chair, but as she leaned forward and the chair shifted the briefcase fell to the floor, its contents spewing out across the smooth parquet floor. Rachel lurched to catch it but she was too slow. The contents scattered everywhere. Luckily Jerrod had turned his back again and was deep in conversation on the phone.

Rachel swore and knelt down on her hands and knees, trying to gather up all the papers so she could shove them back in Jerrod's briefcase before he noticed what she'd done. 'Nice one, Rachel, very glamorous move,' she whispered to herself as she shuffled around the floor in a three hundred dollar dress.

Eventually, Rachel managed to gather up all the papers and shuffled them together into some form of order. There were photographic contact sheets and what looked like layouts, scripts and other bits and pieces of work. Rachel stood up and started to pile everything back into the briefcase on the dining room table. It was clearly all the work Jerrod had been busy with for the pitch. Rachel felt excited just to be holding it. She knew it was confidential and that she shouldn't look at it without first asking Jerrod's permission, but she also knew he would probably say no if she asked him, and there was just no way she could stop herself – self-control wasn't her strong suit.

Rachel glanced up again to make sure Jerrod wasn't watching her. He still had his back turned. 'Mom,' he was saying, 'I told you that I'm happy to help you plan dad's seventy-fifth, but I don't think a surprise party is the best idea. We've discussed this before. If you want to have a party at the club that's fine, but he's a seventy-five year old man, are you sure you want to have a hundred of his closest friends jump out of the dark and startle him? Is that really the smartest idea?'

Rachel smiled and returned her focus to all the work piled up in front of her. The top page was an upside down contact sheet which concealed everything below it. It couldn't harm to take a quick peak, she thought. She wouldn't look at everything; she'd just run her eye over a few of the layouts, just to get the general gist of it. She knew she would have to try hard to act surprised when Jerrod eventually showed her the work himself, but she was sure she could pull it off. The temptation of getting a little sneak preview was too much to bear. Anyway, she told herself, it was Jerrod's fault for leaving it all lying right there in the dining room where she could stumble across it. Slowly, she turned the contact sheet on top of the pile over and studied it. It was a series of small thumbnails and Rachel could tell by the ticks and notes that Jerrod had made in the margins next to each shot that he had started to make his shot selections already. As she scanned the shots Rachel was pleased to note that each one was more beautiful than the next. They were of the same gorgeous car speeding down a highway, the sun setting in the background and the pink sky reflecting off its metallic silver body. Rachel admired the artistry of them and shook her head in impressed silence. They were, in a word, exceptional.

She would look at just one more page, she thought, unable to control herself. Turning over the contact sheet she saw what looked like a rough magazine ad layout. Even in its rough format it was simple, graphic and beautiful. She admired the image and then read the headline that accompanied the picture. As far as print ads went Rachel thought the concept was all right, nothing spectacular, definitely above average, but no stonker. Then her eye automatically dropped to the bottom right-hand corner of the page to look at the logo and the pay-off line. Rachel's heart missed a beat. It was genius. The line at the bottom of the ad was simply brilliant; it tied everything together perfectly. She caught her breath. It was an inspired full stop at the end of a beautiful ad.

It was also her line.

Rachel recoiled like she'd been punched in the stomach. Hands trembling she quickly shuffled through the rest of the pages in Jerrod's briefcase. There it was again on the following layout. Her line! And there it was again on the next page. It was the exact line, word for word, that she'd come up with on the toilet at Target Advertising all those weeks ago. The line she'd written that Jerrod had told her wasn't good enough to present. Yet here it was, clearly the golden thread that pulled his entire campaign together and tied it up in a neat and perfect bow.

Rachel dropped the layout she was holding as if it was on fire. 'Jerrod,' she said loudly. 'You piece of shit!'

Jerrod turned around to face her and looked up from his telephone conversation mid-sentence. He caught her eye then looked down at the open briefcase lying on the dining room table. His smile disintegrated. 'Listen, Mom, I have to go,' he said urgently into the telephone.

Rachel felt like she was going to vomit. She reached blindly for her handbag and ran to the elevator, pumping the button with her finger. 'Come on, come on,' she said under her breath.

'Mom, seriously I have to go, something's come up.' Jerrod slammed the phone down and ran towards her. 'Rachel, don't go ... We need to talk about this.'

Just as he reached the dining room the elevator door opened and Rachel flew inside. She rammed her index finger into the G button repeatedly. 'Please, close! Please, close!' she whispered in desperation.

As Jerrod reached the foyer the elevator door closed. 'Rachel, wait!' he shouted, slamming a fist against the closed metal door.

Rachel slumped against the mirrored wall and let out an enormous sob. When the doors opened on the ground floor she burst out of the elevator and flew past the surprised-looking doorman and out into the street. Then she ran past a long black stretch limousine, waiting outside the apartment, shot her arm in the air and hailed a cab, sobbing uncontrollably.

When Rachel got back to her apartment all the lights were off and for a second she thought Sue had gone out, which was strange, since as far as Rachel knew Sue hadn't left the apartment in weeks. Then she recognised Sue's small figure curled up on the bed under the duvet. Rachel threw her shoes off in the dark and climbed, fully clothed onto the couch, where she curled up in the foetal position and cried herself to sleep.

Rachel Marcus is 'Fuck! Fuck! Fuck!'
July 25 at 6:15am

Rachel slept fitfully and at dawn she got tired of tossing and turning and got up. She slipped the wrinkled emergency dress off, dropped it to the floor and pulled on an old T-shirt. She checked her cellphone but there were no messages or missed calls. She turned it off and tossed it into the depths of her handbag, completely disgusted.

Careful not to wake Sue, Rachel made coffee and logged onto Facebook on her laptop. Sue surfaced as the water boiled. 'Morning,' she said, loping into the kitchen bleary eyed and half asleep.

'Morning,' said Rachel. 'I hope I didn't keep you up?'

'Nah, I took two sleeping pills, not even a bulldozer would have woken me last night,' she said, yawning and stretching. 'Anyway, I wasn't expecting you home, sugar. I thought you were with Jerrod?'

'I was,' said Rachel, bursting into uncontrollable tears.

Sue looked up in surprise. 'What happened, Rae?'

Through heaving sobs Rachel unpacked the whole story for Sue. 'What did he think?' cried Rachel, tears pouring down her face. 'That I wouldn't notice he'd used my line when the ads launched in magazines and on TV screens around the world? Does he think I'm that big a moron? I can't believe this monster, Sue! He's been playing me the whole time and I lapped it up! I'm such an idiot!'

Sue poured coffee and sat down across from Rachel at the table.

'Look at the two of us,' she said. 'What did we ever do to deserve this?'

'And I haven't even had a chance to tell you yet but Justin resigned. He already left Target. He's going to work in a hot new British design studio with a mate from London. My life is a complete fuck-up!'

Sue looked at Rachel, their sad eyes mirroring each other. 'Well,' said Sue, 'that's an excuse to stay in our pyjamas and mope all weekend if ever I've heard one.'

Rachel's tears were like a yawn to Sue – she saw them coming and could do nothing to stifle her own.

'I'm going back to bed,' said Rachel. 'Wake me up when this is all over.'

Rachel Marcus is a cry-fest.
July 25 at 7:40pm

'Rachel, wake up.' Sue shook her shoulder gently.

Rachel opened her swollen eyes and stared into the gloom of the early evening. 'What time is it?'

'It's after six. You've been sleeping all day, sweetie. You need to get up and have something to eat. Look, I made spaghetti ... Will you eat something with me?'

Rachel rubbed her eyes. For the briefest moment between asleep and awake she had forgotten what had happened, but now it all came flooding back. She glanced over into the kitchen and remembered the night Jerrod had made spaghetti. It had been the same night she'd shown him her work. Her stomach tensed. The thought of eating it repulsed her, but Sue hadn't been eating properly, so Rachel decided to pretend to eat to keep Sue company. 'Sure,' she groaned, 'just give me a minute.'

Rachel brushed her hair and her teeth and reminded herself that Sue was mourning a marriage, while she was only mourning the loss of a few words and a relationship that had only lasted a couple of months.

Back in the kitchen Rachel sat down at the table and picked up her glass of wine, half-downing it with her first sip. Then the TV caught her eye. The sound was down, but the picture was vivid and Rachel knew immediately what it was. 'This is it!' she shrieked, yanking on Sue's arm. 'This is the ad.'

Grabbing the remote control she tapped the mute button and watched the rest of the ad open-jawed.

'That's a really good line, Rae,' said Sue as the ad came to an end.

'I know,' breathed Rachel, raw fury exploding through her body. She reached for her purse, rummaged around in it and pulled out her cellphone. Turning it on she dialled Jerrod. He answered on the second ring. 'Rachel!' he said.

'I just saw the TV ad, you fucking thief!' she shrieked. 'How could you do that to me?'

'Okay, Rachel, let's not get hysterical here. Can we just discuss this calmly, please?'

'How you can live with yourself, you bastard?'

'Rachel, don't be like that … Come over, let's talk about this. We make such a good team. I've got a business proposition for you.'

'What is it, Jerrod?' Rachel spat. 'Are you're going to credit me on the award entries and tell the guys at R&P that the campaign line was actually my idea?'

Jerrod snorted. 'Don't be ridiculous, Rachel! I can't do that. The brief was confidential, remember! There's no way I can tell them that I told you all about it, I'd lose my job. No, listen, I have another idea …'

'What?'

'If you don't tell anyone that line was yours and never mention it again I'll make sure you get a job as a copywriter in my group at R&P. What do you say, babe? It's a great idea, isn't it? I would be your creative director. You could work below me. It's perfect. You get what you want and I get what I want. Everyone's a winner!'

'Don't call me, babe, you lying sack of shit! I'm going to call Richmond&Phillips and tell them you stole my line?'

'I wouldn't do that if I were you,' he said, so calmly he could have been talking about the weather. 'Why would they ever believe you?

Since when does a below-the-line writer who's been working on sock packaging for the last six months crack a campaign line like this?' He paused to let his words sink in. 'You would just make a complete fool of yourself and then they'd never hire you. You need to think this through, Rachel. You don't want to burn your bridges here. New York isn't as big as it seems, especially in this industry. I'm mates with the creative directors at every agency. One word from me and nobody will touch you with a ten-foot bargepole. At least think about my offer, Rachel. This doesn't have to be the end of the world. You know I'm crazy about you and we could still be together. Nothing has to change, except you'd have the job you're desperate for. Rachel, don't be foolish. It's not such a big deal, this happens in advertising all the time. Call it collective subconscious, call it borrowed interest, whatever ... But it makes sense for you to take me up on this.'

'The only way this makes sense, you sick, twisted fuck,' spat Rachel, 'is if you die and go to hell! This is not collective subconscious or borrowed interest, it's outright theft and blackmail!'

Rachel took the phone from her ear, turned and threw it as hard as she could through the open window above the kitchen sink. It hit her brick-wall view and exploded, the pieces falling the three stories into the alley below. Rachel squeezed her eyes shut and roared with frustration.

'What a complete prick!' said Sue. 'I never liked him. Now tell me every word he said.'

When Rachel had finished Sue grabbed her by the hand and pulled her up. 'C'mon, have a shower; I'm taking you for ice cream.'

Rachel groaned. 'I don't want to. I want to stay here in my pyjamas for the rest of my life. My heart hurts, Sue.'

'I know, honey, so does mine.'

'I mean it,' said Rachel. 'It's a physical pain. My heart is actually aching.'

'Come on then,' said Sue. 'We need chocolate or ice cream, or both'

Rachel groaned again but eventually she got up and dragged her feet into the bathroom. Once inside she undressed slowly and then climbed under the shower, her head hanging low and her arms pinned to her side, the water so hot she almost couldn't bare it.

'Are you all right in there?' asked Sue after half an hour, banging on the door.

'No!' Rachel said.

Later, they walked down the street to the restaurant on the corner where they ordered one of every dessert on the menu.

'Am I making a mistake, Sue?' Rachel asked.

'What do you mean?'

'By turning down Jerrod's offer? Maybe I should take the job and just forget about what happened?'

'What and work in the same group as that prick? Let him take all the credit and just carry on as if nothing happened?'

'Yes,' Rachel said. 'At least then I could get out of Target. Working under Jerrod would be a bit of a nightmare, but it's definitely a step in the right direction.'

'I don't know, Rachel. I mean, it's up to you, but just think about it carefully before you make any big decisions. Like he said himself, he knows all the bigwigs in the industry, and once he's got you in his group he's not going to let you go without a fight. There's no telling what he'll tell them about you.'

'Well, what are my other options? Am I going to still be a copywriter at Target Advertising in five year's time, living alone in a rat-trap shoebox of an apartment? It's not like any other agencies are lining up to hire me and my portfolio isn't getting any better. The only upside right now is having you living right next door. Maybe I just need to suck up my pride and take the job?'

'Rae, about that, there's something I need to tell you.'

Rachel wondered what more there could possibly be.

'I wanted to tell you sooner, but with everything that's happened over the last couple of days, I just couldn't.'

'What is it?' whispered Rachel.

'I've decided to go back home to Alabama.'

Rachel held Sue's gaze and felt the tears prod at her eyeballs again.

'My marriage is a mess, and I don't think Brian will ever talk to me again. I can't just hole up in denial in your apartment forever.'

'Of course you can,' said Rachel. 'You can stay forever and a day and you don't need to worry about rent. Anyway, it hasn't been that long since you told him. He'll come around.'

'No, Rachel. I don't think so. I did a terrible, awful, selfish thing. And I don't think he'll ever forgive me. Hell, I'm not sure even I can forgive me. I have to face reality. My marriage is over.' Sue looked into her coffee cup and Rachel could see she was also fighting back the tears.

Rachel took a deep breath and swallowed. 'Maybe it's not such a bad idea,' she said huskily. 'It might be time for me to start thinking about going home too.'

'No, Rachel, don't let me ruin this for you, just because I'm running away.'

'You're not ruining anything for me, Sue,' Rachel said. 'I've managed to do that all by myself. I also have to face reality. This is hardly what I had in mind for myself here. I've been here six months already and I still live in a shithole, my job is a joke and I barely scrape through every month. I've hardly got any friends, I don't have an art director any more and my relationship ... Well, there's not much more I can say about that. Maybe it's time to admit that New York has beaten me and go home with my tail between my legs. My mother will be ecstatic; I've gone and proven her right again.'

Sue handed Rachel the last paper serviette. Between them they'd managed to empty the entire dispenser.

Rachel Marcus is thinking some very serious thoughts.
July 26 at 9:14pm

Later that night, with Sue snoring from the depths of a two-sleeping pill slumber on the couch, Rachel lay in bed staring at the ceiling, trying to work out how she was feeling. It wasn't too late, she thought. She could still pick up the phone and talk to Jerrod. She could apologise for overreacting and see if he would still consider getting her that job. A big piece of her missed him terribly; just the thought of not having him in her life anymore was devastating.

Rachel felt overwhelmed and confused. Eventually, she gave up on sleep, sat up in bed and reached for the notepad and pen she kept on her bedside table. It was time to make a list.

STAYING AT TARGET

PROS
– It pays the rent on shithole apartment

CONS
– No art director
– Will work on sanitary pads for the rest of my life
– Dan

Wait, she thought, this wasn't working. Even her pros were actually cons. She tore the page off the pad, crumpled it up, dropped it on the floor and started another list:

TAKING THE RICHMOND&PHILLIPS JOB

PROS
– It's not Target
– It's a step in the right direction
– There's no Dan
– Might get to do work for portfolio

CONS
– Will have to work under Jerrod
– Will have to see Jerrod every day
– No reason Jerrod won't continue stealing my ideas
– Once Jerrod has me in his group he'll never let me go

'Fuck!' Rachel swore out loud. There was no way out of this. Jerrod had her by the throat. He wouldn't let anyone else hire her, but if she worked for him he would have first dibs on all her ideas. Sitting in bed in the rat-trap shoebox, Rachel realised she only had two choices left: stay at Target indefinitely or go home.

Rachel Marcus is stick a fork in me, I'm done.
July 27 at 3:14am

Rachel Marcus is cough, cough, cough, playing sick.
July 27 at 7:42am

Rachel woke up early and decided to bunk off work for a couple of days. She really wasn't in the mood to take Dan's crap and she also needed to figure out what her next move was going to be.

Dan answered after the fourth ring. Rachel knew it was a safe bet calling him so early. When he was in town he always got in around six a.m. to do his meditating without distractions. 'Dan Charter,' he said, his voice a gate in need of oil.

'Morning, Dan, it's Rachel,' she said, putting on her very best sickly voice.

'Ah, Rachel Marcus, good morning.' He breathed deeply as he spoke and Rachel was assailed by an unpleasant mental image of him on the mat in his leotard.

'Hi, Dan,' she coughed.

'Yes, Rachel. What's up?' he asked.

'Um,' Rachel coughed again, this time more dramatically.

'Yes, you were saying?' asked Dan.

'I'm sick, Dan,' she said through another cough, trying to sound as weak as possible.

'You are? Oh. That's terrible. What's the problem?'

Rachel coughed again.

There was silence on the line. Dan wasn't getting it.

'It's my chest, as you can hear,' Rachel wheezed. 'I have an infection. I'm not going to make it in today or tomorrow, and probably not Wednesday either. I'll more than likely be back by Thursday.'

'But Rachel we need to start work on The Charter Method proposal asap. There's a tight timeline on this and I don't want to miss my window.'

'I know, and I'm super excited to get started,' Rachel lied, 'but I don't want to make everyone at Target sick.'

'Okay, I suppose we'll see you on Thursday then ...' Dan sighed. 'But remember, Rachel, we have all the tools we need for healing within ourselves, at our very core.'

'Thanks, Dan, I'll remember that.' But as she put the phone down tears started to race each other down Rachel's face. Dan was right, she thought, she could heal herself, but this time it was going to take a very long time.

Rachel counted out the hours on her fingers – South Africa was six hours ahead of New York – then she picked up the phone, dialled her mom and tried to put on a smiley sounding voice by pasting a big fake smile on her face. 'Hi, Mom, it's me, Rachel.'

'Rachel! Harold, it's Rachel ...' her mother yelled. 'She's on the phone. Pick up the extension. Harold!' Her mother paused for a moment as if listening for some sign that her father had heard her. 'How are you, Rachel?'

'Good thanks, Mom. You don't have to scream; it's a good line.'

'Is everything okay? Are you eating? How's your skin?'

'It's good, everything's good, thanks. Listen, I was thinking about maybe coming home some time soon.'

Her mother shrieked loudly, and Rachel winced at the pain in her ear drum. 'It's about time! I was just saying to your father that you need to stop being so stubborn and come home already ... Harold!' she shouted into Rachel's ear. 'Harold, Rachel's coming home! Pick up the extension!'

'Rachel, your father will be so pleased. I'll call Uncle Jules straight away and find out if the receptionist's job is still available at Zip World. Oh, what should I do about your Five Roses tea? I was going to post it off to you today.'

'Thanks, Mom, but why don't you hold onto it for me. Chances are I'll get there before it gets here.'

'And just wait until Selwyn Schmeisenberger finds out,' her mother cooed. 'I hope he hasn't met someone else already. He's quite a catch, you know.'

Rachel rolled her eyes. 'All right, Mom, I'd better go, will you give Dad my love. I'll call you when I know more.'

'Okay, dear. I'll call Selwyn straight away. Chat soon.'

It was amazing how she could miss her mother so much, she thought as she put the phone down. How the thought of sitting down with her across the cracked Formica kitchen counter felt so necessary. And then how quickly a four-minute conversation could put an end to all that.

Next, Rachel put a call in to an advertising headhunter in Johannesburg who had placed her in one of her first jobs in advertising, just less than a million years ago. The phone rang on the other side of the world and Rachel pictured Tina in her peach-coloured office reaching for it. 'Tina Michaels,' she said.

'Hi, Tina, it's Rachel Marcus.'

'Rachel, what a lovely surprise. How are you?'

'Fantastic, actually, I'm calling from New York.'

'Yes, I heard you left Barker, Massa and Trout and moved over there. How's it going?'

Rachel thought it showed Tina's class that she wouldn't mention the numbers debacle. 'Everything's great, thanks,' she lied, 'but I was thinking about heading back home, and I was wondering whether there's anything happening over there that you think might suit me?' Rachel held her breath. This was it, she was testing the water and all she could do was wait to see how cold it would be.

'Well, it's good to hear you're coming home,' Tina said. 'There are so many talented people leaving to go overseas all the time, it's nice to have someone coming back for a change. What kind of thing are you looking for, Rachel?'

'Anything above-the-line would be great, Tina. Joburg would be my first choice, of course.'

'I tell you what, Rachel, email me the details of what you've been doing over there and let me take a look at what I've got, then I'll call you back in a day or two, okay? Although, I seriously doubt it will be a problem, Rachel. Good talent is so hard to find.'

They swapped details and then Rachel hung up. Sitting in her kitchen she wondered whether Tina was right and enough time had passed for the whole thing to have blown over. She played the conversation over and over in her head. Time would tell. Hopefully her time in New York would be seen as 'valuable international experience'. Nobody would have to know that Target Advertising was a bizarre promotional hole in the wall. Rachel was in advertising after all, and if nothing else she knew how to put a good spin on a story and find a selling point, even if one didn't exist. Rachel held the phone between her ear and shoulder and dialled the number of a South African creative director she'd met at an awards function in her previous life. Then she paged through her address book and phoned everyone she thought might be able to help her. Old advertising partners, colleagues and friends. She wanted to put the word out that she was a gun for hire in Johannesburg. Potentially, she knew nothing might come of it, but she needed options in South Africa to make up for the options she didn't have in New York.

The next call she made was to a travel agent.

'Hey,' said Sue as Rachel put the phone down, rubbing her red, throbbing ear. 'How about some lunch?'

'Sounds good. We need to make the most of the time we've got left together, right?'

Sue pulled a face. 'I don't want to talk about that. It's way too sad to think about.'

Down the street at a deli the girls ordered huge sandwiches, fries and milkshakes.

'So, what did the travel agent say?' asked Sue.

'I got a great deal on a flight.'

'Really,' said Sue.

'Yup. Ever heard of EgyptAir?'

'Not really.'

'They've got really cheap flights ... The only downside is you have to connect in Cairo.'

'Are you sure this is what you want to do, Rachel?'

'Sure, Cairo can't be that bad, can it? It's where the pyramids are ...'

'No, Rachel, I mean are you sure you want to go home?'

'It's not like I have much of a choice, Sue. It's stay here at Target without you or stay here without you and let Jerrod blackmail me. Hardly the winning lottery ticket, is it?'

'I'm sorry I'm leaving you, Rachel,' Sue said, her lower lip quivering.

'Don't be sorry, it's neither of our faults that this has happened to us.'

They ate in silence, both of them too scared to look at the other because they didn't want to start crying again. All either of them ever seemed to do these days was cry. Rachel felt completely dehydrated.

'There's a catch with my flight though,' Rachel finally said, breaking the silence.

'What, other than the fact that it diverts you through the Middle East?'

Rachel laughed. 'Yeah, to get the cheapest fair I had to take a flight that leaves in ten days time, and it's not transferable.'

'Did you book it?'

'I had to.'

'Then I suppose your decision's made.'

'I suppose so.'

Sue nodded and slipped her oversized sunglasses over her eyes. Rachel could tell she was crying but she pretended not to notice.

'Ten days is so soon,' Sue finally said.

'I know but I feel like I've wasted enough time screwing around and being screwed around here. I figure ten days time is as good a time as any to start over one last time, and it's not like I'm rolling in cash right now either.'

Sue nodded. 'That's when I'll go home too then.'

Rachel Marcus – may the fleas of one hundred thousand mangy camels infest Jerrod Craig's testicle hairs!
July 27 at 7:59pm

Rachel was dreaming. In her dream she was sitting on the couch holding the remote control, flicking through the channels, when something started to ring. She picked up the telephone on the table next to the couch, but there was only a dialling tone. The ringing continued. In her dream she walked into the kitchen and checked the timer on the oven, but it was off. Then she went to the front door in case it was the doorbell, but there was nobody there. The ringing continued. Rachel started to drag herself out of her dream, floating up towards consciousness where the phone was actually ringing. She reached for it and picked it up, anything to make the ringing stop. 'Hello,' she rasped.

'Hello, I'm looking for Rachel Marcus?' The man's South African accent was smooth and rich.

Rachel tried to pry open unwilling eyes. 'Yes.'

'Sorry, did I wake you? I wasn't sure if the time difference was six or seven hours, daylight saving always gets me. Shall I call you back in a bit?'

Rachel pulled herself up in bed, trying desperately not to wake Sue, who was asleep on the couch. The alarm clock said 7.15 a.m. 'No, it's okay,' whispered Rachel. 'Who did you say you are?' she asked.

'My name is Zola Madladla, I'm calling from Joburg.'

'Hi, Zola, nice to meet you.'

It was a dumb thing to say, as technically she hadn't met him yet, but given it was only 7.15 a.m. and she was still half asleep she didn't berate herself too much. Zola Madladla, Zola Madladla – the name sounded so familiar. She turned it over in her mind a couple of times, but she still couldn't remember where she knew it from.

'This may seem like a bit of an odd call, but I had dinner with Tom Wooster from Ogilvy last night, and he mentioned that someone at Saatchi's had heard from someone at FCB, whose secretary had told him that she'd heard from a copywriter at TBWA, that you might be moving back home.'

'Ah, the good old African grapevine ...' Rachel laughed. 'I'm actually coming home in nine days.'

'Excellent, I have a business proposition that I think you might be interested in.'

'Hmmm,' said Rachel, her ears pricking up.

'I've been Client Services Director at Ogilvy for some years ...'

Suddenly Rachel remembered Zola. She'd met him several years earlier when she'd done a stint at Ogilvy. He was a charming man who had a reputation in the industry as an honest, no bullshit, old-school kind of guy. Rachel tried to focus on the voice on the other end of the line.

'Recently one of my clients got the rights to start a fourth cellphone operator in South Africa and they're looking for a local agency,' Zola was saying. 'Ogilvy can't take it on because it's conflicting business, and so I've decided to leave Ogilvy and start my own agency.'

Rachel held her breath; this was the call she'd been hoping for.

'So, I'm looking around for a creative partner,' Zola went on, 'and I was wondering if it sounds like something you might be interested in?'

Rachel was more than interested. When she had thought about what waited for her back home it had been with concern. She had been worried that the Barker, Massa and Trout disaster, together with all these months out of the country working on shit, might not have left that many doors open for her. In fact, in her mind ending up the receptionist at Zip World had become a very real possibility.

'Wow, Zola, what an unbelievable opportunity!'

'I know,' he said. 'There is still a lot to figure out, I'm really just in the early planning stages, but I was hoping you'd think about it.

'Of course, I'd love to think about it,' Rachel said. 'I'm thinking about it already.'

Zola laughed.

'Is it okay if I get back to you in the next day or two?' Rachel asked.

'I'll look forward to it,' Zola said.

But dragging her heels was really just a negotiation tool because as Rachel put the phone down she already knew she was going to accept his offer.

Rachel Marcus is pretending to think about it.
July 28 at 10:59am

Rachel Marcus is going places. Finally.
July 29 at 9:06am

The next day Rachel had to force herself to wait a couple of hours before calling Zola to accept his offer in principle. She didn't want to seem as keen as she felt and she knew in negotiating it was always good to at least play a little bit hard to get.

Twenty minutes later Rachel breathed a sigh of relief as she put the phone down. They still had a ton of detail to discuss but she felt relieved to have something lined up. Going home to open her own agency would definitely ease the feelings of embarrassment and failure that she'd been struggling to get her head around.

'Morning, Rae,' said Sue, walking into the kitchen area, rubbing the sleep out of her eyes. 'Let's blow off work again and treat ourselves to a girl's day out, what do you say?

'Why not?' said Rachel. 'I'm resigning anyway ... What's Dan going to do, fire me? Some other lucky schmuck is going to have to do the procurement document for The Charter Method.'

'Somebody's got a treat in store,' said Sue, her face pressed against the front door.

Sue had taken to stalking Brian. Every morning she set her alarm for twenty past seven, when she would drag a chair over to the front door, climb onto it, flatten her body against the wood and stick her eye to the peephole. Then she'd wait in position for Brian to leave for work.

Every evening at around six thirty she would repeat the process. They had yet to speak face-to-face since Sue had made her confession.

'Do you see him?' whispered Rachel.

'No, not yet, but he'd better hurry, otherwise he's going to be late for work. Did I tell you that twice last week he stopped outside our door?'

'No. What was he doing?' asked Rachel.

'It was like he'd forgotten something and was wondering whether to go back and get it.'

'He'll come round, you'll see,' said Rachel.

Rachel's heart still ached for Sue, and she felt pretty sorry for herself too. Jerrod's campaign was everywhere – there were three different television commercials and at least four double-page spread magazine ads gracing just about every major glossy from *Cosmo* to *Time*. Then there were the posters on bus shelters and busses and the rest of the outdoor campaign. Each separate piece had her line slapped on it. Rachel couldn't escape the betrayal. It screamed at her from every street corner. Suddenly, living in New York seemed unbearable.

Rachel Marcus isn't so crazy about the view here anymore.
July 29 at 2:06pm

Rachel Marcus and Sue are out for sushi. We're the birds in the early bird special.
July 29 at 4:00pm

'I can't eat another mouthful,' said Rachel. 'Okay, maybe one more California roll.'

'More sake?' asked Sue.

'Why not? You'll just have to roll me home.'

Sue stuffed another piece of tuna in her mouth. 'You don't get sushi like this back home in Alabama,' she said. 'I'm not quitting till I've finished it, even if it means I have to undo the button on my pants.'

Rachel laughed. 'It's like we're stockpiling for winter; the food and the company.'

Sue nodded and washed down her tuna with more sake. 'Wanna go home and watch a movie?'

'Sure,' said Rachel, 'but we need to pick up more tissues, I think we're all out.'

Rachel Marcus and Sue are putting on their pyjamas at five p.m., just like all good sixty-year-olds.
July 28 at 5:04pm

Rachel assumed the position on the couch. 'Hurry, Sue, *Notting Hill* is starting in five minutes,' she said as Sue came out of the bathroom in her pyjamas.

Halfway through the movie the front door buzzer went. 'Are you expecting someone?' Rachel asked Sue.

Sue shook her head.

'Strange,' Rachel said. 'Nobody other than you, Justin, Brian and all the delivery men from the takeout restaurants round here know where I live.'

Sue looked nervous at mention of Brian. She shrugged her shoulders. 'Maybe it's a Jehovah's Witness?'

Rachel pressed the button next to the small speaker pad nailed to the door frame. 'Hello?' she said.

'Hello,' said a man's voice.

'Who's that?' asked Rachel, pressing down the button again.

'Rachel?' said the voice. 'It's me, Justin. Lemme in.'

'Hold on one second!' she shouted. 'Sue, it's Justin!'

Rachel looked down at what she was wearing. It was an embarrassingly old pair of plaid pyjamas that she'd had for years. The elastic was long gone and Rachel had tied a knot in the waistband to stop them sliding down. The top half was stained and there was a tear in the left sleeve. Sue wasn't much better. She was wearing a pink nightie with a picture of a bear on it and a heart with the words *I wuv you* typed across the front. The girls raced into the bedroom, bumping into each other as they threw off their pymamas and tossed on the first items of decent clothing they could get their hands on – jeans, bras, panties and pyjamas flying across the room.

The buzzer went again. Rachel raced over to the door, pulling a T-shirt on over her head and stubbing her toe on the foot of the couch as she pressed the button 'Yes,' she said, blinking back pain and swear words.

'Oi,' said Justin, 'what are you doing in there? Hosting a political debate? Let me in.'

'Come in,' she shouted through the speaker box, pressing the buzzer.

Rachel tried to calm her wild hair while Sue shoved dirty bowls in the sink and tossed bras into the cupboard and dirty plates into the microwave. A moment later there was a knock on the door. Rachel did one last mirror check and opened it.

'Take your time!' said Justin, smiling.

'I'm sorry,' said Rachel. 'We weren't expecting you. Excuse the mess.'

'Hi, Sue,' said Justin, stepping forward and pecking Sue on the cheek. 'Why do you both have your tops on inside out?'

Rachel and Sue both looked down and started laughing.

'Come in and sit down,' said Rachel as Sue popped into the bathroom to turn her top around. She eyed Justin. It was strange not seeing him every day anymore. He looked great. He was more tanned than she remembered and he'd put on a bit of weight, which was a good thing – he'd looked so drawn and pale when he had lived with her. He'd also had a haircut, so his golden locks framed his face neatly, and his fierce blue eyes shone clearly.

'I thought I'd swing by and see what you're up to,' he said. 'I tried to call but your mobile's been off.'

'Sue and I went to a movie and then out shopping, and then we went for sushi. My battery must have died.' Rachel took her new cellphone out of her bag and plugged it into the charger.

'You didn't go to work today?' asked Justin.

As Sue reappeared in the lounge there was a knock on the door.

'What is this, Grand Central?' Rachel asked with a nervous laugh. 'Two visitors in one night; that's more than I've had since I moved in. Are either of you expecting anyone?'

Sue and Justin shook their heads. Rachel looked through the peephole and opened the door. Brian stood in the hallway. Despite being well over six feet tall he seemed to have shrunk over the last couple of weeks. He was unshaven and wore a crumpled suit and a stained tie.

Rachel gave him a hug. 'It's so nice to see you!' she said. 'Come in.'

Sue cowered in the corner looking pale.

'I was just about to make tea, Brian,' Rachel went on. 'Do you want?'

'No thanks,' said Brian quietly. 'Hi, Justin.'

Justin smiled and they shook hands.

'Sue,' Brian said, 'I was wondering if maybe we could talk?'

Rachel heard Sue gulp from across the room. 'Okay,' she said, wringing her fingers, but she stood rooted to the spot until Rachel nudged her and she trundled awkwardly across the room and out into the passage.

'Rachel, you do know your shirt's on the wrong way around, right?' said Brian.

Rachel smiled and nodded as Brian waved awkwardly and left. She watched him open the front door of their apartment for Sue, and then close it gently behind him. 'That's the first time they've spoken,' she said, turning back to Justin.

'I'm sure they'll figure things out,' he said. 'But what about you? How are things? I haven't seen you in ages.'

'I've been meaning to call you but my life's gotten a little out of control lately.'

'Tell me about it,' he said, accepting a cup of tea from Rachel. 'Rach, I need to apologise to you for so many things, I don't even know where to start.'

'Oh, please!' she said. 'I completely understand why you had to leave Target, it was the best thing you could have done for yourself.

Of all the people who need to apologise to me right now, you're at the bottom of the list.'

'Why? Who's in your bad books?' he asked, blowing on his hot tea.

'You're not going to believe what happened … I mean, I can hardly believe it happened … You know Jerrod was working on that big international pitch?'

'Sure.' Justin nodded.

'Remember when you went to LA on that shoot?'

He nodded again.

'While you were gone I had this idea for his pitch and I scamped it up and showed it to Jerrod. I thought it was good, I wouldn't have shown it to him otherwise, but he bombed it …'

'What does he know?' spat Justin, interrupting her. 'He wouldn't know a good idea if it bit him in the ass!'

Rachel ignored him. 'He stole my pay-off line, Justin,' she said quietly, feeling her chin start to quiver. 'It's on everything!'

Justin looked like his head was going to explode. 'Why didn't you tell me, Rach?' he cried, getting up and pacing the apartment. 'Is that the campaign that's just broken?'

Rachel nodded; she didn't trust herself to speak.

'I told you he was a bastard!' Justin shouted. 'What a complete asshole! I wish I'd been here to support you, Rach. You can't let him get away with this!'

'There's nothing I can do. He got me good, Justin. R&P would never take my word over his and I trashed all my layouts and scripts after he told me the work wasn't any good. I've got absolutely no proof. I was an idiot. I totally believed him and I really trusted him.'

Rachel found herself crying again. She felt pathetic.

Justin sat down next to her and put his arm around her shoulder while she cried. 'Have you spoken to him?' he asked.

'Yeah, and get this, he offered me a job as a writer in his group at R&P if I didn't say anything to anyone or kick up a fuss!'

'Ha, that's a joke!' Justin growled. 'Nice for him, then he can just rip off all your ideas. He's a talentless hack, Rachel!'

'I'm completely screwed, Justin,' she said, through tears. 'Jerrod knows all the creative directors at all the decent agencies. One call from him and nobody will hire me. I thought I'd found something real. I thought he was the one. And it turns out he was only interested in me for my ideas ...'

'I may be clean now, but I still know some pretty dodgy characters,' Justin said as she sniffed into his shoulder. 'I could have both his kneecaps broken for a hundred bucks.'

Rachel laughed through the snot.

'Really, I'm not joking. Something needs to be done about this, Rach.'

'Justin,' Rachel said quietly. 'There's something else I have to tell you.'

He looked at her, his eyes wide and questioning.

'I've decided to go home.'

Justin's arm dropped from her shoulder.

'Sue's heading back South to be with her family – she doesn't think she and Brian will reconcile – and you're not at Target anymore, so unless I do something drastic I'm scared I'm going to spend the rest of my life working on the revolutionary Charter Method.' Rachel grabbed at a tissue and blew her nose loudly into it. 'I've had my heart broken one too many times,' she continued. 'I don't think I can take much more of it. I'm ready to go home, Justin. I made some calls and this guy I know is busy with a start-up in Joburg and he wants me to be his creative partner. It's the opportunity I've been waiting for my entire life. And after this last year I really didn't think I'd ever get it ...'

Justin smiled and reached out to give her another hug. 'Rachel, that's phenomenal news! Congratulations. When are you going?'

'Eight days,' said Rachel, biting her lip.

'Shit, Rachel, that's so soon!' Justin stood up and started pacing around the lounge. 'It looks like the two of us are really getting our shit together at last, aren't we?' he said.

Rachel stood up and gave him another hug.

'I don't know what I'm going to do without you here, Rach,' he said into her ear.

'AA Meetings,' she said. 'Lots and lots of AA meetings.'

Justin nodded.

'And emails, lots and lots of emails.'

Rachel pulled away from the hug. 'What do you think's going on over there with Sue and Brian? It's very quiet.'

'Maybe he's chopped her up into dozens of small pieces, packed her into ziplock bags and put her in the freezer,' said Justin.

Rachel opened the door and stepped into the passage.

'Hear anything?' asked Justin from behind her as she pressed her ear to Sue's door.

Rachel shook her head.

'Look, I'd better get going,' he said. 'It's getting late and we've both got work tomorrow.'

Rachel kissed him on the cheek.

'Hey, Rach, will you at least consider letting me have both of Jerrod's kneecaps broken?' Justin asked as he walked away from her down the passage.

She smiled and shook her head.

'What about a couple of ribs?'

'Call me tomorrow,' she said.

'Of course,' he shouted, turning to blow her a kiss before he disappeared down the stairs.

Rachel put her ear back against Sue and Brian's door. She held her breath, listening for the sound of a chainsaw, but she couldn't hear anything. She felt completely drained. Tomorrow wouldn't be any easier, she thought. It was time to face the music. Or, in Dan's case, the wind chimes.

Rachel Marcus is no longer AWOL, but she is worried about Sue.
July 30 at 9:27am

When Rachel left for work she listened outside Sue and Brian's door again, but she still couldn't hear anything.

At work she dialled Sue's number as soon as she got to her desk. Sue answered on the first ring. 'Hello,' she whispered.

'Sue, I can't hear you,' said Rachel.

'Hold on a sec,' Sue hissed.

Rachel heard rustling, then footsteps and a door closing. Seconds later Sue was back, though Rachel could still only just hear her. 'Where are you?' asked Rachel.

'I'm in the cupboard,' replied Sue.

'Are you okay?'

'Brian's still sleeping and I don't want to wake him up, we barely got any sleep last night.'

Rachel could hear the smile in Sue's voice. 'Did you make up?' she asked.

'First we fought for a couple of hours,' whispered Sue. 'We were both so angry at each other. I was angry at him for putting all that baby pressure on me and he was so angry at me for lying to him. And then I was also angry at him for kicking me out and refusing to talk to me. And we were both angry at the universe for putting us in this situation, and terrified at the same time. Anyway, so we talked, then we sat there in silence for a couple of hours, then we talked some more. He still loves me, Rachel. Even after what I did to him. We've got options and we love each other and that's all that's important, right?'

'Yes, Sue, that's what's really important.' Rachel nodded into the phone. 'I knew your bond was too strong to let something like this get between you.'

'What happened with you and Justin?' whispered Sue.

'What do you mean?' asked Rachel.

'You know what I mean.' Sue giggled.

'What? No! Nothing happened, Sue. I've told you before, we're just friends. I told him about Jerrod and he offered to have his kneecaps broken. And then I told him that I'm going home.'

There was silence. Finally, Sue spoke. 'I'm going to stay here, Rachel. Brian and I are going to make things work.'

'I know you are, Sue, and I'm really happy for you.'

'Why don't you stay too? Nothing needs to change.'

'I'd love to, Sue, but it's too late. There's the possibility of this job and I've booked and paid for my flight. I have to do this, Sue. It's time for me to go home.'

'I don't know how I'm going to live in New York without you.'

'I know, it's going to be weird.'

'Shit, I'd better go,' Sue suddenly said. 'It sounds like Brian's up.'

'Hold thumbs for me, okay,' Rachel replied. 'I have to tell Dan I'm leaving.'

'Good luck, sweetie. You can do it. Go rock his karma.'

Rachel Marcus has a lot to do today.
July 30 at 10:11am

Rachel felt like an entirely different person to the one who had last sat at her desk just a week earlier. The Rachel Marcus who'd last sat behind this desk had been passionately in love with a man she'd believed she had a future with in New York City. The new Rachel that now sat behind her desk felt older and wiser. She'd had her heart broken again and she'd finally decided to allow herself to go home, even though she hadn't achieved what she'd come to New York for. She'd decided to let herself off the hook.

Rachel stared at her computer, feeling sad but also strangely at peace with her decision. She opened a fresh page in Microsoft Word and started to type.

Dear Dan,

I hereby tender my resignation from Target Advertising, effective immediately.

Dan, I've come to find you a man of many surprising quirks and I've thoroughly enjoyed my time here. However, I've been made a once in a lifetime offer to head up a new start-up agency in South Africa, and I plan to return home within the next couple of weeks.

I wish you only the very best for the future and hold thumbs that The Charter Method is a huge success.

Thanks again for everything. Hug on.

Rachel Marcus

Printing the letter out, she signed it and put it in an envelope. Then she typed up a letter to Doreen, giving immediate notice on her apartment, and emailed it to her. She would lose out on half a month's rent but there was no helping that. Finally, Rachel walked across the studio to Dan's office. His door was closed, so she knocked.

'Come in,' shrilled Dan.

Rachel pushed the door open and took a step inside. About two feet away from her nose dangled a tiny wrinkled penis and a pair of small, pink, hairy testicles. Rachel gasped and took a step backwards. She tried to avert her eyes, but it was like driving past a car accident: you don't want to see, but you still can't help staring.

'Ah, Rachel Marcus,' came Dan's voice.

Rachel looked back into the room and tried to see something other than Dan's genitalia. A large metal contraption had been set up in the middle of the office – the desk had been pushed to one side, up against the wall, in order to accommodate it – and Dan was literally dangling stark naked, upside down, attached to it by his ankles. Looking around, Rachel spotted Dan's swami sitting on the leather couch, reading *The Economist*. He had ditched his turban and was wearing a pair of faded diesel jeans, a pair of Puma sneakers and a tight Ed Hardy T-shirt. He nodded a greeting at Rachel, his eyes moving down her face and settling on her breasts.

Rachel ignored him and looked back at Dan, trying hard to focus on his face, which was level with her shins. 'Dan, what are you doing?' she asked, completely bewildered.

'Ah, you're here just in time for a demonstration,' he said. 'This, Rachel Marcus, is the soon to be world-famous Charter Method of meditation. I'm glad you finally got to witness it. Shamandar, come help me down.'

The swami tore his eyes away from Rachel's chest and ambled over to the contraption. He undid each ankle strap in turn, holding onto Dan's ankles as he lowered him onto the ground.

'Thank you, Shamandar, namaste,' said Dan.

'No sweat, homie,' said the Swami, making his way back to the couch.

Dan reached for a small sweat towel, seemingly unperturbed by the fact he was standing completely naked in the middle of his office. 'Now, Rachel Marcus,' he said, wiping his face, 'how can I help you?'

Rachel cleared her throat awkwardly as he started to dress. 'Dan, I wanted to chat to you about this,' she said, holding out the letter.

Dan turned around – he had put on a brightly coloured G-string and a pair of khaki cargo pants, but they weren't done up yet – took the letter from her, opened it and scanned it quickly. 'No, Rachel!' he said. 'You're leaving us? My palm reader told me this was going to happen...'

Rachel nodded.

'We'll be very sad to see you go,' Dan went on, 'but all free souls must travel in order to find their true order within the universe. Now, let's talk leave pay.'

They negotiated briefly. Rachel agreed to sacrifice her amassed leave pay in exchange for leaving before her official month of notice was up. It was a fair trade and she got the feeling that Dan wasn't all that unhappy to see her go. She wasn't surprised; things had hardly gone swimmingly for her at Target Advertising. She hadn't really set the world of below-the-line advertising on fire.

'Wait, Rachel Marcus,' Dan called after her as she left. 'Haven't you forgotten something?'

Dan marched towards her with his arms open, his sweaty chest still bare. Rachel winced, then opened her arms to receive what she vowed would be her very last Dan-hug.

Rachel Marcus is tick, tick, ticking things off her going home to do list.
July 30 at 5:03pm

Rachel Marcus is six days and counting.
July 31 at 9:42am

'So, how's your last day at Target going?' asked Justin.

'It's going,' said Rachel. She was clicking through the client folders on her computer, trying to decide if there was anything worth backing up. She had her telephone cradled between her ear and her shoulder and she was chatting while she clicked. 'I went for lunch with Lisa and a couple of the other girls. They all send love.'

Justin snorted a laugh.

'Even Double D Heather came.'

'What are you busy with?' he asked.

'They had me finish up some loo paper copy and I wrote a press release for Sanitex. Oh, and I signed off my very last sock laser ever. That was a momentous occasion. What about you?'

'I'm supposed to be working on a logo design, but I'm busy with a personal project right now.'

'Oh, that sounds interesting.'

'Yes, and I think you're going to like it,' Justin said.

'What do you mean?'

'It's a surprise. I'll show you when it's finished,' he said with a naughty edge to his voice. 'Hey, I almost forgot to tell you, *Campaign* magazine is doing a profile on us next month.'

'Congratulations, but don't change the subject, tell me about this personal project.'

'Be patient, you'll see,' he said.

'All right, well I'm just about done here. I'm going to pack up my desk and get out of here. Chat to you later?'

'Absolutely,' he said.

Rachel finished packing up her desk, updated her status on Facebook and shut down her computer. Before leaving the office she hovered over Justin's old desk. Since he'd left their office had been almost ghostly it felt so empty. She ran her hand over the hole in the wall from the time she'd thrown her Sellotape dispenser at him and smiled at the memory. Then she ran her eye over his pinboard. All that remained was the half-naked girl torn out of a magazine and some menus from local takeout places. Then, in the bottom right corner of the board, something caught her eye. It was a small sketch done in pen on a torn-off corner of paper. Rachel looked at it closely. It was a sketch of her. The resemblance was amazing. In the little drawing she even had a pencil stuck in her hair, the way she often did when she was copy-checking. Rachel had never noticed it before. She leaned over, unpinned it and slipped it into her handbag.

Rachel Marcus is leaving Target Advertising forever. At last.
July 31 at 4:40pm

'So, what are your plans for your last weekend in New York City?' Sue asked, stirring her coffee.

'I've got a ton of presents to buy and I thought in-between I'd act like a tourist and check out all the things I've been meaning to see. Justin's taking me to the Guggenheim later, if you want to come?'

'We have an appointment at the adoption agency this morning, and then this afternoon we're looking at apartments,' Sue replied. 'I told Brian I couldn't bear to live in this block once you're gone, and you know how he feels about the doorways in here, so he's only too happy to look for something a little taller. How about dinner tonight?'

'Excellent, you can fill me in on the adoption agency, I'm holding thumbs for you guys,'

'Thanks, Rae, I can't believe we're actually doing this.'

'I can,' said Rachel, squeezing Sue's hand.

Rachel Marcus will absolutely, definitely start packing today. If she remembers.
August 3 at 11:19am

Rachel Marcus is 'Oops, I forgot.'
August 3 at 4:49pm

'Shouldn't you start packing soon?' asked Sue.

Rachel pulled her suitcase out of the cupboard and dropped it on the bed. She opened it, picked a flip-flop up off the floor and tossed it into the case. Then she went back to the kitchen and picked up her Johnnie Walker. 'There, now I've started.'

'Are you excited about going home?'

'Kind of,' Rachel said, clinking the ice in her glass. 'I'm excited about the new agency, but at the moment I feel more sad about leaving ...'

'How are you going to fit all of this in there?' asked Sue, gesturing to the clothes and shoes scattered around the apartment and then at the small almost-empty case.

The door buzzed and Rachel was relieved to be distracted from the obviously impossible task awaiting her. She dashed over to the intercom. 'Hello,' she said.

'It's Justin, quick, put your shirt on the right way around. I thought I'd take you out for dinner, and then later I've got a surprise for you.'

'Excellent,' Rachel said, pressing down the speaker button. 'But we need to stop at some shops on the way; I think I'm going to need a bigger suitcase. I'll be right down.' Rachel raced into the bathroom to fix her hair and make-up. 'Wanna come, Sue?' she shouted.

'No thanks, I've got work to do. Do you have any idea what diapers cost? It's astonishing.'

Rachel changed her top three times, changed her jeans once, said goodbye to Sue and bounded out of the door and down the stairs.

'Aren't you supposed to be working?' she asked Justin when she burst out of the apartment onto the street.

'Aren't you supposed to be packing?' he snapped back, pecking her on the cheek.

'Touché,' she said.

'It's still early, so after we've picked up your suitcase I thought we could go past Blue Monkey,' Justin said. 'I want to show you around and introduce you to Dane. Also, I need to pick something up for later.'

'For the surprise?' Rachel asked.

'Yup.'

'What is it?'

'You'll see.' Justin winked.

Rachel Marcus is going to miss riding the subway, even though it stinks like pee.
August 3 at 5:32pm

After Rachel had bought the largest suitcase she could find, and they had dropped it back at her apartment, Justin and Rachel took the subway and then walked a couple of blocks until they found themselves on the street outside the front of a very old brick-faced building. 'Ta-da!' Justin said, sweeping his arms open.

'Wow, this is awesome.' Rachel said.

'This building actually used to be an old firehouse,' Justin said. 'That roller door over there is where the fire engines used to come in and out. We're still busy doing it up, but it's already very cool inside, come see.'

He led her proudly by the hand through the front door and into an old-fashioned cage elevator. It took them up a couple of floors and emptied them out into a large double-volume warehouse space with impossibly high ceilings and lots of natural light. Rachel loved it immediately; the space itself had an incredible energy. Every available surface – the walls and even the floors – had been covered with a shiny whiteboard material and there were jars filled with multicoloured whiteboard markers everywhere. Dozens of ideas, scamps, notes, graffiti and drawings had already been scribbled all over the place. There were ads scribbled on the walls and an idea for some packaging worked out on the floor. Near Rachel's left foot someone had scrawled a brief shopping list: *bread, milk, eggs, light bulbs, toothpaste, pick up laundry*. And on the floor next to a desk someone had scrawled a phone message: *Lisa called for you – Thursday at 2 p.m.*

Rachel smiled. 'Is there a fireman's pole?' she asked.

'Yup, check it out.' Justin led her over to a corner of the room and around a partition to where a giant hole in the floor circled a large fireman's pole.

'That's so cool!' Rachel said. 'Where does it go to?'

'That's the best part,' Justin said. 'Downstairs is our boardroom, a lounge area and a couple of other offices. So you can slide right down into a meeting.'

Rachel laughed. 'How many of you are there working here?' she asked.

'At the moment it's just me, Dane and his business partner Matthew. Oh, and a receptionist and a client service chick ... That's about it.

'I heard my name.' Rachel heard a deep voice with an unmistakeably British accent and turned her head towards it. A very tall, very thin guy with blonde hair walked over to them carrying a cup of coffee. He had a bolt through his eyebrow and one through his ear lobe and a full-colour tattoo chased up his left arm. 'You must be Rachel,' he said.

Rachel shook his hand. She liked him instantly; he had a friendly smile and an easy way about him. 'And you must be Dane, I've heard a lot about you.'

'Not as much as I've heard about you,' Dane said with a grin.

Justin shifted awkwardly, a bright-red blush working its way up past his collar, turning his ears luminous. 'I'll be back in a minute,' he said, 'I just need to grab something from the printer.'

'No problem,' Rachel said as Justin disappeared.

'So,' Dane said, 'Justin told me what Jerrod Craig did to you.'

Rachel froze and wondered how much he knew.

'It's a shame. I'm sorry that had to happen to you. He's a real disingenuous prick; I've never liked him.'

Rachel shook her head, too devastated to speak.

'So, then is it true that the pay-off line on all that work is actually yours?' Dane asked. 'You wrote it?'

Rachel nodded, swallowing back the urge to cry.

'It's really good; without it the entire campaign is bullshit.'

'Thank you,' Rachel managed to squeak.

'I'm glad Justin brought you round,' Dane went on, 'I've been wanting to meet you …'

'Your offices are unbelievable,' Rachel said.

'Thanks, I'm glad you like them because we're on the verge of picking up a very juicy piece of above-the-line business, and in a month or two we'll have space for a writer of your calibre …' Dane paused to asses Rachel's reaction. 'I know Justin said you might be heading home, but I'm just throwing this out there in case you happened to find yourself back in Manhattan looking for a gig.'

'Wow,' said Rachel, 'what a great offer … Thank you, Dane.'

'Think about it, okay?' he said.

'Come on,' said Justin, reappearing clutching a huge stack of A4 pages. 'Let's go get something to eat, I'm starving.'

'What's that?' Rachel asked, pointing at the pages.

'I'll show you later,' he said, shoving them into his backpack and heading for the elevator. 'See you tomorrow, Dane.'

'Thanks again,' Rachel said, turning back to Dane. 'It was great to meet you.'

'You promise you'll think about it, eh?' Dane said with a smile, shaking her hand.

Rachel nodded and followed Justin back into the elevator. 'What an amazing guy,' she said to him as the doors closed.

'Yeah, it's a cool place. I know I haven't been here very long, but so far I can honestly say I haven't been this happy at work in years.'

Rachel believed him; she'd never seen him look so energised.

'So then, where do you want to eat?' Justin asked.

'What about the surprise?' Rachel whined.

'Not yet. Patience.'

Rachel won a ching chong cha outside the building and without a moment's hesitation she made her choice. Seconds later they were on their way to a steakhouse for enormous rib-eyes.

Rachel Marcus is the ching chong cha champion of the universe.
August 3 at 7:16pm via Mobile Web

Rachel put her knife and fork together and pushed her plate as far away from her as she could.

'Are you finishing those?' Justin asked, pointing his knife at her leftover onion rings.

'Urgh, I'm so full, I'm never eating again.'

Justin speared his fork down onto her plate. 'Good steak,' he mumbled.

'The best in the city,' Rachel said. 'I'm going to miss this place.'

'You don't have to move.' Justin said.

'Well, that's a good thing because I'm too full to move. Tell the waitress to order me a gurney or something, you're going to have to roll me out of here.'

'I'm being serious, Rachel,' Justin said, putting his knife and fork together and pushing his plate away from him as he leaned back in his seat and rubbed his own full stomach. 'You really don't have to go.'

'I appreciate that Justin, but I don't have a lot of choice. After everything with Jerrod I ...'

'I wanted to talk to you about that Rachel,' Justin said, tapping his backpack. 'I've got a plan.'

Rachel slid forward on her seat. 'What do you mean? Is this the surprise?'

Justin nodded. 'I don't think Jerrod should get away with what he's done to you, and I've had an idea. It's evil and it's wicked, but it's nothing he doesn't deserve.'

'What is it?' Rachel asked, eyes wide.

'Come, let's go, I'll show you,' Justin said, standing up and gesturing to the waitress for the bill.

Rachel Marcus likes evil and wicked, evil and wicked is good.
August 3 at 10:09pm via Mobile Web

They left the restaurant and hit the street. Rachel was so full she couldn't move very fast, but her curiosity drove her on.

Half an hour later they arrived at the R&P agency offices in midtown Manhattan.

'Justin, what are we doing here ...' Rachel said, hesitating on the street in front of the building. 'We can't ...'

'Trust me,' Justin said, dragging her through the tall glass revolving door.

Rachel had been here only once before, for her interview with Jerrod when she'd first arrived in New York, but the building was as impressive and imposing now as it had been then. The foyer was an enormous space with a series of gigantic, strategically placed arty sculptures that flanked a huge security desk and a bank of elevators. Rachel froze as soon as they were through the door, her body slightly turned towards the exit, ready to run, but Justin carried on walking towards the security desk, seemingly unconcerned by the tired-looking guard behind it. 'Stop looking so worried,' he hissed, turning back towards her momentarily.

'Everything's going to be fine.'

Walking up to the security desk, Justin cleared his throat and the security guard looked up, surprised to see a visitor so late at night. He looked at Justin for a split second and then a huge grin of recognition exploded on his face. 'Justin!' he yelled at the top of his voice.

The two embraced like long-lost brothers and although Rachel was too far away to hear the rest of the conversation she could tell from their body language that they were old friends. Of course, she thought, she had forgotten that Justin had once worked at R&P. It had slipped her mind completely. But questions still raced through her brain. Why had Justin brought her here? What if someone saw them? Even worse, what if Jerrod was here, working late, and he saw them? She gnawed at the side of her thumb, watching Justin and the guard as they talked. Once or twice Justin pointed at Rachel as he spoke and the guard looked over at her, nodding his head. Then the guard spoke, shrugging his shoulders and slapping Justin on the back again. Justin responded, gesticulating wildly and pointing back at Rachel. The guard looked at her again and shook his head in disbelief. Rachel glanced nervously at her watch. She hated being here. HE worked here and she didn't want to be anywhere near HIM. The sheer repulsion she felt just standing in the foyer of the building he worked in made her realise that there was no way she could have worked for Jerrod, ever. She knew then that she'd made the right decision to ignore his bribe and just pack it in and go home.

The security guard lifted his walkie-talkie and spoke into it. Rachel started to panic. They were in shit now, she thought. He was calling the police and they would be dragged off to jail for … for … for what exactly she didn't know, but it was going to be bad.

Two more guards appeared and joined Justin and the first guard. The guard spoke to both of his colleagues earnestly, again pointing to Rachel, and the guards looked at her curiously and nodded as they listened. Rachel smiled at them and tried her hardest to look as harmless and innocent as possible. Eventually, after much debate and nodding, Justin and the security guard hugged one more time, slapping each other fondly on the back again, then Justin shook hands with the other two security guards and walked back to where Rachel still stood, a huge smile on his face. 'It's all cool, come on,' he said, grabbing Rachel by the hand and leading her towards the bank of elevators.

'What do you mean, it's cool? What are we doing, Justin? I want to go home.'

'Rachel, what Jerrod did to you was wrong and we can't just let him get away with it. We need to send a message that he can't mess with people like this.' Justin pressed the elevator button.

'But what if someone catches us? What if we get into trouble?'

'Don't worry, I used to work late all the time when I worked here and I ended up spending a lot of time with these night-shift guys. I spent so much time with Doug over there, we're like this,' he said, holding his two fingers close together. 'Doug and the other guards are totally cool with this; they're going to keep an eye open for us and they'll cover for us tomorrow. He said the creative floor's empty tonight and that's the only place we're going. Come on.'

The lift opened and Justin stepped inside; Rachel followed, too curious not to.

The creative floor at R&P was up on the eighteenth. The entire floor was dedicated to the creative side of the agency. This was where all the teams worked – all the writers, art directors, creative directors, group heads and traffic managers. At least eighty people occupied this floor on any given day and one of them was Jerrod Craig.

Justin led the way into the creative boardroom.

'What are we doing, Justin?' Rachel asked, her voice shaking.

Lifting his backpack onto the boardroom table, Justin unzipped it and pulled out the thick stack of A4 paper he'd picked up at Blue Monkey.

'Rachel,' Justin said, holding the stack tightly against his chest, 'I haven't been able to get what Jerrod did to you out of my mind. When I worked here I thought he was my friend, but he watched my copywriter completely destroy me. He knew what was going on all along, but he never said anything. He never gave me a heads-up; he just acted like everything was cool. He lied straight to my face. What kind of friend is that?'

'I know, Justin, he told me about that,' Rachel said softly. 'I'm so sorry that happened to you.'

'I just kept thinking that he's not a good person and everybody should know that, which is why I made these.' Justin dropped the thick stack of pages on the boardroom table. Rachel picked up the one on top, it had a message printed on it in large black type:

My name is Jerrod Craig and I am not a good person.

She put it down and picked up the next one:

My name is Jerrod Craig and I steal other people's pay-off lines.

And the next one:

My name is Jerrod Craig and I am a shit.

There were dozens of them; each one different, each one scathing and each one closer to the truth than the one before.

My name is Jerrod Craig and I bribe people.
My name is Jerrod Craig and I am a dirty liar.
My name is Jerrod Craig and I'm terrible in bed.

Rachel looked up at Justin when she got to this one.

'I just guessed that one,' he said.

Rachel burst out laughing. 'I can't believe you made all of these,' she said. 'There must be two hundred here.'

'At least,' Justin said. 'So, what do you think? Will you plaster the place with me? Doug and the boys will cover for us if the shit hits the fan. Surprisingly, it turns out none of them are big fans of Mr Craig. Doug says he's never greeted a single one of them in all the years he's worked here. As long as we don't break anything or take anything we'll be in the clear. It will just look like a harmless studio prank.'

Rachel thought about it for a second, there was no doubt in her mind that Jerrod would know that they – she and Justin – were responsible, but what could he do about it? She was leaving any day now and what could he do to Justin? He shouldn't be able to get away with treating people the way he had treated her. Jerrod had betrayed her, he had made her trust him on the most intimate level, he'd made her think she could love him and then he had stolen from her, like a common thief. And on top of that he'd still had the nerve to blackmail her. Justin was right, Jerrod Craig had made her doubt her talent and ripped her heart to shreds, and doing it hadn't seemed to bother him one bit. And now, because of him, she had to leave New York. People should know what kind of monster they were dealing with. She and Justin would be doing the creative department at R&P a favour. 'Let's do it,' she said and smiled.

Justin grinned and handed her a pile of A4 paper and some press stick. They got to work, starting in the boardroom. First they covered the walls and then made their way around the office, ensuring there were at least two flyers on every wall, in every corridor and on every cubicle, pinboard and office desk. They even plastered the backs of every door in the toilets.

My name is Jerrod Craig and I'm not as talented as you think I am.
My name is Jerrod Craig and I have crabs.
My name is Jerrod Craig and I like to wear women's underwear.

Justin had obviously taken some creative licence on some of the flyers and Rachel shrieked with laughter as she pinned them up, picturing the scene that would unfold the following day. People would start arriving at work from about seven in the morning, but Jerrod usually only made it in around nine thirty or ten, so by the time he'd reached the studio and caught a glimpse of the first flyer it would already be far too late for him to do anything about it, the word would be out. Rachel reckoned it would have gone viral by eight thirty and international by nine a.m. – around about the time Jerrod would be leaving his apartment to catch a cab into the office.

By the time they'd put up most of the flyers Rachel and Justin had sore stomachs from laughing so hard. They put the final stack in more creative spaces that people might not discover at first, so that their revenge would have a longer shelf life. One went inside the studio refrigerator, another inside the studio freezer, a whole pile upside down inside the photocopier, so everything photocopied all day would come out on the back of a flyer. It quickly became a competition between Justin and Rachel to see who could find the most ingenious hiding place: in a pot plant, under a telephone, pasted to the television screen.

My name is Jerrod Craig and I will disappoint you.
My name is Jerrod Craig and I think I'm the best thing since sliced bread.
My name is Jerrod Craig and I screwed up.
My name is Jerrod Craig and I thought it was okay to lie.
My name is Jerrod Craig and I should have known better.
My name is Jerrod Craig and I am an embarrassment to the industry.
My name is Jerrod Craig and I should be ashamed of myself.

And then, finally, on their way back down to the ground floor, one went into each elevator.

Back in the foyer Justin hugged Doug again and shook hands with the other guards. Rachel thanked them too and then they stepped out into the cold night air, faces flushed with revenge. 'Come on, I'll see you home,' Justin said, heading towards the curb to hail a cab.

'That was the best time I've had in ages,' Rachel said, grinning from ear to ear. 'Do you think we'll get arrested?'

'If we do I'll take the fall for you, Rach,' Justin said. 'Jerrod's had this coming for a long, long time.'

'Justin, thank you for doing this for me.'

'Hey, you forget, I did it for me too.'

'Yes, I know, but still I really appreciate it. Nobody has ever gone to so much trouble to get revenge for me. In fact, I don't think I've ever even gotten revenge before!'

'Imagining his face when he gets in tomorrow is thanks enough,' Justin said.

'I can't believe we just did that!' Rachel shrieked, adrenalin still pumping through her body.

'I know,' Justin drawled, 'and it was way cheaper than having his kneecaps broken!'

Rachel Marcus is thinking about becoming a career criminal.
August 4 at 2:27am via Mobile Web

Rachel fell out of the cab outside her apartment, still laughing, giddy with excitement.

'I can't believe you're leaving the day after tomorrow,' Justin said.

'I know,' Rachel sighed, 'it's all happened really fast.'

'Rachel, I have to warn you, I'm really crap at goodbyes. Must be my stiff-upper-lip British upbringing.'

'That's okay, I'm not great at them either. Hey, should we rather not say goodbye?'

'What do you mean?'

'Let's just say "see you later", and that will be that ... And it's true, we will see each other again later, at some point.' Rachel said.

The cab driver cleared his throat pointedly.

'I'll be two minutes,' Justin snapped at the driver and jumped out of the cab. 'Okay, then I guess I'll see you later,' he said, hugging her.

'Yeah,' Rachel's voice wobbled, 'see you later.'

Justin got back in the cab and waved out the window as it pulled away.

Rachel Marcus is crap at this goodbye thing.
August 4 at 3:46am

Rachel Marcus is still laughing her ass off at last night's shenanigans.
August 4 at 8:18am

Rachel Marcus is imagining the scene unfolding right now.
August 4 at 9:21am

Rachel Marcus is waiting for the cops to come knocking her door down.
August 4 at 10:15am

Rachel Marcus will really start packing today, Brownie's honour.
August 4 at 10:26am

'Sue! You are not going to believe what Justin and I did last night!' Rachel said. She was standing at the door to Sue's apartment, still wearing her pyjamas.

'Um, okay, that's not so hard to guess, did it involve very few clothes and a condom?'

'Sue!' Rachel shrieked. 'I told you, we're just friends!'

'You could have fooled me ... Look at you, I haven't seen you this happy since before ... you know ... before everything.'

'We have to celebrate,' Rachel went on, ignoring Sue's remarks. 'Justin and I did something completely crazy last night. It's going to blow your mind.'

'You didn't jet off to Vegas and get married did you?'

'No, Sue, you'll never guess, so stop trying!' Rachel laughed.

'Well, how about you let me take you out for lunch and you can tell me all about it?' Sue said.

'Shit, I was supposed to start packing this morning, but packing is so boring,' Rachel whined. 'And it only reminds me that I have to leave, and that makes me feel miserable. And, seriously, you're not going to believe me when I tell you what we did last night!'

'Okay, this sounds like a two glass of wine kind of story,' Sue said, grinning. 'Come on, let's go, and then we'll come back here and I'll help you pack and the wine will help make it all a little more bearable.'

Rachel Marcus and Sue Cooper are both very drunk. It's all Sue's fault that they are in no state to be packing anything. Hic.
August 4 at 11:42pm

Rachel Marcus has pronounced today International Hangover Day. Tomorrow will be International Packing Day.

August 5 at 2:31pm

Rachel Marcus is packing. No excuses.
August 6 at 9:39am

Rachel couldn't waste any more time, she only had a couple of hours left before she had to leave for the airport and packing had become non-negotiable. Making herself a strong cup of coffee, she laid her enormous new suitcase open on the coffee table in the lounge and turned on the TV, letting it yammer on in the background. Then she put her hands on her hips and surveyed the room, trying to decide where to start.

Sue popped her head in and out, taking back some of her things that had gotten mixed up in amongst Rachel's stuff and playing a supporting role in the whole packing effort. At some point, out of the corner of her eye, Rachel saw Sue slip her purple Prada slingbacks into the suitcase when she thought Rachel wasn't looking. Rachel smiled to herself, pretending not to notice. She couldn't imagine a better friend.

Around midday Rachel's phone rang. 'Hey,' Justin said.

'Hey,' she replied.

'How's the packing?'

'Oh, you know, it's packing.'

'Yeah. All right. This is unbearable, you know?'

'I know,' she said.

There was a long pause in the conversation. Rachel could hear Justin breathing on the other end of the phone. 'I'd better go finish packing,' she finally said.

'Okay, Rach. Travel safe. See you later.'

'Yeah, see you later,' she said.

Later, Sue lay on Rachel's bed chatting idly while she packed her last bits and pieces. Neither girl mentioned Rachel's impending departure; it was just too hard to talk about.

Rachel Marcus is leaving on a jet plane.
August 6 at 5:10pm

'Your suitcases are beyond stuffed,' Sue said, sitting on one to try and get it to close.

'You're no good at that, sweetie, you don't weigh anything,' Rachel said, pushing her off and sitting on the bag herself.

Sue knelt down next to her and pulled the zip shut around its bulging seams. Just as she finished the door buzzed and Rachel looked up at Sue with panic in her eyes. 'That must be the car,' she said.

'It can't be time already,' Sue replied with a panicked look on her face. Then she threw her arms around Rachel's neck. 'Rae, remember we love you, always.'

'I love you too, Sue.' Rachel wheeled her bags over to the door and picked up her handbag. Then she ran her eye around the world's smallest apartment one last time. 'It's been amazing, hasn't it?' she said.

Sue nodded. 'Travel safe, okay?'

'You and Brian look after each other, see,' Rachel told her, wiping her eyes on her sleeve.

Sue was crying too hard to speak and when Rachel handed her the apartment key to give back to Doreen all she could do was nod tearfully. Giving her one last hug Rachel grabbed the handles of both her suitcases and dragged them down the corridor, looking back once when she reached the top of the stairs to engrain this place and this time in her memory forever. 'I'll call you as soon as I land,' she shouted back to Sue, tears pouring down her cheeks.

Rachel slumped back in her seat and wiped her damp puffy eyes on her already soaking sleeve. She watched New York pass by through the car window; the radio DJ's voice providing a soundtrack to the city as they drove through it. It was one of the local drive-time shows that accompanied millions of New Yorkers home from work every day. She'd heard it before. The DJ, Tony Tone, was edgy and radical but he was also always very funny.

A snippet of the show caught Rachel's attention. 'So, as I was saying, New Yorkers would have to be blind or in even more of a hurry than usual not to have seen this massive new advertising campaign that hit our streets and our screens this month.'

Rachel's ears pricked up and she sat forward in her seat. It couldn't be, could it?

'We're lucky enough to have the creative director from award-wining advertising agency Richmond&Phillips right here live in the studio to chat to us about the campaign, which was his brainchild.'

Rachel's jaw dropped. 'Please can you turn that up?' she asked the driver.

'Welcome to the show, Jerrod Craig,' the DJ said.

'Hi, Tone, it's great to be here.'

When Rachel heard Jerrod her heart wrenched in her chest. Just the sound of his voice made her skin crawl. He was a lying, thieving bastard and she wanted to kill him with her bare hands. She moved even closer to the edge of her seat so as not to miss a single word. 'Jackass!' she spat.

The driver checked her out nervously in the rear-view mirror.

'So, Jerrod, tell us about the campaign, we've had so many people calling and writing in about it. People just seem to love it. How on earth did you come up with such an ingenious idea?'

'Yes, Jerrod!' Rachel said through a clenched jaw. 'How on earth did you come up with such an ingenious idea?'

'Well, Tone,' Jerrod began, 'automotive advertising is a tough category. Historically, it's one of the most glamorous categories to work on, but on the other hand it needs to be hard-working too, which is why

I think it's so difficult to crack. When I'm working on something like this the old adage is true – it really is ninety-nine per cent perspiration and one per cent inspiration.'

'Try one percent perspiration and ninety-nine per cent appropriation!' Rachel yelled, garnering another nervous glance from the driver.

'That's very interesting, so why don't you tell us a little more about how you actually came up with the idea itself?' the DJ asked.

'First, I always take some time to find out everything there is to know about the product,' Jerrod said. 'You could say that I immerse myself in it fully. Research is invaluable.'

'Right, right,' the DJ said, urging him on.

'And then once I've gathered every shred of information,' Jerrod continued, 'I just let it simmer in my subconscious. And then, after that, the only thing left to do is to work your way methodically through one idea at a time, no matter how long it takes, until the right one comes along. The rest, as they say, is advertising history.'

Rachel's stomach clenched as the bile rose in her throat.

'I see,' said the DJ. 'Now, to be honest, Jerrod, I'm no ad guru, but from what I can tell, other than the physical craft of it, the real genius of this particular idea comes when you read that pay-off line that you wrote. It's just brilliant.'

'Thanks, Tone,' Jerrod said. Rachel could hear his smarmy, self-satisfied ear-to-ear grin through the speakers.

'Now, when I heard you were coming into the studio today I thought I'd better do my homework and check you out a bit, because of course I've never actually met you before, so I Googled you.'

'Oh …' Jerrod said.

'Yes, and I came across a rather interesting snippet. It seems there's been quite a bit of controversy surrounding you over the last couple of days, and it's really lit the industry on fire. The advertising bloggers seem to be going crazy over it.'

'Yes, well we won a Gold Cube at Art Directors Club, so that's been very exciting …'

'No, actually,' Tony interrupted him, 'I was talking about an incident with some flyers that happened just the other night.'

'Oh, that,' Jerrod stuttered. 'No, that was nothing, just a little inter-agency prank …'

'It sounds pretty elaborate to me,' the DJ said, pressing on. 'Let me see if I have this right. From what I can gather someone plastered hundreds of flyers all over the Richmond&Phillips offices, and every single one of them said something different and derogatory about you. And they were all discovered the following morning when everyone came into work.'

'Something like that,' Jerrod said dismissively. 'Like I said, it was just a silly inter-agency prank. But Tone, I thought while I was here we could chat a bit about the TV shoot for the campaign? Did you know we used a camera that we had to import specially from Europe for the …'

'So, what did the flyers say?' the DJ cut in. 'I'm completely fascinated and I'm sure our listeners would love to hear too.'

'I don't remember any of them specifically,' Jerrod said. 'But about the shoot, did you know, we had seven cranes on the set …'

'Not to worry if you can't remember them. Look, I managed to download a whole bunch off the net, and let me tell you, I think some of these are just hysterical.'

Rachel heard Jerrod suck in his breath. She smiled as she imagined him sitting there in the studio with nowhere to turn, starting to lose his cool.

'I just can't believe the time and effort someone has put into making all of these,' the DJ went on. 'And apparently they were plastered everywhere: on the ceilings, on the back of cubicle doors in the toilets, even in the agency fridge. It's quite ingenious …'

Rachel could hear the shuffling of paper as the DJ paged through some of the flyers. 'Oh, this is one of my favourites,' he said. 'It says: My name is Jerrod Craig and I like to wear women's underwear. And I love this one: My name is Jerrod Craig and my middle name is Eugene! Hoo, boy, it's just a classic. That's what I love about your industry; it's just so crazy. It must be such fun to be surrounded by creative people all day, every day.'

'Yes, fun,' Jerrod said through gritted teeth. 'Lots of fun.'

'I don't know what you did to this guy, Jerrod, but he's seriously pissed off at you. Take a look at this one, it says: My name is Jerrod Craig and I take advantage of people. Ouch!'

'You really can't take them too seriously,' Jerrod said, attempting to laugh good-naturedly. 'You know what it's like, a bit of meaningless ribbing between rival agencies.'

'Yes, but it's interesting to me that somebody has gone to so much trouble. There are literally hundreds of these things and every single one of them is different.'

'It's a tough industry,' Jerrod said. 'Think of it as competitive jealousy.'

'Fair enough, but some of these are quite pointed though, aren't they? What about this one: My name is Jerrod Craig and I didn't actually write that pay-off line? Or here: My name is Jerrod Craig and I steal other people's copy lines. Do you think they're referring to the line on the campaign we were talking about earlier?'

'I wouldn't know,' Jerrod said dismissively.

'Here's another one, it says: My name is Jerrod Craig and you'd better not leave me in a room alone with your ideas. And here's another: My name is Jerrod Craig and I ...'

'Like I said,' Jerrod interrupted the DJ, his voice climbing in pitch and intensity, no longer the cool, suave creative director, 'you shouldn't read too much into them. They're not referring to any work specifically; it's just some harmless fun.' Jerrod laughed a fake, nervous laugh. 'What a bunch of kidders,' he added.

'Well, clearly a bunch of kidders who are questioning whether you did actually write that campaign line yourself, if this one is anything to go by: My name is Jerrod Craig and I absolutely did not write that car line myself.'

Jerrod stopped laughing. 'Well, that's just ridiculous,' he snapped, 'of course it's my line! Look, if you're accusing me ...'

'Whoa, whoa, whoa, easy tiger,' the DJ said. 'It's just a bit of harmless fun, remember, and I'm just reporting it as I see it. But let me ask you this, you are technically an art director, right?'

'Yes, I'm an art director,' Jerrod growled.

'Then all I'm saying is that it's pretty impressive that as an art director you have the skills to make the pictures look so amazing, but at the same time you can also come up with such a provocative line of copy all by yourself! I would imagine that's what's gotten people wondering ...'

'The kind of skill I have comes with a certain level of experience,' Jerrod said tightly.

'I'm sure it does,' Tony said, obviously unconvinced. 'Well, this certainly raises some interesting questions. Stay tuned New York, we've got to go pay the bills, but when we come back we've got a traffic update and then we'll carry on chatting to Jerrod Craig, Creative Director at ad agency Richmond&Phillips. Don't touch that dial, we'll be right back.'

The radio went off into a commercial break and Rachel shrieked loudly. The driver just about hit the roof of the car, swerving briefly out of his lane before over-correcting and finally making it back into his own lane with the cars around him honking their horns in outrage. He glared at Rachel in the rear-view mirror.

'Did you hear that?' she shouted at the driver. 'Can you believe what an asshole he is? Seriously, what an enormous, monumental asshole!'

Rachel sat back in her seat, shaking her head as the driver's eyes darted nervously from the road to the crazy lady in the rear-view mirror and back again.

As a commercial for a local car dealership buzzed in Rachel's ears she wondered if Justin had heard any of the interview. His work was famous. Never mind if he wasn't tuned in, she thought, she was sure they would be able to download it off the radio station's website at a later date and listen to it over and over again.

'Welcome back to Drive Time with Tony Tone,' the DJ's voice filtered back through the car. 'We were going to bring you a traffic report next, but you only need to look out your window to see that it's pretty much gridlocked out there as usual. So we decided to screw the traffic, because two very interesting things happened here in the studio while we were on commercial break. For those of you who've just tuned in, before the ad break we were talking to Jerrod Craig, who is the main cheese creative director at ad agency Richmond&Phillips and who claims he was single-handedly responsible for coming up with the new car campaign that you will have seen launched all over the city this month.

'But it seems some questions are being raised in the ad industry about whether the work you see out there did in fact come entirely from the brain of Mr Jerrod Craig. We were hoping to get to the bottom of this, but when we went to the ad break Jerrod stormed out of the studio, claiming we had ambushed him and this wasn't the interview he'd signed up for. Nothing like a bit of a tantrum on a Thursday afternoon. We tried hard to convince him to stay, but he wasn't interested. So, unfortunately, it looks like we won't be able to chat to him any more today. But the other thing that happened while we were on commercial break was that a chap named Luke called us with a very interesting related story. Luke, are you still there? Thanks for holding.'

'Hi, Tony.' The voice sounded young but confident.

'Why don't you tell everyone the story you just told me, Luke?'

'Yeah, dude, I've just been listening to your show and when I heard what you were talking about I thought I had to try and get through. Like I told you before, I graduated from ad school last year, and then I spent a couple of months traipsing around the agencies with my portfolio, like trying to get a job.'

'And how did that go?' Tony asked.

'So far not so great, hey, Tone. If anyone out there is looking for a hot young art director you can find me at www.lukeneedsajob.com, or if you want you can come by Ray's Pizza on the corner of One Hundred and Twenty Fourth and Ninth and I'd be happy to swing you one of our famous pepperoni deep-dish pizza's and show you my portfolio.'

'Okay, Luke, the art director stroke pizza maker, let's get back to your story,' Tony said.

'Dude, I had an interview with Jerrod Craig at R&P and he told me my book was like below average or something, and that I should work on it a bit more before wasting my time looking for a job. And I totally believed him. But then, like two months later, I opened up *FHM* and I see he's completely ripped off one of my ideas for Kodak and gone and sold it to one of his own clients, word for word. I tried to call him a bunch of times, but like he never returned any of my calls. So, when I heard you talking about him stealing that pay-off line, and I realised it was the same dude, and he was in the studio with you, I thought, dude, no way, I'd better give you a call.'

'Well, isn't that interesting,' the DJ said. 'Luke, thanks for your call. Jerrod Craig, if you're out there, and you're listening, and you want to come back up into the studio and chat to us about this new turn of events, we'd love to hear from you. And if anyone out there is looking for a young art director or a pizza maker, I reckon Luke here is your man. If his work is good enough for internationally award-winning art director Jerrod Craig to rip off then surely it's good enough for your agency stroke restaurant?

'Hey, I have an idea, why don't we conduct a poll here on Drive Time? Call in, email or text me here in the studio and let me know what you think. What would you do if you were Jerrod Craig's boss over at R&P? Fire him or promote him? Okay, we're gonna take another quick commercial break and then we'll take some calls.' Tony clicked off and an upbeat jingle for a breakfast cereal burst through the car.

Rachel realised that she was sitting so far forward in her seat that her knees were wedged uncomfortably up against the back of the driver's seat, both her hands were covering her gaping mouth, her eyes were wide open and she'd forgotten to breathe. 'Did you hear that?' she shrieked at the driver, slamming into the back of his seat with both her hands. 'Can you believe it? Can you believe I'm not the only one?'

The driver had been watching her carefully through his rear-view mirror while she had been sitting still but now he renewed his grip on the steering wheel, shaking his head vigorously. Rachel wasn't sure if it was in response to her question or if he was simply shaking his head at her violent outbursts.

Rachel sat back in her seat again and thought about Luke. The poor guy, she knew exactly what he must have gone through: all the self-doubt, questioning his own talent for no reason. She felt a kinship with him. They'd both been betrayed by the same man, a man who had been in a position to protect and nurture them, but who had instead violated and deceived them. Then she thought about Jerrod leaving the studio mid-interview. It surprised her; she'd never thought of him as a coward before. She felt she was really starting to get a good idea of what the real Jerrod Craig was actually like.

'Welcome back, New York,' Tony said, back on the air. 'Our lines have been ringing off the hook here in the studio, but unfortunately still no sign of Mr Craig ... I've got an email here from Terence who says he works at another ad agency here in New York. He doesn't know Jerrod Craig personally, but he thinks he should be strung up by the balls if he stole other people's ideas. That's a little nuts Terence, we were only asking whether you thought he should get fired or get a promotion, I'm not quite sure where the sadomasochism angle came from ... Amy from New Jersey sent in a text and she on the other hand thinks that he's innocent until proven guilty. He should be given the opportunity to defend himself, she says, after all this is America and everyone has rights, blah blah blah. Amy is clearly a bleeding-heart liberal, there's always one of them in every poll, isn't there? But Amy I'm afraid you're pretty much on your own here. So far we've had forty-six votes to fire the guy and only three to give him a corner office. Let's take a call. Hello, you're on the air.'

'Hi, my name's Greg,' a gruff-sounding voice said, 'and I used to work with Jerrod Craig at another agency. I'd rather not name it if that's okay with you?'

'Okay, Greg, that's cool. What do you think, fire him or promote him?'

'He's an arrogant douche bag, fire him.'

'Wow, douche bag hey? I'm not entirely sure you can say that word on the radio, but, hey, too late now. Next caller. Hi, caller, what do you say, fire him or promote him?'

'Hi, my name is Dominique ...' Rachel could hear that the girl on the end of the line sounded nervous.

'Hi, Dom ... You don't mind if I call you Dom, do you?' Tony asked.

'Sure ... I worked for Jerrod Craig about four and a half years ago. I was a junior in his group at R&P then. He was forever taking credit for stuff, and all us juniors in his group started to think that was just the way things were done. This one time I worked on a job with him as his assistant and I ended up doing the entire layout myself. The shoot, the retouching, the illustration, even the typography was all my idea. The ad actually went on to win something at One Show but he never credited me on it, not even as an assistant art director or a typographer. The only name on it was his. There was nothing I could do; he was my boss. I left the agency a couple of months later. I say fire him.'

'Really,' Tony said, dragging the word out. 'What an interesting story, especially in light of everything else we've heard today. The plot sickens. It seems our Mr Craig either has some very sticky fingers or a very short memory. Dom, thank you for calling in, hopefully your boss is listening and he'll give you a sympathy raise.'

'That would be cool,' Dom said.

'Well, I think Dom should get two votes for that story don't you? So, that's two more for having Mr Craig fired. Funny how things start to turn up when you dig a little deeper. Dom, you aren't by any chance the clever little monkey who made all these fabulous flyers are you?'

'No, but I wish I'd thought of it,' the girl said. 'It's classic!'

'Okay, let's take another caller,' the DJ said, moving on. 'Hey, you're live on the air with Tony Tone.'

'Hi, my name's Paul and I'm calling from uptown, and ...'

'Wait, Paul, let me take a wild guess here. You work in an ad agency and Jerrod Craig once stole some of your work and passed it off as his own?'

'Nah, Paul laughed, I've never even met the guy. But as far as I'm concerned if he's got the eye to know a good idea when he sees it and the balls to outright steal it, then that man deserves a promotion!'

'All right, Paul,' Tony said, 'so you're from the take-no-prisoners, screw-your-granny-to-get-what-you-want school of thought?'

'Absolutely!'

'Thanks, Paul. Well, the votes are flying in. We've just received an email from Anonymous in New Jersey who says they have a colleague who works with Jerrod Craig and he says: My friend is too scared to go live on the radio, but he says Jerrod Craig couldn't crack a line like that car line even if his life depended on it. Thanks for your email Anonymous. One has to wonder how many other people out there in the city have a similar story to tell? Let's take another call here on our new segment that I just made up: Fire Him or Promote Him? Suddenly I'm feeling a bit like Donald Trump. Hey, you're live on Drive Time with Tony Tone.'

'Hey, Tony, my name is Laurence Phillips.'

'Hello, Laurence Phillips, and who are you when you're not at home in your pyjamas?'

'I'm the CEO of Richmond&Phillips advertising agency.'

Tony whistled. 'You wouldn't happen to be THE Phillips in Richmond&Phillips would you?'

'I am,' the man said.

'Great to have you on the air, Mr Phillips. We've just been talking about your little shop over there on Madison Avenue.'

'Thanks, Tony, and please call me Laurence. As you can imagine, we've been listening to your show with some interest. And we thought we should call and weigh in on the subject, being as Jerrod Craig is under our employ and most of the work you've been discussing so colourfully comes out of our agency.'

'I'm so glad you called, Laurence. As you heard, Jerrod stormed out of the studio a little earlier, so we haven't had anyone here representing Richmond&Phillips in the discussion. I don't know how long you've been listening, but we've been conducting a little poll here on Drive Time to determine whether your man Mr Craig should be fired or promoted, if indeed he has taken a shine to ripping off other people's ideas and passing them off as his own. And would you believe it, but from our running count so far we've had ... Hold on, let me get this right, my producer is just doing some sums ... Okay, we've had eighty-seven votes to fire him and just six lone cries to promote him.'

'Tony, that's why I called,' Laurence Phillips said. 'I wanted to let you know that I actually just got off the phone with Jerrod Craig a few moments ago ...'

'Oh, I see, and what did he say?' Tony asked.

'We discussed the various accusations and he said he'd be at work in the morning to discuss the situation in further detail with the board.'

Laurence Phillips paused and Rachel held her breath.

'We told him not to bother,' Laurence said, breaking the silence. 'We take these accusations very seriously, Tony. And we're grateful to you for bringing them to our attention. Jerrod Craig has been put on immediate suspension and we plan on investigating each of these allegations thoroughly. Should it emerge that any of them are even vaguely true we will take the harshest measures available to us. We'd like to put the message out there live on your show that Richmond&Phillips will not tolerate plagiarism of any kind and as an agency we take a zero-tolerance stance on this kind of behaviour. This situation has come as a huge surprise to us and we ask that anyone with any information on the subject get in touch with our offices immediately. Ultimately, creating the freshest work for our brands, with integrity and honesty is our absolute first priority.'

'Spoken like a true suit,' Tony said. 'Thanks for letting us know, Laurence. We here on Drive Time salute you.'

'Thanks, Tony.'

'Hey, Laurence.'

'Yes, Tony.'

'Now that you've got a gap over there at R&P for an art director you should think about hiring Luke, I hear he throws a mean pizza.'

Laurence laughed. 'Our team is in touch with him already.'

'Well, there you go New York, once again justice prevails here on Drive Time with Tony Tone, always first to break a juicy story and make your drive home just a little more pleasant. Up next a bit of U2 to keep your commute rocking . . .'

As the song started Rachel clapped her hands loudly. The driver gave her a conspiratorial grin through the rear-view mirror and punched his fist in the air in triumph. Rachel sat back in her seat, her heart thumping in her chest. She felt truly vindicated. Karma really was a bitch.

Rachel Marcus is having the last laugh, at last.
August 6 at 6:01pm via Mobile Web

Rachel Marcus is at the airport in departures, waiting to board her EgyptAir flight to Joburg.
August 6 at 7:41pm via Mobile Web

Rachel sipped a tasteless airport coffee out of a tasteless styrofoam cup. She had half an hour left to kill before her flight started to board. Putting her feet up on her overnight bag she thought about what had just happened. She wondered whether Justin had heard about it yet; she had tried to call him, but her cellphone had beeped at her unresponsively. Knowing she was leaving town she had let her airtime run down and so when she'd changed her status update earlier she had unknowingly used up the last of her credit. She'd also foolishly packed her laptop into the bottom of her big suitcase, so she couldn't even email him. She'd briefly thought about fishing it out before checking her bag in, but she'd been concerned that once she opened that suitcase it would never close again.

From where she was sitting Rachel scanned the terminal for a bank of pay phones so she could call Justin. She was relieved they had decided not to do the whole big goodbye thing. It was definitely better that they'd said their farewells or rather their 'see you later's on the phone. It had been hard enough having to say goodbye to Sue in the flesh.

Rachel craned her neck, crowds surging all around her. She wasn't a big fan of airports and this one in particular. It was always packed, full of people waiting, milling, jostling to get to where they were going, only to sit down and wait some more.

Rachel finished her coffee and got up to see if she could locate the pay phones from a standing position. In the distance, over the heads of the crowd, she suddenly saw the back of a blond head. It was Justin, she was sure of it. It was definitely him: same height, same build. Nobody else had curls like that. She couldn't believe it. He must have raced to the airport to say goodbye to her in person, just like in the movies. Rachel bolted, abandoning her luggage and surging forward through the crowds, never taking her eyes off those familiar curls, not wanting to lose sight of them for a second. 'Justin, what are you doing here?' she shouted, running up to him and grabbing his shoulder.

Before he'd even turned around Rachel knew it wasn't him. This guy had the same hair, but that was where the similarities ended. Startled, the man looked at Rachel like she was crazy. 'Sorry, sorry,' she said. 'I thought you were someone else.'

Rachel slunk back to her seat, her cheeks burning, shaking her head at her own foolishness. Of course he wouldn't come to the airport, that didn't happen in real life. And anyway, they would never just let him through security without a boarding pass and a full shoe and body cavity search. She shook her head again, 9/11 had made big romantic gestures at airports a thing of the past. And why did she even want him to make a big romantic gesture? After all, she didn't feel that way about him, did she? No, they were just friends, old partners, people who had leaned on each other in a crisis, people who had got delicious revenge together. She didn't like him like that. But then why had she felt so excited at the thought that it might be him and so sad now that she knew it wasn't? She thought about the kiss in his apartment that night. It had been rather nice until she'd freaked out and slapped him and he'd fallen through the floor. Questions swirled around in her mind. Then the airport speakers buzzed and flight MS839 to Johannesburg via Cairo started boarding.

Rachel stretched out in her aisle seat, waiting for the plane to take off. The middle seat was empty and an Egyptian man was sitting next to the window. She knew how lucky she was to have an empty seat next to her and someone who didn't speak English on the other side of that but her head was too full of Justin for her to really care.

Two hours later Rachel's plane was still standing on the tarmac. The pilot came through the speakers periodically, first in Arabic and then in poor English. Apparently they were having some 'technical endeavours' which they would be seeing to 'instantaneously'. Rachel groaned loudly and in chorus with over a hundred other passengers on board her flight. Harassed, anxious-looking stewardesses came trundling down the aisles, trying to calm the frustrated passengers by handing out juice boxes. Rachel accepted hers, wishing it was filled with whiskey, not juice. To make matters worse, Rachel suddenly realised that when she'd booked her flight she had failed to take into account the sad fact that a Middle Eastern airline wouldn't serve any alcohol. At the time she'd been astonished at how cheap the flight was; at least a thousand dollars cheaper than any of the other competing airlines who flew between New York and Johannesburg regularly. But now she knew why. At this point in time she would have happily paid double what she'd saved for a stiff Johnnie Walker. She looked at her watch and did some calculations. At this rate she would miss her connecting flight from Cairo to Johannesburg. That was if they ever even got to Cairo.

Rachel studied her juice box, she had no idea what flavour it was, there wasn't a word of English anywhere on the pack and she didn't even recognise the fruit pictured on the front. Maybe this was a sign, she thought. Maybe she wasn't supposed to leave New York. She looked out of the window at the terminal. She loved this city. Granted she'd hated her job and she hadn't been all that crazy about her rat-trap apartment and Jerrod had turned out to be a major disaster, but other than that it had been amazing. She couldn't imagine her life without Sue and Brian living next door. And then there was Justin. She felt completely confused. If he really liked her then surely he would have made an effort to say goodbye to her in person. Rachel shook her head at herself again. Justin was nothing more than a good friend; he didn't owe her a personal farewell, and she was the one choosing to leave, after all. It was time Rachel picked herself up, brushed herself off and went home to Joburg to start all over again.

Just then she felt the engines turn over and they lurched forward as the plane started taxiing onto the runway. There was her sign, she thought. It was definitely time to go home. The entire cabin burst into applause and Rachel clapped loudest of all.

Twelve and a half hours later EgyptAir flight MS839 landed at Cairo International Airport. Rachel and her fellow passengers queued limply at passport control before making their way into the terminal. She had missed her connecting flight and she was officially, according to the Egyptian authorities, 'in transit'. It must have been about a hundred degrees outside and the air-conditioning in the terminal struggled to keep up.

Rachel stood below the flight arrivals and departures boards and craned her neck. Then she groaned. According to the board she had six hours before the departure of the next flight to Johannesburg.

After walking the entire length of the airport and not finding much in the way of anything Rachel settled in to wait. There was a food court, but no Internet access and no shops that could possibly entertain her for more than twenty minutes. This left her five hours and forty minutes with nothing to do but think about her situation. She was miserable and, even worse, she could smell herself. It wasn't pleasant and she immediately felt sorry for the unlucky recipient of the seat next to hers on the flight home.

The closer it came to boarding time the more excited Rachel began to feel about going home. In her mind she packaged up New York and tied it up with a big bright bow, giving herself some closure over it. Jerrod had been reduced to a speck of shit on the bottom of her shoe and with Justin and Sue and Brian she had made friendships that she knew were strong enough to last a lifetime, even from a distance.

Rachel thought about the incredible opportunities waiting for her in South Africa and wondered how she had managed to get so lucky. She was about to open her own advertising agency where she could start from scratch and build the kind of life she'd always dreamed of. She would make a point of not making the same stupid mistakes again. She was going home at last.

What felt like eons later Rachel boarded her flight, exhausted and filthy but completely exhilarated to be on her way home. Just eight more hours, she said to herself.

By the time the plane made its final descent into O.R. Thambo International Airport Rachel had been 'in transit' for almost thirty hours. Excitement bubbled in her stomach. She couldn't wait to see her family and her friends and begin to make her fresh start. This time, she thought, she would do it right.

Hearing the South African accents around her as she shuffled her way forward in the customs queue made her smile. The customs official studied her passport. 'Welcome home, Miss Marcus,' he mumbled in a thick Afrikaans accent.

Home. The word spun around in her mind.

'The prodigal daughter returns,' she said.

'What?' asked the customs official from behind his moustache.

'Nothing,' Rachel said, smiling and shaking her head.

She walked through the terminal towards the baggage claim area. At last the smells and sounds of Africa were all around her. This is what she'd been missing all these months. Rachel hovered at the baggage carousel. She knew from experience that it would take forever for the luggage to come out – the airline workers needed time to go through everyone's bags and pick out the items they were looking for. She considered going to the bathroom to freshen up and then thought better of it. After almost thirty straight hours spent on an aeroplane and in an airport terminal in a Middle Eastern country she knew she would need a hell of a lot more than what she could find in her handbag to make herself even vaguely presentable.

When her bags finally came around on the carousel she pulled them off the belt, piled them on a trolley and wheeled them through the glass door, which parted as she got to it. She scanned the busy terminal, looking for a familiar face, the eyes of other people's loved ones moving over her. Then she saw her parents, waiting patiently on the far side of the barrier. When her mom saw Rachel she bolted forward, waving both arms frantically in the air, shouting 'Rachel, Rachel, over here!' at the top of her voice. As if Rachel could possibly miss her.

Rachel quickened her pace and when she got to her mom she let go of the trolley and sank into her mother's arms, breathing in the familiar smell of her. Next she hugged her dad; it felt so good to be home.

'Welcome home, Rachel,' her dad said, patting her on the back as they hugged. 'That was rather an epic trip, wasn't it?'

Rachel squeezed her eyes tightly shut as she tried to push back her tears, not wanting to cry in front of them. 'Hi, Mom. Hi, Dad,' she said, her voice cracking as she let go of her father and stepped back. 'It's so good to see you.'

'Look who we brought with us,' her mom said, moving aside.

Startled, Rachel stood up straight; she hadn't been expecting anyone else at the airport. She fiddled with her fringe self-consciously, trying to cover as much of her greasy forehead as possible.

As her mom stepped aside Rachel saw a man standing behind her. In his early thirties, he had a doughy body, and Rachel couldn't help but notice that he had attempted to comb some of the longer hair from above his ears over his forehead, which was clearly balding. He was wearing a pair of baggy khaki pants and a yellow-and-blue striped T-shirt and he had his cellphone attached to the side of his belt in some kind of leather holster. Rachel's mouth dropped open.

'You remember Selwyn Schmeisenberger, don't you?' her mother gushed. 'The podiatrist, remember? I'm sure I wrote about him in one of my letters. You met each other at Jewish Camp when you were twelve?'

Selwyn stepped forward. 'Hello,' he said. 'Welcome home, these are for you.' He pushed a bunch of bright pink carnations into her hands. 'I hope you don't mind me coming to meet you at the airport. I know you've had a long flight, but your mother insisted.'

'I thought it would be a nice surprise,' her mother said, clapping her hands together in delight and winking obviously at Rachel.

'Sure!' Rachel said, trying to be polite and too shell-shocked to say anything else. 'Won't you excuse me while I just pop to the bathroom. Sorry, I just need to freshen up quickly.'

Shoving the carnations at her mother, Rachel grabbed her handbag and escaped before anyone could say anything.

In the bathroom Rachel clutched onto the edge of the basin. She was completely horrified: how could her mother do this to her? And in the same breath: why was she surprised her mother had done this to her? This was exactly the kind of behaviour she'd come to expect from her: bringing an almost complete stranger to the airport to welcome her home. And he was so not her type. What was with his hair? Why did guys do that? Did they think nobody would notice they were balding if they combed their hair over the top of their heads? Rachel wondered if this was what she had in store for herself back home: living in her parents' house and being forced to have endless family dinners with unsuitable suitors picked out by her overzealous and clearly blind mother, who meant well, but in that irritating overbearingly intrusive kind of way she had. Was this just the first of many Selwyns she would have to smile at politely before endlessly dodging their phone calls?

Rachel scolded herself; she shouldn't be so shallow. This kind of attitude was exactly what had gotten her into so much trouble with Jerrod in the first place, wasn't it? He had looked so perfect on the outside: perfect hair, perfect body, perfect teeth, perfect career and he would never have worn his cellphone on his belt. And look what a disaster he had turned out to be in the end.

Maybe that was the lesson she needed to take out of this whole experience. Perhaps she had been too picky and it was time to get real. What if Selwyn Schmeisenberger was actually a good guy? Okay, he had bad hair and not the greatest dress sense. So what? she told herself sternly. Those were just physical attributes and nothing a good hairdresser and a bit of a makeover couldn't fix. She should look on the bright side – he was a doctor of sorts, after all. And from everything her mom had said about him he seemed pretty established. It was time to grow up and face reality. Maybe, Rachel thought, she could make this work to her advantage. Perhaps Selwyn had a nice big house and she could stay in his guest room, then she wouldn't have to camp in the craft room at her parent's house. She should at least try to make an effort to get to know him a little and see if there was anything appealing going on behind that comb-over.

Rachel appraised her reflection in the mirror. Her own hair was hardly looking its best. It was a dirty, tangled mess; her roots were growing out horribly. And that was just her hair. There were bags under her eyes and a fresh outcrop of greasy travelling zits covered her chin. She turned her handbag upside down and emptied it out on the counter next to the basin, looking for something, anything she might be able to use. Rachel sifted through the contents of her purse: some sweet wrappers, tissues, half a piece of liquorice, three pens and half a breadstick that she didn't remember collecting. Two unfamiliar folded scraps of paper caught her attention. She picked the first out and unfolded it. It was Justin's sketched drawing of herself that she'd found on his pinboard on her last day at Target.

She picked out the second piece of paper and unfolded that too, smoothing it out next to the sketch on the basin. It was the note from the flowers Jerrod had sent her after their first night together. It was written in a black felt-tipped marker, she reread it.

Rachel, it was a pity you left in such a hurry last night. xJ

Rachel's eyes moved between the two notes. The pen was exactly the same on both pieces of paper and the line work was identical. How could Rachel not have noticed it sooner; they were both made by the same black felt-tipped marker. The same pen Rachel had watched Justin using at the desk across from her every day for months. The penny dropped. The flowers had been from Justin, not from Jerrod. Rachel had assumed the J was for Jerrod, and Jerrod had done nothing to correct her. How could she have been so stupid, she wondered? If Jerrod was so morally corrupt that he could steal the credit for another person's idea, what would stop him stealing the credit for another man's flowers?

All along Justin had known Rachel thought Jerrod had sent them, but he'd never said anything to correct her. It must have burned him up. Suddenly Justin's conduct made so much more sense to Rachael. His bad behaviour started to drop into place: the drinking and drugging, the sulking, the bad moods, all those times he'd slated Jerrod and been rude to Rachel. He wasn't being stubborn, or hung-over, or pathetic, or useless, or childish or brash, he was just being jealous.

Rachel thought about her feelings and she thought about her future. Everything was on the line. She couldn't fuck up again; she was running out of chances to get her life right for once and for all. All these opportunities were laid out before her: her own agency, her partnership with Zola, Selwyn Schmeisenberger ... It was time to make a decision, commit to it and settle down and make it work. She looked up and nodded at herself in the mirror. For the first time in over six months she knew exactly what she had to do.

Rachel did the best she could to fix herself up: she tamed her hair, washed her face and brushed her teeth. Finally, she even put on some of the make-up that she'd found lurking at the bottom of her bag, rounding it all off with a flourish of lipstick. Then she stuffed everything back into her handbag, including the two little notes and raced back out into the terminal with a huge smile on her face.

'That's better,' her mother said.

'You look great,' Selwyn Schmeisenberger added.

'Thank you,' Rachel said, smiling at him coyly.

'Right,' her father said. 'Are you all ready to go? My car is parked in the Ys.'

Selwyn and her dad pulled Rachel's suitcases behind them and they all headed towards the exit together.

'Dad,' Rachel said.

'Yes, dear.'

'You need to make one quick stop for me before you head home, if that's okay?'

'Of course, dear.'

Twenty five minutes later Rachel made her way to the SAA counter in the departures terminal at O.R. Thambo International Airport. She took out her passport and her credit card and slammed them both down on the counter decisively. 'I need a one way ticket on your next direct flight to JFK,' she said. 'And don't even think about making it on EgyptAir.'

Much later, with just forty-five minutes left before her direct flight home to New York departed, Rachel Marcus said goodbye to her parents and Selwyn Schmeisenberger in the small coffee shop in departures and then made her way through the final security checkpoints. Then, as she walked down the concourse and heard the first boarding call for her flight, she stopped off at duty-free and picked up as many boxes of Five Roses tea as she could carry.

THANK YOU FEELS LIKE A BIT OF AN UNDERSTATEMENT . . . but it's unrealistic for you to expect money, so this will have to do.

(Warning: this bit could be boring if you don't know any of these people.)

There are a ton of people who made this book possible. Although sitting down at a computer and writing is a solitary act, done in a small room (often while wearing a grubby T-shirt and drinking copious amounts of tea), it's still somehow a team sport. So as I reread what I've written here I'm terrified I've gone and left someone out. If it's you, please forgive me, you know I couldn't have done this without you and I'm terribly grateful.

Thanks must go to:

Sarah Bullen, who made me put aside the unsellable rubbish I wanted to write and write this (hopefully not unsellable rubbish) instead. Angela Horn, who wrote alongside me and kept me going from word one to word one hundred thousand. My early readers – Chryssa, Stephanie, Angela and Jen – who put their opinions so nicely it never actually felt like criticism. My eternal gratitude and love also goes to Karin – if I had to list what I'm thankful for here we'd be here for another ten pages. Same goes for all the other people on my support team (especially Emma and Warren). My entire family, especially my sisters, my horde of encouraging friends and all my colleagues at King James – I realise how lucky I am to have you all on my side. My personal trainer, shrink and friend, Ian

Waddell, who ran beside me every step of the way. Ron Irwin, my agent extraordinaire, who absolutely, positively was definitely not taking on any new clients when I first met him.

Lovely editor and friend, Jane Bowman. Robyn, my New York correspondent. Judy, who encouraged me to get going. The Good Book Appreciation Society for the weekly inspiration. Alison, Louise, Reneé, Gillian and the rest of the team at Penguin for helping make this one of the most unbelievable, pinch-me-now experiences of my life. My editor, James – for reading every word at least ten times, answering millions of questions without ever letting on that I was being panicky and irritating, and of course for not butchering my manuscript, I can't tell you how grateful I am.

And of course thanks must also go to every crazy art director, mad boss, weird client, bad date, lying-cheating-stealing boyfriend and dodgy guy I've ever met, thank you so much. I knew you'd come in handy somewhere along the line.

FOR MORE ON INTERNET DATING, CLIENTS FROM HELL AND PAIGE NICK VISIT www.amillionmilesfromnormal.com.